T0196009

JACK MURPHY DELIVERS JUSTICE

Detective Jack Murphy can read a crime scene like a book. When the naked, brutalized corpse of a narcotics cop is found, it's not the body that tells him a sick killer is on the loose, but the monkey figurine—of the "see no evil" kind—shoved down his throat. It's a message, not a clue. Then a high-profile judge is set on fire. Another figurine left behind. Murphy has a guess what's next. But it's not what he expects. The torture-killer taking out Evansville's defenders of law and order isn't the only one with secrets. The victims might have a few, too.

Visit us at www.kensingtonbooks.com

Books by Rick Reed

The Jack Murphy Thrillers
The Cruelest Cut
The Coldest Fear
The Deepest Wound
The Highest Stakes
The Darkest Night

Nonfiction
Blood Trail
(with Steven Walker)

Published by Kensington Publishing Corporation

The Slowest Death

A Jack Murphy thriller

Rick Reed

LYRICAL PRESS
Kensington Publishing Corp.
www.kensingtonbooks.com

Lyrical Press books are published by
Kensington Publishing Corp. 119 West 40th Street New York, NY 10018

All Kensington titles, imprints, and distributed lines are available at special quantity discounts for bulk purchases for sales promotion, premiums, fund-raising, and educational or institutional use.

To the extent that the image or images on the cover of this book depict a person or persons, such person or persons are merely models, and are not intended to portray any character or characters featured in the book.

Special book excerpts or customized printings can also be created to fit specific needs. For details, write or phone the office of the Kensington Special Sales Manager:
Kensington Publishing Corp.
119 West 40th Street
New York, NY 10018
Attn. Special Sales Department. Phone: 1-800-221-2647.

Kensington and the K logo Reg. U.S. Pat. & TM Off.
LYRICAL PRESS Reg. U.S. Pat. & TM Off.
Lyrical Press and the L logo are trademarks of Kensington Publishing Corp.

First Electronic Edition: February 2018
eISBN-13: 978-1-5161-0454-3
eISBN-10: 1-5161-0454-4

First Print Edition: February 2018
ISBN-13: 1978-1-5161-0455-0
ISBN-10: -5161-0455-2

Printed in the United States of America

"Death is not the worst that can happen to men."
—Plato, 427 B.C.

"Men may know many things by seeing; but no prophet can see before the event, nor what end waits for him."
—Sophocles, 496 B.C.

"Look not at what is contrary to propriety; listen not to what is contrary to propriety; speak not what is contrary to propriety; make no movement which is contrary to propriety."
—Confucius

Chapter 1

Moonlight fell through the broken windowpanes of the abandoned house, casting squares of light like oversized picture frames across the trash-strewn floor. Detective Sergeant Franco "Sonny" Caparelli lay on his side, naked and freezing. Pain throbbed behind his eyes and skull from the blow to the back of his head.

He remembered sitting in his truck waiting for the go-between. He was going to buy a couple of bricks of heroin for $100K and keep both money and drugs. He caught movement out of the corner of his eye just as he heard a ratcheting sound and the ASP expandable baton shattered his window. Strong hands reached in, grabbed him and yanked him through the opening. He felt a bone-crunching blow land at the back of his neck followed by a loud, insistent ringing in his ears. He woke up bound hand and foot.

Something warm ran down the side of his face and felt sticky under his cheek. Footsteps approached and stopped. In the darkness, he could make out the shape of legs, a shadow, someone standing over him. The shadow moved, a knee pushed down on his bare back, gloved hands gripped the bindings on his wrists. He could hear and feel nylon flexi-cuffs tightening, cruelly cutting into his flesh.

"Hey, you don't have to do this, man. If you want money, I got money. Thousands. It's in my truck. Under the seat. Take it," Sonny said, trying to keep the desperation out of his voice.

Hands gripped his feet and ratcheted down those flexi-cuffs until they ground his ankles painfully against each other.

"I'm not lying. Whoever's paying you to do this, it ain't enough. I'm a cop. I promise you this is a bad move. Take the money and go."

Sonny felt something, a cable or a heavy cord, slip over his head and draw snug around his neck.

"Did you hear me, asshole? I'm a cop. You do this and there's no going back. There'll be no place to hide."

His captor finally spoke. "I'm not hiding. On the contrary. It was you and your conspirators who went into hiding," the man said.

Sonny felt his legs being pulled up, bending his knees, and some of the cable around his throat being slipped between the bonds at his ankles. The man wrapped the end of the cable around a short piece of wood, creating a makeshift handle. Sonny said, "This ain't funny. Don't do this, buddy."

The cable tightened and Sonny's neck jerked back toward his feet. The earlier pain in his head was replaced by choking, gagging, arching his spine to the breaking point. Pinpoints of light drifted across his vision. The cable eased. Sonny gagged until it brought on a series of coughing fits. He got it under control, squinted to clear his vision and spat on the floor. The man stood with his back to the windows, a shadow in deeper shadows. The general outline was that of a tall man, maybe six foot plus. The build and age were indiscernible. The most telling thing was the fact the man was making no attempt to hide his face.

Sonny clamped his eyes shut, not wanting to see a face. Knowing that would spell the end. When he did so, it caused a new explosion of pain behind his eyes. He held his breath, willing himself not to black out. He had to keep talking. The pain eased just enough for him to say, "I haven't seen your face. I don't know who you are." Saying even this much brought on another coughing fit. He tried again. "I don't want to know who you are. I don't even want to know why you're doing this. For all I know you grabbed the wrong guy. It's not too late to stop. You can just walk away."

"And you won't come for me?" The voice sounded sincere. "You'll forget this ever happened?"

For the first time since he awakened in this nightmare, he felt a flash of hope. He didn't want to get caught in a lie and blow any chance he had at being released. "Well, you know it's a serious thing to assault a cop, but if it was a mistake I'm willing to let it ride. You didn't really hurt me too bad. What do you say? Let me go. You can still have the money."

In answer, a boot came down on the side of Sonny's face, the sole grinding his cheek into the floor like someone was putting out a cigarette. Sonny could feel his skin twisting and tearing on both sides of his face. He could taste the boot sole crushing down across his mouth.

The man stopped and said, "Be still. Shut your lying mouth."

Sonny saw only the lower part of the legs. Sharply creased pants were bloused into the tops of tightly laced military-style boots. The only people Sonny knew that dressed militarily were a group of neo-Nazi survivalists he'd busted a couple years ago. He'd taken their money, their drugs, guns, manifesto. He'd kept some of the Nazi memorabilia, money and guns. The skinheads had all gone to prison, and the kids living in the compound were placed in foster homes. He hoped this asshole wasn't one of the men he'd arrested. His best chance of getting out of this was to keep his mouth shut and listen for a clue. When he got out of here he was going to hunt down this piece of shit and flush him. His head felt like a balloon that was ready to burst. He licked at his lips but his mouth was dry and his tongue made a clicking sound.

"Tastes like dirty socks, doesn't it? It should. I used your socks to gag you. If you so much as blink again..." The cable tightened until the blackness swam behind Sonny's eyes again before loosening.

"If you do something I don't like, that is what will happen. The Japanese call this Kinbaku. Can you say Kin-bah-ku? Well, it doesn't matter if you can pronounce it or not. Literally translated it means 'tight binding.' During the Edo period, this form of bondage was used to show superiority."

"You're crazy," Sonny said just before the headlights from a vehicle flashed through the broken windowpanes. The room was bathed in a temporary bright light. Sonny screamed for help but the words came out hoarse, weak, defeated. When the lights diminished and the vehicle had moved on Sonny stiffened, preparing for the punishment he knew would follow.

Instead of the promised punishment, the man said, "I'll give you that one. We're humans after all, and it's human nature to want to live, isn't it?"

Sonny asked, "Why me? I've never done anything to you. And even if I did I can fix whatever it is. Make it right. Just let me make it right. I'll do anything."

The man took something from his pocket, squatted and leaned close to Sonny's face, holding the object in front of Sonny's eyes. The object was a carved figure of a monkey; an inch tall, sitting Indian-style, hands over its eyes.

"Mizaru, this is Sonny. Sonny, meet Mizaru," the man said.

"What?" Sonny asked.

"Who. Not what," the man corrected. "From the proverb of The Mystic Apes? Nod if you've heard of them."

Sonny just stared at the object.

"No? Well, I'll enlighten you. There are four legendary Japanese monkeys known as The Mystic Apes. Mizaru sees no evil, Kikazaru hears no evil, and Iwazaru speaks no evil. The fourth monkey, Shizaru, does no evil. In the Koshin belief, The Mystic Apes teach a desired code of conduct."

Sonny said nothing.

"I can see I'll have to explain further," the man said, as if talking to a child. "Sonny, the Koshin religion teaches that good behavior brings good health. Bad behavior brings bad health. The four monkeys label the behaviors you should avoid. If you engage in any of these unsavory behaviors, you will answer to Ten-Tei, what some believe is the fifth monkey, the most powerful of all Koshin deities. Ten-Tei has come to punish you for your crime in Boston."

Sonny said, "What crime? I've never been to Boston, and I've never even heard of this crap you're talking."

"Liar, liar, pants on fire. Five years, seven months and eleven days ago. I know you remember, because I will never forget what was done to her. The sheer hell she went through." The man squatted. "Tell me something, Sonny. Did she beg? The autopsy report said she wasn't dead when she was set on fire. Did you do that? Or was it your partner?"

"It wasn't me," Sonny said. "I didn't do anything to anyone. I swear."

"The time for swearing has come and gone, Sonny. Tell me the whole truth, and I'll spare you some pain."

"I told you the truth. It wasn't me."

"I know the names of everyone involved in her murder and rape. Tell me, did she struggle? Of course she did. Bits of nylon were melted into her wrists and ankles. Nylon. Like the flexi-cuffs I put on you. They're so easy to use and hard to escape from. You can barely move. I can do anything I like with you. How does that feel? If I rape you, there is nothing you can do to stop me." He flicked a folding knife open and drew the razor-sharp blade down the side of Sonny's face. "Do you have empathy for her now? Do you want to confess your sins?"

Warm blood ran into Sonny's mouth and eyes. The realization that he'd never leave here alive hit him like a fist and at the same time sucked the air from his lungs. His chest hitched in short spasms as tears ran down his face.

"It wasn't me. It wasn't me," Sonny said pitifully.

"Are those tears of remorse? Self-pity? Relief? A real man would have trouble living with what you and your friends did. A compassionate man would have nightmares. I'm not afraid to admit that I've had quite a few nightmares over what I've had to do to even things. But I doubt you have even had bad dreams."

The knife folded shut and he laid it down in front of Sonny's face. He reached into a cargo pocket and pulled out a pair of thin black leather gloves, slipping them on over the latex ones. He took a black brass knuckles—but not exactly brass knuckles—from another pocket and slipped his fingers through the holes, making a fist, gripping them tightly, so tightly the gloves made a creaking noise in the quiet.

Sonny's eyes widened in recognition of the combination brass knuckles and Taser. He'd used a pair similar to these a few times when he was dealing with some scum-bucket, making them talk. He hadn't used anything like it since moving to Evansville. They were made of molded black polymer, with finger holes and four small metal spikes on the top. Now here they were, being held in his face. He could see the man's thumb on the rocker switch. He watched the knucks/Taser come alive, electricity arcing and crackling along the top spikes.

"I found these on Amazon," the man said conversationally and drove the spikes into the soft tissue of Sonny's face, driving the tips deep into the flesh, delivering nine hundred fifty thousand volts of electricity into Sonny's head.

"Did you really think you could hide from me?" The knucks slammed against the side of Sonny's neck and fired again. Sonny's muscles locked in a spasm and a stuttering sound escaped his throat. The fist came down again and again, ripping flesh, scraping bone, infusing each contact with burning electricity.

The man sat back on his heels breathing hard, plumes of breath rising. He placed the Taser/knucks on the floor beside the folding knife. "I don't think you can take much more of this, do you? Bleed if the answer is no."

Sonny lay there unmoving, bleeding.

"I know you didn't land the job here with the feds because of your personality, Sonny. Big Bobby Touhey pulled in a favor for you. Do you know the saying, 'Keep your friends close?' Well, for Big Bobby to send you all the way here, you must be on his shit list."

Sonny's eyes traveled from the weapons to the man's face. It was obvious he recognized the name of Big Bobby Touhey.

"Sam Knight doesn't have that kind of pull. And your partner, Vincent Sullis—what a piece of work that guy is—resigned from Boston PD and went to law school after what happened. Graduated bottom of his class. Touhey got all of you these jobs, didn't he?"

Sonny tried to squint the blood out of his eyes.

Strong fingers grabbed Sonny's face and pulled it up, straining his neck to the breaking point. The man said, "I'm talking to you. You're being impolite. And you're still working for Touhey? That's how you got this cushy job? That's how you're able to live so extravagantly in that fancy house by the river?"

Sonny still didn't speak.

"Maybe your girlfriend will be more talkative?"

Sonny broke his silence. "They're gonna kill you, asshole. You don't mess with Big Bobby. No matter what you do to me, they'll do worse to you. I'm not afraid of you. I spit on your grave." Sonny tried to spit blood but was unable.

The man laughed. "You think so? Well, you may be right. They might get very lucky. But after you, I'll be two for two and they still have no idea who I am."

Sonny looked the man in the eyes. "It was you. You're the one that…"

"Big Bobby's kid was the hardest. Big Bobby—Little Bobby. I swear. Where do they get these names? I could have killed his bodyguards, too, but I knew Big Bobby would do it for me. And he did. You were at the funeral, but the bodyguards were absent. The funeral was beautiful. I saw you and your partner standing close to Big Bobby. That makes you a suck-up, by the way. Yeah. Big Catholic doings. I'm surprised the church would let a person like Little Bobby be buried in sacred ground, but money talks. Am I right? I was counting on every one of you assholes to show up to confirm what I already knew."

Sonny stared at him. "Big Bobby will never rest until he finds you and guts you like you did to his kid."

"I didn't just gut the little bastard. I staked his nuts to the ground. Oh, and he got the first one of the carvings. Shizaru. Do No Evil. But don't worry. I won't give yours to someone else." He set the carved figurine next to the knife and knucks.

Sonny said, "Big Bobby will never stop searching for you. He's killing his own guys to find you. He'll do worse to you than you did to his kid, asshole."

"You're repeating yourself. That's the sign of a weak mind."

"Screw you," Sonny said.

"It's embarrassing how easy it was to get you. Are you embarrassed? Well, you should be. I can't believe you didn't check me out when I asked for a meet. Greed will get you every time. Hey, you're not alone in stupidity and greed. Little Bobby got careless. He had a thing for young Vietnamese girls. Did you know that? No? Well, he agreed to meet me alone. Just like you. And because of him I know everything. I know where Knight is and your partner. Sully's here, by the way. At your house with your girlfriend. Mindy, right?"

Sonny said, "Keep Mindy out of this. She had nothing to do with Big Bobby. You…"

In one swift motion the man slid the knucks back on and slammed them down repeatedly into Sonny's chest and face, burning and ripping flesh.

When the beating stopped, Sonny lay motionless until the man slapped his face and the top of his head until he drew in a sharp breath. The folding knife clicked open. "Tell me if I'm hurting you." The tip of the blade dug into Sonny's scalp and dragged downward, cutting soft tissue and cartilage and exiting through the bottom of the jaw. Blood gushed from the gaping wound.

"G-g-g-god!" Sonny said in a voice garbled by the blood clogging his throat. He made mewling sounds, too exhausted to shiver or cry out.

"God can't help you, Sonny. I could end this, but I've waited a very long time."

The noose was lifted from around Sonny's neck and tossed aside. Sonny was lifted into a sitting position, dragged across the floor and propped against a wall. Heavy steel eyebolts were screwed into the wall studs. Lengths of thin steel cable were attached to each eyebolt at one end, and to a three-inch meat hook at the other.

Strong arms encircled Sonny's chest and lifted him to his feet as if embracing a partner for a slow dance and then shoved him against the wall, impaling him on two of the hooks, his still-bound feet dangling just inches above the floor. The knife slashed through the restraints. His arms hung helplessly, fingers twitching. Sonny's eyes rolled back in his head. He let out his breath and his head lolled forward, chin touching his chest.

"No, not yet," the man said, and felt Sonny's neck. "Good. You're stronger than I thought. I don't guess we're friends anymore. Not after this. But I have one more thing to give you before we part company."

He grabbed Sonny's hair and yanked his face up. With the other hand, he pried Sonny's jaws apart and shoved the carving deep into his throat. The only resistance Sonny offered was reflexive gagging, and his head fell forward again.

The man rummaged in a canvas bag that had been stored in the dark room. He brought out a rubber mallet. He brought out two nine-inch railroad spikes. "I hope you feel everything I'm going to do. It won't bring her back, but it will give us some closure."

Chapter 2

"I don't like it here, Zack," Dayton said. Dayton Bolin had turned fifteen last week. According to her mother, the official age to have a boyfriend was seventeen. If it were up to her dad she would be locked in a closet until she was old. Like twenty or something. If her parents knew she had dated Zack for over a year now, she would probably be sent to a nunnery. She didn't know why her parents didn't like Zack—whom they had met only once for five minutes—but they had taken a disliking to him immediately and forbade her to even mention his name.

Dayton stood on the edge of the frozen sidewalk, cold seeping through the soles of her stylish cowboy boots, icy fingers twining up her calves. She had to admit that Zack had his faults. And he was dirt-poor. In reality, he was poorer than dirt. But he loved her. And she loved him. He thought she was too thin, but he told her that she had a great body. He always said her skin was smooth as silk. He loved her thick red hair, even though her mother was always fussing at her to get it styled. He said she was gorgeous and called her Dy after Princess Diana of the royal family. Princess Diana's hair was blond most of the time but, for a short while, Diana had worn it the same color of copper red and the same style as Dayton.

Of course, right now you wouldn't see any of the things Zack saw in her because she had bundled up in multiple layers of clothing and jackets early this morning before sneaking out of the back door to meet Zack. Her face was entirely hidden behind a wool scarf and a knit hat pulled down over the copper-colored hair. A quilted jacket that belonged to her mother and came down almost to her ankles covered most of her body. The only thing that she had neglected was sensible shoes.

Zackariah Pugh was wearing a pair of scuffed combat boots he'd gotten at Army Surplus, with two pairs of wool socks. He had on two pairs of old jeans with the knees torn out of both, and she suspected they were the only jeans he owned. He had on several T-shirts covered by a flimsy jean jacket that was missing the metal buttons. It was the only coat she had ever seen him wear.

He was a year older than her, having been held back a year in grade school. He said it was because his parents had divorced and he moved around a lot with his dad. She thought his parents had just forgotten to register him for school. They were drunk or high most of the time according to Zack, and he had to hide from them for weeks at a time to avoid being made to steal cigarettes or food.

Zack faced her, his hands in his pockets, that disarming grin on his face, teeth chattering just like hers, but she knew he was trying to pretend they weren't in a bad situation. He was being what he called "a man" and protecting her the only way he knew. She knew him well enough to see behind the smile and the bravado. She could see that he was feeling wretched. Their big plans had turned into this frozen nightmare. She told herself that she would suck it up, for him, because running away to be together was what they both wanted. Her mind and heart were telling her to go home, crawl back under the warm covers, wake up to a big breakfast, and go back to school after the Christmas break. But she wouldn't. She would do whatever Zack decided. That's what you do for the person you love.

He smiled at her and the sun peeked over the horizon, bathing the sky in hues of gold and red. Zack said theatrically, "It is the east, and Juliet is the sun."

She pulled her scarf down with a gloved hand. She wanted him to see her smile. They had taken drama class together. She was Juliet in a play. Somehow Zack had landed the part of Romeo. Not that he wasn't a good actor, but she heard he'd punched out Todd Black and threatened anyone else who tried out for the part.

He smiled back at her and said, "Arise, fair sun, and kill the envious moon, who is already sick and pale with grief..." as Zack said this, he made a theatrical bow and finished the line "...that thou, her maid, are far more fair than she."

Tears ran down Dayton's cheeks. "I love you, Zack."

He gently placed his hands on her shoulders and pulled her tightly against him.

"I love you too, Lady Dy. You don't have to go. I'll take you home." He said this knowing she would never let him go alone. It was all they'd talked about since her dad had forced her to quit the Drama Club because of Zack. She could change her mind, but he could never go home. Not after last night. Not after he'd taken all of his dad's hidden money. It didn't amount to even fifty dollars, but that was an alcoholic's fortune to his old man.

Dayton lifted her face. "I didn't say I *didn't* want to do this, silly. I just said I didn't like it here in this...neighborhood. This is a really bad part of town, baby."

Zack turned away and she realized he wasn't seeing what she saw. This neighborhood wasn't any different from where he lived. Same run-down houses. Same dirty yards and streets, same smell of sewers and open dumpsters. She had never been inside his house. He'd made sure of that. She knew it was because he didn't want her to see how he lived, and he'd told her that his dad would paw at her.

"We'll take a rest and split a Coke," Zack said. "Just a few minutes, though. We've got to get to the highway."

He motioned toward her Western boots. "You should have worn the Army boots I picked up for you."

She didn't tell him that she had a good idea that Zack had "picked them up" but had failed to pay for them. She didn't want to wear anything that was stolen. But right now, she'd steal them herself.

He pointed toward a house all by itself, windows busted out of the panes, front door standing wide open. "I see a place we can get out of the cold." He took her hand and pulled her toward the house.

Chapter 3

Detective Jack Murphy stomped down the ice-crusted snow just inside the crime scene tape to keep it out of the tops of his dress loafers. He was a little under six feet tall, solidly built, with thick, dark hair worn short on the sides and back, pushed up a little in front. His hair showed some gray that his ex-wife Katie said made him distinguished. His eyes were a soft gray that could turn dark and threatening, like a storm you didn't hear coming.

Those eyes didn't miss much, and they were now assessing the neighborhood surrounding the house where the body was found. The streets and yards were empty during the daytime. The "night people"—a term used by local law enforcement—would gather in great numbers after sundown during the summer months. Mobs of one or two hundred or more would fill the streets and yards, playing loud music, shooting craps, drinking, fighting, snorting, more fighting, only temporarily interrupted by shootings and visits from police. When the sun came up, they would skitter off to wherever such people slept, patch up their wounds, restock their drug of choice, and do it all over again when the sun went down. But in this kind of cold they mostly stayed inside.

Seeing the streets empty gave Jack an eerie feeling. Police activity was like a magnet that woke up some innate need to watch "someone else" victimized. Maybe it was a way of affirming that *all was right with their world*. It was that deep-seated psychological need—that moral panic—that the news media preyed on. But the subzero temps had driven everyone inside—even the news crews—and only the hardcore and disenfranchised remained outside, taking shelter where they could find a warm hole, living inside Dumpsters using cardboard and plastic trash bags for blankets. Katie accused him of being too negative. She said he should be more positive. He was positive he was right to be negative.

At one time, this downtrodden community was six square blocks of homes with normal families raising kids, watering their lawns and washing cars while spraying giggling kids accidentally on purpose. Smack in the center of the blocks was a park filled with swings, tables, benches, flowering trees, and a painted, red-roofed gazebo that doubled for a bandstand in the summer.

The decision was made by the city to use the park grounds to build brightly painted row houses with small fenced yards barely big enough to plant small gardens or flowers. It was meant to benefit the elderly poor and down-on-their-luck poor who couldn't afford a house. Within a year, the row houses had turned into a stain on the landscape. The grass—if there was any—was littered with broken glass, cigarette butts, trash, condoms, syringes, rocks, bricks, sticks and other detritus making a scab on an ugly wound. Not knowing what to do, the city built two-story brick apartment buildings around the row houses for the overflow of poor families. This necessitated demolishing several blocks of existing homes, and financial support in relocating those families, many of whom found homes and jobs in other cities or states. Happy Valley had turned into Crack Alley.

Jack's father had walked this beat as a patrolman. Jack had walked patrol here when he was a rookie. The older folks tended to be honest, kind, polite, and worthy of respect. He'd sit with them on their steps, shooting the breeze, listening to their stories about the past, and listening to their complaints about the new generation.

Over the years, the old folks became afraid to sit outside, much less be seen talking to a policeman. Jack couldn't blame them. The kids here, some as young as eight or ten, were carrying guns and mimicking violent gangsta' rap songs. Last week, someone shot through a window and hit a sleeping seven-year-old girl in the head. A few months ago, a baby was hit with a stray bullet and no one saw or heard anything. The young people's ambitions leaned toward becoming sports MVPs, or rappers, or drug dealers, and driving Cadillac Escalades and owning pit bulls. That was what passed for respect now. Middle-class values were being eaten up. This community had a cancer and no one cared.

The city's solution to the violence and decay was to raze the abandoned homes surrounding the row houses and apartment buildings with the promise of building Habitat homes. When the federal funding stopped, so too did the construction. Now the snow-covered, frozen, uneven land seemed empty and tired. Two or three houses remained, standing out like broken teeth in an empty mouth. An even larger portion of the community was riddled with the decay of poverty, unemployment, drugs, gangs and crime. The community here was dying slowly from loss of hope and lack of faith in a system that had turned its back.

A sharp whistle came from the front of the house. Jack saw a uniformed police officer giving him the thumbs up. The show was about to begin. Tarps were on the ground, creating a temporary walkway. Patrolman Lester Steinberg stood beside the door with a clipboard jammed under one arm, hands stuffed deep into the pockets of his Tuffy police jacket. His head was tucked down so far into the neck of the jacket his uniform hat was resting on the coat collar.

"You're one tough SOB, Murphy," Steinberg said. "I'm surprised you didn't show up in swim trunks and flip-flops."

"And a drink with a little umbrella in it," Jack said.

"Heavy on the Scotch, light on the umbrella," Steinberg joked.

"You got it," Jack said and they both chuckled.

Jack was glad to see someone was having a good day. It was his day off, but he had been *volunteered* to teach a criminal investigation class. He had dressed the part—sport coat, shirt and tie, slacks and thin-soled loafers with those sissy little tassels. Cinderella, his mutt, had chewed up the sleeve of his heavy winter coat yesterday. His plan this morning had been to park close to the building, run in, teach the class, and get the spare warm coat he kept in his office. For now, he was making do with a scarf he'd found under his seat and his thick skin. He was freezing.

He vaguely wondered if he should have some uniform cops canvass the neighborhood for witnesses. Einstein's definition of crazy was doing something again and again, and hoping for a different outcome each time. People in this neighborhood didn't talk to cops. Hell, people in the next neighborhood over didn't talk to cops. They would talk to a reporter, or put something on YouTube, but as for actually doing something good, you could forget it. But he reminded himself that someone would have to do a door-to-door sooner or later. It said so in the detective manual.

Steinberg said, "They should be ready for you shortly. Hey, Jack, I just heard someone inside let a big fart. Does that contaminate the scene?" He grinned at his own joke. He probably wasn't lying.

"In that case, you go in first," Jack said. "You can be my canary."

"I hear your ex is taking you back," Steinberg said, the words puffing out of his jacket like exhaust emissions. "My condolences to her."

On that note, Jack was reminded he had agreed to talk to Katie's sixth-grade class at Harwood School after lunch. He didn't have a clue what he'd talk to a bunch of kids about. With rookie cops, he could just tell dirty jokes and some off-the-record, beyond-the-statute-of-limitations stories.

Kids were always raising their hands and asking if he'd ever shot anyone, or telling him their mom or dad was gay or in prison or both. Stuff he'd rather not know.

This couldn't have come at a worse time. Katie, his ex-wife, had taken him back a few months ago and things were going great. He was eating regularly, having sex regularly, wearing clean clothes, having sex regularly, and he was having sex regularly. That bore repeating. He thought she was happy too. But with women you never knew if saying they're happy was code for something else. The only downside to his renewed relationship was he was drinking less. When it was five o'clock it really was five o'clock. No more beer-eal for breakfast and lunch. Beer-eal was his invention. Rice Krispies and Guinness. The breakfast of Irish champions.

Katie was a teacher at Harwood Grade School. Think of a penitentiary with small people. She had asked/told him to talk to her class about how to become a policeman and to stress they should study. He'd asked her if he could just leave his gun on the classroom floor and let nature take its course. She didn't think that was funny. He'd done what any good married man in his right mind would and agreed to visit San Quentin & Sons. But God sometimes smiles on the Irish, and here he was. It kind of made up for missing his beer-eal breakfast.

He'd have to call Katie and give her the bad news. To be honest, he preferred working a murder to talking to a bunch of twelve-year-olds. He could get somewhere with the murder.

Steinberg said, "You dress like a CEO, not like a cop." Steinberg was visibly shivering.

Jack said, "I'm not a pussy like you. Did your wife dress you this morning? No, wait. Your wife dressed me this morning. Well, undressed me, actually." Jack held his hand out for the sign-in log.

Steinberg said, "Well, I'm glad someone got lucky. Maybe I'll dress like you tonight and get lucky. You think?"

"If I call your wife and break our date tonight will you let me sign in?" Jack asked.

Steinberg said, "I'm not taking my hands out of my pockets. You got hands."

Jack pulled the log out from under Steinberg's arm, signed it, and put it back.

"Who found the deceased?" Jack asked.

"Roscoe's down there," Steinberg said, and motioned down the street by tilting his head. Jack saw a black-and-white cruiser parked on the corner. "He got flagged down by two *white kids. Teenagers.* Boy and girl. Probably down here buying dope. Anyway, Roscoe said they told him they found a dead man, and sure enough, they wasn't lying. It ain't pretty, man."

"Where are they?" Jack asked.

"Like I said, they're down there with Roscoe. Walker is inside. Little Casket's been notified."

He was referring to Chief Deputy Coroner Lilly Caskins, who had been nicknamed Little Casket by law enforcement because of her diminutive size, evil eyes, and total disregard for the dead. An officer had once told Jack, "She could eat a plate of spaghetti on the back of a rotting corpse."

"When was it called in?" Jack asked.

Steinberg said, "About thirty minutes ago. Jeez, Murphy. If you keep asking me questions I'll have to insist on my attorney being present. Besides, I got an alibi."

"Lester, you've always got an alibi. You're too lazy to murder anyone." Jack took green paper booties and latex gloves from his pants pocket and bounced from one foot to the other as he put the booties on. If he stood here much longer he'd have to get his feet amputated.

"Where's your partner?" Steinberg asked.

"In-service training. Liddell missed the last three Sensitivity classes. He's in a nice warm classroom, probably sleeping and dreaming of being nice to the citizens of Evansville."

Steinberg snorted and said, "Sensitivity training, huh? How can they teach someone to be sensitive? It's like teaching ethics. Either you got it or you don't. Am I right?"

"If he's nice, he can come over here later and play," Jack said.

"If he's smart, he'll flunk the class and retake it in the summer months. Anything's better than what you got in there."

Crime Scene Officer Tim Morris came to the door. "Aren't you freezing?" he asked Jack. "Where's your coat?"

"My dog ate it along with my homework," Jack answered, and Morris snickered.

"Where's the Cajun?" Morris asked. Liddell Blanchard, aka Bigfoot, had been Jack's partner on the Homicide Squad for several years. Liddell stood six foot six, and weighed in at a full-grown Yeti. Hence the nickname Bigfoot, although Jack was the only one who called him that to his face. To the rest of the department he was Detective Blanchard, or the Cajun because he had come from a Louisiana Sheriff's department and worked water patrol in and around the Mississippi River.

"I can run out to the car and get you a blanket to cover up with," Morris offered. Morris was suited up like an Eskimo. He was like the Stay Puft Marshmallow Man from the *Ghostbusters* movie.

Steinberg asked, "Could you bring Detective Murphy some warmed-up Scotch and read him a story?"

"I'd say yes to the Scotch, and no to the blanket. But thank you," Jack said.

"Follow me," Morris said. "My boss is waiting for you." His boss was Sergeant Tony Walker.

Jack stayed directly behind Morris. He followed the tech into a room that seemed to be growing a crop of discarded McDonald's boxes, pieces of shattered drywall, broken glass, Styrofoam cups and food wrappers.

McHomeless: Over 1 million NOT served daily.

In one corner of the room was a small pile of ashes where someone had built a fire. He imagined the fire-builder was trying to get warm, or maybe cook someone's pet. He idly wondered if the two teenagers had made the fire.

To his left were the intermittent flashes of crime-scene cameras. Straight ahead a tech snapped photos of a naked corpse that was suspended from the wall like a grotesque marionette, arms and legs bent, head cocked to one side. A blackened tongue protruded from the mouth. Deep cuts slashed across the chest muscles, upper arms and legs. The side of the head was gashed open as well, and large spikes were driven through the victim's eyes.

Frozen blood and fecal matter was pooled on the floor beneath the body. The subzero temperature almost masked the smell that accompanied the kind of violence that had been visited upon this victim. But not quite.

Shards of glass lay on the floor beneath the windows, covered with ice crystals and years of grime. The window frames held jagged pieces of glass like broken teeth. There were holes in much of the drywall where someone had punched or kicked it to strip out the copper wiring. Kids probably. Old damage. Across the room in the far corner some items of clothing were haphazardly piled up. A pair of faded and scuffed combat boots lay on the floor ten or twelve feet away from the clothes.

"Are we having fun yet?" asked a familiar voice from behind Jack.

Jack turned to find Crime Scene Sergeant Tony Walker. Tony was fifty years old and, except for the salt-and-pepper hair, could pass for twenty years younger. He was as tall as Jack, but without an ounce of fat on his sturdy frame. He had been Jack's mentor and partner when Jack first made detective a decade ago. They made a formidable team until Walker was promoted to sergeant and transferred to Crime Scene. At first it seemed like a bad thing that Batman and Robin were split up, but since Tony had taken over the Crime Scene Unit, things ran much more smoothly. The brass was afraid to cross him, and the other detectives respected him. It was the best of both worlds, as far as Jack was concerned. Jack was glad to see Tony was at this scene because it had all the earmarks of a gift that kept on giving. In other words, a case that kicked your ass for months.

Jack said, "What I think is, I wish Bigfoot was here to share in the fun." Jack was unable to take his eyes from the hanging man.

"Where is your partner anyway? He's not coming?"

"You're the third person to ask. No. He's not coming. He's making up an in-service that he missed. Sensitivity training."

Walker said, "They should make you teach sensitivity, Jack. You're the most sensitive guy I know."

"I mean this in the most sensitive way, Tony. Bite me."

"See what I mean," Walker said. "Somebody really didn't like this guy. Let me show you." He said to the tech taking pictures of the body, "Take a break, Jim."

The tech said, "Hi'ya Jack. Where's your partner?"

"Not coming," Jack said. "That's four," Jack said to Walker, as the tech walked away. "Can we identify him?"

"No wallet. There's a pile of clothing over there. Boots there." A ruler and a small red flag set beside each boot. "We haven't finished searching inside and around the outside of the house."

The tech finished taking photos of the clothes and began the collection process. Each piece went into a separate paper bag. Paper bags were used because of the possibility of ice crystals or bodily fluids. The clothes would need to be dried completely to collect any evidence.

The tech said to Walker, "Nothing in the pockets, Sarge."

Walker put his head close to the wall. "Come here Jack. See those," he said, a gloved finger pointing behind the victim's back.

Jack saw the large metal hooks buried in the victim's back, upper arms near the elbows, and legs near the knees. "What the hell, Tony?"

Walker said, "One of my guys says these are used to hang meat in a butcher shop."

"The killer took his time," Jack said.

Walker said, "His bowels evacuated while he was up there."

Jack recognized the signs of livor mortis—the dark purplish coloring that appears on the skin from the pooling of blood after the heart stops pumping. The blood settles in the lowest extremities. "He was hung up there close to his time of death," Jack offered, and Walker agreed.

The victim's head was tilted forward and cocked to one side, effectively hiding the face. Jack stooped down to see the face more clearly. The tongue was swollen, blackened, pushed out of the mouth, but not as pronounced as would be seen in a strangulation-type hanging. The guy's face and head had taken a beating. A two- or three-inch cut on the back of the head was crusted with dried blood. A knife wound ran from above the left ear, continuing down through the jaw. The ear was sliced vertically and teeth showed through the gaping wound. The face, head, neck and shoulders showed small circular burn marks, but something worse caught Jack's eye.

A large piece of black metal protruded only slightly from both eye sockets. Streaks of blood underlined the objects and had run down the cheeks like red tears.

"Are those what I think they are?" Jack asked.

"Yeah," Walker answered. "Railroad spikes." He pointed out the direction of the blood streaks beneath each spike. "This was definitely done after he was hung up here. Maybe when he was still alive."

The scalp was shredded in places, and chunks the size of a quarter were missing in others where bare skull showed through. The hair was burned to the scalp around some of the small circular burn marks. Jack felt numb, and not from the cold.

"Taser burns," Walker suggested, pointing to one of the places where the hair and scalp were burned. "He has them all over his body."

Jack was no stranger to Taser burns. He had volunteered to let himself be Tasered during an in-service training class on the use and effect of Tasers. The Taser uses compressed gas to fire two small metal darts, each with a thin wire attached. The darts strike the target's body, the barbed end of the probes catch in the skin, and at the same time an electric charge flows from Taser to target, interrupting the body's own electrical signals to the muscles. When a Taser is deployed, it runs through a five-second-cycle jolt. Jack could only describe the experience as akin to being struck by a *Star Wars* lightsaber. The muscles lock up, the pain is immediate and severe, but the person is aware of the entire experience. Five seconds was a lifetime, and Jack came away from the event with two small, circular burn marks on his skin, similar to but not as severe as the burns on this body. Whoever did this held the trigger down for a very long time.

Walker pointed to several places. "See these patterns? Four spots in a row. Some of these are overlapping. This isn't a regular Taser. I found a brass knuckle/Taser combination on the Internet. The knucks are made of polyprenco instead of brass. Polyprenco is hard. The advertisement said it has a high melting point and will insulate the person using the knucks from the electric charge."

Jack said, "I'm impressed, Mr. Wizard. I know what polyprenco is. My bagpipe chanter is made of that."

Walker showed Jack a photo on his phone. The weapon was indeed a Taser, but it fit in the hand like brass knucks with pointed studs over each knuckle. This photo was advertising something called a Zapper personal protection device.

"Personal protection doesn't get much deadlier than this," Jack said.

"You can buy them on Amazon or in a sporting goods place."

"I wonder if I can find the killer on Amazon," Jack said sarcastically.

Crime Scene Tech Morris came up to them. "You want us to wait for Little Casket? We're ready to move the body."

Walker said, "No need. Just give her a set of the pictures."

"We didn't find much in the other rooms, Sarge," Morris said. "The only thing I thought strange was the clothing is expensive, brand-name stuff. The boots are crap and don't seem big enough to fit someone this guy's size."

Jack thought something was off about the clothes, but the marionette body with spikes in the eyes had distracted his thought process.

Morris didn't seem to be finished.

"You got something else?" Jack asked him.

"The body has an impression on the ring finger. No ring," Morris said.

A white cotton sheet was positioned on the floor below the body, carefully avoiding the fecal matter. An open body bag was placed on the sheet. Two of the techs snipped the wires and lowered the body slowly. Rigor mortis—stiffening of the muscles—had fully set in and the joints were locked into the position in which he was found, arms and legs akimbo.

"Put him on his side. I want to see his back," Walker told the techs.

A third tech had to forcibly manipulate one of the arms before they were able to put the body on its side.

"Is he frozen in that position? I mean literally frozen?" Jack asked. He knew from experience that rigor mortis set in within two to six hours of death because the muscles lacked some type of chemical process. Rigor could last as little as twelve hours if the body was in a warm or hot environment, and as much as three to five days in cold such as this.

"You'll have to ask the coroner that one," Walker said.

The metal hooks buried in the upper back, arms and legs corresponded with splashes and smears of blood that stained the wall behind the body.

Walker said, "Below-zero temperatures will slow rigor mortis. I suppose Lilly will want a core temperature before we move him."

Jack would skip that part. Core temperature was what it sounded like, and could only be obtained with a rectal thermometer.

To the techs Walker said, "Let's leave him as is and let the deputy coroner decide."

The techs carefully pulled the black bag around the extended limbs. Jack said, "Wait a second. Did you already bag up the boots?"

A tech handed Jack two paper grocery bags. One was sealed with red evidence tape but the other was open. Jack took the boot out of the open sack and knelt. He held the sole of the boot near the bottom of the victim's bare foot. It was obviously too small.

"Don't seal that one, Tony," Jack said. "Corporal Morris. Did you find a ring?"

"No," Morris said. "But I should have mentioned the jacket that was with these clothes is probably worth less than these boots. You think someone came in here and helped themselves to the jacket and boots?"

"Steinberg said the kids that found the body were runaways, right?" Jack asked Walker.

"He didn't tell me that," Walker said. "I know Roscoe was holding them down the street until you got here."

"Tony, can you get the jacket and boots and come with me?"

Walker was given the bag containing the jacket and opened it, but didn't take it out of the bag. He grabbed the single boot and he and Jack went outside.

Chapter 4

Jack and Sergeant Walker hurried through a freezing fog of exhaust plumes to the back of the police car where the two witnesses were being held. Through the windshield, Jack could see a young male and female. The female sat with her back against the passenger door as if she were trying to keep her distance from the male.

Jack rapped on the car window and stuffed his hands under his arms.

The officer turned his head and said something inaudible to his passengers. He braced himself before opening the door, stepped out and pulled his jacket up around his face. The wind wasn't moving much, which made the cold barely tolerable. They walked to the back of the car and Jack could see the boy rubbernecking at them and mouthing something to the girl. She turned her face away, arms crossed. Jack didn't know much about teenagers, but he recognized a pissed-off female when he saw one.

Officer "Roscoe" Dean said, "Hold on a second, guys." He rapped hard on the back windshield, made eye contact and pointed at the young male. The boy faced forward, but Jack could tell his lips were still moving. Undoubtedly, he was saying something age appropriate, like "Screw you, man," or "Up yours, cop."

Roscoe stood away from the exhaust cloud and shifted from one foot to the other, hands jammed in his pockets. Police love to nickname everyone. It comes with the job. The only rule is that you don't get to nickname yourself. Another detective in Jack's office had wanted to be called Magilla Gorilla because of his muscular physique. You never, ever, want to show a weakness around policemen, and it was well-known this detective had a low gag threshold. If someone even pretended to hawk up a gob of spit he would run from the office, hand over his mouth. He was promptly named Loogie, as in *hawking up a loogie*.

"Roscoe" had earned his nickname when he had threatened to beat a child molester with his "roscoe," the old-timer name for the long-barreled revolver police carried back in the day.

Roscoe had as many years of service as the number of lines that cut across his craggy face. His uniform was crisp, with razor-sharp creases in his pants. Even in this cold he wore the eight-point police cap and dress shoes that most officers had traded for BDUs and baseball caps. Roscoe was a veteran policeman in every sense of the word. A throwback to the days when Jack's own father had walked a beat. His gunslinger's eyes told of the suffering he'd seen and somehow shoved into a place in the back of his mind that didn't open except in nightmares.

"Let's make this quick," Jack said.

"Where's your coat?" Roscoe asked.

"I'm not supposed to be here, and Liddell is in sensitivity class," Jack said, wishing they could skip this part.

"None of us are supposed to be here," Roscoe said.

Roscoe pulled a sheet of paper from a small notebook and handed it to Jack. On the paper were the names Zackariah Pugh and Dayton Bolin, aged sixteen and fifteen respectively, along with their addresses and Roscoe's notes on how he came upon them. "I'm finishing the incident report," he said. "I'll do a supplementary report on what the kids told me. I didn't read them their rights. I went in and saw the body." He made a face. "No way these two done what I saw in there. I know the boy and he's a puke, but he could never do something like this."

"I'm going to pull my car up behind you," Jack said. It was too cold to talk outside. "Send the girl back first."

Jack and Walker hurried to the car. Jack cranked it up and made a three-point turn, pulling behind the police car. Roscoe opened the back door and helped the girl out, pointing toward Jack's car. Jack cranked his window down in time to hear Roscoe say to the boy, "Sit still, or I'll get the cuffs out, boy-o." Roscoe was good with kids that way.

Sergeant Walker sat in the back seat and Jack pushed the passenger door open. The girl got in and put her gloved hands against her face to warm it, even with his car heater running like a politician's mouth.

"I'll give you a chance to get warm," Jack said. She didn't respond. Eyes straight ahead.

According to Roscoe's notes, the teens were on Christmas break from Reitz High School. They were both in their junior year. She wore a jacket that swallowed her petite size. Strands of thick, copper-colored hair stuck out from under a fashionable, knit plaid tam, the color of which perfectly complemented her jacket and skintight slacks. In this neighborhood, in this cold, with this guy, she was totally out of place. Jack wondered what this nice girl was doing with this scum-bucket. They belonged together like Donald Trump and Hilary Clinton.

Zack had turned in his seat and was watching them through the windshield. Jack said, "Don't worry about him. Zackariah. Is that his name?"

"Yes."

"I'm Detective Murphy. This is Sergeant Walker. Your name is Dayton Bolin, right?"

"Yes."

"I need to ask you a couple of questions," Jack said.

She opened her mouth to respond but stopped when Sergeant Walker showed her the scuffed combat boot. He opened the bag and took out the rolled-up jacket.

"Where did you get those?" she asked.

"Do you know who they belong to?" Jack asked.

"They're his. Zack's."

"I think you two have some property that doesn't belong to you," Jack said. "If you give it to me...right now...I won't charge you with robbery and murder." He didn't intend to charge them with anything. The boy probably wouldn't talk, but the girl was soft, respectable, law-abiding. She'd break like Humpty Dumpty.

In a voice barely above a whisper Dayton said, "We didn't touch anything. Honest."

"You're not a liar, Dayton." Jack tried to keep a comforting tone, but he didn't do comfort well. Especially when someone stole from a corpse. "Talk to me."

She hugged herself and words spilled from her mouth. "I didn't know Zack took those things. We went in there to get warm and Zack was... we saw..." Her voice broke and she began shaking from more than cold.

Jack softened his voice. "Slow down. Take a deep breath. Now let it out." She did. He said, "Start again. Did you go inside or just Zack?"

"Both of us. It was freezing and we'd walked forever. Zack saw this house and said we should go in and get warm. I didn't think it would be any warmer but Zack said we could start a fire. Zack said he was going to find something to burn. I told him not to."

"How long were you in the house before you saw the—victim?" Jack asked.

She stared at Jack before saying, "I...I'm not sure."

"Guess," Jack prompted.

She turned her head away and said, "I'm not sure. Maybe a few minutes. We came in the back door. I stayed in the kitchen. I didn't know what he was doing. I never thought…"

"And what happened?"

"When Zack came back in the kitchen I knew something was wrong. I went to see and that's when I saw… I just ran to find a cop…I mean a policeman."

"Did Zack go with you to find the cop?"

"I don't know. No. I saw the police car and when the policeman brought me back Zack was standing out front."

Jack saw her stealing glances at the boot in Walker's hand. "Did Zack take anything from the house besides these boots?" He could see the wheels turning in her mind and added, "I'll know if you're lying, Dayton."

"I didn't know Zack took anything. I swear!" she said. "That's Zack's boot, but he's not like that. He's a sweet guy."

"Dayton, what kind of jacket was Zack wearing this morning?" Walker asked. He opened the paper sack and showed her the tattered blue jean jacket.

Her expression told Jack that it was Zack's jacket.

"Does he have anything else?" Jack asked. "If you don't come clean you will be an accessory to theft at the least, and maybe obstruction of justice."

"The policeman had Zack come and sit in the back of the car with me and he went in the house. While Zack was in the house he must have found the boots and he was wearing a different coat from what he had on this morning. That's Zack's blue jean jacket in the sack," she said. "He showed me a bunch of money. He said he found it in the pocket of the coat along with the ring."

"Dayton, I want you to stay right here. Do you have anything from the house? Did he give you anything? I'll search you and these cars before we take you downtown. You might as well give it to me."

She shook her head. "I didn't take anything. Zack tried to give me the ring, but I couldn't stand the thought of…you know."

Jack and Walker left Dayton in Jack's car and took Zack from the back of Roscoe's car. Zack was wearing a heavy winter parka and a newish pair of Wolverine lace-up boots.

"Can you help Sergeant Walker search the car?" Jack asked Roscoe. To the boy Jack said, "Come on."

While Walker and Roscoe searched the car, Jack took Zack to the side and said to him, "Nice coat."

Zack's mouth twisted into a sneer. "You haven't read us our rights. Anything she said to you isn't usable. I know that much. And I don't have to tell you shit, man."

"Why should I read Miranda rights to you?" Jack asked, and Zack turned away.

"What do a pair of those boots cost?" Jack asked. They were dark brown, suede leather. They were too big for the boy's feet.

"What? These?" Zack said like a practiced liar, "My dad bought me these for Christmas. I don't have any idea what they cost. You like them? He can tell you where to go."

Jack watched Walker pop the back seat loose. In police cars, the seats were made to be easily detached because it was a favorite place for those inclined to hide things. It was police policy to search the back seat before and after transporting a prisoner or anyone else. Walker straightened up almost immediately, holding something in his hands.

Zack said, "Whatever that is, it's not mine. Even if it was mine—and I'm not saying it is—it don't mean nothing. Money's money. I'll bet you've got money in your pocket. So what? I don't know how it got in the car but I didn't steal it and you can't prove shit. Someone else could have left it. That cop probably stuck it down the seat."

Dayton got out of Jack's car and came forward. "Give him the rest of the things you stole, Zack, or we'll go to jail. He's not kidding."

"I didn't steal nothing, Dayton," Zack said. To Jack and Walker he said, "She's just scared. You're bullying her."

"That money wasn't ours, Zack. Those aren't your boots, or your coat, or any of it. You took them from...from... the dead guy? What is *wrong* with you?"

"It ain't like I was gonna keep it. I just wanted to show the badge to my buddies. You know?" He dug in his pocket, pulled out a black bifold wallet. *Badge?*

Jack took the wallet from Zack. Sure enough, inside was a police badge. A gold sergeant's shield on one side of the fold, police credentials on the other that identified Detective Sergeant Franco Caparelli. Evansville Police Department.

Jack grabbed the boy by the shoulders, spun him around and shoved him face down over the police car's trunk. He patted Zack down, reaching in his pants pockets and turning them inside out. A couple of wrinkled dollar bills and some change came out on the frozen ground. Jack stripped Zack's coat off, searched it, and shoved the boy toward Roscoe. Walker and Roscoe had snapped the backseat in place and Jack shoved the kid onto it. He yanked the boots off of Zack's feet and when he did a gold-nugget ring fell onto the street.

Jack scooped up the ring.

"That's the ring I told you about," Dayton said.

"Now you," Jack said. He patted down Dayton's jacket. He asked her to unzip it and hold it up while he checked her waistband. She slid her shoes off while he searched them. He said to Roscoe, "Sit her in the front. Put him in the back. Don't let them talk."

Dayton said curtly, "I wouldn't talk to him anyway. How could you, Zack?"

Roscoe put a hand on Dayton's shoulder. "Come on," he said, and put her in the passenger seat. He leaned in the car and said, "You heard the detective. No talking. Do we understand each other?"

"Are you going to put us in jail?" Dayton asked.

Zack said, "Seeing as we ain't done nothing, I guess they won't. You guys wouldn't have found this guy if it wasn't for us. So are we free to go?"

"No," Jack said.

Roscoe motioned for Dayton to put her seat belt on. Zack started to do the same and Roscoe said, "Hold up there, champ." He leaned Zack over and put him in handcuffs.

Jack handed the nugget ring and the badge case to Walker. He came around to Zack and said, "Stick your feet out."

When Zack did, Jack yanked the socks from his feet. "These probably aren't yours," Jack said, and handed two pairs of socks to Walker.

"Roscoe, can you call Juvenile and tell them these two are coming. I want them separated until I can interview them." Before Roscoe shut the door, Jack asked, "Is there anything else you need to tell me before it's too late? For example, did you find a gun?"

Zack said, "I'll sue your asses. You can't leave me out here without a jacket or nothing on my feet. You got no right to take my stuff. This is police brutality."

Jack lost his patience and started to climb in the back seat. "Cop killing is a capital offense punishable by death," Jack said through clenched teeth.

Zack recoiled. He'd lost the cocky attitude. "I swear to God, man. I'm telling you the truth. I didn't take nothing. Someone must have left that money back here. I only took the coat and shoes because I was freezing. The ring and the badge were in the jacket pockets. I didn't touch the money and I don't have anything else… I swear. Ask Dy."

Jack stared at him and Zack wisely turned his head away.

"Roscoe, take these young people to Juvenile," Jack said.

Roscoe asked, "You want me to charge him with theft? Desecration of a corpse? Being stupid?"

"Forty thousand in one-hundred-dollar bills." Walker had counted the money. "Four bundles. Ten thousand to a bundle. Still in bank wrappers."

Zack whistled.

"Shut up," Jack said. "Just take him to Juvenile for now, Roscoe. I haven't made up my mind."

"I'll have one of my people get their fingerprints downtown," Walker said. "I won't be able to get Zack's real boots downtown for a bit. I have to get shoe prints and photos of the soles of both of their footwear for comparison."

Roscoe said, "I'll have Juvenile notify the parents to bring shoes and warm clothes."

"Zack won't be going anywhere for a good while," Jack said.

"I'm not a thief. You can check your records all day and you won't find nothing. I only took the stuff 'cause we got nothing. That guy didn't need it no more. We needed money to get us started, but we didn't kill him. I'm telling the truth now. The money was in the pocket of the jacket too. I swear to God!"

"Where were you going?" Jack asked Zack.

"We *were* on our way to Hollywood. Plays, television, movies, commercials...well, commercials if the other stuff don't work out," Zack said. "We're actors."

Jack said, "Here's the deal. If...and that's a big if...you aren't more involved than what you've told me, I'll let you both go. But part of that deal is that you and Dayton don't speak a word to each other until you're interviewed and give a statement. If you so much as breathe on each other, I'll charge you with interfering with a corpse and an IC-Seventy and Thirty-Five." He counted on them not knowing he was making up charges.

Roscoe got in the car and said to Jack, "I'll take Brad and Angelina here to headquarters. Maybe Juvie will find them a talent scout."

Jack said, "I'll settle for finding their parents. I hate to ask this, Roscoe, but do you mind staying on this for a bit? Juvenile might need help running down the parents."

"I always wanted to be a detective," Roscoe said with a fake grin. He put his seat belt on and said, "Nah. I never wanted to be a detective," and drove off.

Walker said, "Little Casket's here."

Jack watched the police car drive away. He could see Zack's profile in the side window. The kid was destined for prison, or worse. Kids like that didn't have a chance.

"Let's go see Lilly," Jack said.

Chapter 5

Little Casket climbed down from the driver's side of the black Suburban and walked carefully to the curb. That she had made this run herself suggested two possibilities. One, she was bored and needed something interesting, like a good murder. Or two, she was just going to be angry and nasty for its own sake.

She pulled on latex gloves as she walked toward Jack and Walker. "Heard it's Sonny Caparelli," she said.

Jack gaped at her, wondering how she knew who the victim was when he'd just found out himself.

"Close your mouth, Murphy, you'll catch pneumonia," she said. "I got a call from the dispatcher who got a call from one of your guys." Little Casket said something that was totally out of character for her. "Too bad. Sonny was one of the good ones." She pushed her way between Jack and Walker. "I haven't got all day. Let's get to it."

The men followed her up to the house, listening to an unending stream of complaints about being short-handed, underpaid, tired of this shit, and so on.

As she signed into the crime scene, Walker said, "A couple of teenage runaways found the body about an hour ago."

She nudged her glasses up the bridge of her nose and scowled. "Well, are you going to take me in, or shall I just wander around until I trip over the body?"

After Jack and Walker signed the crime scene log again, Lilly went directly to the body. She knelt down and zipped open the body bag. "Huh," was her only remark upon seeing the damaged body with metal spikes driven through both eye sockets. She examined the eyebolts and wires still buried in the drywall, and then the body. The wire that was wrapped around the knees, wrists and neck had been left in place by the techs.

She pointed to the chain hoist and asked, "What gives?"

"He was hanging from meat hooks and steel cable. There were three-inch hooks in his back and the same in his buttocks," Walker said. "His arms and legs were suspended by more wire but no hooks."

"Huh." She felt the skin on the side of the neck. "Did someone get the temperature in the room?"

Walker said, "Two degrees below zero in this room. Same as outside. The back door was standing open. Front door is missing. The window is mostly gone."

"Duh," she said. "I only asked for the room temperature."

Lilly was even more foul-tempered than usual.

"She's having a bad day," Jack mouthed at Walker.

"I'm not deaf," Lilly said. "Every day is a bad day. But I'm not complaining."

She pinched several of Sonny's fingernails and watched for a reaction. "No blanching," Lilly mumbled. She pushed at the skin on his throat to check for resilience. His muscles were stiff. Skin was stiff.

"Help me turn him," she said. Walker and another tech lifted the body, allowing her to see underneath. When she was satisfied, she said, "We need to get him in the freezer, chop chop."

"I'll get the gurney," Officer Morris said. He headed out to Lilly's Suburban, where a gurney was stowed like in the back of an ambulance.

Without thanking Morris, she said, "I called Dr. John as soon as I heard who the victim was. How did you identify him?" she asked. "Not by his face."

Jack told her about the badge, but didn't mention the money they'd found. He hoped Roscoe wouldn't say anything about it either.

"I'm going to guess for you, Jack, but I can be way off depending on when he was last seen."

"I'll keep that in mind," Jack said. Sometimes Lilly's guess was as good as an autopsy. She'd been around death since Moses parted the Red Sea.

"My guess is six to twelve hours." She checked the clock on her cell phone. "Estimated time of death is nine p.m. yesterday to around midnight. Maybe more, maybe less. That's the best I can do. He didn't freeze to death anyway, but he may be frozen by now."

She added, "I went to a medico-legal death class a few months ago. On my own dime, of course. An average-size person will freeze completely in twelve hours at zero degrees. We need to get him in the freezer at the morgue to stop the freezing process. I'll get a core temperature there. If you're through with it, I'll take the body. I may need one of your guys to help load him and unload him. I don't have any help right now."

Walker said, "I'll send Officer Morris with you."

Morris came back with the gurney. He and Walker and Jack helped get the body bag on it. It was like picking up a block of ice. A heavy block.

"Call me when the autopsy is set," Jack said.

"Where's Bigfoot?" Little Casket asked. She was probably the only other person who dared call Liddell that.

"He's learning how to be sensitive," Jack said.

"Thank the gods!" Lilly said, and her mouth turned up a little at the corners.

"Did you just make a joke, Lilly?"

She scoffed and said to Officer Morris, "What are you waiting for? I get cold like everyone else."

Morris said, "Yes ma'am," and pushed the gurney out the door.

Jack followed them outside, got in his car and cranked up the heat. As fast as word was traveling, Captain Franklin would surely have heard the deceased was Sergeant Caparelli. Jack would be remiss in his duty if he didn't tell him in person, and that thought led to another. The news media would know too.

Murphy's Law says: *The news media's idea of what the public needs to know is directly proportional to media ratings.* He figured he'd have just enough time to get Liddell out of class and notify Sonny's next of kin before the murder was on the air.

He took out his cell phone and called the dispatch supervisor directly.

"Connie," she said, coming on the line. Not "Vanderburgh County Central Emergency Dispatch. How may I help you?"

She had explained to Jack once that by the time she spit out that entire preamble, the caller probably forgot why they were calling, or the problem had resolved itself, or everyone was dead. That's why Jack loved her. She was a bitch. But she was their bitch.

"Connie. I need a favor," he said and heard a laugh, of sorts.

"What a surprise. Okay. Go ahead."

He said, "I need you to find any vehicles belonging to Sergeant Caparelli, and I need—"

Connie interrupted him. "Already done, Jack. He drives a black 2016 Dodge Ram Laramie dually. I called the sector sergeants by telephone and put out a description and plates. I was just getting ready to call you. Car 13 found it in the Royal Food Market parking lot with the keys left in it and the window down. Car 13 is standing by," she said.

"I'm on my way, Connie," he said.

She said, "Sonny was one of the good ones, Jack. Who would want to do this to him?"

Jack didn't know Sonny very well. He knew Sonny was recruited by EPD and immediately assigned to EPD's part of the Federal Drug Task Force. The FDTF was made up of Evansville officers, Vanderburgh County deputies, Drug Enforcement Agents, and ATF Agents—Alcohol, Tobacco and Firearms. Jack avoided any involvement with narcotics cases like the plague. Jack's idea of hell on earth was being assigned to the Narcotics Unit.

Five Evansville Police officers were assigned to the Task Force, and Sonny was their sergeant. Sergeant Caparelli must have been a good guy, because everyone was saying so. Even Little Casket, and she wouldn't spit on her own mother if she had one. He shuddered at the thought of Little Casket as a newborn. All pink and wrinkled, already wearing thick-lensed glasses and bitching at the delivery doctor.

Chapter 6

Jack drove north on Fulton Avenue from Columbia Street. Royal Food Market was seven or eight blocks away from where the body was found. The keys were left in Sonny's truck. Maybe Sonny was waiting for someone. They came up. He got out and left the truck running. He was taken from there by force. He wouldn't wait with his windows down. Not in this kind of weather. Whoever took Sonny must have rolled down the windows and left the keys, hoping the truck would be stolen.

The killing scene was such a trash pit it would be hard to tell if there was a struggle. Jack's mind turned to Sonny's job. Sonny could have gone to the house on a drug deal. The forty thousand might be "buy money." The killer dumped the truck at Royal Market. It wasn't far away. But why leave the money behind?

Jack called Walker. "Did you know Sonny's truck was found at Royal Foods? I'm headed there now. I'll let you know if I find anything. Can you see if one of your guys is on their way?"

"I knew, and someone is already there," Walker advised.

Jack saw a white crime-scene SUV parked behind a new Dodge Ram truck in the parking lot of Royal Foods. The truck was facing Fulton Avenue. The driver's door stood open.

Jack turned into the parking lot and asked Walker, "Have you found Sonny's weapon?"

"Not yet," Walker said.

"I'm just pulling up. Thanks." Jack disconnected and parked behind a relatively new Mercedes SUV with EPD Crime Scene markings. He could see the butt, legs, and feet of someone digging under the driver's seat of the truck. The back hatch of the Crime Scene SUV was open and no one else in sight. No sign of Car 13.

"You need some help?" Jack asked.

"Hi'ya Jack," Joanie Ryan said, and got to her feet. "I found something."

Joanie was one of the first civilian crime scene technicians hired by the city. Using civilians with degrees in forensics was the brainchild of Mayor Thatcher Hensley. Surprisingly, it turned out to be a good idea.

Hensley peddled his decision to hire civilians as *forward thinking* and a *savings to the city*. He said the civilian techs were paid half of what the sworn officers made, and were given fewer benefits because they weren't full time. Chief of Police Marlin Pope had argued against the change because of the lack of control the department would have over these individuals. Pope predicted there would be a more frequent turnover rate, and you usually get what you pay for. Joanie Ryan seemed to be the exception to the chief's fears. She did good work. She was thorough and wrote readable reports. She listened instead of arguing.

"What have you got?"

"Just a sec, Jack." She snapped some pictures of the driver's side floorboard and under the seat. She reached under the seat and pulled out a large manila mailing envelope. "It's not sealed. Think we should peek inside?"

"We'd be crazy not to," Jack said.

She carefully undid the clasp that held it closed and opened the top. "Holy shit!"

She held the envelope open for him to see inside.

"Holy shit!" Jack said.

* * * *

Inside the envelope were six bundles of one-hundred-dollar bills held together with mustard-colored wrappers. Each bundle was ten thousand dollars, according to the wrappers.

"Sixty thousand dollars," Joanie said, sounding like she didn't trust her own eyes.

"Yeah," Jack said. This made an even one hundred thousand dollars.

"I'll take the truck to the secure garage so I can go through it better," Joanie said. "The money? I've never dealt with this much money."

Jack scanned the area. He wasn't going to leave her out here, alone, with sixty thousand dollars cash.

"Call for a flatbed wrecker," Jack said. "I'll stay with you until it arrives and you can follow it to the garage. Bag the money. Don't tell anyone, and don't let it out of your sight until you give it to Sergeant Walker."

"By the way, I didn't see anything else in the truck. No gun, phone, notes, letters. Nothing. He kept it spotless."

Jack had asked Walker if they had found Sonny's gun and they hadn't. Not in the truck either. "None of this goes on the air. Use your cell phone. A flatbed wrecker is on the way. Do your supplemental report but don't turn it in to records until you run it by Sergeant Walker or myself."

"Do you think Sergeant Caparelli…"

Jack said, "I don't think anything yet, and neither do you. Oh, and if Deputy Chief Dick asks questions…"

"Lie to him," she finished his sentence. "No problem."

Jack felt some empathy for her. She was in possession of evidence that might reflect negatively on a fellow officer. Sides would be taken. She could get hurt no matter how it turned out.

"Good find, by the way," he said, and she smiled. They chatted some more while they waited for the wrecker. She left following the tow truck and he headed downtown to break his partner out of class. He would try to be sensitive.

He called Captain Franklin while he thawed out in his car.

Chapter 7

Franklin had very few questions, and like a good supervisor got right to the point, saying very wisely, "You've got to solve this quick, Jack. Come to my office."

Jack did, and was greeted with a grunt by the chief's secretary, Judy Mangold. "You can go right in. Where's your partner?"

"In prison," Jack said, and she grunted again.

He entered the captain's office and was greeted by the chief saying, "Tell me."

Jack told Chief Pope what he'd told Captain Franklin concerning the discovery of the identity of the victim, the money found on the kid, the money found in Sonny's truck, and the absence of a weapon. The chief and captain didn't ask a lot of questions. They just wanted to know something to tell the Mayor in case of a news-media invasion. Murphy's Law says: *If shit rolls downhill, at the top it must be one huge turd.* The Mayor was a well-known turd, and would shit all over the chief if it suited his own interests.

"Can I borrow Liddell?" Jack asked.

"Of course. I'll contact Narcotics and the Task Force. Do you need more detectives?" Captain Franklin asked.

"If I need detectives, I'd like to pick my own," Jack said. "I still have to notify Sonny's next of kin. As far as Narcotics or the Task Force, I won't be able to get to them immediately."

Captain Franklin asked the million-dollar question. "Is there any chance they've been compromised?" In other words, could one or all of them be involved in the death or what led up to Sonny's death?

"Considering the world they live in, I can't rule anything out," Jack answered.

Chief Pope said, "The cat's already out of the bag. Claudine Setera from Channel 6 has called, and I've agreed to do a news release at nine. She's asking about thousands of dollars in cash found with the body. I'm only going to confirm it's Sergeant Caparelli, and that we are investigating a suspicious death."

Jack bit back a nasty remark. Channel 6 knew more than he wanted released. He'd hoped to keep knowledge of the money in a very tight circle.

"They didn't say anything about the money in the truck?" Jack asked.

"Not yet," the chief answered.

"Captain, when you call the Task Force will you ask them to stay in their office until I get there? Say, in an hour," Jack said.

Franklin said, "I'll round them up. You'd better get going."

* * * *

Jack made a quick stop in the office to get a heavier coat and headed downstairs. The door to the Police Training Room was closed, lights off, a PowerPoint presentation playing on the projection screen. This was supposed to be Sensitivity Training, but the photos the class was seeing were anything but sensitive. The current slide was a split-screen picture of bullet entry and exit wounds, brain matter, tissue disruption and all the trimmings. The next slide showed a circular puncture wound on a baby's chest. The next showed a two-inch round chunk of meat missing from where the bullet exited the baby's back.

The slide changed to a picture of the FBI emblem. The lights came on and Jack recognized the instructor. FBI Special Agent Frank Tunney of the National Center for the Analysis of Violent Crime (NCAVC) in Quantico, Virginia. Tunney was a profiler.

Jack opened the door in time to hear Tunney say, "Remember kiddies, be back in ten minutes or you'll be marked absent." There was chuckling and the general chaotic sounds of chairs scraping as the herd of policemen thinned.

Liddell came from the back corner of the room, yawning. "Did you miss me?" he asked Jack.

For a large man, he had a soft side. Talking to the juveniles and their parents would require finesse that Jack didn't have. Notifying Sonny's family would likewise need a gentle touch, and Jack was better at shooting people than being nice to them.

"I need you," Jack said, and immediately regretted his choice of words.

"I've told you before, Detective Murphy, I'm already spoken for. Besides, what would Katie say?" Liddell said, and batted his eyes at Jack.

"We've got a case," Jack said, not wanting to encourage Liddell or he'd never get him stopped. "I've already briefed the captain and chief."

"Sonny Caparelli," Liddell said. "I heard."

"Captain Franklin has given permission for you to skip the sensitivity class. I told him if you got any more sensitive you'd cry and wring your hands like an old woman."

"Hah," Liddell said. "They're only making me take this class because you're my pod'na."

"Speaking of sensitivity, what's with all the blood-and-guts pictures? And for that matter, why is Tunney here?"

"Oh. The sensitivity class was cancelled," Liddell said. "Frank was in town for a meeting or something and offered to do a criminal profiling class. Frank was just explaining the difference between organized and disorganized killers."

"There's no difference, Bigfoot. A killer is a killer. Dead is dead. What's with the dead-baby pictures?"

"He was using that to get everyone's attention. You know how policemen are. You have to piss them off to get them to focus."

"Let's go," Jack said. He wanted to get things moving. Before long, the Task Force guys would be out beating the bushes for the suspect, and afterwards beating the suspects. He'd seen the aftermath of guys they said had "resisted" arrest. He'd strong-armed suspects before, but he drew the line at old ladies, nuns and children. Sometimes he wondered why the chief didn't put them on a shorter leash. Or a choke chain. In their defense, he could never do what they do. Dealing with meth-head zombies wasn't his forte.

"Hold on, pod'na," Liddell said. "I have to tell you something. Frank showed us a picture of a guy who was found in the closet with the handle of a Hoover vacuum cleaner shoved up..."

"Please," Jack said, and put his hands over his ears. He didn't even want to think about it. Luckily, he didn't have to, because FBI Special Agent Frank Tunney approached them and held his hand out to Jack.

"Good to see you again, Frank," Jack said, shaking hands. Tunney was tall and lean with an athlete's aura. His eyes were light gray and he was dressed in the traditional blue suit that was the school uniform for FBI agents. Jack always thought the FBI should wear kilts like their founder J. Edgar Hoover—like ancient Highland warriors.

"Hello, Jack. Been a while. You never write, you never call..." Tunney said and gripped Jack's hand in both of his.

"Oh great," Liddell said. "An FBI guy with a sense of humor. I certainly don't need the competition."

Jack said, "I haven't needed your expertise for a while, Frank."

Tunney had earned his PhD in Psychology from Harvard at the age of twenty and had spent almost ten years teaching before being recruited into the FBI's famous behavioral analysis unit. He had assisted in high-profile cases not only in the United States, but had been requested and loaned out to several other countries. For someone in his forties, he'd had a full life. Tunney had a reputation as the FBI's Serial Killer Hunter. His job was to detect, track and apprehend serial killers, and he was very good at doing just that. Jack had worked the "Cleaver" case with Tunney a while back, when a serial killer was literally taking his victim's faces for souvenirs.

Jack said, "Frank, I'm going to steal the teacher's pet. I need him to make a death notification."

"Oh, that's too bad," Tunney said with a boyish grin. "His snoring was the only thing keeping the rest of them awake. If you need some help on the Caparelli case I'll be in town a few more days."

Jack must have looked surprised, because Tunney said, "I heard it through the grapevine."

Jack said, "One man's grapevine is another man's megaphone. But I appreciate the offer."

"Sonny was with Narcotics. Do you think it was a drug deal gone bad?" Tunney asked.

"To be honest, Frank, I don't know all that much yet. It has all the earmarks of a revenge killing."

"Revenge?" Tunney asked. "Hmm. I might be interested. It's not a serial killer, but I use this type of murder in my lectures. If you want I can run the manner of death through our database."

"Good idea. I'll have Sergeant Walker send you a copy of his report. We've really got to go. Thanks for the offer," Jack said, and thought he was crazy not to pick Tunney's brain. If he didn't get a lead real quick, he'd have to run the murder profile through ViCAP—Violent Criminal Apprehension Program. It was part of Tunney's unit. It would search for similar methods of killing—signatures—to track and maybe identify the killer.

"If we catch the bastard, you can put him in your system," Jack said.

"You'll catch him, Jack. I have confidence in you."

"I don't know about that, Frank."

Tunney said, "I heard some runaway kids found the body. And I heard you haven't found the sergeant's handgun."

"Yeah. The kids are upstairs. And speaking of that, we need to get hustling."

"Do you think the kids took the gun?" Tunney asked.

"I turned the boy upside down and shook him till his teeth fell out," Jack said, and Tunney chuckled.

"I'll just bet you did. Is there a connection between the kids and the victim? Was he married?" Tunney asked.

Liddell said, "No. A live-in girlfriend."

Jack said, "I haven't really had a chance to talk to them. That's a good question though. You're always good for an idea or two, Frank."

"You know I normally advise on cases that have gone cold, but if you need my help I'll be here. I've got a couple more classes scheduled for tomorrow." He gave Jack a business card. "Here's my cell number in case you lost it. I'm in room 45. Or I'll be in the casino spending my per diem."

Jack put the card in his pocket. "I'm glad to know my tax money is going to such a worthy cause," Jack said. "Thanks, Frank."

"Hey, I hear you're back with Katie," Tunney said. "Why don't you join me for dinner tonight." To Liddell he said, "Bring Marcie. I hear she's eating for two now."

Jack grinned. "Bigfoot's eating for two. Or three."

An officer got Tunney's attention and he excused himself.

"How does he know all this stuff?" Jack asked as they left the classroom. They walked up the back stairs and Jack stopped Liddell before they exited onto the main floor. "I'm going to call the captain before we leave."

He got Captain Franklin on the phone. "Captain, I think I may need some help on this."

"What do you need, Jack?"

"Two detectives on each shift for the neighborhood checks around the scene and Royal Food Market. Also see if there's any video in either area. Businesses, drug houses. Some of the houses around there have personal security cameras."

"Will do," Franklin said.

Jack thanked the captain, hung up and asked Liddell, "What do you know about the case, Bigfoot?"

Liddell told him, and apparently Channel 6's Claudine Setera had more information than had leaked inside the police department. He caught Liddell up on the scene, the kids, the money, and the investigation and let him chew on it as they left headquarters.

Chapter 8

"I'll drive, Bigfoot. According to dispatch, Sonny lives out by my cabin." Jack headed southeast to Riverside Drive, east to Waterworks Road, past Two Jakes Restaurant and Marina, and turned onto a private drive marked with a metal sign tacked to a tree: *NO TRESPASSING*. A hundred yards down the drive sat half a dozen locking mailboxes. No names. No house numbers. Only a number stenciled on them. Past that was an eight-foot-high iron gate with a massive stone entrance. A bronze plate set into the stone read, *RIVER POINTE ESTATES*.

"I've passed this drive hundreds of times," Jack said. "You can see some of the houses from the river, but I've never come back here." Jack's cabin was a mile or two east of Sonny's.

Jack pulled forward to an intercom box with a camera that swiveled to face the car. There were six buttons on the intercom with names and no numbers. Jack was impressed. It was a decent security setup. He pressed the button marked for Caparelli and waited.

A woman's slurred voice came over the intercom. "Come on in. I'm at the end." The gate automatically opened.

Jack pulled through the gate. "Have you met Sonny's girlfriend, Bigfoot?"

Liddell said, "Me and Marcie ran into her and Sonny at The Log Inn once. They said hello, we said hello. She seemed nice."

They continued down the drive, past expensive homes with spacious yards landscaped with hedges and small decorative trees and nameplates for each house, with names like River Castle and River View, all river-something except for one that read Casa Thatcher.

"What do you want to bet that place belongs to our illustrious mayor?" Jack said pointing to Casa Thatcher.

"I'm not a gambler, pod'na."

"Probably five-acre lots," Jack said. "The three on the left have a riverfront view. This is not a cheap place to live."

"Rich people always name their houses," Liddell explained.

The road continued straight and disappeared around a bend. They came to another gate, this one open. Ornate but serious-looking spikes topped the double gates and fence to discourage trespassing. There was another camera and intercom.

At least an acre of the property inside the gate was dotted with low trees, the branches of which swept to the ground and were full of pinkish-white blossoms.

"Isn't that beautiful," Liddell said. "Not many trees bloom in this cold. I wonder what they are. Marcie would love it."

The gate swung shut behind the car. In the side mirror Jack saw the camera swivel, following their progress.

"Big Brother's watching," Jack said.

"Maybe Bill Gates lives here," Liddell said. "Get it? Gates? Oh, never mind."

The driveway was lined with more blossoming trees. The road continued to climb gently and turned toward the river before opening into a landscaped lawn. At the back of this was a monstrous sprawling ranch with a gabled roof and a four-car attached garage. One of the bay doors was open. A black four-door Mercedes was backed in.

"She's got company," Jack remarked and parked in front of the house.

Liddell let out a low whistle. "Wow! This place makes my house a shack. And speaking of shacks, how does it feel to live in a real home again?" Liddell was referring to Jack recently moving his things from his river cabin back into the house he shared with his ex-wife, Katie. "How many trips did it take you to move all of the Scotch?"

"You're implying my cabin is a shack and I'm an alcoholic. Is that what you're saying, Bigfoot?"

"Well...yeah."

"Well. Bite me," Jack said.

They walked up to the front door and Jack pushed the doorbell.

The door was opened immediately by a cadaverous man in a three-piece suit. He was nearly as tall as Liddell and had a prominent nose. It was like a doorknob with varicose veins. "Can I help you gentlemen?"

Jack pegged the guy at forty-five to fifty, not into exercise, vegetarian, and the too-tight dark green suit said car salesman or butler or personal injury attorney—or a reanimated cadaver.

Jack and Liddell showed the man their police credentials. Jack said, "We're here to see Miss Middleton."

The man didn't offer to introduce himself or ask why they wanted to talk to Miss Middleton. He frowned and said, "This way, please."

Jack and Liddell followed the man down a hallway. Double doors on the right looked into a book-lined study with a wet bar in one corner and a stone fireplace with several tall brass candlesticks on its mantelpiece. The room was decorated with expensive leather furniture.

"*Mr. Green* in the *library* with the *candlestick*," Liddell whispered.

The man slowed and fixed Liddell with a glare. "What did you say?"

"I said this is a great house," Liddell answered. "By the way, it's kind of you to lead us around. We could get lost in this place." He smiled. The man did not.

"This way." The man turned down an intersecting hallway.

"*Liddell* in the *hallway* with the *lead pipe*?" Jack said.

"Hey," Liddell said to the man. "You're going to show us the way out when we're done, right? I mean, I forgot to bring a pocketful of bread crumbs or M&Ms."

The man ignored the remark. They came to the end of the hallway. The man opened a set of pocket doors and motioned them inside.

They entered a spacious great room that was over-decorated for Jack's taste. But then, a bed, a chair and a box for a wardrobe were fine with him. Leather furniture was strewn around the room like the aftermath of a bar fight. No doubt an interior designer was paid handsomely for this reckless placement. Thick rugs were scattered strategically. Two full suits of armor stood on either side of a wood-burning fireplace. The fireplace was large enough for a man to walk into without ducking. Several hutches were placed around the room, displaying odd collections consisting of music boxes, ceramic figurines of children, dogs, frogs, and other detritus Jack would have thrown on a burn pile. In one hutch were a number of carved figurines of monkeys in various poses and states of activity. Some were sitting, some were hanging from a branch attached to an imaginary tree, their mouths peeled back as if screeching, and some were just being monkeys. It reminded Jack of a congressional hearing in progress.

One entire wall of the room was made of glass, giving a view of the ice-covered lawn and white-blossoming trees. At the far end of the room, French doors opened onto a brick patio with an in-ground Olympic-sized pool that was covered for the winter. Beside the pool was a cabana with a tiki bar and a stone outdoor fireplace. *Throw a little sand on the ground, set up a chair, a bottle of Scotch—instant Bahamas.*

"So, this is how the other one-half of one-half percent live," Liddell quipped.

"Yeah, ain't it somethin'," came a breathy voice from somewhere off to their left.

Draped on a white suede sofa was a thirty-something-year-old woman, wrapped in a filmy, leopard-patterned robe. Behind her was another hutch, this one filled with Santa dolls of all sizes, wearing clothing from around the world, some in costumes of golfers, baseball players, ninjas, even a scene of samurai warriors battling with katanas, Japanese swords.

On the coffee table in front of the woman were a dozen or more ceramic miniatures of Mr. and Mrs. Santa Claus in various poses, some of them sexually explicit. *Sorry, Santa.* A silver cigarette case sat open next to an overflowing ashtray, next to an empty magnum-size bottle of wine. She held a burning cigarette in one hand. In the other hand was a Big Joe wineglass filled to the rim. She took a drag off the cigarette, followed instantly by a sip of wine. A sip, in her case, was half the glass. Jack had seen gutter drunks with more manners. He was glad she was sloshed. It would save her time after they gave her the news.

"Hello, Miss Middleton," Liddell said. "I'm Liddell Blanchard."

"I met you and your wife. Right?" Mindy said, cocking one eye at him.

"At The Log Inn a while back," Liddell said.

She said, "Yeah. I remember. Marilyn, right?"

"Marcie," Liddell corrected. "This is Detective Jack Murphy."

Mindy unsteadily lifted herself from the sofa. She extended a hand that was heavy with jewelry. Her face might be called pretty if she wasn't toasted. Bottle-blond hair with dark roots was piled on top of her head. She removed a clip and shook it down around her shoulders. Jack took a hand that was cold despite the heat from the blazing fire.

"Mindy. That's short for Miranda, ya' know? You gonna read me my rights, officer?" She held her wrists out, Big Joe glass in hand, almost sloshing wine onto the sofa. She tried to avert the spill and dropped her cigarette. Reaching for the cigarette, she spilled wine onto the white fur rug, and the white suede sofa.

"Oh, shit," she said, and sat down again, sloshing more red wine on the sofa and into her lap. "You must think I'm a terrible person."

Jack said, "I would never."

She smiled and affected a pose that was meant to radiate sexiness, but came off as what she was—drunk, going on very drunk. "Aren't you the gentleman," she said. Keeping her eyes on Jack's she took another *sip* from the remains of the glass and emptied it.

"My last name is Middleton," she said. "You know." She seemed to expect some type of reaction, but seeing none she said, "Kate Middleton."

Jack couldn't see a resemblance except that they were both female. "Oh," he managed to say.

"Oh my God! The princess. She's English royalty, ya know?"

"Pleased to meet you, Mindy Middleton," Jack said.

She said, "My Sonny talked about you. You're that cop that saved those people on the riverboat. He said you're a real hero. He said you shot a lot of people."

Jack hadn't saved everyone. A lot of good people had died on that riverboat. Some attorneys, too.

Liddell said, "Mindy, we have bad news. Sonny has been…"

She cut him off with a waggle of her hand. "I already know. Sonny's dead." She headed for the wet bar in one corner of the room. "Sully told me this morning."

Sully made no attempt to introduce himself or explain how he already knew Sonny was dead. Jack wasn't aware the news media had reported anything yet.

Mindy was barefoot and the robe just barely concealed what was underneath. She took another bottle of wine from behind the wet bar, leaning over the top and allowing her robe to part.

"They was a present from Sonny," she said, seeing where everyone's attention was drawn.

Her accent was East Coast—Jersey or Massachusetts or New York. Jack said, "Miss Middleton, would you care to sit down, please? We need to ask you some questions."

Her eyes went to the man she'd called Sully.

"Don't say anything else, Mindy," Sully advised.

Her eyes went from Sully to Jack to Liddell. "It's okay, Sully. They're cops. I was just going to tell them that my Sonny got me this place, too. I always wanted a house like this and Sonny got it for me." Her smile turned quickly into a frown, like a switch was thrown. "Too bad my ma' didn't live to see it."

"That's enough, Mindy," Sully said.

Jack held a hand out to Sully. "Detective Jack Murphy. And you are…?"

"Vincent Sullis," the man said, ignoring the proffered hand. "Okay, Detective Murphy, you've notified Miss Middleton of Sonny's death. You can see she's in no condition to answer questions." He made a gesture toward the door.

Mindy was drunk but she didn't seem to be eager for them to leave.

Jack said, "Mr. Sullis, we have police business with Miss Middleton. We take the death of a policeman very seriously. I hope you won't take this wrong, but unless you're family, would you please be quiet and take a seat. We'll get to you."

Sully smirked and said, "I'm Miss Middleton's friend, but I'm also her attorney. I insist you stop questioning Miss Middleton and leave her house. *We* will get to *you*."

Jack turned his attention to Mindy and asked, "Is that what you want, Mindy? Do you want us to leave?"

Mindy's eyes went to the floor.

Sully answered for her. "Miss Middleton has retained me to represent her. You've done your duty, detectives. Miss Middleton doesn't wish to speak to you at this time. Any further questions can go through me. I'm going to have to insist you leave my client to grieve." More forcefully he said, "I'll see you out."

"Mr. Sullis," Liddell said, leaning into the attorney's face, "This is Mindy's house and we're not here to charge her with anything. You're not representing her regarding our investigation. In fact, you're interfering."

Jack had seldom seen his partner get angry. If Vincent Sullis were a smart attorney, he wouldn't go poking a Bigfoot. But Sullis stood his ground and traded glares with Liddell. The guy had balls.

"Charge me?" Mindy said. "What do you mean? Charge me with what?" Her eyes widened and her complexion paled.

"Don't say anything else, Mindy," Sully said.

Mindy's expression said she was caught between a shark and a bigger shark. "I don't care if they stay, Sully. I'm okay. I want to know what he means. Charge me with what? My Sonny's dead. What are you gettin' at anyway?"

"Sonny was murdered," Jack said.

"Murdered! Sully told me he was killed but he didn't say nothin' about murder."

"Mr. Sullis," Jack said, "how did you hear that Sonny was killed?" Neither he nor Bigfoot had mentioned that Sonny was killed, just that he had died.

Sully said, "I'm sorry, Mindy. You don't have to be here for this. These men have no right—"

Jack interrupted him. "We have every right, counselor."

"What exactly did Mr. Sullis tell you about Sonny's death?" Jack asked.

"He told me Sonny was killed, you know, dead, but I didn't know he'd been murdered." Tears welled in her eyes and trickled down one cheek.

Jack couldn't see a distinction between killed and murdered, but he'd give her the benefit of the doubt. Jack asked Sully, "Who told you Sonny was murdered?"

"I don't have to answer that, Detective Murphy. Am I a suspect?"

"No, counselor. Not at this point. But I'm sure you know the meaning of investigative detention. That gives me the right to detain you for questioning to determine if you're involved. I can take you downtown until I verify who you are. Would you rather do this here or at the station?"

Sully smiled. "You know full well you can't take anyone anywhere without some type of probable cause. Which you don't have, by the way. But since Sonny was a personal friend, go ahead and ask your questions, Detective Murphy. You're on notice that anything you learn from me, or Mindy, is under my objections and may be in violation of our constitutional rights. You do remember what those are?"

"Quit wasting my time. Who told you Sonny was murdered?"

Sully said, "I got a call from my secretary. I don't know who told her. I can give you her phone number. You can ask her."

"When did you get that call?" Jack asked.

"Am I a suspect now?" Sully asked. "If so, read me my rights and I'll tell you to arrest me or let me go."

"Oh, for God's sake, Sully," Mindy said. "Someone called a little while ago. I heard him on the phone. He said Sonny was killed. Sully wouldn't hurt Sonny. Besides, he was here all night."

Jack hadn't told them when Sonny was murdered.

"Mindy. When was the last time you saw Sonny?" Jack asked.

"You don't have to answer that," Sully said.

Jack asked, "Was Sonny working last night?"

"Don't answer that, Mindy," Sully said.

"It's okay, Sully," Mindy said. "Sonny ain't been at home for a couple of days."

Before Sully could object again, Jack asked, "When did Mr. Sullis get here?"

"Detective, I don't see what—" Sully said and Jack interrupted.

"Mr. Sullis, I'll take you to headquarters and read you your Miranda rights and call the prosecutor and maybe the news media because the public has a right to know what a shit you're being. You can sue the hell out of me if you like."

Sully rubbed his temple when Mindy said, "Sully, I want to talk to them. I need to know. I appreciate you lookin' out for me, but shut up."

Sully leaned against the wall and crossed his arms.

Jack didn't think Mindy had killed Sonny, but Sully was being overly defensive. It didn't make sense.

"When did Mr. Sullis get here, Mindy," Jack repeated.

"Sully came yesterday morning," she said and smiled at Sully. "Sonny didn't come home two nights in a row. He always came home before, didn't he? Only not this time."

"You say Sonny didn't come home for two nights. Did you call Sully, or did he come on his own?" He wondered where Sully had slept. From the way Sully was acting, Jack also wondered if Sully was giving Mindy more than legal advice.

"Sonny's been acting kind'a funny the last couple weeks. But he's never not come home, ya' know," Mindy said.

She didn't say who initiated this visit, but in either case it didn't explain why Sully was here.

"Has Sonny ever gone missing before? I'm asking because you said he always came back. Back from where?"

"Sonny watched people. What's that called?" Mindy said.

"Surveillance," Jack said.

"Yeah. He worked some nights doing that kind of shit—excuse my language. You're going to think I'm a potty mouth."

"It's okay. Please continue," Jack said.

"Sometimes he was gone overnight. I'm sure you've been on those things. You know, my Sonny always talked about you."

Jack said, "Go on."

"He was never gone more than a night unless he told me he was gonna be gone a while. Sometimes he was off fishing for a week. He took his boat to some lake in Kentucky. He has a boat, you know?" she asked and winked at Jack. "Really nice. But I get seasick. Sonny said I could get seasick in the shower. So I never went with them."

Jack was about to steer her back to the present when she said, "He's got a really nice boat, don't he, Sully?"

Sully didn't say anything and Mindy continued reminiscing. "Sully's the one who introduced us. They're like best friends."

Sully still said nothing.

"Twice a year. They took his boat and would be gone for a week. But I always knew where he was, didn't I," she said in Sully's direction, not quite a question. "He caught murderers in Boston. Went out and raided places. But after we moved here he promised me he'd never do anything dangerous. I told him I wouldn't stand for it. I told him if he got himself hurt I wouldn't stay. I told him…" She stopped talking and tears welled in her eyes.

"You're saying that you'd know if he was watching people the last few nights?" Jack asked.

"Oh yeah. I would'a known." She wiped her eyes with the back of her hand. Jack found a box of tissues. He gave her several and she smiled.

"You're a real gentleman. My Sonny was right about you, wasn't he?"

"Gentleman Jack," Liddell said.

"He never told me who or where, but he always told me. He was a swell guy." Her eyes grew wide and she said, "He got shot at once! Did you know that?"

"I didn't know that."

"That was part of the reason we moved here," she said and stared into space. "He never told me what happened."

Jack could tell by her eyes that she was lying. *Why?*

"He got mad at me for even asking. It wasn't long and we were moving here. He said he'd already found a job and I wouldn't have to work at the bar no more. Did I tell you I worked at a bar in Boston?"

She lit another cigarette, took a puff, watched the end burn, and said, "He lived in a trailer until the house was built. I stayed in Boston for a while."

She smiled at a memory and said, "He built some of this stuff himself. He did that tiki bar outside. He's got a regular woodworking shop out behind the garage. He was..." Her words trailed off.

Sully laid an arm across Mindy's shoulders. "Do you want to lay down, Mindy? You've had a shock. These men can come back later."

Mindy said, "He always came home, didn't he?" She poured another glass of wine and took a drink. "His people ought'a know what he was doing. They was all close, ya know. You talked to Jerry yet? Jerry would know."

That reminded him that Jerry and the others on the Task Force were waiting.

"When was the last time you saw or talked to Sonny?" Jack asked.

Mindy took a deep drag off her cigarette, sucked the smoke into her lungs and eyed Jack as she slowly released it. "Let me think a minute," she said, and began a hacking cough that turned into what Jack called a smoker's death spasm. When she could get her breath, she tried to continue, squinted at Jack, holding a palm out in a "wait a second" gesture, and gave a few more hacks. Jack once saw a cat do the same thing, only it wasn't smoking.

Mindy downed the wine and poured the glass almost to the top again before continuing. "Sonny called the first night he was gone. That was a few days ago. No, it was day before yesterday. I don't really remember. But I was mad at him still, wasn't I? You should talk to Jerry. I tried to call Sonny last night but his phone was turned off."

Sonny's cell phone... Jack would check with Sergeant Walker. Zack didn't have it, but Jack hadn't searched the girl very thoroughly.

Sully said, "I think that's enough. We've cooperated with you." To Mindy he said, "I'm *strongly* advising you not to answer any more questions." He handed Jack a business card.

Jack read it. Vincent Sullis. Attorney at Law. Boston, Massachusetts. "You're from Boston?"

"That's what it says on the card."

"Did you drive here?" Jack asked.

"We're done here," Sully answered.

Jack handed the card to Liddell. "Time to leave."

Mindy followed the men to the front door with Sully attached to her like a Siamese twin.

As Jack stepped outside he turned to Mindy. "Mindy, we may need to talk to you again."

"Do you need me to...to identify Sonny?" Mindy asked.

Jack didn't think that was a good idea. Sonny was messed up. But it gave him an idea how he could get Mindy alone.

"We'll wait for you to get dressed and take you to the morgue," Jack offered. He could let a Juvenile detective talk to Zack and Dayton. Sonny's crew could wait too. He had the feeling there were more answers here. Something didn't add up.

Sully stepped outside and placed himself between Jack and Mindy. "Should she need to go, I'll take her. She should be with a friend."

Mindy blurted out, "Maybe two weeks ago. We went to eat at The Log Inn. Sonny knew it was my favorite place. While we was eating, Sonny's phone dinged. You know that kind of ding when there's a message. Anyway, he just didn't seem okay. Like he was scared. I never seen him scared before. He went outside and came back and I said to him, "What?" And he said, "I got to do something." And that was that. He took me home and he went out."

"Two weeks ago?" Jack asked. "Do you know what day and what time?"

Jack was thinking he could get Sonny's phone records and find out who he had talked to.

"It was a Friday night. Had to be after five. I don't know exactly. Is it important?"

"Maybe," Jack said. "Did you find out who it was?"

"Nah. But he got a call here the last time he was home. He went out by the pool and got his keys and took off in that truck of his. He was proud of that truck. He ain't never had a new truck before he came here. Or a boat. Sometimes I thought he liked them more than me. But he got me this house, didn't he?"

She was rambling. Jack tried to get her to focus. "When he left did he say anything? What was his mood like?"

"He was acting anxious. He was anxious a lot lately."

Sully said, "Mindy, I think..."

"Go on," Jack prodded.

She said, "I thought maybe it was another woman. I thought that's who ding'd Sonny while we were at The Log Inn and he was scared I would find out. Later he got the call here and he seemed kinda put out, mad. He took off in a hurry. I thought maybe she was threatening him, you know. I knew some guys, some cops, in Boston that cheated on their girlfriends and got caught. One guy's girlfriend caught them in bed together and shot him with his own gun. He had it coming, I said to Sonny. But I couldn't believe Sonny would do that to me." She deliberately let her robe fall open and asked, "I ain't so hard to look at, am I?"

Jack sidestepped her question and asked, "What was Sonny like after the call at The Log Inn? Did he do anything unusual? You said he was scared."

"Nah. Well. He started putting guns everywhere; in the bathroom, under his pillow, on top of the refrigerator. He wasn't never like that. Not even that time he got shot at. Not the whole time we was together."

Jack said, "One more question, Mr. Sullis. You said you got a call from your secretary this morning. That's in Boston, I take it?"

"That's right."

"How did they know about the murder?" Jack asked.

Sully's face turned red. "You got me there. Okay, it wasn't my secretary that called. I've got other friends here in common with Sonny. I'm not telling you who called. I don't want you harassing them."

"Why did you come to Evansville? When did you arrive? Where are you staying?" Jack asked.

Sully said, "You'd better leave, now."

"Mindy, if you need to talk, or you remember anything else, just call me or Liddell. Call the department. They know how to reach us. Anytime. Okay?"

Sully shut the door on them before she could respond.

* * * *

Back in the Crown Vic, Jack cranked up the heat.

Liddell said, "She never asked where we found him. Or how he was killed."

"Sully didn't ask either. He knew Sonny was murdered before we got here and he didn't want to give up the name of the person that told him. We don't know how long he's been here."

"Mindy said she thought Sonny was cheating on her. Maybe she wanted Sully to talk to Sonny and see what was what. Maybe it's just a coincidence Sully's a lawyer. But he could have done all that stuff on the phone. Why come all the way from Boston?" Liddell asked.

"Maybe a lot of money is involved," Jack suggested. "They're not married. This is her dream house."

"Hell hath no fury like a woman scorned," Liddell offered.

Jack said. "Maybe Mindy and Sully have something going."

"Let's explore that," Liddell mused. "Sonny and Mindy aren't married. He was going to kick Mindy to the curb. Leave her penniless. Sully to the rescue. He seemed like more than a friend."

Jack said, "Mindy might have a reason to kill Sonny. Sully seems capable of murder. But she seemed genuinely surprised when she realized Sonny was murdered. It would be hard to fake that expression, even drunk."

"Or maybe that's why she was that drunk," Liddell said. "Where to now?"

"Let's go back downtown and question Zack. We still have to talk to Sonny's crew."

Chapter 9

Jack spoke to Lilly Caskins at the morgue while he drove to headquarters. "Lilly?"

"Jack?" she said. "Now that we know who we're talking to maybe you can get to the point. I'm kind of busy watching mold spores grow on our budget request."

Liddell could hear the conversation and chuckled.

"Sonny's girlfriend is Mindy Middleton…" Jack said.

"That's nice to know," Lilly said. "Are you going to tell me who his dentist is? Or maybe his banker?"

"Lilly. I'm calling to ask you to call Miss Middleton, Sonny's live-in girlfriend, and her attorney to come identify the body."

"She doesn't need an attorney for that."

"I know. I'm the one that suggested it," Jack said before she cut him off again.

"So why in the hell would you do that? We know who he is. We don't need a troop of people getting in the way."

"I'm trying to tell you." *Bitch!* "I want to get Mindy away from her attorney for a few minutes. She wants to talk but he doesn't want to let her."

"I eat attorneys for breakfast," Lilly said. "Why didn't you just say that's what you wanted? You always go the long way around."

Jack took a deep breath. "Can you tell them you need them in an hour? We need to do something else first."

"I can give you all day."

"Just an hour will do, Lilly," Jack said, but she had already hung up.

"Pleasant as always, our Little Casket," Liddell said.

"Let's go to Juvenile and talk to Zack and Dayton."

* * * *

Zack Pugh and Dayton Bolin were being held in the Juvenile Detectives Unit where day shift handled the bulk of the complaints—runaways, missing, thefts, underage drinking, drugs—and spent a lot of their time dealing with Child Protective Services.

Jack and Liddell found Juvenile Detective Tom Woehler leaned back in a chair at his desk with a phone jammed against his ear, nodding, saying few words, and rolling his eyes at what must have been a very one-sided conversation. He hung up and said to Jack, "CPS" as if that explained anything.

"Any luck finding Zack's parents?" Jack asked, hooking a thumb toward Zack, who was sitting in front of Woehler's desk looking even cockier, if that was possible.

Woehler said, "Zack's father stays scarce. Mom's not in the picture. Zack's been here a few times." He asked Zack, "Isn't that right?"

"You getting senile, old man?" Zack said.

Woehler continued, "Nothing bad. Couple of thefts, trespassing, fighting. Today I find out the girl's parents have a restraining order to keep him away from their daughter."

Zack interrupted him. "That's only outside of school. I got a right to go to school."

"You weren't in school this morning," Woehler pointed out.

"That paper don't mean shit and the judge is full of it. Dayton loves me and I love her. We're like Romeo and Juliet."

Woehler said, "Zack's dad has a record. Aggravated battery with injury, drunk and disorderly, a couple felony drunk-driving arrests. He went up for negligent manslaughter around the time Zack was born. Drove a motorcycle through the glass doors of a tavern because they cut him off and told him to leave. There was a passenger on the back of the motorcycle at the time. The passenger died."

"Where is your father?" Jack asked.

"I'm not talking to you, asswipe," Zack said.

Woehler said, "We beat on his dad's door. No answer. The neighbors wouldn't admit they even knew him. We're checking taverns, but he's probably passed out drunk in the house. Hey. Want to go kick the door?"

"Not me," Jack said. "Any chance a judge will declare Zack a ward of the court?"

"I said I'm not talking to any of you," Zack leaned back in the chair. "I been a ward of the high and mighty court and I know I don't have to talk to you."

Woehler said, "I've already sent the papers to Judge Knight. He'll probably give you the warrant." Woehler checked his watch. "Let's talk to Dayton and her folks." To the unit secretary, he said, "Keep an eye on him for me."

"I got to go to the bathroom, Mister Detective, sir," Zack said.

"You can't wait?" the secretary asked.

"Dr. Oz said holding it when you gotta pee will cause postate problems. I don't need my postate going bad," Zack said, grinning.

"Your 'postate' huh?" Woehler said and grinned at Jack. "I guess I have to take him to pee before his 'postate' falls out. Dayton's parents are waiting in the soft interview room. I'll be right back."

The 'soft' interview room was where children under the age of eight, or with special needs, were generally kept until they could be taken to CPS or released to a family member. These children were usually the victims of abuse. In this case, the use of the soft interview room was appropriate considering the trauma of seeing the body.

They entered the room. Dayton's father was in his late thirties, solidly built, wearing a dark power suit, white button-down shirt, red tie and highly polished wing tip shoes. His arm was around Dayton's shoulders. The wife sat on her daughter's other side, hands clenched in her lap. Except for the mother's deeper tan, Jack couldn't have told mother and daughter apart from a distance. The mother's clothing said "classy" and made you examine your own lack of taste.

"I'm Detective Murphy," Jack said. "This is Detective Blanchard."

Mr. Bolin's handshake was a vise grip. Mr. Bolin was obviously a gym rat. Jack had known a PT instructor like him at the police academy. The guy even exercised his jaw and neck muscles. Imagine the cartoon character, Popeye, without the ever-present can of spinach. He asked Jack, "Do I get to talk to him? Just a few minutes."

"Mr. Bolin, we have some questions for Dayton," Jack said. "Given the circumstances, I decided this was the safest place to ask them. And, no, you can't 'talk' to Zack. But we'll be glad to answer some of your questions before we start."

Liddell interjected, "We know this is a terrible shock to your family, but time is always important; memories are fresher if we do this now."

Mr. Bolin took his arm from around his daughter and Mrs. Bolin's arm took up the empty post. Mr. Bolin said, "Go ahead."

Liddell gave them the basics. Mr. Bolin took it all in without a reaction. Mrs. Bolin sucked in a breath like she'd been gut-punched when Jack told them the role Zack and Dayton played in the finding of the body, and again when told that Zack had taken some of the deceased's property.

Mrs. Bolin asked, "Why couldn't she have been brought home right away? Why is she still here? Should we be talking to a lawyer?"

Mr. Bolin patted her hand. "It's what they have to do, Sarah. It's okay. Let's just let them talk to Dayton and we'll take her home."

"She's not in trouble with us," Jack confirmed. Dayton was going to be in trouble enough when she got home. "Dayton, do you think you can answer some questions for us?" Jack asked.

Doe-eyed, and in a voice so soft it could barely be heard, Dayton answered, "I guess."

"Speak up, honey, so the men can hear you," Mr. Bolin said.

"Okay, Daddy," Dayton said, and sat up straighter.

Liddell would usually do the questioning, because Jack was scarier than the Yeti for some reason. But in this instance, Liddell hadn't been to the scene.

"We'll get to why you were in that house later, Dayton," Jack said, and saw her flinch. "Right now, I have more important questions. Okay?"

"Yes."

* * * *

Jack took her back to the beginning.

"Dayton, I know this will be hard, but I need you to think about your answers. Can you do that for me?" Jack asked.

She looked at her father. "I'll try," she said.

"You and Zack were on the street. It was cold. He led you to the house. How did you get in?"

"The back door was open. Zack wanted to go in," she said. "We didn't break anything."

"I know you didn't, Dayton," Jack said. "What rooms did you go into?"

"It was empty. There wasn't any furniture or anything. No one lived there," she said.

"Answer the detective's question, Dayton," Mr. Bolin said.

She kept her eyes down and said, "We came in the back. The door was standing open. I guess it was the kitchen. Zack said we could get warm in there but it was cold. Like outside. It smelled bad too. I wanted to go back outside, but Zack went into the room where that guy was." She stopped and Jack could see the terror building.

"You're doing good, Dayton," he said. "Zack went into the room where the body was found. Did you go in there too?"

"I didn't at first."

"What do you mean?" Jack asked.

"Well, Zack went in the other room and I stayed by the back door. Then I heard him say something. I thought there might be someone else there. You know. Maybe a homeless person. I was scared and wanted to leave, but I couldn't leave Zack by himself."

Jack gave Mr. Bolin a cautioning look. To Dayton he said, "And you what?"

"I went in to get Zack. I wanted to leave there. It was scary. It smelled like an..."

"It smelled bad," Jack said. "But what did you see?"

She swallowed, clasped her hands tightly in her lap, and said, "I saw him. He was hanging there. His face was all..."

"Was the body a man or a woman?" Jack asked.

"A man. At least I think it was. Yes. It was a man. And he was. He was naked and hanging from the wall."

"Where was Zack?"

"He was over by the body. He didn't even look at me when I came in. I screamed and ran outside."

"Did you run out the front or back of the house?" Jack asked.

"The front. The door was shut, but it didn't have a lock on it I guess. And I ran down the street screaming. That's when I found the policeman. The car was coming down the street and I ran into the street and he stopped and he got out and was asking me like a lot of questions and..."

"Okay, Dayton. Let's go slower. Okay?" Jack said and she nodded. Mr. Bolin had taken one of her hands. Her mother held the other. "How far from the house were you when you saw the police car?"

She didn't remember.

"Did you notice a vehicle or any person around there?" Jack asked.

"I don't know," Dayton said. "Am I in trouble for going in that house?"

"No, you're not," Jack said. *It would be trespassing at best.* "Where was Zack when you came back with the policeman?"

"He was standing outside. By the door."

"Front or back?" Jack asked.

"Front."

"Was Zack wearing the same clothes as earlier?" Jack asked.

She looked to her mother and said, "I didn't notice until the detective came over to the car. I swear."

"But you knew that he'd taken some things," Mr. Bolin said.

"Not until this detective came to the car, Dad."

Jack looked at Mr. Bolin and put a finger to his lips.

"What was Zack wearing when you went in the house?" Jack asked. Dayton didn't answer.

"You saw Zack standing outside when the policeman brought you back to the house. Did you notice if Zack was wearing a different coat from the one he'd had on earlier?"

Tears welled in her eyes but she didn't answer.

"Did you know Zack took anything?"

Dayton's cheeks turned red and she turned her face downward. "He had on different shoes and the coat. In the police car, he showed me the money and tried to give me the ring. I guess I knew he'd stolen all of it, but I was just so scared..." She said to her father, "I'm sorry, Daddy."

"Tell the detective the whole truth, hon. You know what your mother and I think about lying."

It was obvious to Jack that Dayton cared for this boy. He hoped her eyes were opened by Zack's lack of judgment, not to mention lack of ethics.

"I believe you, Dayton," Jack said.

Jack asked Dayton to close her eyes. He told Mr. and Mrs. Bolin not to talk. He took Dayton back through her story again. He'd already asked these questions, but sometimes you took a traumatized witness through what they'd seen in layers. The first time they only remembered what was on the surface. The following times they remembered things they smelled, heard, the feel of the ground under their feet, the emotion of things they saw around them. With their eyes closed, they weren't distracted by anyone. Jack called it emotional interviewing. He lent support when she needed it with a "Keep going" or "You're doing fantastic, Dayton."

They kept at this for another twenty minutes before Jack knew he'd squeezed every brain cell dry. He hadn't found out much else, but he didn't think she or Zack had seen the killer, a car, or Sonny's truck along their path. He knew the money Zack had taken was Sonny's whether it was in Sonny's jacket or not. He knew this because Dayton didn't recall stopping anywhere along the way. They had only gone in that house because she was freezing. She knew Zack only had forty-three dollars. She hadn't told Zack she'd brought the two hundred thirty-five dollars she'd been saving. When she revealed that tidbit, Jack had to scowl at Mr. Bolin to keep him from saying something.

Jack finished with the interview, and the Bolins agreed that Dayton would provide fingerprints, and allow Crime Scene to take photos of her and impressions of her shoes to eliminate from the scene.

Jack and Liddell asked the Bolins to follow them and they headed for the hallway. Zack stiffened when he saw Mr. Bolin.

"I'll deal with you later," Bolin said to Zack.

Zack sneered but said nothing. Jack had no doubt Bolin could take him apart with one finger and had to wonder if he himself would have had that much control if it was his daughter who was running away with a future convict.

He took them to the front lobby, where they agreed to wait for a Crime Scene tech. Mr. Bolin took Jack aside and asked, "Tell me honestly. Is our daughter going to be charged with a crime? She's never been in trouble before. Do we need to hire a lawyer? She and *that boy* are the only witnesses, right? But they're only witnesses? I mean, you don't think Zack killed that man, do you?"

Jack asked, "How well do you know him?"

Bolin's jaw stiffened. "Like I told you in there, I don't know much about him. I'd like to know even less. Listen, my daughter takes in stray dogs and cats. We, her mother and I, have to feed them and find homes for them."

Jack said nothing. He knew there was more.

"To my daughter, this boy is someone to be saved. We've done everything to discourage her from seeing him. We even took out a restraining order to keep him away from her and our house. Quite frankly, he's going to get our daughter into serious trouble. And, well, I guess today proves me right."

Jack saw Bolin obviously loved his daughter, but he seemed to love being right and in control even more.

"Mr. Bolin, we may need to talk to Dayton again," Jack said.

"She said she didn't see anyone. Do you think she was...? Do you think she saw something?" he asked, and before Jack could answer he said, "Of course you would have to be certain, wouldn't you. And if you suspect that she did see someone or something important, the person that did this might think so as well." He lowered his voice. "Is my daughter in danger?"

Jack handed him a business card. "There's no reason to think Dayton's in any danger," Jack said. "You might want to keep her home today and consider taking her to a counselor, someone she can talk to." He didn't say that a counselor would also help discover why Dayton had run away from home in the first place.

Mr. Bolin turned Jack's card around in his hands, saying, "She can talk to me and her mother."

"It's just a suggestion," Jack said. "Some people talk easier to an outsider."

Chapter 10

"It might take a while for a judge to sign a ward-of-the-court order," Jack said. He and Liddell crossed Sycamore Street going to the Federal Building. The law said Zack couldn't be interviewed while he was in custody without being read his Miranda rights, and with a parent or guardian present. Since he wasn't free to leave, Zack was technically in custody. The court order would allow someone from Child Protective Services to stand in as guardian while they talked to Zack.

Liddell said, "That boy is incapable of telling the truth, but I think the girl was being honest."

"Woehler said he would call us if we can get to Zack."

"I call shotgun," Liddell said.

"We're not driving anywhere," Jack said. "We're going to see Sonny's people."

"I know. But I'm going to tell Sonny's people that you're to blame for not getting to them earlier, pod'na. You're in the driver's seat. I'm riding shotgun. I've got your back."

"Whatever," Jack said. Sonny's crew would be all kinds of pissed off that they had sat around for a couple of hours before Jack and Liddell even came to talk to them.

Jack's phone rang. It was Angelina Garcia.

"About time," Angelina said. "I've called a dozen times."

"Sorry, we were tied up," Jack said. His phone showed repeated calls. He hadn't heard the phone ring once. Technology could be stupid sometimes.

She said, "The captain called and asked if I wanted to work with you two yahoos again. I said no, so he offered to pay more."

Jack said, "Wait a minute. I'll put you on speakerphone." They stopped walking and Jack punched an icon on the phone that somehow ended the call.

"Shit! I hate these things. The square thingies on the screen are too damn small," Jack complained. The phone rang again.

He answered. "I'm sorry, Angelina. We must be in a blind spot." He put the phone to his cheek and it disconnected again.

"Give me the phone," Liddell said. It rang again and Liddell punched the answer button, the speaker button, and held the phone up where they could both hear.

"You hung up on me, Jack. Twice. You're lucky I understand how technology-challenged you are. Anyway, the captain filled me in on what you've got and gave me a list of names. I'm sending you a text with the list. If there's something you need immediately, let me know. Otherwise I'll take them in order. Okay?"

Liddell said, "I'll do it. My pod'na has spastic fingers. Glad you're on this, Angelina. How's Mark?"

Mark Crowley was her fiancé.

"You mean Sheriff Mark Crowley? The future father of my children?" she asked.

"Yep," Liddell said. "Unless you've hooked up with another guy by that name."

"He's fine. I'm fine. We're all fine. Got to get to work on this list. I'll text you the list Captain Franklin gave me and you can add whatever. Bye," she said.

The list came to Liddell's phone only seconds later. "She has Sonny, Sully and Mindy on the list. What else do you want me to give her, pod'na?"

Jack told Liddell to tell her to pay particular attention to Sully.

* * * *

Jack would have preferred to just drop in on Sonny's team of detectives before they had a chance to talk among themselves. Keep witnesses separated. Says so in the police manual. But that wasn't possible with the way word of Sonny's murder was spreading. He hoped the discovery of the money would be kept quiet, but Roscoe had witnessed them finding the money on Zack, so hope was not on the table.

They walked into the Winfield K. Denton Federal Building and handed their weapons over to the two U.S. Marshals at the metal detector. Their guns were put in lockers and they were given the keys. They were on their way to the third floor when Jack said, "Katie! Oh shit! I forgot to call." Jack hadn't called to tell Katie that he couldn't give a talk to her sixth-grade class this morning. "What time is it, Bigfoot?"

"Almost ten, pod'na. I remind you we haven't ate. I'm getting hungry and when I do I get cranky."

They stepped off the elevator. Jack said, "I'll be right in there."

Liddell walked on and Jack dialed Katie's cell phone. He hoped he would catch her between classes. He knew Katie would understand why he couldn't make it to school, but it wasn't a good precedent to start. His being unavailable—going back on promises, bringing the job home, putting the job ahead of everything else—was one of the reasons for their divorce. Not the only, or even the biggest reason, but it was right up there with not putting the seat down on the toilet, or leaving dirty clothes on the floor, or getting in bed with cold feet.

Katie answered the phone with, "I know. Something came up."

Jack broke a smile. "Sorry, Katie. A policeman was killed last night."

"Oh my God, Jack!"

"Katie, you know I would have been there..."

She interrupted and said, "You don't have to explain. I was going to call you anyway. The three students who really needed your attention are out today. They were taken to the Detention Center for breaking into a building last night."

Jack suppressed a laugh. The majority of the kids in Katie's school had multiple problems: abused kids, violent kids, runaways, addicts, kids placed there by family court in lieu of going to a juvenile detention center, and on and on it went. Hers was the last school most of these kids would attend, the last transfer they would be allowed, the last chance at an education. She was passionate about helping them. It was one of the things he loved about her.

"You can tell me tonight," she said. "I know you're busy."

Jack heard raised voices in the background that turned into outright yelling.

"Gotta go," she said. "Love you."

"I love you too, Katie," Jack said to an empty line.

Jack made it to the door of the offices the FBI had loaned to the Federal Drug Task Force, or FDTF, when his phone rang again.

"Jack," Captain Franklin said, "I just wanted to warn you that Deputy Chief Dick is on the warpath. I told him you were unavailable and he's in with the chief right now. Are you going to be able to come back here and brief him?"

"Not now, Captain." Jack could feel the impatience at the other end of the call. It almost matched his own. Deputy Chief Richard Dick, aka Double Dick, wanted some dirt he could give the media during an *impromptu* news conference. *Well, Dick ain't getting dick.*

"I was hoping you could give me something for Chief Pope. At least he'll know what he's lying to the deputy chief about."

"I hear you, Captain," Jack said. "We notified Sonny's live-in girlfriend. Her name is Mindy Middleton. An attorney named Vincent Sullis, from Boston, was with her."

Captain Franklin said, "Sonny was from Boston. Why was an attorney from Boston at his house?"

"We don't know," Jack said. "We think Sonny's girlfriend called this Sully character. He was an overnight guest the night Sonny was murdered. Mindy said Sonny wasn't home for two nights, and they made it sound like that was part of the reason Sully was there. Sully said he got a call from his Boston secretary this morning telling him that Sonny had been murdered. But he admitted he lied and he refused to tell us how he found out. I seriously doubt that our grapevine reaches Boston or Sully in particular. Mindy didn't seem to know that Sonny was murdered until we spoke to her, but Sully had told her Sonny was killed. She was drunk. Who knows what she thought. Anyway, Sully won't stop interfering with our questioning. I don't want to arrest him. Yet. So we're going to try to separate her from Sully to see what she knows."

"Whatever you think, Jack. I won't ask how you plan to cut the attorney out of the conversation. Have you talked to the Task Force yet?" Franklin asked.

"No. We went to Juvenile first to talk to the kids who found the body. We were only able to interview the girl. She didn't see anything, but she confirmed that Zack stole Sonny's things. We're just getting to the Task Force office."

"Thanks for keeping me up to date, Jack. Do you need anything?"

"Just one little thing, Captain," Jack said.

"Uh oh," Franklin said.

"I'm sure Angelina has other things to do with her business, but I want her to be able to work exclusively on this," Jack said. "It'll cost you."

Angelina Garcia was a computer genius. She started her career as the IT person for the Evansville Police Department, fixing glitches in the data systems that linked EPD to other law enforcement agencies in the state and federal database. She was working with the Vice Unit when she came to Jack's attention. He was searching for a serial killer who was using nursery rhymes to select and kill children. She had proven herself invaluable in digging up information and using her connections with other agencies and in the cyber-world.

After that case, Angelina had gotten engaged and had semi-retired from EPD and moved into her fiancé's cabin on Patoka Lake. She was on a consulting basis with the Evansville Police Department and several other law enforcement agencies. Jack suspected she was also working for the federal government. He and Liddell had worked a human trafficking and murder case in Louisiana during the summer. Angelina had given them a hand with that and had ended up getting chummy with the FBI, ICE, DEA, and ATF.

He'd asked Angelina recently if the Feds had offered her a job. She'd responded, "If I told you, I'd have to kill you." She may have been kidding. Maybe not.

"I think that can be done. Keep me informed," Captain Franklin said.

Jack promised, ended the call, and walked into the office. It was empty. Angry voices were coming from a room in the back. When Jack walked in, no one was sitting. The three detectives that made up Sonny's team had surrounded Liddell.

Jerry O'Toole, Bertha Claudel, and Ernestine Simpson were not happy with whatever Liddell had told them. Bertha and Ernestine, nicknamed Bert and Ernie for obvious reasons, stood with arms raised over their heads. Either they were declaring a field goal, or they were just declaring.

The third member of the team, Jerry O'Toole, claimed he was Irish, but he spoke with a Southern drawl. Their faces were taut, lips tightly pressed together, and all eyes turned and targeted Jack when he came in the room.

Jack took a chair and sat. Liddell eased his way out of the circle and followed Jack's lead. Jack maintained eye contact with O'Toole, whose face was fire-engine red.

"It's damn effing time, Murphy!" O'Toole said.

Jerry was a big man, a little taller than Jack, smaller than Bigfoot. If he wore a nametag, it could have said "Bouncer." Jerry had worked in the detectives' office before he was loaned out to the Feds. Jack remembered working a few cases with Jerry. Jerry would crush walnuts in his hand, pop the whole thing in his mouth and spit pieces of hull on the floor of the car. Jack liked Jerry. Respected his work. But there could be only one alpha dog in this room.

"If you like, we can leave, Jerry," Jack said. "You can talk directly with Chief Pope. Maybe he'll put up with your shit."

Bert pushed Jerry into a chair. She and Ernie took seats on each side of Jerry. "Go ahead, Jack," Ernie said and glared at Jerry.

Jack pulled his chair closer and waited for the questions he knew were coming.

Jerry again. "You ain't got shit, have you? What about that little puke, Zack? I busted his daddy's balls a couple of times for dope charges. I hope you're at least busting Junior's balls."

Liddell said, "That's strange, Jerry. Zack told us *you* were his daddy."

Jerry sniggered and said, "The best part of that boy ran down his momma's leg."

"This ain't the time or place, gentlemen," Ernie said. "Jerry, you want to shut your pie hole and let them fill us in?"

And Jack did. They weren't happy with the lack of information. They were hurting. Upset would be too soft of a term for the emotions they were telegraphing. "Going postal" came closer to describing the atmosphere in the room. He sympathized with them. They were a small team and had undoubtedly formed a strong bond. What you did to one, you did to all of them. But he had to keep this under control.

"I'm working directly for the chief," Jack said. "Pope said you three were not to go vigilante. You can still work the case from your end. I got you that much leeway from the brass. You get what information you can and pass it on to us. Do not step on our investigation. If you screw up, Sonny's killer takes a walk."

"Not if he can't walk," O'Toole said. "You want us to read him Miranda rights? Maybe tuck him in?"

Liddell said, "You know Miranda. She ain't ever been right."

That got a snicker from everyone.

"First question," Jack said. "I need to know the last time Sonny was seen or talked to by any of you." He surmised that Jerry was the one he needed to question. "Jerry?"

"I saw him yesterday," O'Toole said. "Maybe around seven. I was getting ready to leave for the night. Sonny came in and told me to get my ass home. I did."

"Can you be more precise on the time?"

He thought and said, "It was close to seven-fifteen or seven-thirty. I remember because when I got home, my wife had put my dinner in the freezer. Said she'd cook for me again when hell freezes over."

"Was that unusual?" Jack asked.

Ernie said, "Yeah. It's unusual that his wife would cook at all."

Jerry gave her the finger and said, "Sonny was in a bad mood. That wasn't unusual, but he seemed, I don't know, agitated. Don't go reading anything into that. Lots of things piss us off."

"Did he seem pissed off?" Jack asked.

"What's the difference between being pissed off and agitated?" Jerry asked. "This is just wasting time."

"You have somewhere else to be, Jerry?" Liddell asked. "Maybe something more important to do?"

"Yeah," Bert said. "Answer his questions, numbnuts." To Jack she said, "I didn't see Sonny last night or talk to him. He wasn't in the office yesterday as far as I know. Did you talk to him, Ernie?" Bert asked.

Ernie said she hadn't.

Jery said, "His demeanor was like when he was going to meet one of his asshole CIs. He acted like he needed to take a bath in holy water after talking to some of them."

Jack twirled his finger in the air for Jerry to get to the point.

"Anyway, Sonny acted like he was going to see someone," Jerry said.

"Do you have any idea what he was working on? Who he was going to meet?" Jack asked.

"We just wrapped up a big case," Jerry said. "Five hundred thou and a couple kilos of heroin. All to Sonny's credit. He's got connections like you wouldn't believe."

"Jerry? Answer the question," Ernie prodded.

"Oh yeah. I have no idea who he was going to see, but now that I think about it, maybe it was someone new. He seemed more contemplative than usual."

Ernie jumped into the conversation. "Jerry, you don't even know how to spell big words like that. Better stick to picture books."

"I was making a point," Jerry said defensively. "Sonny didn't share his contacts. Well, none of us really do unless we have to. But he was real paranoid about it. I didn't know any of his CIs." Jerry looked at Bert and Ernie, and they said they didn't know any of them either.

"That don't mean nothing," Bert said. "He was making all our big cases for us. If I was Superman I'd keep my identity secret too."

Jerry said, "When he took over the unit, he insisted we all carry a burner cell phone to avoid using the phones we're issued. I thought that was a little extreme, but he was the boss."

"Any chance you have a number for that phone?" Jack asked.

Ernie wrote something on a piece of paper and handed it to Jack. "There're the numbers for the burner phones and official phones we all use. None of us use our personal phones unless it's an emergency. But you won't get anywhere calling Sonny's. We've tried them all morning. They must be turned off. We have tracking software on all of them. Well, except the burners. We're not getting a signal for his personal or issued phone.

We don't have any idea what his burner number is. He changed phones like most people change underwear. Well, except for Jerry."

Without having to ask, Jack knew why they'd been calling Sonny's cell phones even after they knew he was killed. If someone had Sonny's cell phone and it rang, it would be a gut reaction for the thief to answer it. If they couldn't get a signal, the phones were most likely turned off or destroyed.

"How do you log property?" Jack asked.

"We keep all of our property seizures in a log, but it's locked in Sonny's desk," Jerry said.

"Money? Drugs? Everything?" Jack asked.

"It includes all that down to the last molecule of drugs."

"Let me guess," Jack said. "One of you—probably you, Jerry—broke into Sonny's desk and checked the log?"

"No one did. I swear, Jack," Jerry said.

That told Jack that they broke in but didn't find anything. "I swear" was always the precursor to a lie.

"Okay, let me ask you this. Was Sonny messing around with anyone? Did he have something going on the side?" Jack asked.

Jerry answered with a question of his own. "What did Mindy tell you?"

"She said she suspected something."

Jerry said, "Have you seen the rack on that woman? Sonny bought those for her. Anyone who would cheat on those puppies needs to have his head examined!"

"I have to broach a subject with you, and I'm hoping you understand why I'm getting into this," Jack said. "No. I really don't care if you understand."

"Screw you too, Murphy," Ernie said. "And the Cajun you rode in on."

"Hey, I haven't said anything," Liddell protested. "But, yeah, what Jack said."

"Have any of you known Sonny to carry large amounts of money?" Jack asked.

Ernie answered. "We all have at one time or other. How much you talking?"

"In the neighborhood of 100K," Jack said.

Jack took their silence to mean, no, they had never carried that kind of money around.

Jack said, "I'm going to have Internal Affairs do an audit and—"

Bert asked, "What are you implying?"

"I'm not implying anything, Bert," Jack said.

"He's not implying shit, Bert. You want to just come out and call me a thief, Jack?"

Jack held up a hand. "I'm not calling you anything, Jerry. You don't do your own audits now, right?"

Bert turned away. Jerry reluctantly agreed. Ernie said, "What if he was working something really big and didn't want us in on it?"

"Would any of you do that? Do you really believe that's possible?" Liddell asked. "You knew Sonny better than us."

Ernie said, "Okay, probably not. But even if he did have that kind of money on him, there's still a chance he was doing something legitimate."

"From what I remember," Jack said, "Internal Affairs does a random audit on all monies and seizures of drugs, vehicles and other property in possession of the EPD Narcotics unit. Since you're part of a Federal Task Force, does Internal Affairs do yours? Or does the FBI do it?"

"Agent Dave Carrell, DEA," Ernie said. "Along with Sonny. There are two logs. One in the safe and like Jerry said—one locked in Sonny's desk drawer."

Jack suspected a lot of money passed through the FDTF and there would have to be extreme measures taken to account for everything.

"None of us has a key to his desk or the combination to the safe," Bert said.

"What do you want to find?" Jerry asked. "I heard you found forty grand on that little shit, Zack. Do you think Sonny stole that? Or do you think it was maybe one of us? Zack's dad is into meth and heroin and anything you can shoot, snort or rub on your gums. Maybe he was offering Sonny some good info and turned on him. That's just as possible as Sonny stealing."

"I didn't say Sonny stole anything," Jack said. "I wasn't going to bring up the money until the audit was done but I need to know if he was working on something. Why he would have that kind of cash."

Bert said, "You said one hundred thousand, not forty."

"We don't have an accurate count on the money yet," Jack lied. The amount had slipped out. "But it's at least forty."

"We can't get in the safe. And it takes one of us with Sonny to get into the evidence room where the safe is."

"Could Sonny get in the safe or the property room without one of you?"

"No," Ernie said.

"Yeah," Bert said.

"He wouldn't," Jerry said.

"What about buy money?" Jack asked. *Buy money* is the cash kept on hand for narcotics officers to make small drug deals. Buy money is almost always recovered, but sometimes the loss is a necessary evil. You buy the little fish to dangle as bait in front of the whales.

"We checked the ready cash—the buy money—and it's all there. We only keep a thousand dollars in ready cash," Bert said. "The last bust we made netted five hundred thousand plus. It's locked in the safe."

"Do you know if the money is still there?" Jack asked.

"That was eleven days ago. The money will still be there," Jerry said.

"And none of you have the combination to the safe?" Jack asked.

Ernie gave them DEA Agent Allen's phone number. "He's the guy to call. He's the only one besides Sonny that has the combination."

"What kind of plan is there to handle a situation like this? What if you couldn't find Agent Allen? What would you do?" Jack asked.

Ernie answered this one. "Agent Allen's boss has the combination. There's always a failsafe in case of shit like this."

Jerry added, "Push comes to shove, we'd blow the damn thing open."

Jack ignored the remark, and told them that under orders from the chief, they were not to get back in Sonny's desk or try to get in the safe. Jack asked a few more questions, and left them with a promise to keep them in the loop.

As they were going out the door, Jerry said, "When this investigation is over, all promises are null and void. The asshole that killed Sonny won't need a lawyer."

"Jerry, don't say something that can come back to bite you in the ass," Jack cautioned. "I know how you feel, but keep it to yourself."

"Look who's talking," Ernie said. She and Jerry bumped knuckles.

Jack and Liddell picked up their weapons and left the Federal Building. Double Dick came striding across the parking lot, spotted them and waved his arms to get their attention. They double-timed it to their car, got in, and Jack sped out onto Sycamore Street.

"Think he wanted us?" Liddell asked.

"Don't care," Jack answered.

Chapter 11

"I'll be quiet as a mouse if we go by Donut Bank. The drive-thru window is okay by me," Liddell said.

"You drive, then," Jack said, and pulled over.

They went to the drive-thru of Donut Bank on First Avenue. Liddell placed his order while Jack took a call from Detective Woehler.

"Judge Knight signed the court order," Woehler said. "I'm in no hurry and his 'postate' is still intact, so take your time getting back here."

Jack thanked him and hung up while Liddell paid for a box of donuts.

Liddell stopped in the parking lot and took a chocolate long john from the box. "Want one?"

Jack declined. "I'm surprised you don't have diabetes."

"Yetis are immune to human diseases," Liddell said, and pulled out onto First Avenue heading back downtown.

Instead of trying to text with Angelina, Jack called and gave her the names of the members of Sonny's team at the FDTF. He then called Sergeant Walker and asked if Sonny's cell phone had been recovered. It hadn't been. Not from the scene or from his truck. Jack called Jerry O'Toole.

"I know you don't have a number for Sonny's burner cell phone, but I need you to get subpoenas for his personal and work cell phones, Jerry. And while you're at it, can you get a subpoena for these numbers?" Jack gave him Mindy's home phone and the phone numbers on Vincent Sullis's business card. He didn't ask for a call history for the desk phones in the Task Force office because they were on a trunk line to the Federal Building, and a nightmare to track down.

"I've already put a subpoena in for our phones. I'll add Mindy's and the attorney's phones to the subpoena."

"Thanks, Jerry," Jack said and disconnected. "Hey, Bigfoot, can you chew with your mouth closed? I'm getting a sugar high from the secondhand breath."

"Donut interruptus," Liddell said.

"If you're facetiously trying to compare withdrawal from donuts to the withdrawal method of coitus interruptus, I need to tell you it works for Planned Parenthood. The withdrawal method doesn't hurt you. Maybe we should start weaning you off Donut Bank. You can wear one of those collars that give you an electrical shock every time you get near the place. Like Pavlov's Bigfoot."

"You a funny man. The key word here is *withdrawal*, pod'na. If I start sweating and slapping a vein, you'll be sorry."

Liddell took a cinnamon twist from the box and said, "Did I tell you Marcie joined the Police Wives Society?" The Police Wives Society was a group of spouses formed to support each other.

"Good for her," Jack said.

"Yeah. Having a baby makes you think way differently. If something ever happens to me, I want Marcie to have some help. Raising our son will be a full-time job."

"You found out the baby is going to be a boy?" Jack asked, surprised. "Why didn't you say something?" Marcie was eight months pregnant now. Jack found out Liddell was going to be a daddy while he and Liddell were working a case in Louisiana and Katie had let the news slip. She had warned Jack not to tell Liddell, but it turned out Liddell had known all the time.

"Just positive thinking, pod'na."

"What if the baby is a girl?" Jack asked.

Liddell said in a deadpan voice, "If we have a girl we'll name her Jacqueline. A boy, Jack."

"I'm honored, Bigfoot," Jack said. And he was.

"Who said I was naming him after you? I'm naming him after my favorite actor, Jack Nicholson."

"Bite me," Jack said.

Liddell parked on Sycamore Street and they hurried into the Juvenile office.

Detective Woehler was sitting behind his desk again and rubbing the back of his neck. "I've got to get away from this desk more often. It really is giving me a pain in the neck."

"Where's Zack?" Jack asked.

"June Baldwin from Child Protective Services is babysitting Zack in the interview room. We struck out on finding Zack's father. He got out of jail a couple weeks ago. He wasn't at home, or at any of the local watering holes. The warrant allows us to take fingerprints, photos, etcetera, and that's already done. We'll add the new photo to his album right next to his baby picture."

The secretary came over. "Jack, Captain Franklin wants you and Liddell to meet him in his office as soon as possible. Double Dick."

"Shit!" Jack said. "That man's like herpes."

Liddell added, "The gift that keeps on giving."

Jack and Liddell went into the interview room. June Baldwin from CPS handed Jack a Juvenile Miranda form. It was unsigned.

"Zack, are you still refusing to talk to us?" Jack asked.

"No. I'm just not signing anything. If I don't sign it you can't use anything I say against me."

June said, "I guess he's got us there." Zack was an idiot. It didn't matter if he signed the form or not. All that mattered was he was willing to talk and was being represented by a guardian. In this case, June Baldwin.

They talked for twenty minutes and Zack told them basically the same thing as Dayton, leaving out the part where he took the nugget ring from the dead man's finger. He refused to close his eyes and imagine going to the house, saying he didn't trust Jack, who he thought might try to hypnotize or brainwash him. He didn't see anyone near the scene. Didn't hear anything. But he did add some important facts.

"Dayton was in the back. She didn't take anything. I found the body. The guy was dead. His clothes were folded in a neat pile in the corner, the jacket on top. I was cold. I took the jacket," Zack admitted.

"Where did you get the money?" Jack asked.

"It was in his coat pocket," Zack said, and feigned a disinterested demeanor although Jack could see the boy was both excited and pissed off that the money had been taken from him by the police.

"And the badge case?"

"In his jacket pocket," Zack said, looking directly at Jack.

"You've got a tell, Zack," Jack said.

"A what?"

"A tell. You know, like playing cards. When you lie, you keep good eye contact, and when you tell the truth your eyes wander. Where did you learn that?"

"I don't know what you're talking about," Zack said, and looked away when he caught himself doing exactly what Jack said he did.

Jack believed most of the important items because Zack wasn't a good liar, although he'd had lots of practice. Zack never once asked how Dayton was doing. Maybe he didn't really care. Or maybe he was biding his time, waiting for her parents to let their guard down so he could coax her away again. The only way to stop that from happening was to charge him with theft and destroying evidence. The court probably wouldn't send him away because every juvenile institution was full to bursting. The most he'd get was temporary detention, like Katie's hoodlums. He'd be released today or tomorrow.

"I'm going to release you to CPS, Zack. Don't leave town or I'll track you down and arrest you. Understand?" Jack asked. When he said arrest, he made a sweeping motion across his neck with one finger.

Zack said, "Detective Murphy, huh? One a' my old teachers was named Murphy. Katie. She's a knockout. She had a husband that was a cop."

Jack reached under his jacket and put his hand on his gun. He said, "What do you know? I'm a cop. Do you want to see my gun up close? Like up the side of your head if you say my wife's name again?"

"No, sir," Zack said hurriedly.

Jack talked to June Baldwin outside of the interview room and explained that Zack had stolen the boots belonging to the deceased and had left his own boots in the crime scene, so both pairs were evidence. Zack's jean jacket and Sonny's coat had also been seized. Zack wasn't getting his own boots or jean jacket and socks back for a while. June said CPS would take care of finding him clothes. She also agreed with Jack that criminal charges were almost a waste of their time. Jack could always file a warrant if he wanted. June walked Zack out of headquarters.

Jack thanked Woehler for his assistance.

Woehler said, "I know you don't want to hear this, Jack, but that kid is a victim, too. His dad is an abusive drunk when he's conscious. His mother abandoned him. He's had to fend for himself most of his life. All of his contact with police has been negative. To tell the truth, I'm surprised he's stayed in school. There's no way we can make him go. Maybe he's worth saving? Who knows?"

Jack said, "He's a murder victim waiting to happen. But you may be right." *Not!*

* * * *

Jack and Liddell went to Captain Franklin's office to update him and get Double Dick's ass-chewing session over with.

They made it to the front lobby and saw a mob of reporters. The mob quieted and turned as one, like a tank of great whites sensing blood in the water, pencils like sharpened teeth, notebooks held like the tips of dorsal fins, and they swam at Jack and Liddell in a feeding frenzy.

Captain Franklin stepped out of the executive offices and shouted for the reporters' attention. Jack and Liddell bulled through the crowd and made their way past the captain to the relative safety of the office.

"I wish we had a flash-bang like SWAT uses," Jack said.

"You think that would work?" Liddell asked.

"Not for the reporters," Jack said. "I was thinking of using it on Double Dick. Maybe we could make a break for the car."

Judy Mangold said, "Deputy Chief Dick is waiting for you two in the captain's office."

Jack opened the door to the captain's office. Deputy Chief Dick was sitting in the captain's chair behind the captain's desk, as was the right bestowed on him by his rank.

"First, let me say I'm saddened by the loss of a valuable officer," Double Dick began. "Now come in and shut the door behind you."

Chief of Police Marlin Pope came out of his office and said, "I'll join you." They stepped inside and Chief Pope followed them in and stood, leaving the door open. Captain Franklin came in and sat in one of the visitor's chairs.

Pope said, "I've briefed Deputy Chief Dick on this investigation. He is in charge of the Public Information Office. All news releases will go through the captain, him or myself. I've also advised the deputy chief that all news releases or comments will be approved by me first."

Double Dick fidgeted. "I understand, Chief. But if the media thinks we're withholding information…"

Pope wasn't finished. He said, "Information will be on a need-to-know basis from here on. I want tight control of this for the investigation's sake. If there is any backlash from the press or anyone else, it will be handled by me. Is that understood, gentlemen?"

Everyone but Double Dick agreed immediately. Double Dick asked, "Does this mean you won't be keeping *me* up to date on the investigation?"

"I'm doing you a favor, Richard," Pope said. "What you don't know, you can't comment on. This is not a news blackout by any means. We will share with the public what we can. But if there are any more leaks in information," he pointed down the hall toward the reporters, "I will deal with the person responsible and I'm not just talking a suspension. Deputy Chief, I know I can trust you implicitly, but I expect you to get word of that to every officer and civilian in this department. No one talks to wives or husbands or anyone else. Detectives Murphy and Blanchard will be the hub. All incoming information will be reported to them, or the captain. I'm depending on Captain Franklin to keep me apprised when necessary. Clear?"

Double Dick asked, "If we don't tell the media something, they'll report the rumors that are already going around."

Pope surprised everyone. "Captain Franklin told them I will be talking to them in a moment. Captain Franklin, you're with me. I don't want them to get nasty with the deputy chief since he's the PIO."

Dick was stunned. He stood behind the desk. "I don't think..."

Pope said, "Deputy Chief Dick, this will all fall in my lap anyway. Don't worry. I have a very important job for you. You will be helping with the investigation by gathering all the background information for Detectives Murphy and Blanchard. You will need to see to this personally. I don't trust anyone else."

Dick had been frowning but the praise did its job. His face lit up. "I'm yours to command, Chief. Anything you need."

"I knew I could count on you, Richard. I know you and Detective Murphy haven't seen eye to eye in the past, but I expect you both to put that behind you. This is too important to let past feelings get in the way."

"Of course, Chief," Jack said. He held his hand out to Double Dick, who grudgingly took it, gave it a limp shake and pulled away like he'd put his hand in a toilet.

Double Dick sat again, but Chief Pope said, "Step into the hallway, Richard. You need to get on this. Talk directly to me if you need anything."

Dick was disappointed that he wouldn't be in on the briefing, but he did as ordered. As Double Dick and the chief went out the door Pope was saying, "Richard, we need all the records..." and the rest was silenced by the shutting of the door.

Jack asked Captain Franklin, "Is the deputy chief really going to help us?"

"Someone shot their mouth off, Jack, and the media has Caparelli's name as a murder victim. I was just asked by a reporter if Caparelli was assassinated. The deputy chief wasn't told about the money involvement yet. Chief Pope is trying to keep the deputy chief busy," Franklin said. "If Richard contacts you, he should only do it to *give you* information."

Jack understood that to mean he wasn't supposed to give Dick dick. He hadn't planned on it. Life was good.

Chief Pope came in. "I know you two have a lot on your plate. Give me the bare bones. I'm going to talk to the media."

"Yes sir," Jack said. He replayed the conversation with Sonny's crew, the statements of the teens, and the curious run-in with Vincent Sullis at Sonny's house. They knew about the forty thousand dollars found at the scene in Zack's possession but not about the sixty thousand found in Sonny's truck. The chief and captain were genuinely surprised when Jack told them about that money.

Jack ended by giving his opinion that Sonny was living too well for a policeman's salary. He added that Angelina was checking everyone's backstory. Sonny's weapon and cell phones were still missing. Jerry O'Toole was getting a subpoena for the phone records. The briefing was brief.

"What next?" Chief Pope asked them.

Jack answered. "Morgue."

Chapter 12

"Lilly should have called already," Jack said as Liddell drove to the coroner's office.

"Maybe she has Sully in one of the freezers," Liddell said.

"You can't freeze attorneys," Jack said. "Ice in the veins."

Jack called the morgue. No answer. He hung up and called Lilly's cell phone. It rang several times before she answered.

"Lilly?" Jack said.

"Who'd you expect?"

"Lilly, when will Mindy and her attorney be there to identify the remains?" Jack asked.

"They're here," she said. "Join the party."

"Be right there," Jack said and put the phone in his pocket.

"Maybe Sully is in town to negotiate a severance package for Mindy," Liddell said as they got in their car.

"You're suggesting Sonny was paying the hundred thousand dollars to settle with Mindy?"

Liddell said, "Whoever did this is a maniac. Someone without a conscience. Bloodthirsty. An attorney is a logical assumption."

"How long would it take to drive from Boston to Evansville?" Jack asked. "Ten? Fifteen hours?"

"At least," Liddell answered.

Jack pulled Sully's business card from his pocket.

"Let me see," Liddell said, and Jack handed the card to him. "Lawsuits 'R' Us. Good name for a firm. All the names on the firm are mob names. Guido, Jimmy Fingers, Pot Luck Sal." He turned the card over to the back and said, "*Omerta or your money back—guaranteed.*"

"Stop it," Jack said. "We need to get Mindy alone."

"Maybe she's claiming a common-law marriage to clean him out."

Jack called Angelina and put her on speakerphone. "What did you find for us?" Jack asked.

"How long have you got?" Angelina said.

"We're on our way to the morgue," Jack said.

She gave him the abridged version. Sonny's background was need-to-know because of his employment with the Task Force, and she was still working her way around it. Same for Sonny's team. She could get EPD personnel files, bank records, birth records, etcetera for anyone on the police department, but the feds protected their own.

"Angelina, we're pulling into the morgue. I'll have to call you back," Jack said. She hadn't started on Mindy or Sully.

Chapter 13

They arrived at the coroner's office. Liddell parked next to a black Mercedes sedan with deeply tinted windows and Massachusetts tags. "Sully's probably serving papers on the corpse, pod'na," he said.

Jack and Liddell went to the front door and the lock buzzed open immediately. Little Casket was standing with her arms folded across her chest, her face set in an expression that could either be normal for her, that is, a resting bitch face, or it could mean she was ready to throw someone through a window. Minus the profanity, the gist of what she said was, *"If I talk to this man anymore I'll gut him."*

"Where are they?" Jack asked.

She crooked a finger and they followed her to a room marked *PRIVATE*. Jack opened the door and Sully jumped to his feet. "Did you put this woman up to this? I demand you stop jerking the widow around and let us see the body," he said to Jack.

Lilly pushed Jack aside and got into Sully's face so fast he stumbled backward and plopped down in a chair.

"Number one," Lilly said angrily, "no one puts me up to anything. Number two, you aren't in a position to demand squat. Number three, *you* aren't going to view the deceased. If you can count, which I seriously am beginning to doubt, that adds up to 'keep your ass in that chair or get the hell out of my building'!"

Sully said, "I protest and—"

Lilly's thick-lensed glasses focused on him like a mean kid burning ants with a magnifying glass.

"Miss Middleton is in my office," Little Casket said to Jack. "You *detectives* can go with her to identify the deceased."

She shooed Jack and Liddell out of the room and stepped out, pulling the door shut with a bang.

"That went well," Jack said.

"Asshole," Lilly said, loud enough for the corpse to hear, and led them to her office.

"Lilly Eastwood." Liddell said softly to Jack. "Did she count to six or only count to three? Well to tell you the truth in all the excitement I kind of lost track myself."

Without turning, Lilly said, "Do ya feel lucky? Well—do ya, Bigfoot?"

"No ma'am," Liddell said.

Jack and Liddell entered Lilly's office. Mindy was staring out of the window. Lilly said, "I'll give you a few minutes," and shut the door gently.

Mindy turned toward the detectives. She was a different person from the one they had met earlier. This Mindy had sobered considerably, unless this morning was all an act. Third option—Mindy was bipolar.

"Thank you for being patient with me this morning," Mindy said. "It was—it still doesn't seem real."

"Do you want to talk to us without your attorney, Miss Middleton?" Jack asked.

She smiled. "Yes. I'd like that. I'm sorry about this morning. That's just Sully being Sully. He can be overprotective sometimes," Mindy said. "Can you tell me what happened? How did he…?"

Jack wasn't sure how to answer that question. He didn't want to give her a detailed description of the wounds. "That's what we're here to find out," Jack said. "The autopsy will be performed and give us those answers. Finding Sonny's killer is our first priority," Jack said.

She blinked and it was like someone turned the lights off behind her eyes. The other Mindy was back.

"I mean, yeah. Sure," she said in her strong Bronx accent. "My Sonny would want me to talk to you. He liked you two guys. My Sonny was always saying what a cop's cop you was, Detective Murphy," Mindy said. She smiled at Liddell and said, "He thought a lot of you too, Detective Blanchard. I remember seeing you and your wife while we was out eating."

Jack was pretty sure they'd covered all this earlier.

She continued, "Sully can be an asshole, but he's always been good to me and Sonny. When we moved here he loaned Sonny enough to build the house. And don't even ask how much it cost. Sonny never told me, and my ma always said, 'Never look a gift horse in the mouth.' Ya know?"

"Nicer than the place you came from, I'll bet," Liddell said.

"Not only 'yeah' but 'hell yeah'! It's a mansion compared to the two-story brownstone we had in Boston. I was sick of that place, sick of that whole neighborhood. Sonny came out and got us set up. The house was built when I got here. Said he wanted to surprise me. And boy was I surprised." Her eyes lit up. She was adrift on a sea of emotions with no one at the helm.

"I'm sorry. I don't think I can do this. See Sonny, I mean," she said. "Sully said Sonny was really messed up, but he said Sonny died quick-like. He wouldn't say how."

"You don't have to do this," Jack said, wondering just how much Sully knew. "But if you want to say goodbye, I'll go in with you. Sonny will be covered with a sheet."

She asked timidly, "What would you do, Detective Murphy? Do you think he'd want that?"

Jack put a hand on her arm and Liddell opened the door. Jack said, "I would say goodbye. Sonny would want that."

Jack grabbed a handful of tissues from Lilly's desk and handed them to Mindy. She gripped his arm and let him lead her down the hall to the viewing room. Any doubt he'd had regarding Mindy as a suspect melted away. She was just what she seemed. Lost and alone.

* * * *

Jack didn't remove the sheet from Sonny's battered face. Mindy gently put her palm on the sheet where it covered the side of Sonny's face. She leaned over, her voice hitched, and tears fell on the sheet. "You was always the one. Wait for me. Love you, Sonny."

She turned to Jack, eyes brimming, face contorted in grief. Her voice cracked as she said, "Sonny told me you was the guy that made things right. You make him pay for what he did to my Sonny. Promise me."

Jack wanted to say something comforting, but he heard himself saying, "I'll pull his wings off."

She gave him a weak smile.

"Can we call someone to stay with you tonight, Mindy?" Jack asked.

"I'll be fine," she said. "Sully's staying."

She looked at Jack's face. "Why are you surprised? Sully's not such a bad guy. He's always been there for me. And I need someone right now. I don't know what to do next. I mean with Sonny and the house and all."

Jack said, "I understand."

She took Jack's arm and let him lead her back toward Little Casket's office.

"He thinks he's protecting me," she said. "He was worried about me when he called a few days ago. It's like Sully has a second sense—a pre-something—you know, like that Tom Cruise movie where he could see things before they happened."

Jack knew what she meant, but the fact that Sully had called a few days before the murder, and Sully had called *her*, not the other way around—he found that very interesting.

So Sully lied when he said Mindy called him.

"Did he call you before or after Sonny hadn't come home?" Jack asked.

"I think it was after. Maybe I'm not remembering too good."

"Did he call for Sonny?" Jack asked.

"I'm not sure. Is it important? You can ask him."

"Did Sonny talk to him?" Jack persisted.

"Not really. Sully talked to me," she said. "He's like that. He just called to check up on us. Why you asking?"

Jack said, "That's my job, Mindy. I ask questions."

"Oh," she said.

"What time did Sully come to your house yesterday?"

"You don't think Sully…"

"Mindy, I don't know enough to think anything yet."

"Sully showed up early yesterday morning, before noon I guess. He drove all the way from Boston. That's a real friend, ya know. He'd never do anything to Sonny. They were like brothers. We was all close."

"You said Sully was worried," Jack said.

"Yeah," she said. "It was strange. It was like Sully knew something was going to happen."

"What did you and Sully talk about while he was with you?"

"Oh. He asked the usual stuff. How are you? How is Sonny? That kind of stuff. But he just sounded different. Worried. Ya know?"

"Why did he come to see you, Mindy? Was he coming to see Sonny?"

"I'm not sure why he came. Just being a friend, I guess."

Jack said, "Liddell will be in the office. You can wait with him."

"Ain't you coming with me?"

"I want to talk to Sully to straighten some things out," Jack said truthfully.

"Of course," she said. "Thanks for being kind, Detective Murphy. My Sonny always said you was a stand-up guy. And you was right. I feel better."

Jack watched as Mindy entered Lilly's office and when she was safely out of earshot he opened the door to the room marked *PRIVATE* to find Lilly standing toe to toe with Sully. Again. Literally. Her tiny feet were almost on top of Sully's highly shined wing tip shoes, her face turned up, his face bending down. The proverbial shit had hit the fan.

Jack had to yell to get their attention. "What the hell is going on in here?"

Color crept up the collar of Sully's shirt and spittle formed in the corners of his mouth. "Detective Murphy, I don't see any reason that this little woman won't let me accompany my client, my friend, in this most distressing time. She put her hands on me. I want her arrested for battery."

Little Casket spit the words out. "You will not refer to me as 'this little woman.' I'm the Chief Deputy Coroner for Vanderburgh County, State of Indiana. I don't know where your attitude comes from and I don't give a shit. You don't make the rules here. I'll have *you* arrested for trespassing."

Sully smirked. "I'm sure that's not the law even in a backwoods town like this."

Jack said, "Mr. Sullis, you're correct about the law, but that doesn't mean she can't make you leave. As far as viewing the deceased, only a law enforcement officer, preferably the investigator, is allowed to be with the person identifying the remains. You should know that."

Screw you if you don't.

Sully's jaws clamped shut and he said, "I apologize to you Detective, and to you, Deputy Coroner of Vanderburgh County, State of Indiana. In my grief for my old friend I've forgotten my manners. Can I have both of your business cards?"

Time to go.

Jack took Sully by the arm and hustled him toward the front exit, saying, "You need to come with me, Counselor." It wasn't a request. He muscled Sully outside and pushed him an arm's distance away. Before the door shut, Jack could see Little Casket standing in the hall mouthing the word "Asshole."

"Keep your hands off me," Sully growled. "I'll have your job."

Jack said, "You wouldn't want my job. You'd have to deal with assholes all day."

Sully was taken aback, no doubt wondering if Jack had just insulted him, but he slowly calmed and said, "You win. I didn't think I was being the asshole, but I get it. I've used your exact words before."

"I appreciate your understanding, Counselor. Here's another one. 'Some of my best friends are attorneys,'" Jack said, and Sully chuckled. It was at that moment Jack knew Sully for what he was. Or what he had been. Sully was an ex-cop in lawyer's clothing.

"You used to be a cop," Jack ventured.

"Good guess," Sully answered. "Yeah. I had the displeasure for twelve years. I wised up and saw where the real money was at without worrying I'd be sued or killed every minute of the day."

"Boston PD?" Jack asked.

"Boston PD," Sully said.

"Can you say 'Park the car' for me?" Jack said, and grinned.

"Oh, screw you," Sully said, but he cracked his first real smile. "That's bias and labeling and all that good civil rights shit. Just for you, Murphy, and only because you asked nicely." Sully said, "Park the car." It came out "Pa'k the ca'h."

"Yep. You're from Boston," Jack said.

"What do you want, Detective Murphy?" Sully asked. The niceties were over.

"I want you to tell me about Sonny, for starters," Jack said. "I'm not holding anyone's balls over the fire. Sonny's only been here a few years, and you two apparently go way back. Did you work together in Boston? I know he came from Boston PD."

Sully said, "Short version. We were detectives with Boston PD. The job got too complicated. YouTube, Facebook, Twitter, Instagram—all that kind of instant shit. Police were being made to wear body cameras. Honestly, I think everyone should wear a body camera and we could all have a good laugh. Cops are being charged with murder because some asshole D.A. wants their head on a platter. I took a partial pension and went to law school. I defend a lot of scumbags, but I also defend cops. You probably think I'm a traitor."

"I agree with most of what you say, Sully. Still, someone has to do the job. The military is getting the same crap," Jack said.

"When I quit, Sonny cashed out and came here. We keep in touch. Get together a couple times a year. Like Mindy said, we go fishing."

Jack asked, "When was the last time you saw him?"

"Been a while," Sully said noncommittally.

"How long's a while? A week? A month? A year?"

"Listen, I'll save you some digging. The last time I talked to Sonny was a few months back. He thought his bosses were out to get him, just like every cop. But he never said anything about someone physically out to harm him. He wasn't in trouble financially with anyone dangerous— unless you think the bank will kill you over a large mortgage. And Sonny was a tough guy. He could take care of himself. If he'd had problems that he didn't think he could handle he would have called me. But he didn't."

"Are you talking trouble here, or back in Boston?" Jack asked.

"He's got no enemies there. In Boston, I mean. But doing the job he did here...who knows?"

Jack asked, "You mentioned a large mortgage with a bank. Sonny had to take a huge cut in pay to come here. How deep in the hole was he?" Mindy had said Sully loaned Sonny the money to build the house.

Sully said, "He doted on Mindy. He'd give her both kidneys if she asked. You've seen the house. What do you think something like that with the view and acreage would cost around Boston? I'll tell you. At least five times what it costs here. I didn't ask him for a financial statement, if that's what you're getting at."

Sully rubbed his hands together and blew into them. "Sonny was the superhero type. He needed a cause, a purpose. He felt like he was making a difference here. And Mindy was as happy as I've ever seen her. He gave her everything she asked for. Those boobs alone cost him a mint, I can tell you, but she wanted 'em, and Sonny got 'em for her. He was that kind of guy. He'd give you the shirt off his back."

This didn't jibe with Mindy saying she thought Sonny was cheating on her. And if Sonny was rich, why did Sully have to loan him the money to build the house? Jack asked, "If Sonny would do anything for Mindy, why would she think he was fooling around? Why did she call you? When did she call you? Why did you have to loan him money?"

"Mindy tell you I loaned Sonny the money for the house?" Sully asked. "All she knows is how to spend it." Sully raised his hands, and said, "That's it. No more questions. I'm getting Mindy and taking her home. She hired me, and in that light, I've advised her not to answer any more of your questions."

"Thank you for your cooperation, Mr. Sullis," Jack said.

Sully walked past him to the door, hit the buzzer and was admitted. A minute later he came out with Mindy in tow. She was once again subdued and timid, and didn't speak or glance in Jack's direction. They got into the black Mercedes sedan that had been backed into Sonny's garage earlier. He now saw it had Massachusetts license plates that read SO SU ME.

* * * *

The Subway sandwich shop on Walnut Street gave him an unobstructed view down S. Morton Street to the front parking lot of the Vanderburgh County Coroner's Office. He'd watched a black Mercedes park in front of the coroner's office. A tall man and a Dolly Parton clone exited the sedan.

The tall man was Sully, Vincent Sullis. The busty female was Mindy Middleton, Sonny's woman.

He had watched Sully put his hands on Mindy's shoulders and lean down to speak. It was too distant to hear voices, but he could imagine the conversation. It was about Sonny. It was about the boogeyman.

After Sully and Mindy went into the building, he'd unwrapped the six-inch BMT, careful to keep the wrapper across his lap, and took a bite. He had finished eating the BMT when a gold-colored Crown Vic parked near the Mercedes. The detectives working on Sonny's murder. Jack Murphy and Liddell Blanchard. He didn't want to go up against those two—many had tried and failed—but if they got between him and his prize...

He wadded the sandwich wrapper, stuffed it inside the plastic bag, and set this on the seat beside him. He'd seen what he needed to see, and besides, he had an appointment a few blocks away. He put the car in gear and thought of how these men had raped his daughter and burned her alive. They had thrown her in a Dumpster like garbage and set her on fire.

He had planned to get together with her the day she was killed. It would be the first time they'd met. He'd talked to her on the telephone and she'd told him she was coming to town early. She'd said, "The early bird catches the worm." Of course, she meant something entirely different from what he was thinking of doing. He would get this worm too. He'd get them all.

Chapter 14

Jack and Liddell were waiting in the garage at the morgue when the Forensic Pathologist, Dr. John Carmodi, arrived. Sergeant Walker pulled into the lot and they all came in through the garage entrance. Dr. John took off his North Face parka and slipped on mint-green Tyvek coveralls. He tucked a yellow tie embroidered with little black hearses inside the coveralls and zipped up.

"Nice tie, Dr. John," Liddell remarked.

"I got it at a medical convention last year. Pretty cool, huh?"

Little Casket was waiting in the autopsy room. "Hmpff," Lilly said, and zipped up a pair of white coveralls. She pulled up the hood and adjusted the protective faceplate over her glasses. Her head resembled a bizarre depiction of a spaceman with bulging eyes.

"Good thing you showed up in there, Jack," Lilly said.

"I think you could have handled Sully without my help," Jack said. Sully should never have called Little Casket "this little woman."

"Wasn't me that needed help."

Dr. John stood beside the autopsy table, hosing some of the detritus from around the body, washing it down the stainless-steel table into a drain in the deep, steel double sink. Sergeant Walker watched this operation closely, stopping Dr. John here and there to snap photos or collect some item of interest.

A set of X-rays was clipped to the light box. Several others lay in a pile on the shelf underneath. Lilly had been busy taking X-rays while Jack talked to Sully. One of these showed the victim's skull and neck.

Lilly motioned to a spot on the X-rays. "Poor bastard," she said, in a rare display of compassion.

"Jesus H...!" Liddell said, pointing to the thick spikes driven through Sonny's eye sockets and traversing to the back of the skull. This was the first time he'd seen this. "I guess that's the cause of death."

"How would I know? I'm just a glorified receptionist." Lilly clipped more films to the light box. "Above my pay grade."

Dr. John moved the X-rays around until he had viewed each. He began his examination of the body starting with the top of the skull. As he carefully parted the hair, he said, "We call the top of the head the skullcap. Did you know skullcap is also a flowering plant? Part of the mint family, I believe." He continued examining the top and sides of the skull and continued his dissertation on the plant. "Skullcap is used as a medicine for insomnia, anxiety disorders, even strokes." Under the autopsy table were pedals that operated a boom microphone for a recorder. He depressed the pedal with his foot and described the location and description of cuts, bruises and burns on the scalp.

"Are those spikes part of the mint family too?" Liddell asked.

Dr. John smiled and said, "Those would be a permanent cure for insomnia, wouldn't they?" He pointed to patterns of black circular burns on the scalp and side of the neck. "Tony, can you get some shots of these?" Walker did.

"We noticed those marks at the scene," Jack said. "We thought they might be Taser burns."

Dr. John said, "Maybe. They're definitely burns. My guess is some type of electrical device. The consistent pattern indicates some type of handheld weapon that I'm not familiar with. See how the scalp hair is scorched around the burns. Do any of you know of something that could make that?"

Walker took a set of black plastic brass knuckles from his back pocket and slipped them on. On top of each knuckle was a pointed nub made of metal. A pressure switch was on the side where it could be operated by the thumb. He pressed the switch and electrical arcs danced across the top of the knuckles. Walker slipped them off and handed them to Dr. John.

"I'm not going to get zapped, am I?"

"Don't press the switch on the side, Doc and you'll be okay. Right there," Walker said and showed Dr. John where the switch was located.

Dr. John held the metal nubs near a set of burn patterns on the chest. They matched.

"Where in the world did you get these?" Dr. John asked.

"Army Surplus store on First Avenue," Walker answered.

Jack said, "Zack got his boots at the Army Surplus store. There's only one in town, to my knowledge."

"That's interesting," Liddell said.

Walker said, "Before you get too excited I talked to the manager at Army Surplus. If you're thinking of finding the killer by getting sales records you'll be disappointed. He said these are sold as fast as he can buy them and he doesn't keep records. You can get them off the Internet or in just about any sporting goods store."

"There's something else interesting," Dr. John said, and motioned for the men to follow him back to the light box.

"More interesting than spikes through the eyes?" Liddell asked.

"Well, let's see."

Dr. John selected another X-ray, clipped it in place and put a finger on a shadow almost hidden by the jaw. He clipped up a side view of the skull. The shadow became an object about one and a half to two inches by three quarters to an inch in size. It had a definite shape, but Jack had no idea what it was.

"What's that?" Liddell asked.

"It's too far back in the throat for it to have been accidentally ingested," Dr. John answered. "It's not food. Food has softer edges. This is something solid. I think someone shoved it down the victim's throat."

"Any ideas on a time of death, Doc?" Jack asked.

"When was the last time someone saw the victim?" Dr. John asked.

Chapter 15

Sam Knight had gone to Harvard Law School in Cambridge, Massachusetts. To pay for this, he'd burned up an inheritance, worked two jobs, and gave up any kind of life outside of study and more study. After graduation, he had turned down lucrative job offers with prestigious law firms in Boston, opting instead to become a deputy district attorney.

He soon gained a reputation as a tough but fair deputy district attorney, handling the toughest cases: drugs, organized crime, money laundering, etcetera, and he'd successfully prosecuted two death-penalty cases. If it was mob-related, Knight was the D.A.'s go-to guy.

Knight's tenacity and success in prosecuting these types of cases brought him to the attention of Big Bobby Touhey. Touhey had reached out to him by sending four very large men who had asked Knight not so nicely to come with them. Knight was placed in the back seat of the limo between two of the men. Not a word was spoken until the car arrived at the Arlington Street entrance of the Boston Public Gardens. Knight was let out and one man asked him, "Do you know where the statue of George Washington is ridin' that horse?" Knight had said, "Yes." The man got back in the car and drove away.

That was seven years ago, but Knight remembered it like it was yesterday. Knight had walked east toward the sixteen-foot-tall stone pillar that held a twenty-two-foot statue of George Washington sitting atop a horse, sword drawn and held high over his head leading a charge. A few hundred yards further east was a manmade lake/lagoon where swan boats could be rented. A hundred yards north of that was the famous park bench where Robin Williams sat with Matt Damon in the movie *Good Will Hunting*.

Sitting on Robin Williams's bench overlooking the lagoon was a slight man, dressed in faded brown corduroy pants, a beige button-down shirt and brown and beige two-tone wing tip shoes—the kind favored in the early 1920s. All the man was missing to make the outfit complete was a straw boater hat called a skimmer, a bow tie, and a bamboo cane.

Big Bobby Touhey was in his late sixties or early nineties. It was hard to tell; he had drooping earlobes but a head of thick, jet-black hair. He was around five foot two, one hundred twenty pounds, and no muscle tone. The only thing big about him was the enormous gold-and-diamond studded ring he wore on his right ring finger. Touhey had a reputation for making big money and big violence. He had more than a little interest in gaming, prostitution, money lending, trucking, protection, knock-off clothing, and even garbage collection. You wanted an Apple watch, a Mac computer, or a designer purse, you could get it from one of Touhey's people cheaper than from the Apple store or off the rack at Nordstrom. It was well known that Big Bobby also had more than an interest in politics. It was said, "No one gets elected without Big Bobby's blessing."

That meeting took place seven years ago. The meeting was short and Big Bobby was deliberately vague, but his message was crystal clear. Knight had seen the wisdom in working for Big Bobby and not against him. He would continue to prosecute organized crime, just as in the past, with the exception that he would get the go-ahead nod from Touhey first. Touhey would throw one of his own people under the bus every now and then to make Knight appear legit.

In exchange, Big Bobby would give Knight firsthand information. Knight had stagnated at his current position with the D.A.'s office. This could be his ticket to bigger things. He had to decide if he wanted to be rich and successful, or dead. Knight had chosen rich and successful. The relationship had become mutually beneficial. Knight was on his way up. A judgeship. Maybe appellate court judge. Maybe Massachusetts Supreme Court.

There had been one hiccup in all of this, and more than one person was involved in the hiccup. He had handled it, just as he handled everything. Knight's word was gold with the District Attorney. Coupled with Big Bobby's clout, Knight made most of the decisions whether charges were filed and what cases the D.A. would pursue. He had made the hiccup go away. He had no choice in the matter, since the crux of the problem involved Touhey's son and two of Boston's finest. Knight had made the problem go away, but at great risk and cost to himself. Touhey's kid wouldn't go to prison. Wouldn't even be a suspect.

Big Bobby had suggested to Sonny and Sully that they resign from Boston PD. But by that time Knight had had enough. He wanted to quit.

Quitting wasn't an option. Knight had been offered a position as a Circuit Court judge in Vanderburgh County, Evansville, Indiana.

Sonny was also offered a job in Evansville, similar to the one he'd held in Boston. Sonny had been accepted by the Evansville Police with open arms and allowed to keep the rank of sergeant when he transferred. Sonny wasn't a problem for Knight. They had a good working relationship.

It was Vincent Sullis that had caused the problem for Little Bobby in the first place. If Sully had handled things differently and not made such a big mess, there wouldn't have been as much fallout. Little Bobby brought a shitstorm down on his own head time and time again.

Knight thought it ironic that Sully would go to a private Jesuit Catholic research university, Boston College in Chestnut Hill, to study law. And now Sully was a lawyer working for one of Touhey's casinos. Sully was an idiot. A retard. A wannabe gangster. He had even started touting himself as Touhey's consigliere—counselor, advisor to a mob boss.

Instead of dumping Sully in the harbor, Big Bobby thought Sully was hilarious. Knight knew Sully didn't know a legal brief from Michael Jordan's underwear. It was Sully who had called him at work to give him the news that Sonny Caparelli was found murdered. Knight much preferred never to talk to Vincent Sullis again, but Sully said Big Bobby himself had ordered him to meet with Sully.

Knight felt a chill of unease run through him as he sat in his book-lined office in the City-County Courts Building. He couldn't help but think of all the deaths around him. The judge he'd replaced was barely forty years old and had been killed during an attempted robbery. Knight had no doubt that Big Bobby was behind it.

When Little Bobby died—murdered, really—Knight had gone to the funeral in Boston because it was expected of him. He'd told a small lie to his wife, telling her it was a business trip. At the service, he ran into Sonny and Sully. They appeared to be uneasy. Truth be told, he hadn't thought they should be seen together, much less with Big Bobby. He didn't see any sign of it, but the Feds were likely photographing everyone who showed up.

Little Bobby had been brutally murdered and now, from what Sully told him, Sonny Caparelli had been tortured. Who would be next?

The top of his desk was stacked with legal tomes covering precedents of decisions for cases like the one before him now. Knight made a neat pile of the folders, opened a side drawer of his desk and locked them inside. The petitioners, four families suing the plaintiff, were obviously motivated by twenty million dollars each. They were insignificant. Just working Joes.

The plaintiff, however, was a close friend of the Indiana governor. He was going to decide in favor of the plaintiff. It was what Big Bobby wanted.

He wrapped a scarf around his neck, pulled on a heavy wool overcoat, made sure he had gloves in the pocket and exited his office into the hallway that separated the judge's chambers from the back of the courtrooms. Sheriff's deputies guarded the hallway, and this allowed the judges to enter and exit the courtroom without being accosted.

"Hello Judge," the sheriff's deputy working the metal detector said, and waved Sam through the door. "Hard day, Your Honor?"

Sam smiled and said, "Not as hard as yours, I'm sure."

The deputy gave him a tired smile. "See you tomorrow."

Sam exited into the Civic Center courtyard, strode down the marble steps, past the enormous winter-dormant water fountain, past the Evansville-Vanderburgh County School Corporation offices, to the pedestrian crossing on SE 8th Street, where traffic stopped for him.

He felt good. He'd made the right decision. Sully hadn't said as much, but this sudden meeting had to involve Sonny Caparelli's death. Knight would attend the meeting, fix whatever needed fixing, and by this time next year he'd be on his way to Indianapolis. He was a shoo-in for an appointment as a federal judge. He was already anticipating the next step. Anything was possible now. The world was his oyster. Evansville had been good to him, but it was just a pond and he was a very big fish.

He walked for what seemed like an hour before he spotted his car, a cream-colored 2017 BMW Z4 sport convertible. He got his key fob out and spotted a big glob of something white on his windshield and another glob on the driver's window. Some bastard had spit on his car! No doubt just because it was new and expensive. He took a slow tour around the car to be sure there wasn't any other vandalism. There wasn't.

He muttered, *Shit on a stick!* He punched the trunk button on his key fob and the trunk lid popped up. He was fixated on cleaning off the mess and didn't notice when a shadow fell over him.

Chapter 16

The purpose of an autopsy is to determine if natural conditions could have contributed to the person's death. Autopsies also help police establish the identity of the deceased. Ultimately, the autopsy is performed to determine the cause and manner of death.

Cause of death is the most plausible reason the person died. In Sonny's case, there were several plausible reasons. The manner of death is the method or methods that explain the type of death, be it asphyxiation, exsanguination, or, in Sonny's case, two heavy railroad spikes shoved through the eyes and into the brain.

Dr. John made a Y-incision starting from high on each shoulder, cutting to midchest, and then down to the pubic area. Even wearing a surgical mask, Jack had to turn his head away at the smell of a stomach being opened. The intestines were empty. The heart was normal size and weight. The brain was normal—except for the metal spikes.

Dr. John examined the site in the throat, removed the object, and said, "Gentlemen, I think we have a possible cause of death. Asphyxia." The shadowy object found in the victim's throat turned out to be a figurine. An inch-and-a-half tall, less than one inch wide.

"What the hell is that thing?" Jack asked.

Dr. John gently removed the carving using a pair of Kelly forceps and held it up to the light. "It's a carving of a monkey. Sitting with its legs crossed." Dr. John rinsed it off and turned it different angles.

"See no evil," Sergeant Walker said.

"I think you're right," Dr. John agreed.

* * * *

Jack and Liddell left the morgue. Sergeant Walker was still doing paperwork and talking to Dr. John.

"So, according to Dr. John, the time of death could be anywhere from seven last night to six this morning," Liddell said. If a time of death couldn't be proven as a fact, it became a legal guesstimate on the coroner's part. Dr. John used the time Sonny was last seen by Jerry—seven-fifteen the previous evening—to the time his body was discovered this morning— around six. The extreme cold hadn't helped.

"Off the record, Dr. John said he thought it was closer to midnight," Jack said. "We have to work with what we've got, but it would be nice, just one time, for something to go our way."

Jack's phone rang. It was the chief's secretary.

"Let me guess. Double Dick's on the warpath again," Jack said.

"He's on the path to hell if you ask me. But, no, that's not what I'm calling about," Judy said. "You've got a visitor in the lobby. And before you ask, no, the man wouldn't give a name or reason for the visit. He asked specifically for Detective Murphy."

"Thanks, Judy. We're on our way," Jack said.

"I'll drive," Liddell said.

Jack got in and turned the blower off. It was cold air until the engine heated up anyway. "What do we have? Dr. John gave the cause of death as the spikes through the brain. The secondary cause of death was the monkey carving blocking his airway. *See no evil.* What's it supposed to tell us, Bigfoot?"

"Maybe Sonny saw something he shouldn't have."

* * * *

The man waiting in the police lobby was somewhere in his late sixties and what you would call "well-preserved," with a heavily tanned six-foot frame, ocean-blue eyes and white hair worn long and slicked back. He was dressed in a dark suit and tie and dark wool knee-length overcoat. He reminded Jack of George Clooney except for the hair.

"Marty Crispino," the man in the police lobby said, and shook hands with Jack and Liddell.

Jack said by way of introduction, "Detective Murphy and Blanchard."

"I know who you are," Crispino said.

Jack didn't know if this guy knowing who he was, was a good or bad thing. Crispino's expression gave nothing away. "What can we do for you?" Jack asked.

"My nephew was Herbert Crispino. You knew him as Cubby. Cubby Crispino. That ring a bell?"

It did. Jack remembered Cubby Crispino as a hired gun from New York. Cubby had tried to carry out a contract on a guy in Shawneetown, Illinois, but got killed himself. In fact, that was how Jack ended up stuck with Cinderella, the mutt who was currently being tended by Jack's sister-in-law, Moira Connelly. He hoped Marty Crispino wanted the dog, but he knew it was something else that had brought him downtown.

"I remember the case, Mr. Crispino. What can we do for you?" Marty and Cubby bore a clear family resemblance. He wondered if they shared the same occupation.

"Everyone calls me Uncle Marty," Crispino said. He gave Jack and Liddell a disarming smile. "I always wanted to come here and thank you gentlemen personally for eliminating the guy who killed my nephew. Cubby's father—God rest his soul—would be here himself if he could. Cubby's mother thanks you, too."

Uncle Marty gave the impression that he wasn't someone you wanted to meet outside an Italian restaurant without a bulletproof hide and backup.

Liddell, being the sensitive one, said, "You and your family have our sincere condolences."

Jack made a guess where he was from based on the accent. "You came all the way from New York just to see us, Marty? Or do you have other business here? I hope not. Cubby's death has been avenged. It's over."

Jack saw the corners of Marty's mouth tilt up minutely. "I get it. That's a good one, Detective Murphy. You joke. That's good. Means you have a sense of humor. A sense of humor is important in your line of work." He reached up and smoothed his hair back.

Jack noticed Marty had used his right hand. He could see the right side of Marty's overcoat was wider at the hip.

"I won't keep you long. I can see you're busy, but I wanted to meet you," Marty said, but he obviously had something on his mind.

Jack smiled and said, "Here's some more cop humor for you, Marty. Is that a banana in your pocket, or are you just happy to see me?"

Marty's hand started inside his coat and Jack grabbed his wrist and said, "Let's take it slow, why don't we? May I?" Jack patted down the side of Marty's waist and felt something hard under the coat.

Marty cracked a smile. "Another good one, Detective Murphy," he said, and held his arms up, palms outward. "I got a permit for the banana. New York has a reciprocal handgun carry agreement with Indiana. I checked before I left home. I checked my gun at the airport and got it back when

I arrived in this happy little city. All legal. I'll be happy to show you my permit, and we can compare bananas if you like." He chuckled. Jack didn't.

"I like that idea," Jack said, and relieved Marty of the semi-auto he carried in a holster on his waist. Jack said, "Here's another oldie. Assume the position."

Marty smiled but turned around and put his hands on the wall, spreading his legs. Jack patted his outer clothing down from his neck to his socks and felt nothing else that could be a weapon.

"Why don't we go somewhere more private, Mr. Crispino?" Jack said. "And keep your hands where I can see them."

Crispino said, "Lead on."

"After you. I insist." Jack pointed toward the door leading to the detectives' offices.

Interrogation Room 1 was available. Jack ushered Marty in. Liddell came in and closed the door. Marty retrieved a New York concealed-carry permit and allowed Jack to inspect the weapon, a Beretta 9mm, model 92S. Liddell left long enough to check on the reciprocal agreement between Indiana and New York. Marty was legal. The gun wasn't stolen.

Preliminaries over, Jack popped the magazine out, worked the slide to be sure there wasn't one in the pipe, and handed Marty's gun and magazine back. "I apologize for the cold reception, but as you said, we are pretty busy at the moment. You can reload the gun when you're out of my sight if you don't mind. I like knowing which guns are loaded when I'm around someone I don't know. I'm funny that way."

Marty put his pistol and permit away. He put the magazine in his coat pocket. "You guys are okay. Thorough—like the cops back home. But nicer. I guess you already figured out that I came here for another reason than to just say hello. I came to ask for your help. I need to find someone. But now I think maybe we can help each other. I know you're working a murder case. Maybe I know some things you don't know. In return, you can help me find that certain someone I came for."

Chapter 17

Knight was confused and regained consciousness in stages. It was like coming out of the after-surgery fog where the nurse makes sure you can say your name and pee before letting you go home. But if he was in the hospital, his bed was jarring and bumping and jarring and bouncing the side of his head against something hard. The bouncing stopped. He heard a pop and then bright light flooded his vision. He tried to raise a hand to block the light but his arm wouldn't move. He tried again and realized his wrists were bound behind his back. His knees were drawn up under his chin. He couldn't move his feet. The light dimmed briefly and he could feel someone was near.

"Who's there?" Knight asked. He was answered by gasoline being sloshed over his naked body, his hair, running into his eyes and mouth, burning and choking. Panic ripped through him like a knife. "Who are you?" he sputtered through burning lips.

A man's voice said, "I guess you're wondering why I asked you here?" A slight chuckle. "I hadn't planned on taking you this soon, Judge. But I couldn't pass up the chance." More cold liquid poured across Knight's face and eyes. "That was just water. Sorry. I think I got the gas in your eyes. This will help." More water poured on Knight's head.

The water didn't help. Knight's eyes still burned, but he cracked them open. His vision was blurred but he could make out the outline of a tall man framed above him and he realized he was tied up in the trunk of a car. Knight wasn't a big man, but the space was a tight fit.

The fumes were making him dizzy, nauseous. The man was speaking again, his lips were moving, but the words were hollow, mere echoes fading in and out. The voice was unthreatening, educated. He tried to place it but he couldn't. He tried to form words but couldn't because of the fire burning in his throat.

"Did you want to say something? No? Well, feel free to express yourself. No one will hear, but I'll listen. Promise."

Knight heard a click and felt a deep burning sensation run slowly from the top of his cheekbone, dragging down across his teeth and lips and exiting the side of his mouth. The burning in his throat was nothing compared to the flash of burning pain that followed. Knight sucked in breath, the fumes burning deep in his lungs, causing a coughing fit. Bloody froth bubbled through the gaping wound in his cheek.

"You know who I am, Judge."

Knight fought the urge to cough and squinted his eyes to focus. His eyes widened before clamping tightly shut. There was an almost imperceptible nod of Knight's head.

"You recognize me. That's good. I want you to know why you're going to die." He buried the knife blade into Knight's shoulder until it struck bone, then pressed and twisted.

Knight's scream came out as short squeals. Vomitus spewed out of his nose and through the gaping cut on his face, splattering across his naked knees.

The man closed the knife. "I don't want you to choke."

Knight gagged and vomit dribbled down the side of his face. "W-w-why?" he managed to say.

"You're an educated man, Sam. Every crime must have a punishment. The four monkeys are the crimes. Ten-Tei is the punisher." He held a small ivory-colored figurine in front of Knight's eyes and said, "This is Kikazaru. Hear No Evil. As a judge, you've heard a lot of evil. You were too late to save her from them but you helped them escape justice. Your job was to protect people. You allowed evil to exist for your own personal gain. You have no dignity. For that I sentence you to death."

Knight's mouth was forced open and the monkey shoved deep into his throat. Knight's eyes bulged, his throat spasmed, his entire body lurched in a futile attempt to expel the blockage that was robbing him of oxygen.

"One more thing, and the Devil can have you," the man said, and took a heavy iron spike from his pocket. "Hear no evil," he said, gripped Knight by the throat, and drove the spike into his ear. Knight's body convulsed once.

Chapter 18

Marty Crispino asked, "Hey, you're not locking me up, are you?"

"Why?" Jack asked. "Did you do something?"

"I'll tell you everything I know in exchange for your promise to help me," Crispino said.

"That depends on who you're looking for and what you plan on doing with them."

Crispino said, "Please, call me Uncle Marty. Can I call you Jack and Liddell?"

"No," Jack said.

"Hey. You won't have a problem with me. No reason we can't keep this informal. I only ask—and this part isn't negotiable—that we go somewhere that I'm not being taped or filmed. I've been in police station interrogation rooms before. I don't want my talking to you to come back and bite me in the patootie."

"Okay. Uncle Marty. We'll go to the coffee shop. The mayor's too cheap to put cameras in every room in the Civic Center."

"Except in the women's bathroom. Right?" Marty said and grinned.

Jack was starting to like this guy. They walked down the narrow hallway and into the cafeteria/break room. That's what the sign over the doorway said, at least.

The room was huge, filled with vending machines, napkins, straws, more vending machines, a couple of trash cans, tables, plastic-and-chrome chairs, even more vending machines, a bill-changer machine, and a homeless guy sleeping in the back of the room.

"We've got a place exactly like this back in Boston. Government buildings must come equipped with homeless guys and vending machines."

"The coffee's not good, but the food will probably kill you," Jack said.

A refrigerated vending machine offered cold sandwiches and single-serving soups that were freshly made during WWII. A tiny microwave in a steel frame was bolted to the countertop. No one in their right mind would eat the crap available here. Except Liddell, who, of course, was slipping one-dollar bills into the sandwich and soup machine.

Jack took Marty to one of the tables. They sat and Liddell brought an armload of mini-donuts, SunChips, Fritos, pretzels, and four petrified cold cuts. He laid these in the middle of the table and sat down across from Marty.

Marty put his hands up. "Thanks, but no thanks. I got ptomaine on the flight. If you're ever in New York or Boston it'll be my treat. Is the coffee safe?"

Liddell got up again and headed to the coffee machine. Jack pulled his chair up closer to the table and said, "Uncle Marty. Tell me what you have for us and I'll decide if we can help you."

Liddell came back with three coffees and a pocketful of cream and sugar packets.

Marty said, "I came here to see Franco Caparelli. He goes by Sonny."

Without a pause Jack asked, "You know he's dead, right?"

"Yeah. I found out when I landed."

"It hasn't been on the news," Jack said.

"You got your sources, I got mine," Marty said. His eyes narrowed. End of discussion.

"Why would Sonny Caparelli interest you, Marty?" Jack asked.

"Okay. Here's where I tell you something and you get out the handcuffs and off we go. If you think it's important and help me out, I'll tell you everything."

Jack made a mental note that twice now Marty Crispino had mentioned being locked up. *Guilty mind? Or just guilty?* He'd have to find out when Marty had really arrived in Evansville.

"We're listening," Jack said. Even Liddell was interested now. The snacks and sandwiches had gone untouched.

"Sonny owes a guy I work for. I came here to work out payment arrangements."

"How much?" Jack asked.

"Let's just say it's a lot of money. Sonny paid back some of it, but there's an outstanding balance due, if you get my meaning."

"Was he supposed to be making a payment last night?" Jack asked.

"I wasn't in Evansville last night," Marty said without any hesitation. "I was going to..."

"Surprise him?" Jack finished for him.

"I know what you're thinking." Marty took his airline ticket from his jacket on the table. It was an open-ended round-trip ticket from Boston to Evansville, dated today. He'd arrived in Evansville several hours ago.

"You can check with the airport. I picked up my gun there maybe three hours ago."

"We will," Jack said. "Continue."

"Okay. Sonny still owes my boss five hundred big ones."

Liddell whistled. "I can see why it was worth your trip out here."

"I wasn't going to shoot him," Marty said. "I brought my gun for protection. I mean, Sonny's a cop. I believe in keeping balance in a discussion involving five hundred grand. My mama always said, 'Never bring just your mouth to a gunfight'."

Jack countered with, "My mom said, 'You get farther with a kind word and a gun than just a kind word'."

Marty snickered and Jack asked, "Who do you need our help finding?"

Marty pulled a picture from his suit coat and slid it across the table between Jack and Liddell. "This is—"

"Vincent Sullis," Liddell said.

Marty tapped the photo with a finger. "You met him already?"

"Before we answer your questions, maybe you should tell us why Sully is here," Jack said.

Marty thought it over. "Sully indirectly works for my boss. He's a close friend of Sonny's and a second signature on the loan. When I got here and heard Sonny was dead, I called my people and they checked on Sully's whereabouts. He wasn't in Boston. I figured he must be here."

And you just happened to be carrying a picture of him. And a gun.
"Would he know Sonny's loan was due?" Jack asked.

"Sully was in a position to know," Marty said. "Maybe my employer sent him ahead of me."

"You just said you came here to collect a debt. If your boss sent you, wouldn't you know if he also sent Sully?"

Uncle Marty said, "My boss doesn't tell me everything."

"When exactly did you hear Sonny was dead?" Jack asked.

"I told you. Someone called me when I landed at your airport. It doesn't matter who, unless you think I killed him."

"Did you?" Jack asked, not missing a beat.

"I don't even know the guy personally," Marty said. "If that's not plain enough for you, no, I didn't kill him. Pinky swear."

"I had to ask."

Jack didn't ask, but he was pretty sure Uncle Marty had another picture in his pocket. This one of Sonny.

"I knew you would ask. Getting back to a topic that won't get me arrested, Sonny and Sully were partners on Boston PD. They went their separate ways, but stayed friends."

"Old news," Jack said.

"Okay, here's something you don't know. For this I expect a trade."

"*If* you've got something I need," Jack said.

"Not good enough," Marty said. "With Sonny dead, I'd think you'd be wanting to talk to Sully. But maybe you don't care what I know. Eh?"

Jack said nothing and Liddell tore open a pack of powdered-sugar mini-donuts. He offered one to Marty.

Marty declined and said, "Both Sully and I work for a guy in Boston who owns a couple casinos. Atlantic City, Missouri, even the one you got here. The Blue Star, right?"

"Yeah," Jack said. "They've got more money than God. Does Sonny's death have something to do with the casino?" Jack asked.

"You get right to the point," Marty said. He picked up a donut, turned it over, put it down and wiped the powder off his fingers with a napkin.

Liddell asked, "If you're not going to eat those, do you mind if I have the rest?"

Marty pushed the package across the table to Liddell. He ran a hand through his slicked-back hair and wiped his palm on his suit pants. "I'm not saying it has a direct connection to the casino and I'm not saying it don't. I'm simply telling you Sonny borrowed five hundred thousand from my employer via the casino operations to facilitate his move to Evansville. I know Sonny's got expensive tastes that his pay doesn't half cover. He has a house here that's worth close to what he owes us. He's got a boat worth forty thousand or more. I did my due diligence before I came."

"So you're casino muscle?" Jack asked.

"Crispino muscle," Liddell said.

"You make jokes, but I'm not a leg breaker like you are suggesting, my friend. My job is to make sure people are aware they have to pay. Do I think Sonny's death has something to do with the money he owes? Truth is, I don't really know. To be brutally honest, him dying doesn't get my employer a penny. We don't make money off dead guys. That's lawyers." Marty took a sip of the coffee, grimaced, and took another sip. "Not bad. A little Scotch and it would be—fair."

Jack said, "A lot of Scotch and it wouldn't matter."

Marty toasted Jack with his paper cup and continued. "Let's start with Sonny. You may not want to hear some of this. Like you know Sonny was with Boston PD. He was a detective with the Vice Unit, and went to the Violent Crimes Unit. But he was on loan sometimes to a special Narcotics task force."

"Did he work undercover?" Jack asked, and Marty pointed at him.

"Sully was Sonny's partner. He's one crazy bastard. Reckless. Know what I mean?"

"Reckless? In what way?" Jack asked.

"Well, for one thing, he's sexually addicted. He'd put his dick in a knothole. Or another cop's girlfriend, or wife, or sister, or even his best friend's girl."

"I get it," Jack said. "So what's your point?"

"Sully's bipolar too. He's fine one minute and screaming and tearing ass the next. He hurt a couple of these—ladies—because the hubbies found out Sully was banging them. He didn't care if the husband watched or not while he beat the women up. You see where I'm going with this now?"

Jack thought he did, but he wanted Marty to say it. He waited.

"Sully was poling Mindy right under Sonny's nose," Marty said.

Jack and Liddell were silent.

Marty said, "Oh for God's sake, I'll spell it out for you. Sonny gets killed and Sully is here. Mindy gets all the money and property. Sully gets Mindy. Two plus two equals a dead Sonny. Get it?"

Jack asked, "How does that help Sully if he's co-signer on the money owed to your employer?"

"I lied," Marty said. "He's not a real co-signer, but he vouched for Sonny. I guess you could say he would be on the spot to repay the money. Sully was supposed to come here to get the money for our employer."

Jack asked, "How do you know all of this?"

"I know lots of things," Marty said. "For example, I know that Sonny resigned from Boston PD five years ago and moved here. I know he worked here for the Federal Drug Task Force. He's a sergeant, which means he is in charge of operations. He's got to be good at what he does to keep a job like that. On the other hand, there's Sully. His old partner with the one-eyed roving monster in his pants. Within a week of Sonny retiring from BPD, Sully puts his papers in, goes to law school, becomes a defense attorney of all things, and stays in Boston. He ends up working for my boss."

Jack remembered Sully telling him that he had resigned first and *that* was the reason for Sonny's quitting and moving away. Everyone was lying. What a surprise.

"Now Sully's defending the same guys he used to arrest," Marty continued. "That didn't make him popular with the boys in blue. He might as well have a target on his back. But..."

"But what?" Jack asked.

"But you guys play it mostly by the rules. You got to read someone their Miranda rights before putting a bullet in their brainpan," Marty said, and smirked. "At least most of the time. Am I right?"

"I think our conversation is over, Mr. Crispino," Jack said and rose to his feet.

"Sorry for that. I just admire anyone that can do the job you guys do. So, I'll get to the end of my story and you decide if you owe me." Marty took a sip of the now-cold coffee. "Did Sully tell you why he's here?"

"He said he's Mindy's lawyer," Jack said. "He's being supportive."

"You haven't asked me why Sonny and Sully retired from a promising career with Boston PD," Marty said. "You woulda found out when you checked out these guys' history—and I know you guys woulda done that."

Jack noticed that Marty's accent became more pronounced when he was telling a story he figured was particularly interesting, one man to another.

Jack said, "Tell us why Sonny and Sully gave up an exciting career, and why I'm going to reciprocate. That means respond in kind."

Chapter 19

While Jack and Liddell were talking to Uncle Marty in the Civic Center cafeteria, Engine No. 3 rolled out of Firehouse Station No. 5 on Maryland Street, emergency lights flashing, speeding down St. Joseph Avenue. Engine No. 3 is what is known as a "quint," a ladder truck that has pumping capabilities. Pump House No. 7 on Barker Avenue and Perry Township Volunteer Fire Department were also en route with pumper trucks.

The fire was in Dogtown, an area along the Ohio River that the city annexed from the county a few years ago. A farmer who lived on Duesner Road, over a mile distant, called in the fire.

Fire Captain Taylor Swenson drove his ten-year-old Crown Victoria, equipped with a bar light and siren that sometimes worked. He was overdue to get a new Ford Explorer, but there were budget concerns and so on. He followed Engine No. 3, saying his usual prayer when responding to a fire call. "God please let me wreck this piece of junk and get a real vehicle." He added, "Oh, and don't let anyone get hurt."

Swenson was a hands-on administrator. He worked his way up through the ranks, worked every position within the department, had seen everything and then some. The procession was passing the Blue Star Casino when another pump truck and rescue truck passed him. He fell in behind them.

In less than two miles they were on Old Henderson Road, which ran parallel to the Ohio River. Thick black smoke rose in the distance and created an intermittent fog across the road. The stilt cabins were the start of the fishing/party structures running along the banks of the Ohio River. Most were built with enough space between to give them some privacy, but many were built like older homes, with just an alleyway separating them.

When he arrived at the scene, Township Volunteer Firefighters and a pumper truck from Station 7 were already laying out hoses. Alleyways barely wide enough to walk through separated three cabins. The cabin in the center was fully engulfed. The quint was a bustle of activity as firefighters rolled hose in the direction of the blaze. Two teams of firefighters dressed in heavy gear risked life and limb checking the structures for signs of occupancy. Like police, a firemen's first job was to protect lives, even at the risk of their own.

Swenson parked a respectful distance away, put on his white helmet and walked to the quint to meet his crew chief.

The crew chief said, "Three cabins are involved, Captain. I don't think we'll save any. No sign of anyone but we're checking them now."

Two ancient pickup trucks, one of them with no wheels and resting on cinder blocks, sat in front of the center cabin. The pickup closest to the fire was completely engulfed, its doors open and the front hood lifted, looking like the charred skeletal remains of an ancient beast.

Swenson called dispatch on his cell phone. "Call in Howard," Swenson told the dispatcher. Howard was Richard Howard, a veteran of EFD and one of the best investigators Swenson had ever known. In his experience, this fire had the earmarks of arson.

No civilian casualties so far. "We'll save what we can," Swenson said to the crew chief. "I don't want anyone taking chances. No one's hurt so far. Let's keep it that way."

The crew chief hurried away, shouting out orders and lending a hand rolling out hose. Swenson watched his people and the Volunteer Firefighters knocking the fire down. One of the pumpers had laid hose to the river to draft water from the Ohio. There was a shortage of hydrants in the river camps.

Along the riverbank, willow trees and river birch leaned over the water, their flaming limbs dripping embers like a child's sparkler.

The fires were knocked down. The cabins were reduced to wet ashes, with charred telephone-pole-sized stilts sticking up out of the rubble.

Crews began overhauling—sifting through—the ashes. Swenson's own report to his chief would be on a loss of property only. He turned the scene over to his crew chief. It was the fire investigator's job to make out the reports and distribute them to the needed agencies. A copy of the report would be sent to the Chief of the Perry Township department.

"Good job," he yelled to the firefighters, and was walking to his car when one of the line firefighters yelled to him.

"Captain! Over here."

Swenson waded through the wet ashes. The back of the center cabin had had an upper deck with parking beneath. The telephone-pole stilts there had burned through and the cabin had collapsed onto a vehicle, a small car.

Chapter 20

Uncle Marty had told Jack there were rumors that Sonny and Sully left their jobs under a cloud of suspicion. Uncle Marty denied knowing anything more than that an Internal Affairs investigation was coming their way. He unconsciously ran a hand through his hair again and wiped the hand on his slacks. "I don't know for sure what the Internal Affairs thing is about."

"Are you talking criminal charges?" Jack asked.

"I'm telling the truth. I don't know any specifics."

I'm telling the truth is like saying "Honest to God." Or "I swear." He waited for Marty to continue.

"Honest to God. I don't know for sure," Marty said.

He's lying his ass off.

Jack said, "Come on, Bigfoot. This guy has got shit in his mouth. We can get the 'truth' from Boston P.D. We don't need to trade favors." Jack got up to leave.

Marty said, "Something tells me you're going to need me before this is over. I can either work with you or by myself. I'm good at what I do. You ever heard that saying, 'Keep your friends close, and keep your enemies closer?' I'm not saying I'm an enemy, but even if you think I am, you should keep me close on this."

Jack thought about it and said, "Here's a better one. 'With friends like you, who needs enemas?'"

Marty grinned like a kid. "Okay, I get you. But I wasn't lying. I was just saving something back to trade in case you reneged on our deal. I figure if anyone can find Sully—besides me, that is—it will be you guys. I'll tell you what I know if you let me know when you find Sully, and give me five minutes with him. How about that?"

"First of all—Uncle Marty—we don't have a deal. You're not in a position to trade with us. We'll get the information. We'll find Sully. So here's my deal. You tell us everything you know about Sully and Sonny right now. You tell us what you suspect happened to Sonny. And if *you* find Sully first, you tell us before you approach him. If you don't, I'll arrest you for obstruction of justice and whatever else I can think of. And I can think of a lot," Jack said. "That's the best deal you'll get out of us."

"That's not a deal," Marty said. "You should at least buy me dinner before you screw me. Know what I'm saying? That ain't even worth me putting lipstick on."

He ran the hand through his hair again and wiped it on his leg. "Okay. In the interest of me not going to jail on some trumped-up charge, I'll come clean."

Jack sat back down.

"Okay. A reporter friend of mine back home approached me a couple of weeks ago. They were asking questions about Sonny and Sully and heard Internal Affairs was interested in talking to them. That's who told me Sonny was killed. I was already here to find Sully. You know how reporters are. If there's dirt they want to wallow in it. Especially dirt on a cop. My reporter friend is no different. But time to time I get stuff I can't get through normal channels."

Jack said, "Go on."

"Like I said, I don't know the details, but this reporter seemed to know an IA investigation concerning Sonny and Sully was in the works. The reporter knew I'd been sent to Evansville. Don't ask me how. I don't like being in the news, if you catch my drift?"

"You can save me some time, Marty. What is the Internal Affairs investigation concerning? And why now? These guys have been gone from BPD for five years."

Marty said, "All I know is it has something to do with an old case. Sonny and Sully worked a murder five years ago. I don't know the details, like I said, but the Boston D.A. is interested. This has to be big to get the D.A.'s fur up."

Jack raised an eyebrow. Marty was right about that. If the District Attorney's office was investigating Sonny and Sully, it could only be a criminal investigation.

"Are you here to make sure Sully doesn't talk to Internal Affairs?" Jack asked.

"I told you I didn't kill Sonny," Marty said. "I wasn't here. You saw my airline ticket. I'm here to make sure my employer gets paid. That's all."

"Does Sully have something to do with Sonny's death?" Jack asked.

"I knew Sully was on his way here. I don't know about the murder."

Jack wanted to point out that Marty had just told them he didn't know Sully was in Evansville until after he was told that Sonny was dead. Marty changed his story to fit his mood, kind of like a politician.

Mindy said Sully came to Evansville two days ago. Sully said he got into town yesterday. Now Marty was saying Sully left Boston the day before that. Two of them were lying. Maybe all three.

"If I had to put my money on someone killing Sonny, I'd bet on Sully. He and Sonny weren't as close as people might have you believe. I'm sure this IA thing had them worried, and I assure you they knew about it too."

"How can you be sure they knew about the investigation?" Jack asked.

"I just know. Besides, the reporter told me she called Sonny a couple weeks back. She's very thorough. She would have called Sully too."

Jack didn't necessarily agree with all of what Marty just said. Police departments' Internal Affairs units were forced by police policy to review every complaint or possible violation of police procedure, no matter how small. Some ended with a suspension from duty, very few resulted in dismissal or criminal charges. However, the D.A.'s office was only limited by the statute of limitations.

It has been said that the criminal justice system is built on a wedding cake model. Only the top layer of the cake, the celebrity layer, gets the true procedural protections intended by the U.S. constitution. The rest are dealt with in an expedient manner. Think of O.J. Simpson, Casey Anthony, and George Zimmerman. Now think of a town drunk breaking into a department store to get out of the cold. You know who will get the best lawyer and the highest caliber of police effort? The truth was, not everyone is treated equally under the law.

"What's this reporter's name?" Jack asked, and was surprised when Marty gave it up without trying to trade.

"Danny Diego."

Liddell took a notebook out of his pocket and wrote down the name.

"Do you think he'll talk to us?" Jack asked.

"You ever know a reporter that didn't like to talk to a cop?" Marty asked, with a smirk playing on his face. "And she's not a he. Danny is short for…hell, I don't know what her name's short for, but here's her number." Marty took his cell phone out, found her number and gave it to Liddell.

Jack's questions about the ties to the casino or Marty's employer were reticently answered or minimized. The tabletop was filled with empty paper cups by the time they finished talking.

"I appreciate you coming to see us," Jack said.

"I've worked with the authorities before," Marty said. "No offense, but they usually act like they have a stick up their ass. You guys are okay. We'll make a good team. I think we'll both get what we want."

"No offense—Marty," Jack said, "but we're not a team." *And I don't give a rat's ass if you find Sully. Just stay out of our way.*

"Keep my gun in my pants. Got it," Marty said and stood. He handed business cards to Jack and Liddell. "My room number at the hotel, work number, and my personal cell number are on there. The work number gets you my secretary. A guy named John Smith." He raised his hand and said, "Swear to God. That's his real name."

Marty held his hand out and said, "How do I get in touch with you?"

Jack didn't offer him a business card or shake his hand, both of which would imply they were working with him. Jack said, "You found us. Just call 911 and tell them it's Uncle Marty for Jack."

Marty took his hand back. He said, "You're both honorable men. I know you'll do the right thing. Me, I'm not so honorable. I'm doing this because I owe you for flushing that piece of shit that killed my nephew. I always repay a favor." Marty turned and walked away.

"And collect a debt," Liddell said when Marty was out of earshot.

Liddell asked, "You don't believe him, do you?"

"Does the Pope shit in the woods?" Jack asked, using one of Bigfoot's aphorisms.

"Do you want to talk to the reporter, Danny? Or should I talk to Boston PD Internal Affairs?" Liddell bumped his palm against the side of his head. "What am I saying? The only time you talk to Internal Affairs is when you're in trouble."

"Let's go back to the office. I'll talk to the reporter. Only because I'm better with news media types." Jack hated talking to news people but he hated talking to Internal Affairs more.

They walked through the Civic Center and ran into Captain Franklin coming out of the detectives' office.

"I've got something for you," Franklin said.

* * * *

What Captain Franklin had for them sent them out of the station in a hurry. Jack and Liddell rolled up behind Captain Swenson's Crown Vic.

"What a mess," Liddell said. "I hate fire crime scenes. You can't get the smell out of your clothes."

"Do you still have boots in the trunk?" Jack asked. They'd taken Liddell's car. He kept rain boots in the trunk, a pair for both of them. When they were going to a fire scene, Jack always suggested they take Liddell's car, because of the boots and he hated to smell up his own car.

Liddell watched firefighters sloshing through black, ankle-deep muck and said, "I guess we'd better get the boots on."

Liddell popped the trunk and they pulled on the boots. He spread a sheet in the trunk and another on the front floorboard for when they returned to the car.

The smell of steam and smoldering wood made their eyes water and burn. Captain Swenson got out of his car wearing a heavy coat, boots and an eight-point uniform hat.

"Captain Franklin says you have a crispy critter," Jack said to Captain Swenson. "Crime scene is on the way."

"I know they're busy with the murder from this morning, but you're going to need them here," Swenson said.

A black Chevy Suburban pulled past them and parked in front of the chief's car. Little Casket had arrived.

Sergeant Walker's SUV parked behind the Suburban. Walker waved at them and busied himself gathering equipment and pulling on rubber boots and latex gloves.

The Suburban's door opened and a young man nearly the size of the Suburban squeezed out through the opening. He made tentative eye contact with the men and hurried around to the passenger side of the Suburban. Little Casket used the Suburban's chrome step bar to climb down. The giant reached out to help her and she slapped at his hand.

"Hands off, Igor," Little Casket said, and his arms dropped to his sides. She looked at the men gathered and said, "What?" To her helper she said, "Come on, Igor. Chop chop."

Jack wasn't surprised Little Casket called her driver Igor. She had a nasty temperament and was equally rude regarding the living and the dead. But in this case his size and appearance must have prompted the name. The guy was a behemoth but he seemed pleasant and respectful—or scared. He was somewhere in his late teens or early twenties at best, with dark skin and blond hair worn in a tall crew cut. He topped Liddell's six-foot-six by at least two inches, maybe more, and had at least forty pounds of muscle on Liddell. His shoulders were broad, and the sleeves of his parka were bulged to bursting. Jack's first impression was of a young Dwayne "The Rock" Johnson, a Samoan-Canadian WWE-wrestler-turned-actor.

"You forgot my bag, didn't you? Go back to the Suburban and get it. We need some equipment." She pointed to Igor's feet. "I don't suppose you brought any rubber boots to work?"

He said nothing and she flapped a hand at him dismissively.

When he was gone, Jack asked, "Who is that?"

Little Casket said, "You got wax in your ears. That's Igor. My helper. For a while anyway. He's on internship from Ivy Tech College. This time they sent me one big enough to do the heavy lifting. They keep sending these little girls who think they're going to be all *CSI: Miami*. Most of them faint dead away when they see blood, puke when they see gore, chip their French nails if they touch something, or don't like wearing caps because it messes up their hair. They don't grow 'em tough anymore. Mommy and Daddy tell them they can be anything they want. They don't tell them how hard it is to feed themselves."

"Not everyone can be as tough as you, Lilly," Jack said. "But I think you calling him Igor is insensitive even for someone as—experienced—as yourself."

Walker retrieved his camera and boots from the trunk of the crime scene wagon and stood back watching the banter between Jack and Lilly.

Lilly trained her horn-rimmed glasses on Jack. Her mouth drew down on the sides. "You want me to call him Aloysius, or maybe "hey Dummy"? Maybe I should imitate you—being that you're so sensitive and all—and call him Bigfoot."

"She's got you there, pod'na," Liddell said.

Jack said, "You don't mind me calling you Bigfoot."

"I wasn't going to say anything but now that you bring it up, I can't sleep some nights," Liddell said. Swenson chuckled.

"Igor" came back from the coroner's vehicle with the bag.

"Are you going to introduce us to your intern?" Jack asked. He still didn't believe Little Casket.

Lilly said, "Igor, this is Jack Murphy. The other one is Bigfoot. The little guy with the cab driver's hat is Captain Swenson."

"Ivan Ivansky," the giant said. "Glad to meet you."

"Pleased to meet you, Ivan," Jack said.

"She calls me Igor," Ivan said. "You can too if you want. I don't mind. She's nice."

Lilly walked away, saying, "You can share recipes later."

Chapter 21

Mindy shrugged out of her winter coat, pulled on a coffee-colored cable-knit sweater and opened a bottle of Rombauer Chardonnay. She filled a Big Joe wineglass, lit a cigarette and plopped down on the sofa, splashing the wine onto her Talbots wool slacks and the bottom of her sweater.

"Shit! Shit!" She jumped up and cast around for something to wipe at the stains. She threw the glass of wine at the fireplace, and the cigarette after it. Her hands pulled into fists of rage and she screamed, "Goddam it!"

"Why don't you just open a bottle and pour it on yourself. Save you some time," Sully said from the doorway.

"Screw you, Sully."

"I thought you'd never ask." He took her by her wrists, pulled her close and held her until she could feel the hardness of him.

"No, Sully," she said in a soft voice.

His eyebrows rose, and he released her.

She put her palms against his chest and lay her head against him. "Not here," she said. She could feel her heart beating and her eyes softened as she pressed herself against him. He stooped and cupped her buttocks in his large hands, lifting her from her feet. A soft moan escaped her lips as she wrapped her arms around his neck, her legs around his waist.

"I need you, Sully."

"That's why I came," he said.

"Won't be the last time you *came*." She loosened his tie, pulled it off, and unbuttoned his shirt.

* * * *

Later, as she lay satiated and holding the sheet beneath her ample breasts, she watched Sully dressing. She turned the sheet down, waggled her bosom at him, and said in a pout, "No round two?"

Sully buttoned his shirt and pulled the tie over his head. "Mindy, I told you we have to go. We've been here way longer than I wanted. Get dressed." He slipped on his suit jacket.

"Just like you to *come* and *go*," she said teasingly.

Sully pulled his tie into place. "Sonny's gone, Mindy. Do you understand what that means?"

She patted the mattress beside her. "Yeah. We're all alone."

Sully said, "Unbelievable."

"No, Sully. I don't know what that means. What does it mean?"

He rummaged through the scattered clothes she'd left on the floor. She would never be confused with a housekeeper. He dug around until he found a pair of her jeans. He opened a dresser drawer and pulled out a clean wool sweater—one that wasn't stained with red wine. He tossed them on the bed. "Get dressed."

Mindy got up, knocking the clothes onto the floor. She stood, naked. "I'm not leaving, Sully. I finally got a house I like. I got friends. I got a life, ya know. I loved Sonny, but what happened to him's got nothing to do with me."

He said as if to a child, "Your boobs are big, Mindy, but your brain's the size of a pea."

She grabbed a brush from the bedside table and threw it at him. "You bastard! You wasn't complaining a minute ago. If Sonny was here he'd kill you for what you done."

"What *we've* done," Sully corrected her. "And Sonny's not here."

He looked down at the clothes he'd given her. "Put those on and don't back talk me again."

Mindy reluctantly bent down and picked the clothing off the floor under Sully's scrutiny.

He said, "I took the liberty of leaving a letter with the coroner telling them the body will be cremated. I've made arrangements for it. You don't need to be there. I signed the papers for you, and witnessed as your attorney. As soon as the coroner releases Sonny's body, he'll be a box of ashes."

"I got to give him a proper funeral, Sully. You should be there, too."

"Don't you get it?" Sully asked. "Whoever killed Sonny won't stop at him. There are things you don't know. Sonny was my friend and he'd want me to get you somewhere safe. I'm doing this for him—and you—and risking a lot."

Mindy's jaw clamped tight. She sat on the edge of the mattress sans underwear and pulled the tight jeans up over her legs. She bounced and squeezed into them and slipped on the too-tight sweater. "What am I supposed to do with the house? We got bank accounts. Cars. The boat. The stuff in the safe? I'm not losing it all, Sully. I'm not. Give me some time to think."

"I'll do the thinking," Sully said, and lifted a wooden blind to see the front of the house.

"What, Sully? Is someone here?"

He watched for a moment longer and let the blind drop. "It's nothing. I thought I heard something."

"I'd better go see," she said. "Maybe those detectives are back."

"Don't worry about it." He opened the walk-in closet. One entire wall at the back was filled with shelf after shelf of women's shoes.

"Here," he said, and threw a pair of serviceable flats to her. He selected a carry-on size bag and brought it to the bed. "Take only what you need for tonight. Nothing else. Understand?"

"But what about my things, Sully?"

Sully said, "We'll get new things."

Mindy walked into her closet as if in a trance. She touched sweaters, evening wear, and stood in front of the wall of shoes biting her bottom lip.

Sully made a disgusted sound, shooed Mindy out of the closet and grabbed a pair of jeans, another sweater, and one pair of tennis shoes. He stuffed the clothing into the bag. "Get some underthings. Only whatever crap you need for tonight."

She stood motionless in the middle of the room, arms hanging limply by her sides with tears streaming down her face. "It ain't crap, Sully. It's my life."

He put an arm around her and pulled her head against his chest. "I know this is hard for you. It's a big change. But you've been in worse shape. Right?"

She dabbed tears away with the back of a finger.

"I just don't understand why I have to go. I don't mind talking to the cops. They were Sonny's friends. I don't know anything, Sully. I ain't done nothing to make anyone come after me."

He led her to the bed, sat her down and sat beside her. "I'm going to tell you some stuff you may or may not want to know, but listen closely. You need to understand some things. Sonny was working for Big Bobby. You might think you're safe here, but distance doesn't mean anything to these people. They have a long memory and a longer reach. Sonny's being a cop only meant one thing. He was a resource. The cops here *were* Sonny's friends, but they don't know what he was doing. They'll come after you just like the mob is going to do. Only the mob will get to you first."

Mindy started to say something and Sully stopped her. "Yeah, Sonny was busting drug dealers," he said in a singsong voice. "But he was dirty. The drug busts were competitors of Big Bobby's. How do you think Sonny got all his information? Made all those busts?"

Mindy's eyes had widened at the mention of Big Bobby. "Sonny wasn't working for him!" she said. "Just that one time in Boston. That's why we had to move. Sonny promised me nothing like that would happen again. He took me away from all that. Got us this house. Sonny was a good man."

Sully said patiently, "Do you remember the trip you and Sonny made to Atlantic City two years ago?"

"I remember."

"Sonny was meeting with Big Bobby," Sully said.

"No he wasn't. He was gambling. He won a bunch of money that night."

"He was paid a bunch of money," Sully said. "Do you remember what we were doing while Sonny was in that meeting?"

Mindy said, "I remember you giving me a tour of the casino while Sonny was playing roulette." She also remembered Sully had given her a tour of an unoccupied suite. It wasn't the first time, either. She had dated Sully first. He had introduced her to Sonny.

Sully always took her to upscale places. But he was a slam-bam-no-thank-you-ma'am kind of guy. Sometimes she had that kind of need. But sometimes she needed to feel wanted. Sonny was solid, dependable. He knew what he wanted out of life. And what Sonny wanted was her. But now Sonny was dead. She was alone. Vulnerable. She needed someone. For a little while at least.

She brushed her thigh against Sully's. "Those were some good times, wasn't they?"

"Good times," Sully agreed.

"What am I going to do now, Sully? I don't have any friends. I don't have no one."

Sully said, "Friends? You're worrying about friends? You've got real problems, Mindy. If I didn't like you I wouldn't be here. I've always been there for you. Right?"

Mindy said nothing. She'd been passed from man to man before Sonny came along. She didn't want to go back to that kind of life.

"Don't lie to me, Sully. You're just after one thing. Well, two, and you already got one of them," she said. "What you want is in the safe and I don't know how to get in it. Sonny never showed me. I didn't want the money." But she did. It was her ticket to a new life.

Sully stood and gripped her shoulder until it hurt. "If it wasn't for me you'd still be living in that shitty, roach-infested walk-up in Boston. I know a lie when I hear one and you, Mindy, are lying your pretty little ass off." He let go of her shoulder.

She stood and moved away from him, rubbed her shoulder and said, "Big Bobby didn't have nothin' to do with the money. Sonny had his severance pay. His 401K and some other stuff. He made good money. I'm his beneficiary."

Sully said, "Show me the safe, Mindy."

Mindy pointed to the walk-in closet. "It's in there. But you can't get in it, I told you."

Sully said, "Stay right there." He walked into the closet and pushed clothes around, stomped on the floor listening for a difference in sound. Nothing.

"Mindy," Sully said.

"I don't know the combination anyways, Sully. Honest to God."

He forced her into the closet and towered over her. "Where is it?"

"It's behind the shoes."

Sully pulled at the shelf and felt for a switch. He knocked shoes onto the floor from several shelves. "There's nothing there, you dumb bitch!"

"Don't you dare call me names, Vincent Sullis," Mindy said, finding her nerve. She flipped the light switch and the switch next to it into the On position. There was a click and the wall of shoes swung open. Sully pulled it further open, revealing a six foot by three foot steel safe. In place of a combination lock or keypad was a box with two LCD screens.

"Sonny always went for high tech," Sully said. "Open it."

"I told you I don't have the combination, Sully," Mindy whined.

"It's not a combination, Mindy. It's biometric. Put your thumb on it."

"What are you expecting to find, Sully? You can't take Sonny's stuff. It's not right."

Sully took her hand and held her thumb on the screen. Nothing. "What's wrong with the damn thing?"

Mindy put her thumb on the other LCD screen and gears could be heard. Sully turned the handle and pulled the door open. Inside the safe were shelves and drawers and a gun rack. In the rack were a Colt AR-15 with laser sights, and an old Winchester 30-30. A Czech Skorpion 9mm machine pistol lay on one of the shelves with two extra 20-round magazines, loaded. The Skorpion had a folded wire stock that could open up into a compact rifle. Sully picked it up, folded out the stock and lifted the weapon to his shoulder. Sonny had shown Sully the gun when they were on BPD and told him it was a trophy Sonny's old man brought back from Vietnam.

From behind, Mindy said, "Sonny loved his guns. Said it was part of history."

Sully's expression hardened. "Now Sonny's a part of history."

Several shoeboxes were stacked on the floor. Sully opened one of these. It was full of stacks of one-hundred-dollar bills still in bank wrappers. He lifted the lid on the other boxes and they were likewise full of cash.

"I seen the guns, but I ain't never seen any of that," Mindy said, and reached for one of the stacks of money.

Sully pushed her hand away. "This doesn't belong to you. Or me, for that matter," he said. "This is why I came."

Sully found a small duffel bag rolled in the closet and dumped the money inside. He saw some jewelers' trays stacked on another shelf, filled with gold and diamond jewelry, bracelets and precious stones.

"Where did he get this stuff?" he asked Mindy.

"They're presents from Sonny. He gave them to me. I need to take them."

Sully left the trays and shut the safe door without waiting to see if it locked.

"Sully, that's my jewelry in there."

Sully shoved her out of the closet and shut the door. He poured the contents of the duffel bag on the mattress and counted.

"Screw me!" he muttered, and shoved the money back in the duffel.

"What's the matter, Sully?"

"It's not all here," he said. "Shit!"

"Can I get my jewelry first?"

"No! We've got to go. When they send someone, they'll find the jewelry and guns and take them. They'll think Sonny laundered the money or hid it somewhere else. You don't want to be here when that happens. These guys don't ask questions."

"Why would they take my jewelry? I don't understand any of this, Sully."

Sully said, "Oh for Christ's sake, Mindy! We don't have time for this."

"I'm not going anywhere until you tell me what's going on," Mindy said.

Sully's hands clenched into fists, relaxed, and his shoulders slumped. He sat on the mattress beside her. "Sonny isn't the only one working for Big Bobby. We both had to resign from the police in Boston, but that wasn't enough. We knew things we shouldn't have, but we were smart enough that we put some evidence away. Insurance. If either of us got hurt or disappeared, the other would tell where the evidence was."

Mindy's hand went to her mouth. "Is that why Sonny told me to call that number if he didn't make it home?"

Sully said, "I'm glad you didn't call. Do you remember the number?"

"I forgot it. Sully, you're scaring me."

"You're lying again. But it doesn't matter now. I'm protected. But this house, everything you have is because of Big Bobby. As far as he's concerned, he owns it. Sonny forgot that. He tried to cheat Big Bobby."

Sully said as if to himself, "Big Bobby's kid was killed last week and he thinks either we were behind it, or it was because of someone coming after us. Either way, we are now loose ends. The money in that bag is Big Bobby's money. He knew Sonny scored half a mil two weeks ago and, well, never mind the rest."

"He wants to kill *me*?" Mindy said. "I ain't never done nothin' to him. I wouldn't know him if I saw him, Sully."

"Maybe he wouldn't kill you. Maybe he'd put you in one of his whorehouses and make you work off what you and Sonny owe him." Sully peeked out of the blinds again. He let them close and said, "Don't give me any more shit, or I'll leave you here."

* * * *

A plume blew from the dual exhaust pipes of the white Jeep backed into a wooded area. Marty Crispino wore the heavy wool overcoat, scarf and gloves. Even with the heater blasting on his feet and face he was cold. In Boston it was colder than this. Icier too. But cold was cold. He hated it. He hoped the next job was in Florida.

He had gone off-road with the Jeep to get around the first gate. He hoped the surveillance camera wasn't recorded anywhere. He watched Sully's sedan drive away and leave Sonny's gate open. Crispino couldn't see faces but there were two people in front. The sedan was definitely Sully's car with vanity Massachusetts plates that said SO SU ME.

He let them drive away. They wouldn't get far before he was done here, thanks to a couple of gizmos he'd brought with him. One was a real-time GPS tracking device that he had synced with his iPhone. Another was a GPS counter-surveillance device. He'd put the tracking device under Sully's back bumper. He'd use the counter-surveillance device to make sure he didn't have a tracker on *his* Jeep. The Jeep was a rental, but you could never be too cautious.

He knew Murphy didn't believe him about why he was really here. He just hoped Murphy didn't figure everything out too quickly. Marty had known a lot of killers in his time. Murphy had a badge, but he was the real deal.

When Sully's car was out of sight, Marty drove through the gates Sully left open and parked in front of the house. It didn't matter if anyone was home, but he rang the doorbell just to be sure. Maybe Sonny had a housekeeper. Most likely not. From what he'd gleaned from those who knew her, Mindy wasn't much good at anything except screwing and drinking.

There was no answer. He took out his tools and set to work. The lock popped and then something behind his eyes popped.

Chapter 22

Jack and Liddell stood in muck up to their ankles. The back wall of the cabin was made of heavy split logs and had partially survived, but the part over the carport had collapsed and partially buried a small convertible car. The ragtop of the car was burned down to the metal frame; all that was left inside were naked springs and steel and hot coal. The trunk of the car was open and the charred remains of a body could plainly be seen.

The body was curled into a ball with hands drawn into a pugilistic pose, knees drawn up to the chest. The sight and smell of fire victims was always nightmarish.

Walker took pictures while Lilly instructed her intern on the physical anomalies caused by fire.

"Is that what I think it is?" Liddell asked Lilly.

"It's a railroad spike," Little Casket said. "Just like Sonny Caparelli. Except this one's stuck through his ear instead of his eyes."

"And he was set on fire," Liddell added.

"Ya think?" Little Casket said.

Richard Howard, fire investigator for Evansville Fire Department, walked over. He was wearing extra-large Dickies winter coveralls. The pant legs were tucked into a pair of lined hunting boots. On his head was a fur-lined aviator hat with the earflaps down.

"Hey. It's Rocky, the Flying Squirrel," Liddell said.

Howard came back with, "Gee Bullwinkle, we're not in Kansas anymore."

"Did you identify him yet?" Lilly asked the fire investigator. When he didn't answer immediately she said, "Didn't think so."

Lilly took several photos with her iPhone. She said. "He was naked."

Liddell said, "At the risk of sounding stupid, how do you know he was naked? His clothes could have burned off."

Lilly speared him with a stare. "You never worried about sounding stupid before. What's gotten into you?"

Liddell said, "That hurt, Lilly. You know Marcie and I are having a baby girl and we were thinking of naming her Lilly."

"So you said," she scoffed and turned back to the body. "His wrists and ankles were bound. See?"

"She's right," Howard said.

"A'course I am."

"The license plate has melted," Jack said to Walker. "We'll need to get the VIN from the door or engine." VIN stands for Vehicle Identification Number and is usually on a small plate stuck to the inside driver's door panel, the front dash near the windshield, or on the engine.

"We'll have to wait to see." Walker asked Howard, "What do you think?"

"This one was pretty hot," was all Howard would commit to.

The unmistakable smell of charred human flesh was both disgusting and somehow pleasant. Jack suggested they move away. Walker and Howard stayed behind and the rest moved to the street. The temperature near the fire scene was twenty degrees warmer than back at the cars.

"That's a new BMW," Igor said. "Z4. Sport convertible. 2017. I'll bet there's not many of these around Evansville."

Jack called dispatch. "Connie, can you do something for me?" He listened. "You have? How did you get the information? I see. No. Thanks. Can you text me the information? Thanks."

"What?" Liddell asked.

"Connie at dispatch said she already knew the model of car and ran a list of similar makes registered in Evansville and Vanderburgh County. She'll send us the names and addresses."

Lilly said, "I'm glad to see my tax money isn't being wasted."

Sergeant Walker came over. "Hi Lilly. Who's your intern?"

"Don't you start on me too," she said with a scowl and stomped off.

"What's wrong with her?" Walker asked.

Liddell grinned. "Well, first the dinosaurs roamed the earth. One of them didn't go extinct."

The cabin resembled burned Lego blocks. The victim's car was barely visible from the road. Water was freezing at the outer edges of the fire scene and steaming where it was hottest.

"Most of my people are still working Sonny's murder scene," Walker said. "I told Dr. John we had another body. I'll let you know what I find here. Guess I'll see you at the autopsy."

Richard Howard approached the men. He was holding something in a gloved hand. "See what I found."

Jack could see it was a man's bi-fold wallet. The wallet was soaked. Howard had scraped most of the muck from it and held it open. The driver's license was melted and unreadable, but the next plastic frame held a Vanderburgh Superior Court identification card for Judge Samuel J. Knight.

Jack called police dispatch and got Connie again. "Connie, we have a possible name. Can you see if Samuel Knight is on the list of cars?"

"I don't have to. It is."

"Who have you told?" Jack asked.

"I'm not a blabbermouth."

"Sorry, Connie. Can you get his address, work, and home phone numbers for me?"

"I'll text them to you," she said. "And Jack. He has kids."

"Connie, on second thought, can you connect me to Judge Knight's office?"

There was a click, and a young man answered on the first ring. "Judge Knight's chambers. Jason speaking."

"Jason, Detective Murphy here. Is Judge Knight in today?"

"He's taking a late lunch, Detective Murphy. Can I take a number and have him call you? The judge is really covered up today. It may be a while. Is there something I can help you with?"

"Jason, I need to find the judge right away," Jack said. "Can you tell me where he is? I only need a moment of his time."

It turned out that Jason didn't know exactly where the judge was. He suggested a couple of restaurants on the Main Street walkway, and another on the west side of town. Jason gave Jack Knight's cell phone number.

Jack turned back to Captain Swenson. "Can you keep this quiet? No talking. Not even to nosey dispatchers. Not even to wives."

"Do guys still talk to their wives?" Swenson asked. "Just joking. Hey. You think this is related to Sonny's murder? He was a great guy."

"Hell of a way to die," Liddell said.

Chapter 23

Judge Knight lived on the east side of Evansville near Harrison High School. There was nothing Jack and Liddell could do at the fire scene. They rode in silence until they reached Fielding Court on the city's east side. Liddell said, "If his kids are home, we need to have someone come and sit with them while we talk to the wife. Her name is Michelle."

He turned left onto Outer Lincoln Road. Their destination was a few blocks ahead.

"His law clerk, Jason, said his calendar was crowded today." Jack said. "Maybe the wife can tell us who he was meeting during his lunchtime today."

The house was just ahead. Jack said, "She may not know anything. We'll have to talk to his clerk. The judge might have handled cases for the Task Force."

"I'm not sure what kind of cases Knight heard," Liddell said. "He was in Superior Court, so he could have heard drug cases. Sonny didn't make any friends dealing with druggies. I'm sure if Knight dealt with that garbage, he cost a bunch of people their livelihood. Revenge is as old of a motive as they get. Hell, between him and Sonny there could be a thousand suspects, pod'na. That's not including the enemies Sonny made in Boston."

"Knight's death may not be connected to Sonny's. We need to talk to Sonny's crew and bring Angelina up to date. Maybe she can work some magic and find something all these people have in common." Jack texted Angelina telling her to add Knight's name. She texted back "leave me alone."

"You need to add Marty Crispino to that list, pod'na," Liddell said.

Jack texted her again, adding Marty Crispino—Boston. She didn't text back.

"I'd add you to the list, Bigfoot, but these killings weren't over picnic baskets."

They arrived. Sam Knight lived in a brick ranch-style home with empty lots on both sides and a privacy fenced backyard. He wasn't starving, but he wasn't living high on the hog like Sonny. Christmas lights were strung on the eaves and in the holly bushes. Wreaths decorated the front door and the dormers. A Christmas tree, heavy with lights and ornaments, could be seen through the picture window. On each side of the front walkway were a deflated blow-up Santa, sleigh, and reindeer.

Kids.

Jack could read the angst on Liddell's face. Marcie's pregnancy had changed him. Plus, he'd just had a run-in with some pretty dangerous characters in Louisiana involving the kidnapping of his niece and a human trafficking ring involving children. Liddell wouldn't admit it, but situations involving kids hit him harder now. Jack's heart sank. "I'll make the notification, Bigfoot."

"Nah. You're better at shooting people, pod'na. No offense," Liddell said.

"None taken."

The driveway curved around to the back of the house. One door of the two-car garage was open. A maroon Chrysler Pacifica minivan was pulled in one of the bays with the back hatch open. A woman, thirtyish, wearing a hooded parka, was unloading grocery bags. Liddell pulled up behind the minivan and stopped. She gave the approaching Crown Vic a cursory glance, but, being the wife of a judge, she'd seen many detectives' cars.

Mrs. Knight set the bags of groceries back down and waited for them to exit their car.

Liddell said, "Ma'am. We're here to…"

"Vincent Sullis said you might come by," she said without letting him finish. Liddell nudged Jack with his elbow.

"Help me with the groceries and come inside," she said. She picked up several environmentally unfriendly plastic bags of groceries and went to the back door of the house. "My kids aren't home. I'll make tea. Sam's not here but I expect him any minute."

Jack and Liddell brought the rest of the groceries into the kitchen and set them on a counter. She busied herself making a pot of tea, putting the frozen things in the freezer, and chattering on, the weather, her children, the new Aldi grocery store that had opened in Evansville, how the prices were half of Schnuck's—anything other than why Sully had told her Jack and Liddell would be coming there.

"We have twin boys. Bryce and Timmy," she said. "They're four years old next week. I let them go on a playdate with a family we know from their preschool. I have to pick them up in an hour." She motioned them to seats at a kitchen island. The electric teapot whistled. She placed matching china cups and saucers in front of them and poured steaming water into each of their cups. Seeing Jack and Liddell had made no attempt to fix their drinks, she said, "Sorry. It's just a habit. I didn't even ask if you wanted tea. You're probably in a rush. You guys always are." She said this last with a wry smile. "Can I offer you something else until he gets here?"

Liddell said, "Mrs. Knight. Please have a seat."

Her smile faded gradually. Liddell took the teapot from her and placed it back on its stand. He pulled a barstool out for her and helped her sit. She remained silent, her eyes never leaving Jack's.

Jack said, "Mrs. Knight, I'm afraid we have bad news. Is there any one we can call for you?"

"Call for me? I don't understand," she said. "Is Sam in trouble? Has he been arrested? He didn't do anything bad in Boston. I can promise you that. Sully said he might be arrested and taken back to Boston. It would be completely humiliating for Sam. For us. What would I tell the boys?"

"Mrs. Knight, have you talked to your husband today?"

"Not since this morning when he left for work. Oh God! He has been arrested! He said Boston was not a problem."

"No, he hasn't been arrested, Mrs. Knight. Does your husband drive a BMW?" Liddell asked.

"Yes. It's a little blue convertible. Did he have an accident? Was he hurt?"

Liddell said, "Mrs. Knight. We're very sorry to tell you this."

Her face tightened and turned white. "Is he...?"

"I'm so sorry, Mrs. Knight," Liddell said.

Her hands went to her mouth and she drew in a sharp breath and stared into nothing. "I warned him about that car, but he said it made him feel good. He was always under so much pressure. Always working. Always..." The dam broke.

Liddell took some napkins from a holder on the kitchen island and put them in her hand.

She took several deep breaths and let them out slowly. When she calmed slightly she said, "I have to see him. The kids...?"

Liddell asked, "Can we call someone for you? Family? A neighbor?"

She put the napkins on the table and wrapped her hands around the teacup, not seeming to notice the heat. "We don't have family here. I'll call his dad in Boston. My mother lives in Connecticut. I have to see him."

Jack saw she was struggling with the reality of this. It was times like this he wished he was better with people. "Mrs. Knight," he said. "You won't be able to see him for a little while. His body was taken to the morgue for an autopsy."

Her eyes searched his. "An autopsy? I thought it was an accident. You don't know how he died?"

Liddell said, "Mrs. Knight, let me call a neighbor or a friend to come stay with you."

She said absentmindedly, "No. No. We really don't know the neighbors. We've been here over five years and we've never made friends with the neighbors. That's why our boys were spending the night with a family we met at preschool. And Sam didn't even want to do that. He's very protective of us."

"I see," Jack said.

"And my best friend lives in Boston. But it would take her too long, wouldn't it? I mean, she'd come, but—I just don't know what to do," she said and buried her face in her hands, crying again.

Liddell held his finger and thumb up to his ear, mimicking a phone, and mouthed "Marcie" to Jack. Liddell went in another room and Jack could hear him on the phone with his wife.

Jack asked, "Mrs. Knight, you mentioned a call from Vincent Sullis."

"Sullis?" She sounded confused. "Oh yes. Vincent Sullis. He called this morning."

"You said he told you we might be coming by?" Jack prompted her. "Do you remember what time that was, Mrs. Knight?"

"Was he in the accident with Sam?"

"It wasn't a car accident, ma'am," Jack informed her. "If you can remember when you spoke with him…"

She gave Jack a quizzical look, but answered his question. "Umm, maybe an hour ago. Around eleven I guess. I was on my way to the store when the phone rang. I remember because I thought it was Sam saying he wasn't going to make it home this evening until late. He worked late some nights."

"Can you tell me exactly what Mr. Sullis said?"

"Detective Murphy, I…I… Let me see. He asked to talk to Sam. I told him he wasn't here and he said he knew Sam from Boston. I knew who Mr. Sullis was because Sam spoke of him recently."

Jack didn't interrupt, but that was interesting.

"He said it was important. I didn't give him Sam's cell phone number. I thought if Sam wanted to talk to him, he would already have the number. I didn't get a good feeling from him. I can't tell you why. I just didn't."

"Did he give you any idea why he wanted to talk to your husband?"

"He didn't say."

"You said he talked to your husband recently. When was that? What did they discuss?" Jack asked.

"It was weeks ago—a weekend. Sam was still putting one of the boys' Christmas presents together. Sam was never very good with assembly instructions. I answered the phone and a man asked for Sam. Not Judge Knight. I asked who was calling and he said "Sully." I didn't recognize the voice but I got the impression he was from back home. From Boston."

Boston again.

"And this was the same man that called approximately an hour ago?" Jack asked.

"Yes. Sam didn't want to talk to him when he called before. He seemed to be angry. He got that way when someone bothered him when he was playing with the boys. He wanted me to hang up and I told Mr. Sullis that Sam wasn't available. He said, "Tell Sam it's about Boston, and he might be arrested.""

"Who might be arrested?" Jack asked.

"I assumed he meant Sam. It was ridiculous."

"Did your husband talk to him?"

"He took the phone and went into his study. I could hear him raise his voice but I didn't hear what was being said. It wasn't like my husband to raise his voice. When he came out I asked who that was. Sam said it was about an old case, but he wasn't involved. Did you know Sam used to be an Assistant District Attorney in Boston before we moved here?"

Here's the connection. Sonny, Sam Knight, and Sully. All in law enforcement or the legal system. All from Boston.

* * * *

"It's things just like this that make me thankful we have a Police Wives Society, Bigfoot," Jack said as Liddell drove toward headquarters.

Marcie had come to Knight's house in less than ten minutes. She had things well in hand by the time Jack and Liddell left. Marcie had called the woman taking care of the twins and the very nice woman had offered to keep them for another night. She told Mrs. Knight the boys were having such a good time they wouldn't notice for a while.

Jack convinced Mrs. Knight she would be unable to identify the body because of the injuries, but if she wanted to have a few minutes with him—like Jack had afforded Mindy, albeit for a different reason—someone would take her and bring her home. One of the wives volunteered to spend the night at her house if needed.

Michelle Knight knew Sonny Caparelli because Sonny had been to their house several times over the years to get warrants signed.

Liddell pulled into the detectives' parking area just across the way from the Courts Building. They went to talk to Judge Knight's law clerk, Jason. Jack's phone rang.

"Jack, did you make the death notification?" Sergeant Walker asked.

"We just left and are going to Knight's office," Jack answered.

"You didn't happen to ask who their dentist was?" Walker asked.

Jack gave him Knight's home phone and told him to talk to Marcie. He told Walker, "We made the connection between Sonny and Judge Knight. Sully too. They all left Boston about the same time. Sonny resigned and moved here. Sully resigned and went to law school. He has a practice in Boston. Knight resigned to take a judge's appointment here. Plus, Judge Knight had dealings with Sonny through work, and Knight's wife said Sully called the judge at least twice in the last few weeks."

Jack discussed this with Walker for a minute before continuing to the Courts Building. Inside the Courts Building, Jack and Liddell went through the usual routine of giving up their weapons, belts, and the contents of their pockets before they walked through a metal detector. Judge Knight's offices were on the first floor at the end of the hallway. As they entered, a young man came from behind a desk and asked, "Can I help you?"

"Detectives Murphy and Blanchard," Jack said.

"Jason Atwood," the young man said. "I'm the one you spoke to. Judge Knight's law clerk."

"Thanks for your help, Jason. If you can answer just a few questions for us I'll explain why we're here," Jack said.

"Of course. I'll answer what I can."

"Do you keep the judge's calendar?" Jack asked.

"At least for now," Jason said and smiled. "I take the Indiana Bar exam next month." His smile faltered. "Is the judge okay?"

Jack explained only what he had to. There was a car fire. Jack described the car. Jason confirmed the judge owned that type of car. He told Jason there was a body in the car. They were in the process of identifying it. He thought Jason Atwood, the soon-to-be-card-carrying barrister, was going to cry.

Jason said in a barely audible voice, "Do you think it's Sam? He was here a couple of hours ago. I thought he was going by his house or to lunch."

Jack asked, "Can you tell us where the judge was going? Did he have a meeting?"

"Well. He eats at Milano's on the walkway. Or maybe DiLegge's near Garvin Park. And he goes a few other places. I don't know exactly. Most days he runs by his house for a few minutes. He didn't say he was meeting anyone for lunch. If he had a meeting I would have known."

Jason asked, "Do you need someone to identify the body?" He put a hand on his forehead and said, "Oh Christ! Shellie. That's his wife."

"Michelle? We've already talked to her," Jack said. "Jason, I'm afraid the body can't be identified that way."

"Oh…"

Jack said, "Can we see his appointment calendar?"

As if by reflex, Jason said, "I think you need a court order or a search warrant to do that, Detective."

Liddell took out his cell phone and stepped away.

"Have you tried to call the judge's phone?" Jack asked Jason.

"Yes. Several times. He's been absent from several court hearings this morning and he's never missed a hearing. He's supposed to be in trial tomorrow and he always prepares for trial the evening before. Was he…?"

"Has anyone called for him? Besides for court business, that is? Anyone you don't know?" Jack asked.

"I can't discuss the judge's business with you. You understand. Confidentiality."

Liddell handed his cell phone to Jason. The young man said hello. Listened, said okay and handed the phone back to Liddell.

"Follow me," Atwood said. "You can view the calendar on his desk. But you still can't go through any of his files without a court order. I don't make the laws, gentlemen. He has numerous calls every day. This morning was no different. If the caller asks to leave a message, I stick a note on his desk."

Jason stood in the doorway of Judge Knight's office keeping watch while Jack and Liddell flipped through the judge's appointment calendar going back several months. Mrs. Knight said Sully had called Knight two weeks ago, but there was nothing in the appointment calendar that would correspond to a call.

"When you say you leave notes, Jason, do you also put the telephone calls on the judge's Outlook calendar?" Jack asked.

"Sometimes," Jason said. "But not every call unless they specifically ask for a callback. Otherwise I just make out a Post-it note and leave it on his desk."

"Have you heard the name Vincent Sullis?" Jack asked.

Jason's expression said volumes, but he was quiet. Jason needed to take Lying for Dummies 101 again.

"I'm not asking you to betray a confidence, Jason. I just want to know if this guy called your boss in the last couple of weeks," Jack said. "It's very important."

Jason cringed like a dog shitting a pork-chop bone. "I may get in trouble for telling you this, but Sam—Judge Knight—was my mentor. Yes. A Mr. Sullis called for Judge Knight a couple of times two weeks ago. He just identified himself and asked if he could speak to Sam Knight. I assumed he knew the judge, but the procedure is that I screen the calls. He didn't want to leave a message. I didn't record it on the judge's electronic calendar. I didn't put anything on the calendar on his desk either. When Mr. Sullis called the second time, I told the judge the man was on the line. Judge Knight said he didn't want to speak to him. I didn't transfer the call. Mr. Sullis left a phone number and said it was important. He left a message of sorts, but I didn't write it down. I just told Judge Knight what he said."

"What was the message?" Jack asked.

"He said to remind the judge about Boston. I asked him what that meant and he said the judge would know."

"You don't have the phone number he left, do you?" Jack asked.

"I don't. But it was a Boston prefix." He blushed slightly. "The guy sounded like a jerk."

"That's Sully," Liddell said.

Jack showed Jason the business card Sully had given him.

"That might be the number," Jason said. "I'm sorry I can't remember more."

"You've been a great help, Jason," Jack said.

Jack flipped through the calendar on the judge's desk. The judge was a busy man. He recognized some of the names of local attorneys, judges, and there was a notation to pick up dry cleaning and buy an anniversary card. Nothing saying, "Secret meeting today." Nothing with Sully or Sonny's name, just a lot of court docket numbers. There was one interesting notation on today's date. Scribbled at the bottom of the date was *MC*.

Liddell wrote the names on the file binders in his notebook. One name he recognized as a corporation that was embroiled in a class-action lawsuit. Another file concerned a drug case with numerous defendants. He made note of the docket number. He wrote down the names of the attorneys and others that Knight had penciled in over the last two weeks. All of these would need to be contacted.

Jack pointed out the initials MC on the desk calendar. "Uncle Marty?"

"This is just getting better and better, pod'na."

"Do you know who MC is?" Jack asked Jason.

"I haven't seen that before. It wasn't there this morning."

"Any ideas?" Jack asked.

"Maybe M is for Michelle, his wife," Jason suggested. "Maybe it means Michelle and cleaners. He jots reminders on his calendar, or leaves sticky notes on the desk to pick stuff up at the cleaners, etcetera. She might have asked him to do that and he made a note."

"Can I take this calendar to study it?" Jack asked.

"You only have a verbal order from the prosecutor who, by the way, can't issue court orders. I'm giving you more leeway than I should. The prosecutor promised I'd have the signed court order in my hands shortly."

"Understood," Jack said. "So that you can't be blamed for any of our actions, I'm lawfully ordering you not to touch anything in this office. As of now, this office is a secondary crime scene in a murder investigation. Don't open the door for anyone except a detective or for EPD Crime Scene. They will have a court order in hand. Nothing in here is to be taken or moved by anyone for any reason before then. If you can't comply, I will have a policeman stand at the door. Tampering with *possible evidence* is enough to get your *possible* new license to practice denied even if you pass the Bar exam." Jack said the last part loud enough for anyone outside the office to hear.

Jason caught on. He said, "I know the law, Detective. This office has to keep running. But I'll do what I can to assist you in your homicide investigation." He said this last a little louder than necessary.

"I never said this was a homicide investigation. How did you know the judge was murdered?" Jack asked.

"I didn't know, until now."

Jack was tempted to say, "Bite me," but the kid had bested him fairly.

"You should come work for us," Jack said.

"I can make three times the money going into my own practice."

Jack lowered his voice. "You got me again, Jason. I'm counting on you to keep that door shut until the court order arrives. I promise we'll make the search quick and try not to complicate your job."

Liddell was talking to the Prosecutor's office again as they left Superior Court chambers. The deputy prosecutor who had talked to Jason on the phone was Moira Connelly, Jack's sister-in-law. She was working on the court order and would include copying or seizing the calendar and anything in the office that might be relevant.

In the hallway Jack said, "We need to go work the phones, Bigfoot."

"Okay pod'na. But first I've got to go Code Three to the little boys' room," Liddell said and rushed down the hallway.

Chapter 24

Jack sat at his desk with a cup of coffee. Liddell was in donut heaven.

"Donut Bank sent six boxes of donuts to the detectives' office when they heard about Sonny's murder. These guys are the best." Liddell said this like a kid who had just gotten a Red Ryder BB gun for Christmas.

"You took two of the boxes," Jack said. "What about everyone else?"

"These two had my name on them. See?" His name *was* written on the side of two of the boxes. "We donut aficionados take care of our own. And speaking of our own—let's call our FBI friend. We're getting out of our depth here, pod'na."

"Maybe Frank can help narrow down our suspect list from everyone, to maybe a hundred thousand people."

Jack called Tunney's cell phone and it immediately went to voice mail. He was leaving a voice message when Tunney's phone number showed up on his display.

"I wondered if you were going to call," Tunney said.

"Let me put you on speakerphone, Frank."

"Hi Frank," Liddell said around a mouthful of donut.

"Didn't your mother teach you not to speak with your mouth full?" Tunney asked.

"It's not completely full," Liddell said, "or I couldn't be talking."

"We're hoping you can tell us who we should be looking for," Jack said. He could hear a shower running in the background. "Listen, if this isn't a good time I can call back."

"No. It's okay. I was just at the Casino and I smell like cigarettes and cigars and liquor."

The shower stopped and Liddell said, "Speaking of smoke. The most recent victim is a Superior Court judge who was burned to death in the trunk of his own car."

"I can meet you at headquarters in say, an hour," Tunney said.

"Hey Frank," Jack said. "If this is going to cause you a problem with your bosses I'll have the chief make the request official."

"See you in an hour," Tunney said and hung up.

They got busy reading the reports that were steadily drizzling in from crime scene, motor patrol, dispatch, and the fire departments.

Jack handed Liddell half of the reports and skimmed through his half. "Can you believe it? No one saw anything. There's nothing here. Must be a dozen cameras around the place Sonny's truck was found, but none of them recorded diddly and no one saw squat."

"Too cold," Liddell suggested.

"Yeah. I guess. You got anything?" Jack asked.

"Maybe." Liddell handed Jack a spreadsheet. "Jerry O'Toole sent Sonny's cell phone records for his work phone and personal cell phone. Two calls came to Sonny's phones between five o'clock and six on the evening he was killed. Jerry said he saw Sonny at the office around seven that evening. These calls came before Jerry saw him. There's another call early this morning. Six-twelve a.m."

Jack went over the phone record. "Mindy said she tried to call him a couple of times but his phone was turned off."

"Jerry sent a note with this. He said all three calls were made from pay phones. Evansville is probably the last place in the country that has pay phones. Anyway, one call was made on the north side, one west, and one downtown. The north side call was to Sonny's personal cell phone. The west side was to his work cell phone. The last call came from downtown to Sonny's personal cell phone. If it was Mindy who called Sonny, she had to do it from a pay phone," Liddell said, and added, "Jerry said Sonny had a burner phone. Maybe Angelina could check Mindy's phone records to see if she called anyone for the last two or three days?"

Liddell called Angelina and made the request. He told Jack, "She said she already cross-referenced the telephone numbers for all of these people. She couldn't find any number that might have been Sonny's burner. She confirmed Mindy had called Sonny's office and personal cell phone. She's taking another look at the calls made from the phone booths Jerry told us about."

Jack said, "There won't be many phone booth calls in this weather. Are you thinking the person that called Sonny might have made other calls from the booths?"

"No loose ends," Liddell said.

Jack made a sweeping motion with his arm over the piles of paper. "Whoever this guy is, he's savvy. He avoided video cameras. He left the truck to be stolen. He left the money, but he took Sonny's cell phone and gun. I wouldn't imagine Knight carried a gun, but what do you want to bet Walker doesn't find Knight's cell phone?"

"I understand taking the cell phones. Maybe the killer didn't want anyone to get hurt with Sonny's gun," Liddell suggested. "Or he didn't take the gun. Maybe that boy, Zack, hid it? You said he had some time alone there before Roscoe arrived at the scene."

Jack thought that was possible. He dialed the Motor Patrol sergeant's office and talked to Sgt. Mattingly. He asked to widen the search around Sonny's crime scene for the missing gun.

While Jack was on the phone, Liddell called Angelina Garcia.

"FCI. Angelina Garcia," she answered.

"Hello, Miss FCI. How's Mark?"

"With the wedding coming up and all, he's a little crazy right now."

"Yeah. Guys get a little nutty with weddings," Liddell agreed.

Angelina laughed and said, "It's not the wedding. You already know we're staying at his cabin on the lake. We're arguing because I want to move his furniture around. He has a disgusting deer head over the fireplace. It's a small cabin and you can see the fireplace from the bed. I said, "No way, buddy. I'm not having some dead Bambi staring at me while we're—"

"Whoa there, girl," Liddell said. "Too much information. We were just wondering if you have anything for us. We're meeting with Frank Tunney in a few minutes."

"The famous serial killer hunter. That Frank Tunney?"

"That's the one. He'll have his own graphic comic book someday," Liddell said.

"Like the Blade character, but in a suit and tie," Angelina quipped.

Jack had just hung up, and Liddell said, "Let me put you on speakerphone."

"Tell me you have something," Jack said.

"Hello to you too. I've got some interesting information for you regarding Judge Knight."

"Samuel Knight?" Jack said, unable to hide his surprise. "How did you hear?"

"Your partner called me from the fire scene," she said. "Don't you guys talk?"

Liddell shrugged and said, "I told you, pod'na."

Angelina continued, "Judge Samuel Knight bought the house he and his wife and kids live in five and a half years ago. He paid two hundred seventy-five thousand in cash. Old fashioned paper money, Jack. I found the transfer of deed and talked to the previous owner."

"I take it that's not all," Jack said.

"You are correct. He has two offshore accounts. How many judges do you know who have offshore accounts with two hundred thousand dollars in each? He also has a bank account here at Fifth Third Bank and one in Boston at Fidelity Credit Union. Together they are another three hundred thousand. And he has a safety deposit box at Fifth Third Bank."

"Is his wife on any of these accounts?" Jack asked.

"She's second signatory on the bank accounts. She doesn't have access to the deposit box."

Jack said, "Give us the financials on the rest of them. I want any connections you find."

Jack and Liddell listened without questions while Angelina related what she'd found. Knight purchased the house in Evansville several months before he resigned and took the job in Evansville. Sonny retired from Boston PD at near the same time as Knight and Sully and built the house here. Sonny'a house was paid for in cash to the tune of three hundred fifty thousand plus.

Sonny had an account at Fifth Third Bank in Evansville, direct deposit from his police pay. It wasn't a big account. She found nothing else, no offshore holdings or accounts at other banks.

Mindy Middleton's name was on a Teachers Federal Credit Union bank account and an Old National Bank account totaling over $325K. She was sole signatory on these and had opened both a year before she moved to Evansville. Her tax records showed she earned $100K yearly from Garp Investments, which had a New York address. That $100K was split evenly into direct deposits to her bank accounts. There had been no large withdrawals from hers or Sonny's accounts. It was interesting that Mindy was the sole name on the deed to the house.

"Vincent Sullis was never in private practice, according to a friend of mine," Angelina said. "He's a member of the Bar in Massachusetts like you said, but he works for Garp Investment, the same company that is paying Mindy. According to Sully's tax records, he earns $100K a year."

More connections.

"And get this, Samuel Knight was a reference, or sponsor if you like, on Sully's application to enter law school," she said.

"Did you run down Garp Investments?" Jack asked.

"Now you're insulting me," she answered. "Garp Investments is a man named Robert Touhey Sr. And before you ask if Garp is his alias, I'm saying he's the owner, CEO and the board for Garp Investments. The business is like the mythological Hydra. He owns dozens of other businesses that then own other businesses and so on. I could send you a flow chart but you'd go bonkers."

"Marty Crispino?" Jack asked.

"He's interesting," she said.

"Interesting how?" Jack asked.

"There's almost no background on him, that's how. I couldn't even get a real address for him. I found him in IRS records."

"Let me guess. He works for Garp Investments," Jack said.

"You should be a detective," Angelina said. "So, he shows a reported income of $100K a year, but there are no bank records to show where the money goes. If he's hiding money, he's very good at it. Even my friend that I can't name on an open telephone line couldn't find anything."

"When I see Crispino again I'll rattle his cage for you," Jack said. "Can you check on Robert Touhey and see if you can make any other connections with the ones I gave you? Also, keep on Crispino. Check divorce records, lawsuits, and that kind of stuff.

"Already done that. There was nothing you'd be interested in."

Jack thanked her and hung up. He said, "Bigfoot, will you call the captain and ask for a quick meeting? We need to update them. I'll call Tunney back and see if he'll come to the meeting too. Make it fifteen minutes."

Liddell talked to Captain Franklin. Jack talked to Frank Tunney. They agreed to meet in the chief's complex. Jack spoke to Sergeant Mattingly again before calling the morgue.

Chapter 25

Jack and Liddell made their way to the meeting with the brass. Liddell said, "The monkeys are interesting."

Jack said nothing, so Liddell continued. "Johnny Hailman told me something about monkeys that I've never forgotten." Johnny Hailman was a K-9 handler with a bomb-sniffing partner. He was also known for his extremely bad, and poor taste in, jokes.

Resistance was futile. Jack said, "Go for it."

Liddell grinned. "Okay. Hailman said a guy takes his wife and pet monkey to his favorite bar. The monkey jumps down from the guy's shoulder, runs up and down the bar, knocking over drinks, grabbing handfuls of peanuts, pissing on customers, screeching the entire time. The bartender hurries over to the guy and says, "I thought I told you to keep that animal out of here!" The guy turns to his wife and says, 'Go wait in the car.'"

"Have you told that one to Marcie?" Jack asked.

"I'm going to be quiet now," Liddell answered. He ducked his chin as they entered the chief's complex.

The chief's secretary mouthed the name "Double Dick." She said out loud, "They're waiting for you in the conference room. Go on in."

Liddell said, "Oh boy. We're going to get a spanking."

His premonition was proved right. When they reached the conference room door Deputy Chief Richard Dick came storming out.

"You're late," Dick said, his Aryan-blue eyes blazing.

Jack thought, *We've been kind of busy working a couple of high-profile murders, Dick-face.* Jack said, "My apologies, Deputy Chief. It won't happen again."

Double Dick straightened the award ribbons on his starched white shirt. "See that it doesn't, Detective." He stalked back into the conference room. Jack and Liddell followed him in.

FBI Special Agent Frank Tunney was seated facing the door and stood at attention when Double Dick came back into the room. Liddell stifled a laugh and Double Dick turned to him.

"Is something wrong, Detective Blanchard?" the deputy chief asked.

"No sir. Nothing. My spit went the wrong way down my windpipe and kind of…" He coughed into his hand.

"That's disgusting," Dick said and turned away.

"Take your seats," Chief Pope said. "Sergeant Walker won't be here. He and all of his crew are busy at several crime scenes, as you know, and I don't want to interrupt them. You can begin, Jack."

Jack told them about the money found in Sonny's abandoned truck.

Pope interjected, "We know about the money, Jack. It's been counted. Forty thousand recovered from the teenagers who found the body. Sixty thousand found in Sonny's truck."

Double Dick was smirking. Enjoying himself at the expense of the police department's reputation. Jack was sure in Dick's mind were visions of his mug on a Channel 6 News Special revealing a dirty cop.

Jack told them the financial information Angelina had given him. When he was finished, the room was quiet.

"Definitely a corrupt cop," Double Dick said to no one in particular. To Jack it sounded like he was rehearsing for the news cameras. "Someone should have seen this coming," the Dickster added.

Chief Pope ignored the implied insult. "I guess we're not jumping to conclusions anymore about Sonny. IA finished the audit of Task Force money. Nothing was missing, which makes me think he was skimming off the drug-raid seizures."

Deputy Chief Dick said, "We should check everyone on the Task Force."

Dirty cop, news media and drugs. Oh my! Jack thought.

Jack hurriedly said, "We've done that. Nothing there, Deputy Chief, and if nothing was missing from Task Force–seized money…?" Jack left the question open. "We collected some stuff of the judge's for a DNA analysis," Jack told the chief. He was sure Double Dick already knew all of this. Dick had almost as many snitches as the news media.

Double Dick was sitting on the edge of his chair. "Sam Knight's murder is connected to Sergeant Caparelli's?"

"I haven't been able to make a solid connection yet," Jack lied.

Jack hadn't told them everything he'd learned in the last hour. For example, Sully's call to Judge Knight. Sully's suggestion there was a legal, possibly criminal, issue in Boston involving Knight. And he hadn't told them Uncle Marty's possible involvement in this circus of liars.

Chief Pope said, "Richard, we first of all need verification that the body is Judge Knight. I think it's safe to assume there will be a connection, but first things first."

"My thoughts exactly," Double Dick said. "I'm just thinking out loud. Judge Knight handled mostly civil cases, didn't he? And Sonny only worked drug cases."

"Yes," Jack said, knowing it wasn't true because Jason, the law clerk, had told them so.

"I see," Double Dick said. "We definitely have a murder. No one would get in a car trunk and set it on fire."

Captain Franklin cleared his throat and said, "You're right, Deputy Chief."

Double Dick smiled. It was like when a baby farts or fills their diaper kind of smile.

"Stay on top of the judge's autopsy," Pope said. "I guess that's all for now."

Deputy Chief Dick started out of the room. Pope said, "Jack, Liddell, stay a moment. And can you stay as well, Agent Tunney?"

Deputy Chief Dick went back to his chair. "Should I stay too, Chief Pope?"

"That's not necessary, Richard. I'll be in touch as soon as we get any news," Pope said.

Dick was disappointed but he left.

As Jack and Liddell took their seats, Jack's phone rang. It was Sergeant Mattingly reporting that no one appeared to be at Sonny's house. The front desk of the Tropicana let Mattingly check the floor, and Crispino wasn't in his room.

Jack said, "I appreciate you doing this, Sarge. One last thing and I'll owe you. Can you check the Blue Star? Crispino told me his company is connected to the casino."

"Will do, Jack," Mattingly said, and Jack heard him say to the clerk "get me the security chief," before the line went dead.

Jack stuck the phone back in his pocket and checked the hallway to be sure Double Dick wasn't hanging back. Judy Mangold saw him and said, "All clear."

"Okay. Now tell us everything," Pope said.

Jack told them everything, the connections between Sonny, Sully and Knight. He told them Crispino's revelation that he and Sully worked for a guy in Boston that owns a couple of casinos in Atlantic City, Missouri and even the Blue Star Casino in Evansville. He told them about Garp Investments and Robert Touhey Sr. He told them of Mindy's possible financial connection as a source of hiding or laundering illegal funds. He told them about the monkey carving found in Sonny's throat, holding back no scrap regardless of how insignificant it may seem. Most of this was for Tunney, who had helped with a case a few years back, successfully profiling a serial killer and ending his murderous spree.

Tunney leaned back in his chair, hands behind his head, eyes closed as if he were going to sleep. Jack knew that he was absorbing every word, every inflection, hesitation, and tone of what was being said.

When Jack stopped speaking all eyes went to Tunney.

"Agent Tunney. Do you have questions?" Pope asked the FBI profiler.

Tunney opened his eyes. "I'd like to see this animal carving your forensic pathologist found."

Jack said, "I'm sure Dr. John is still at the morgue. Judge Knight's autopsy should be starting soon. Which reminds me, I haven't heard from Little Casket or Walker."

"I think I should attend the autopsy with you," Tunney said.

Chief Pope stood. "Thanks for volunteering your time, Frank. If you want I'll contact your office and make the request official?"

"I've already called them, Chief. I'm all yours."

Captain Franklin and Chief Pope left the meeting.

"I like him. He's not your typical Chief of Police," Tunney said.

"Yeah boy! You can say that again," Liddell said. "I'm surprised Double Dick showed up without his chauffeur and cameraman. He needs to record his every thought and action for his presidential library."

"Let's go check on the autopsy," Jack said.

"Hey Frank. Want to hear a joke?" Liddell asked. "This guy takes his wife and his pet monkey..."

Jack tuned him out, stepped into the hallway and closed the door behind him to call the morgue. "Hi Lilly. Ready for us?"

"They were having trouble extricating the corpse from the trunk. In one piece, anyway. Come on over."

Chapter 26

Little Casket was waiting at the open garage door when the men drove up. She was already dressed for the autopsy in a mint-green Tyvek suit, latex gloves, and paper booties. A surgical mask was pulled into place covering her nose and mouth.

"'Bout time," she said, the sarcasm in her voice muffled by the mask. "Dr. John already started. He said he's not like us. He has a life." She said over her shoulder as they followed her inside, "He's dreaming."

Judge Samuel Knight's partially cremated body lay in a semi-fetal position, legs and arms drawn up, fingers of one hand curled into a fist, the fingers of the other hand missing, the feet and lower parts of the calves reduced to charred bone. Most of the scalp and face were crispy black, teeth bared, eye sockets empty. Three inches of a thick metal spike protruded from the right ear.

Dr. John said, "Frank. Good to see you again. I heard you were in town."

Sergeant Walker said, "I heard you were teaching this morning. Sorry I had to miss it."

"You've been busy," Tunney said.

Dr. John said to Jack, "I've got something for you."

"We saw the spike at the scene, Doc," Jack said.

"Not the spike. This." Dr. John clipped a set of X-rays on the light board. Both were taken of the neck and skull. A thumb-sized object appeared to be lodged deep inside the throats of each.

"The one on the left is Sergeant Caparelli. The one on the right is Sam Knight," Dr. John said.

Walker reached in his top pocket and produced a sealed evidence bag. "This is the carving Dr. John took out of Sonny's throat."

"Can I see that?" Tunney asked. Walker handed him the evidence bag.

Jack's heart raced the way it always did when his gut told him he was nearing the fulcrum of a case.

"Maybe the carvings can be identified," Tunney said, turning the bag in his hands, examining the object.

Dr. John said, "I can send a picture of that to a friend at Indiana State University."

"I think I can save you some time. If Sergeant Walker can send me some digital photos I'll forward them to our people," Tunney said.

"I can send them for you," Walker offered.

"I think I can get a faster response if they come from me."

"Of course," Walker said, and Tunney gave him an email address.

They all went back to the table and Dr. John went to work. Little Casket and Walker helped Dr. John draw the legs down and roll the corpse onto its back. When the right leg was extended, the joint made a squishing sound and the femoral head separated from the pelvis.

"You found him on his left side?" Dr. John asked Walker.

Lilly answered, "Yeah. He was stuffed in that trunk in a fetal position."

Dr. John said to Jack, "The left side rested against the floor of the car's trunk. That protected some of the muscle and ligament on that side. See how the leg is more intact." He pulled the leg down next to the other and this one extended without separating from the body.

"The arms will be the same," Dr. John said.

He was right. The humeral head of the right arm separated from the joint when the right arm was manipulated. It reminded Jack of a baked chicken coming apart.

Most of the scalp and face were gone. Dr. John used an electric bone saw to remove the skullcap, revealing a railroad spike eight to nine inches long and three-quarters of an inch thick. The chisel end had been shoved—or hammered—into the victim's ear, through the brain, and fractured the skull on the left side just behind the ear.

Sergeant Walker photographed everything, collected the spike and bagged it as evidence.

Dr. John said, "I think given the lack of evidence to the contrary, I'll rule that spike as the cause of death."

No one disagreed. Dr. John moved on and opened the trachea. The carved figurine was lodged just below the epiglottis, completely blocking the airway.

With a pair of plastic forceps Dr. John carefully removed the object and held it up. It was indeed a small carving of a monkey. This one was squatting with its hands covering its ears.

Tunney, who had been examining the bottom of the first figurine, said, "Can I see the bottom of that one?"

Dr. John adjusted his grip to turn the carved figurine upside down.

Tunney compared the bottoms of each figurine. He asked Lilly, "Do you have a magnifying glass?"

Lilly said, "I think we got a magnifying glass back in 1950. That was the last time we had money for equipment." She rummaged in one of the cabinet drawers and came back with a magnifying glass.

Tunney took it and said, "Tony, can you shine a light here for me?"

Walker trained a light on the bottoms of the carvings while Tunney examined them with the magnifying glass.

"Huh," Tunney said. "What's this?" He held the magnifying glass while the men took turns.

"It's my magnifying glass," Lilly groused.

"Sorry, Lilly," Tunney said and held it lower for her.

She asked, "Is that Chinese?"

"I think this is ivory. Real ivory is very valuable. The symbols on the bottoms are Chinese or Japanese. The maker's signature," Tunney said.

"Will that help us identify who owned them?" Liddell asked.

"It would be a place to start," Tunney said.

"What do you think they're worth? I mean, if they're ivory like you said?" Liddell asked.

"I really don't know. One thing I can tell you." Tunney handed the evidence bag to Walker. "This isn't over money. This is revenge, or honor. Something personal."

Dr. John promised to call when he heard something. Jack and Liddell walked with Tunney to their cars. Jack said, "Hold on. Let me call someone."

"O'Toole," Jerry answered.

"Jerry. You said you made a big bust a while back. How far back and how big of a bust are we talking?" Jack asked.

Jerry said, "No money is missing."

"Humor me, Jerry," Jack said.

"A week or so ago we did a multi-state bust. DEA, State Police, County Sheriff, you name it and they were involved. It was a big roundup on federal warrants. Our part was up north of here. Jasper, Indiana if you can believe that."

"Was Sonny involved?" Jack asked. No answer. "Come on Jerry. Don't make me call Bert and Ernie on you."

"Yeah. Sonny was there. It was his tip that got us there. Arrests were made all over the place, but the big bust was in Jasper. All told, forty-something arrests with ten of those being in Jasper. We found guns and cocaine out the wazoo. Sonny said we personally seized close to two hundred thousand in cash."

"Were you with Sonny in Jasper?" Jack asked.

"Jack. You can go through our books. You can search me. In fact, you're close to doing a cavity search right now."

Jack waited.

"Sure. We were in Jasper," Jerry said. "We did the same house. There was money seized at every scene, but the money from every bust is accounted for."

"Who found the money?" Jack asked, and Jerry didn't answer right away.

"Before you go crazy…"

"Jerry, who found the money?" Jack asked.

Jerry reluctantly told him.

When Jack finished the call, he told Liddell and Tunney, "Jerry said he didn't actually count the money. Sonny seized it, transported it, and put it in the safe. Sonny was responsible for keeping the log. The log shows two hundred thousand, but Jerry heard one of the suspects say something about half a million or more."

"I thought the log was part of the audit. How come they didn't report this?" Liddell asked.

Jack said, "Jerry admitted there was a lot of to and fro during the bust. Officers coming and going. It was kind of an honor system of evidence collection due to the number of people found in the house and the cache of weapons they had available to them. I can understand how the process could get a little loose."

"We don't have any accurate count on the money that was seized. That means we have no way of knowing what Sonny might have taken for himself," Tunney said. "But according to Mr. Crispino, there is a large debt owed to his employer, who happens to be Big Bobby Touhey."

Jack pointed out, "They're all from Boston. Sonny and Sully were detectives. Knight an Assistant D.A. They all change careers close to the same time. They seem to have the means to get their hands on large sums of money. Crispino came from Boston to collect from Sonny. Sonny is murdered and the killer leaves forty thousand at the scene and sixty thousand in Sonny's truck. It looks like Sonny was skimming money from the drug busts; either for himself, or to pay the bill he owes Touhey. That still doesn't get us any closer to identifying the killer except to say it's not Big Bobby Touhey. He wouldn't leave that kind of money behind."

Tunney said, "The personal nature of these killings points to organized crime. It's possible that Sonny or Knight, or both, got on the wrong side of the mob via Touhey. Whatever he or they did, it would be something that involves all the players—Crispino and Sully are included. A criminal enterprise of some sort. I think honor is at stake."

"See No Evil. Hear No Evil," Jack said. "That leaves Speak No Evil."

Tunney said, "The killer isn't finished."

Chapter 27

Vincent Sullis had settled a sometimes nervous, sometimes belligerent Mindy into a room at The Peaks Inn on the outskirts of town. The billboard advertising the place showed a ski chalet on the side of a snow-covered mountain. This wasn't that. It was more of a hot-sheet motel for shift workers. The inn consisted of four rooms and none were occupied. Sully paid cash for all of them. The goth clerk was glad to take cash without requiring a name. Sully paid four times what the rooms were worth but he needed the privacy. He put Mindy in one of the rooms with strict instructions not to go anywhere, make any calls, order out, or open the door for anyone. Mindy was coming down from a drunk and alternately screaming threats or crying uncontrollably. Plus, he needed somewhere to bring those two kids.

He had only gotten away from Mindy's little bipolar tantrum by promising to go to the store and buy her a couple of bottles of wine and some snacks. At the rate she was drinking, he would have to buy a cask and a spigot.

He'd picked up two bottles of wine and a bag of junk food at a mom-and-pop liquor store and drove back to the inn. While Mindy was unscrewing the top of one bottle he walked down the block to a pay phone in front of the American Legion Post. He'd done some thinking while he was trying to find a liquor store. He'd maybe figured a way out of this mess. At least for himself.

He was in possession of most of the money that Big Bobby knew Sonny had skimmed from the drug busts. How Sonny could be that dumb he'd never understand. No one cheated Big Bobby and lived. But the money Sully found in the safe was shy more than a hundred thousand from what Big Bobby said there would be. He could make it up with his own money, but he wasn't to blame for this mess. *Screw that!*

He took the phone off the hook and saw the number pad was missing several keys. He punched zero on the phone and when the operator came on the line he gave her a phone number in Boston.

The phone was answered after one ring but no one spoke.

"This is Sully," he said.

"Go," the man's voice at the other end said.

"I need to speak to him."

"Wait one." The line went to some Muzak shit.

Big Bobby Touhey came on the line. "Sully." The voice sounded tired.

Sully knew Big Bobby wasn't thinking straight after the death of his kid. Normally he would never use names on the phone. Never.

"I have some good news, sir." Big Bobby didn't respond. The silence said, "About damn time."

Sully recounted what he knew of Sonny's murder, the two juveniles' discovery of Sonny's body, the $40K the police found on the boy, and the subsequent murder of Samuel Knight. He held back the fact that he'd found most of the five hundred thousand in Sonny's safe.

"You got a cop you can work with?" Big Bobby asked.

"The two detectives here are hard-asses. I was hoping you had someone here," Sully said, meaning a cop on the pad.

"I did. He's dead, you dummy. What am I paying you for? You're an ex-cop. You should have some damn connections."

"These two won't be a problem."

"You see to it that they aren't. Listen to me, Sully. My kid was tortured. His dick was cut off and...he was left there...like garbage to humiliate him. And me. You're gonna find this guy, or I'm gonna find him. You better hope you do it first."

Sully knew exactly what was done to the younger Touhey. He'd had a chat with the coroner right after the autopsy. Gone to the funeral. But he was surprised to hear Big Bobby talk like that over an open line. His son's death had hit him hard. Big Bobby was in a murderous rage. Little Bobby's bodyguards had dropped the ball on that one. They should have gone with his kid even over the kid's objections. Big Bobby made them aware of their failure.

The call had come in anonymous. Another dead body in Boston didn't raise many eyebrows until they identified the victim. A homeless man was found sleeping in a box near the scene. The homeless guy was brought in for questioning by the police and released. Two of Big Bobby's guys were waiting outside the police station and picked him up. He didn't know anything. And because he didn't know anything, Big Bobby decapitated him with a sledgehammer.

Afterwards, Big Bobby had given orders to round up some people he thought had a grudge against him or his kid. Sully had brought in some of these unfortunate souls. Big Bobby interrogated them one by bloody one.

To be truthful, Sully hadn't felt bad over Little Bobby getting whacked. Little Bobby wasn't particular whose wife or sister he slept with. Not that he himself wasn't a sex addict. But at least he knew it. Little Bobby acted like having sex with whomever he wanted was his right. Big Bobby had been told about his son's proclivities and only laughed at the tales of forcible conquest. Sully figured the little creep was a murder waiting to happen. He knew the kid's dick would get him in trouble someday. He remembered Little Bobby shoving the barrel of a .44 Magnum revolver up one woman's snatch and pulling the trigger. It had blown her pubic region to hell and back. Little Bobby had laughed and said, "Look. She's on her period."

For that little shit, everything was fun and games, but Sully had to clean up the mess. Seems he was always cleaning up one mess or another for Little or Big Bobby.

"I want this guy, Sully," Big Bobby said.

"And the money?" Sully asked. "Do you want me to find it?"

"Screw the money. You find those kids. And hold on to Sonny's punch. What's 'er name. She might have been behind Sonny stealing from me. You get them and squeeze hard. They know something. No one touches my family. You hear me?"

"I understand," Sully said. "If I come across the money I'll bring it to you along with the guy's head."

"Forget the money, I told you. Your first priority is to find this guy. He hurt me. Sonny getting hit was just a matter of time, but Knight was important to me."

"I'm working on it," Sully said.

"Work harder. I sent someone to help you. He should be there already. Get with him, Sully. This kind of stuff is his specialty. You do good work, but you ain't a cop anymore. You lost your edge. I don't want to hear any excuses. You work with Marty. Get this guy. You said you'd bring me his head. I'm holding you to that. You hear me?" The line went dead.

Sully hung up, trudged back to the car and got in. He had only agreed to come to Evansville because he was Sonny's pal. He thought he had the best chance of getting the money without killing Sonny. He should have known Big Bobby had no intention of just getting the money back. It was getting dangerous to be around Big Bobby, friend or foe. Now Marty, known as "Uncle Marty," was here too. Big Bobby had sent his version of mob RoboCop. *To help. Right.* Uncle Marty made things go away. Sully wasn't going to get anywhere near the man.

It had crossed Sully's mind that he and Sonny were being set up. It might have been Marty that did Sonny and Knight. It made sense. Both he and Sonny had worked with Knight back in Boston, and Sonny continued working with Knight. Knight handled the cases that didn't go federal. Sonny would discreetly dispose of any record or evidence that might tie Big Bobby to the distributor. Big Bobby was smart, and threw some of his own people to the wolves.

Sully had suspected Sonny was siphoning off some of the money. Hell, Sonny's house, boat and Mindy were worth a fortune. Sonny should have known Big Bobby had a long reach and even better hearing.

Now Sonny is dead. Knight is dead. Marty is here. And Big Bobby isn't concerned with half a million dollars. Not on your life.

Sully cranked the heat up and positioned the vents to blow on his freezing hands. The damn steering wheel was like ice. He hated this shithole of a town. He hated Sonny and Mindy and Knight and especially Big Bobby. That man was more than crazy. Sully wouldn't be surprised if Big Bobby himself whacked his own kid. It would give him the excuse he needed to go after anyone his paranoid brain felt threatened by. Maybe Big Bobby was rolling up the Evansville portion of the operation.

Sully had a sick feeling that he was next. Big Bobby was a scorched-earth kind of guy. Sully knew some of what Sonny and Knight were doing, but he didn't know who Sonny's source was. He suspected whomever Big Bobby was using to feed drug info to Sonny was with the DEA. Maybe not a DEA agent, but someone close to them. A wife, a girlfriend, maybe even a kid. Whoever it was, they had to have access to the inner drug circle. He wondered if the person who was calling him, giving him tips and information concerning the murders, might not be the same source that was calling Sonny.

He hadn't told Big Bobby everything that happened since he arrived in E-ville. For instance, he hadn't told Big Bobby he'd gotten an anonymous call the morning Sonny was killed. He was warned the police were on their way, and sure enough, Murphy and his big partner showed up at Mindy's a half hour later. The number that showed on Sully's phone wasn't one he recognized. He'd almost not answered, but Mindy was snoring in his ear and her breath was disgusting.

Whoever was calling knew his name. Knew his cell phone number. Sully had called a friend with Boston Police Department and asked them to see who the number belonged to. It was a pay phone in Evansville.

Then the guy called him back after the detectives left and told him not to worry. The cops didn't have squat connecting Sonny and Sully and Knight. The guy was right about the cops being clueless. Murphy and that other Neanderthal detective didn't know shit. But Murphy could become a real problem. Sully had known a couple detectives like him on BPD. Murphy wouldn't quit until someone cancelled his ticket. Maybe that was why Uncle Marty was here? Or maybe it was Uncle Marty who was calling him.

Sully learned a proverb in law school. In Latin it goes, "Praemonitus, praemunitus." Loosely translated it means, "forewarned is forearmed." The caller had given him just enough information to stay on top of this. Unlike Sonny and Knight, he'd be ready to put an end to this asshole.

One thing worried him. His caller hadn't told him that Uncle Marty was in town. Of course, if it were Uncle Marty calling he wouldn't have. Would he? Another thing that bothered him was the caller's mention of a connection between him and Sonny and Knight. Only a handful of people knew about that. If this guy wasn't working for Big Bobby, who was he working for? He only knew of Uncle Marty by reputation.

There was no doubt in his mind that Sonny's murder was connected to Little Bobby's. The murders were retaliation for something they all had done. This was all connected to Big Bobby and Little Bobby.

Big Bobby's hand-wringing grief and swearing of vengeance might be just another ploy. What if he was the one who ordered the hits? Big Bobby might be eliminating them for reasons known only to him. The only thing that came to mind was the murder of the girl a few years back. He, Sonny, Knight, and Little and Big Touhey had been involved in some way. Was Big Bobby getting rid of any connection between himself and that murder? It was a good question.

Five years ago, Big Bobby had called him because Little Bobby had a problem. He and Sonny were in Big Bobby's pocket, so they couldn't say no. No one said no to Big Bobby. He and Sonny got to Little Bobby's apartment and walked into a nightmare. Little Bobby had raped some young woman, sodomized her, and cut her female parts to shreds. Little Bobby said he'd picked her up on a train and took her home. Translation—he'd forced her into his car at a train station.

They put her body in a Dumpster, poured in gasoline, and lit her up. Sully made an anonymous call reporting the fire. Big Bobby didn't need the heat, so he arranged for a guy to take the rap. Sully and Sonny had to resign not long after to get IA's attention off of them. Big Bobby used his influence to have Sonny relocated and get Sully admitted to law school. And Knight. Knight was the Assistant D.A. who helped with the cover-up. Now he was burned to death. Just like the girl. It was ancient history, but couldn't be a coincidence.

He dragged his thoughts back to the problems at hand. Mindy was safely stashed. He'd torch Sonny's place when the cops left. If Sonny was stupid enough to steal from Big Bobby, who knows what was sitting around his house. There were lots of papers inside the safe. He kicked himself for not taking time to go through them.

Right now, he needed a plan. He had to find those kids. From what his caller told him earlier, the kids didn't have the money. The cops had taken forty thousand from the boy that he had stolen from Sonny's body. The boy had balls. He might know something important. Sully was a detective long enough to know witnesses were unreliable, or they lied for all kinds of reasons. These two were running away together. To do that they would need money. Maybe they were smart enough to hide a nest egg before they got the cops involved.

Chapter 28

Jack and Liddell sat in the chief's complex conference room with Captain Franklin, Chief Pope and Sergeant Walker. Deputy Chief Richard Dick was currently in the basement classroom giving a press conference. Chief Pope had given Double Dick a script to read from and admonished him to stick to the script. Pope was wise enough to know that if you didn't give the media something to report, they would report what they thought were the facts, which occasionally put them at cross purposes with the police department's efforts. He was also wise enough to know that he had to feed Double Dick a spoonful of importance now and again.

"Is Frank coming?" Liddell asked.

"Present," Tunney said, coming into the room. He took a seat next to Jack. "Sorry if I'm late. I was on the phone getting the run-down on the monkey carvings."

"We were just starting," Captain Franklin said. "Thanks again for helping, Frank."

Tunney waved the comment away. "My people said the monkeys are very unique. Collector quality." He took out a notebook and flipped through some pages. "Rio Kawara," he said. "Anyone heard of him?"

No one had.

Tunney referred to the notes again. "The Japanese symbols on the bottoms of the two figurines are identifiers for an artist named Rio Kawara. He was one of a handful of Japanese artists during the Edo period—the 1500s—who became famous for netsuke carvings. Netsuke is typically small carvings of fish, peasants, and animals—like these monkeys, for instance. Kimonos, or robes, had no pockets to carry needed items, like money or tobacco or a pipe. Those things would be carried in a small pouch closed with a drawstring. The pouch was hooked to a sash with the netsuke. As time passed, the need for these diminished and they became valued collector's items. Original carvings can sell for five hundred to fifty thousand dollars, depending on the creator and the material used."

"You are quite the expert, Frank," Captain Franklin remarked.

"My people are the experts," Tunney said. He continued. "Some netsuke were carved from bone and some from wood, but the more expensive ones were carved from ivory. The most valued by collectors were carved from ivory that is ten to twenty-five thousand years old."

"Are these that old?" Chief Pope asked.

"They would need to be carbon dated," Tunney said. "There are a lot of fakes in circulation, as you can imagine. I emailed the pictures Sergeant Walker provided to Quantico and my researcher thinks they may be the real deal."

"That's good. Right?" Liddell asked. "We can trace them."

Tunney said, "You can try. It will take some time. First, you would have to get the figurines evaluated, dated, and start searching databases of auctions, antique dealers, and the whole nine yards to see if they ever carried such items. When we have all those names we search through all of the purchases and...you see where I'm going with this?"

Jack waited for Chief Pope to make that decision. This would take manpower, time and money and EPD didn't have any experience in such research.

Chief Pope asked, "How fruitful do you think a search like that would be, Frank?"

Tunney replied, "If it was my decision, Chief, I would hold up starting down that path until your investigation stalls. It's a Hail Mary pass for sure. Even if you find the owner, these may be stolen. You will have to send a nationwide request out to ask other departments if such a theft was reported. Or it might point directly to the killer. Your call, Chief."

Jack broke the silence. "We're not dead in the water yet, Chief. I've put out a BOLO on Sully and Mindy and Marty Crispino. Angelina is still working on backgrounds. I'm going to contact the Boston Police Department. With all the principals coming from Boston, the reason for the killings must have come from there. It's on my list." Jack didn't have to say it was probably the end of his list. They were almost at the end of their rope.

"I agree with Jack," Tunney said. "This Marty Crispino stands out in my mind. What do you know about him?"

"Very little," Jack admitted. "Even Angelina seemed to get little on his background."

"We need to pick him up," Captain Franklin suggested. "Can you run him through your system, Frank?"

"I can, but your computer whiz, Angelina, has probably gotten everything I can."

"Crispino is staying at the same hotel you are, Frank," Jack said.

"Is he?"

"Can we release those net-sushi things to Frank?" Liddell asked.

Tunney smiled. "Netsuke. It's pronounced *neh-sook*. I'd be happy to take possession and see what I can do with them."

"I'll get them ready," Walker said. "Chief?"

"Chain of custody might be an issue."

Tunney said, "I've gotten permission to work this. I can do this officially. The FBI is always here when you need us."

"Do it," Chief Pope said to Walker.

Deputy Chief Richard Dick swept into the room. "What did I miss?"

Chief Pope said, "Not anything important, Richard. How did the news conference go? Are you still on board with running that end of things?"

Deputy Chief Dick said, "I will do whatever you want, Chief. I just wish I could have told them we have a distinguished FBI profiler involved in the investigation."

Chief Pope said, "Agent Tunney asked that we not do that just yet, Richard."

Tunney sat stone-faced while Chief Pope continued. "Right now, we're thinking the killer is keeping pace with the news media reports, and that means you're our only contact with him. We will feed him what we want. We don't want to show our cards too soon."

"Absolutely, Chief." Double Dick made as if to sit down and Chief Pope stood.

"That's it for now, gentlemen. Let's get back to work," Pope said.

As they filed out of the room, Tunney took Jack's arm. "I'm interested in Mr. Crispino. He bothers me. If you find him, would you allow me to be present at the interview?"

"Sure, Frank," Jack said. "Thanks for getting all that background on the monkeys. I think you are dead-on with your notion the monkeys are the killer's signature. I know the legend of the wise monkeys from when I was a kid. There are four."

Tunney said, "I'm with you, Jack. If the killer is following a pattern, the next murder will be Speak No Evil or Do No Evil. Or maybe both."

Tunney left and Liddell said, "If we find Uncle Marty, what grounds do we have to pick him up and hold him? I know we can ask him to come downtown, but if push comes to shove, we can't detain him for long."

"We'll have to play it by ear." He knew he'd never get a judge to issue a warrant based on a suspicion. They'd need more.

Chapter 29

Jack and Liddell went to their office. Most people think murder investigations are worked in the field. Car chases. Gunfights. Foot chases. More gunfights. Roughing up witnesses. Sex with hookers. Bribing Johnny the shoeshine boy. In the real world, drinking coffee in the office, eating donuts, making phone calls, reading reports and sometimes going door to door to door are the real winners. Television shows have given people a mistaken impression that if a case isn't solved in the first twenty-four hours, *the trail* goes cold. In Jack's world, that was horseshit. You work until you have the bastard's throat in your hands and *he* goes cold.

Liddell made a fresh pot of coffee. Jack called the Boston Police Department. So far, Jack had listened to three foreign languages before being prompted to press '4' for English. He was told to pick from a menu for departments, prompted to punch in the extension if he knew it, select the word that most closely described his reason for calling, and press '1' or wait on the line for the next operator. He left the speakerphone on during this to let Liddell share the joy. At least there wasn't Muzak or advertising.

"I think we could have walked to Boston as fast, pod'na," Liddell remarked.

"At least the machine nazi didn't ask us to take a short 'satisfaction survey' at the end of the call," Jack said.

Liddell pretended to snore.

A woman's voice came on the line. "Police Department."

"This is Detective Murphy, Evansville Police Department in Indiana," Jack said. "I need to talk to one of your detectives."

"We got a bunch of them. Who do you want?"

"Preferably someone familiar with Vincent Sullis and/or Franco 'Sonny' Caparelli," Jack said.

The woman said, "I think Captain Baumeyer is the guy you want."

"Can I speak to Captain Baumeyer please?" Jack asked.

"No."

"Can I ask why not?" Jack asked.

"'Cause he's not in."

"She reminds you of Little Casket, doesn't she pod'na?" Liddell said.

"What was that?" the woman asked.

"That's my partner," Jack said. "He's talking to the undertaker. Can I talk to someone in the detectives' office?"

"You're talking to the detectives' office," she said.

"Are you a detective?" Jack asked testily.

She snorted and the line clicked. Jack thought she'd hung up. She hadn't. A slightly friendlier voice answered. "Detective Yankowski."

"Detective Yankowski, I'm Detective Jack Murphy from Evansville Police Department. I'm on speakerphone along with my partner, Detective Blanchard."

"Where's Evansville?" Yankowski asked.

Jack was wrong. He wasn't friendlier. He sounded like a smartass. "Indiana. You know? John Cougar Mellencamp. 'Small Town.'"

"Never heard of any of them. What can I do for you, Murphy?"

"We're working a couple of murders, and I need to ask you some questions."

"Okay."

"One of our murder victims is an ex-Boston PD detective, Franco Caparelli."

"Sonny?"

"Yeah," Jack said. "Do you have some time? If not, I can call you back."

"I got time. Let me get some coffee first."

Yankowski raised his voice. "Millie. We got any coffee brewed?"

"You want me to drink it for you too, Dick?"

Liddell said under his breath, "*Dick* Yankowski?"

Yankowski said, "That's right. Dick. I've heard it all, Detective Blanchard. Dick Yank-off-ski. Dick Yanker. My mom and dad had a sense of humor. Give me a second. Millie thinks she's the captain instead of the secretary." He said this last in a loud voice.

Jack and Liddell took advantage of the wait and refilled their coffees. Yankowski came back on the line and said, "Okay. Shoot."

Jack told Yankowski about the Caparelli murder scene and the autopsy findings, holding back nothing. He waited to see what Yankowski had to say about Caparelli before he told the detective about Knight's murder, or about Uncle Marty.

Yankowski said, "I always suspected Caparelli was in bed with the wrong people. I heard he got a job working for the Feds in Evansville."

"Yeah. Caparelli was part of a Federal Drug Task Force," Jack said.

"Figures," Yankowski said. "Was he still living with Mindy?"

"You know her?"

"Mindy was a troll," Yankowski said. "She hung around cop bars, precinct parking lots, that kind of thing." He didn't have to tell Jack the reason for that. It was obvious she was a police groupie. "She was hooked up with Sully—excuse me, I mean Detective Vincent Sullis—who introduced them. He was also one of ours, but he's gone over to the enemy camp. Sonny fell in love with Mindy. You know how some guys are always trying to fix hookers? Sonny was that kind of guy. Generous and desperate. He wanted to marry her, get her off the streets. Were they married?" he asked.

"No. Cohabiting," Jack said.

"Yeah? What a pair. And I'm not just referring to her tits. Did she tell you Sonny bought them for her?"

"Funny you should mention that," Jack said. "She bragged about it like she'd gotten a Harvard degree. Let me warm this sludge and I'll be right back."

They all filled up on brain fuel and resumed the conversation.

"Okay," Yankowski said, and slurped loudly. "I can get records on all of this, but I'll just tell you what I can remember if that'll do ya?"

"Sounds good," Jack said.

"Sonny Caparelli was with BPD about fifteen, sixteen years. He was good. He made detective quick and was partnered with Sully in the Vice Unit. They both went to other units but it was during their time in Vice that the rumors started. They were good at their job. Maybe a little too good, if you know what I mean?"

"How's that?" Jack asked.

"There were rumors that they were both on the pad—Big Bobby Touhey's pad," Yankowski said.

"Let me guess. Sonny and Sully were busting Big Bobby Touhey's competition," Jack said.

"You must be a detective," Yankowski said. "Sonny transferred to Narcotics and Sully stayed in Vice, but he gave Sonny tips on dealers. Anyway, after a few of these big busts the other units started talking. Some of it was petty jealousy, but even the outside agencies were talking, Sheriff Narcotics, State Trooper Narcotics, DEA. No one, and I mean no one's sources had come up with any information close to what Sonny and

Sully seemed to be getting. No one could guess who their snitch was. Of course, most cops keep their friends close, snitches even closer."

"So, what happened to them?" Jack asked. "Why did they resign?"

"A little over five years ago, Sonny and Sully worked a homicide. The Homicide Unit guys didn't raise a stink about two Vice detectives working a murder because Sonny and Sully were rising stars. They did one hell of a job on other cases. The victim was a twenty-year-old woman, found mutilated, burned to a crisp inside a big construction bin. The killer must have used ten gallons of gasoline on her. The coroner had a devil of a time determining the cause of death. Officially, cause of death was attributed to the fire, but she had some deep stab wounds—chipped the bone in one thigh, broke a rib—that kind of stuff. She may have been sexually assaulted. Her breasts were gone, her genitalia was destroyed. The coroner thought she'd been sliced and diced before she was burned. Soot in her lungs indicated she was still alive when she was set on fire."

"So how did Sonny and Sully tie into this?" Jack asked.

"Hey, you called me. Let me finish."

"Sorry," Jack said.

"You're forgiven. The original call came in from a phone booth. Anonymous. The run was dispatched and Sonny volunteered to take it," Yankowski continued. "Said he was close. He was there even before the fire department. The body was so badly burned the coroner couldn't give us much, like I said. We couldn't identify her for a while and she was going to be a Jane Doe. Missing Persons took a report a couple of days later from a woman saying her college roommate was missing. Missing Persons swore they told Sonny. Sonny didn't follow up for weeks. The missing person report worked its way up the chain of command and Captain Baumeyer gave it to Sonny."

"At the time, it was still Sonny's case so he had to talk to the roommate. His report said she didn't know when her roommate went missing, and that she thought the girl was going clubbing in Boston."

"In his report, Sonny had information the victim was dating a boyfriend the family didn't approve of, but he couldn't get the guy's name. Sonny said he was getting a DNA sample to compare the missing girl with the dead one. Anyway, the case sat on Sonny's desk for a couple of weeks and he added follow-up reports that said absolutely nothing. It went unsolved for a couple of months.

"I got involved because the roommate was a friend of a friend of my wife. The friend told my wife that Missy's mother called Sonny almost every day, but he told her the case was dead in the water. Missy's mother must have believed Sonny. I never got to talk to the mother because she died before I got the case.

"When I took over the case, I talked to the roommate and she denied saying any of what Sonny had in his reports. She said Missy—the victim's name was Missy Schwindel—never went 'clubbing.' Missy didn't drink alcohol or go to parties on campus. She told me Missy wasn't dating anyone or she would have known. Missy was totally focused on school. Missy had no family left after her mother died. She never knew her father."

"Sonny never really worked the murder," Jack said.

"Turned out that Sonny had only talked to the roommate on the telephone and she called him. He never collected anything for DNA comparison. I took this to Captain Baumeyer, and he reassigned the case to me, unofficially in case I didn't turn up anything. Sonny was still a star and the captain didn't want to start a pissing match."

"I went to the roommate's place and collected several samples from stuff that belonged to the victim. We sent it off to the lab and got a match. I talked to one of the uniforms that was on scene that night and they said Sonny was there, and Sully was there too. Sully wasn't mentioned in any of the reports, but wherever you found Sonny, you found Sully."

"What happened?" Jack asked.

"The captain got IA involved after we got the DNA match. They were already looking at Sonny and Sully with a magnifying glass. The case was officially assigned to me, and I started working it hard."

Jack took out a notebook and pen. This had all happened before Sonny and Sully left the Boston PD. Sully had recently told Mrs. Knight and Judge Knight's law clerk he needed to speak to the judge because of what happened in Boston. Was this what he was referring to?

Yankowski said, "Internal Affairs ran down a guy that saw Sonny and Sully at a bar, drunk off their asses on one of the nights Sonny was supposedly talking to the victim's roommate. The witness was a bartender at a club that most cops avoid because of its reputation. He remembered the date because he knew Sonny and Sully and they were giving him a hard time that night. Translation, they were shaking him down for drugs or money or both. The bar is a regular hangout for some of Big Bobby Touhey's cronies. I don't know how IA found this guy, but they were excited. They had caught Sonny in a lie and maybe tied him and Sully to Big Bobby."

"Did that ever go anywhere?" Jack asked.

"Not really. Circumstantial evidence at best, and no one wanted to get in disfavor with Big Bobby. Or Sully for that matter. Sully was kind of a loose cannon. The witness—the bartender—recanted his story. He didn't see anything because he was drunk himself. Couldn't have seen shit if it was on him. He didn't know what day it was and so forth."

"Convenient," Liddell mused.

"Exactly. But IA never let up on Sonny and Sully. Out of the blue, a guy comes in to the station and asks for me. He says he wants to confess. He claimed he was hopped up on drugs when he killed the girl. He told me she was walking down by the overpass. He thought her car might have broken down. He made a pass, she seemed to be willing, but he got a little rough and she changed her mind. He admitted to raping her. She threatened to call the cops, so he stabbed her. He panicked. He supposedly didn't remember anything about slicing and dicing her breasts, but the Assistant D.A. figured it could be because he was high on drugs. The guy had a long record for drugs and sexual assault.

"Anyway, he said he put her in a big trash bin and set her on fire. I asked where he got that much gasoline and he told me he went to a gas station and borrowed a can. Of course, he couldn't remember where the gas station was. I checked every place he could have gotten the gasoline and no one had loaned a gas can to this guy. I asked him why he was coming forward, and he said his conscience was bothering him."

"Did you believe him?" Jack asked.

"Didn't matter. He was convicted by a jury of twelve fine citizens and sentenced to five years."

"Five years!" Liddell said.

"Yeah," Yankowski said. "Sam never was a believer in long sentences, and that was the plea deal he made."

"Sam?" Jack asked.

"Deputy District Attorney Sam Knight. We called him "Plea Deal Sam." I'm glad that asshole is gone," Yankowski said.

Jack said, "He was a judge in Superior Court here in Evansville. He was killed by the same guy that got Sonny. Spike through the ear. Monkey carving stuck in his throat. Set on fire."

"Well, I can't say I'm unhappy about either of them—Sonny or Knight. Hey, hang on a minute. I don't know how I could have forgotten this. Be right back."

Jack heard the phone put down and rustling of papers before Yankowski came back. "I forgot about Little Bobby. Robert Touhey Jr. He's Big Bobby's kid. He was killed a couple of weeks back. Not my case. But I remember hearing something about a monkey carving."

The papers rustled again. "I've got some crime scene pics here. Jeez, what a nasty way to go. He was disemboweled and castrated. His body was hung with steel cables. Is that what you have?"

"Yeah. Sonny was hung by steel cables and meat hooks. What about the spikes?"

Yankowski let out a low whistle. "He was castrated and his man parts were staked to the floor with a railroad spike. He was cut from stem to stern."

"The carving?"

"Yeah. Stuck down Little Bobby's throat."

"Do you have the autopsy report?" Jack asked.

Chapter 30

Dr. John had called after they finished talking with Detective Yankowski. Jack and Liddell drove back to the morgue.

"This can't be a coincidence," Liddell said, and turned down Walnut Street. Yankowski had told them Little Bobby was found by a wino in a vacant house near a housing project. He was stripped naked, with Taser burn marks on his chest, neck, and back. He was hanging from a wall with wire cable wrapped around his neck. He was eviscerated. His penis and scrotum had been cut off and were nailed to the floor with a nine-inch-long railroad spike. The kicker was the carved figurine of a monkey that had been found during the autopsy, jammed far down his throat. Steel cable tied his hands over his bloody groin area, mimicking the pose of the monkey carving, Do No Evil. The coroner ruled the death due to exsanguination—blood loss. Secondary cause of death was strangulation. Little Bobby hadn't died quickly.

"I don't think Uncle Marty is our killer, but I'm starting to agree with Tunney that he is an important piece of this puzzle, Bigfoot."

"Yeah. Me too. I mean, even Angelina couldn't find anything much on the guy. If Angelina can't find it, it's not there. Funny that he disappears at the same time that Mindy and Sully take a hike. You don't think they're dead too?"

"Took a hike more than likely," Jack said.

"I don't think the killer's going anywhere until he kills Speak No Evil. I guess that's Sully. Think about it. Attorneys are referred to as a 'mouthpiece'."

Liddell turned off Walnut heading toward the morgue.

Jack said, "The next victim could be Uncle Marty."

Liddell said, "Maybe killing Sonny was only a way to get Sully here? Sonny and Knight were already here."

"Could be," Jack said. "Sonny, Knight and Sully are all connected by circumstance to Missy Schwindel's murder. All three of them resign their jobs in Boston and scatter."

"Knight basically gives a confessed murderer a walk. Five years, pod'na." Jack added, "And don't forget Yankowski said the guy was killed in prison."

"Big Bobby?" Liddell said.

"Probably," Jack said. "Mindy is connected to all of this through Sonny and Sully. We don't have anything on her."

"Mindy's a life-support system for a pair of jugs, if you believe Jerry O'Toole and Yankowski," Liddell said, and parked in front of the coroner's office.

"You really have a way with words, Bigfoot."

Dr. John showed them inside and said, "I might have something for you." He handed Jack a paper. "Toxicology on Sonny Caparelli."

Jack handed the paper back without reading it. "You know I can't make heads nor tails of this stuff, Doc."

Dr. John said, "Sonny was poisoned. Cyanide."

"Are you sure, Doc?" Liddell asked.

"Prunasin is a form of cyanide. It's found in some plant leaves, twigs, and blooms, flowering trees. The cyanide level in his blood wasn't lethal, but if it increased any more it would have killed him."

Jack remembered the trees on the lawn around Sonny's house. "There were cherry trees in Sonny's landscaping. They were still blooming."

Dr. John said, "Cherry blossoms are used to make tea. They contain small amounts of Prunasin."

"But why would Sonny eat that stuff?" Jack asked.

"He may not have known," Dr. John explained. "The Japanese make tea from cherry blossoms and leaves. If they are dried properly before making tea, they are not quite as poisonous. But if wilted leaves, twigs, or wilted blooms were introduced in enough quantity, the poison created could act on the lungs as a nerve agent. Cyanide is one of the oldest poisons used to commit murder."

Everyone Jack had talked to in Evansville had praised Sonny as a good guy, although Yankowski in Boston had a different opinion. The only one from Boston who had consistent access to Sonny's food or drinks here in Evansville was Mindy. Maybe she wasn't just a dumb blonde.

"I guess we're going back to Sonny's house," Jack said. "We'll need a search warrant this time. We may have enough probable cause to detain Mindy for questioning. If we can find her, that is."

Liddell called dispatch and asked them to tell Sergeant Mattingly to call via cell phone. "What are we looking for? I need to name something for the search warrant."

"Tea leaves, plant material. You're the experts," Dr. John said.

Sergeant Mattingly called and Liddell said, "Sarge, can you send a car by Sonny's house again? We need to find Mindy." He listened then said, "We're getting a search warrant for the place. If you find Mindy or this Vincent Sullis guy, hold on to them."

When he hung up, he called Sergeant Walker and told him what Dr. John discovered in the toxicology report. Walker said he'd take care of getting the search warrant.

Dr. John said, "Japanese cherry trees. Japanese monkey carvings."

"Shit!" Jack said.

* * * *

Henderson County Deputy Sheriff Bart Findlay walked along the bank on the Kentucky side of the Ohio River. An anonymous caller reported that a body had washed up on the shore west of the Twin Bridges. He was freezing his ass off checking the shoreline on foot. There was no way to do it in a vehicle—which is where he wished he were right now. He hoped with all his might that what the reporter saw was a log or something else. If it was a body, he'd be standing out here all day. When he was a rookie, almost twelve years ago, his training officer had told him, "Bart, there's three things a cop never does. Get wet, get hungry, or get cold. Especially cold." How he wished it were his training officer standing here right now instead of him.

He cursed out loud as he pushed his way between rows of tall sticker bushes. Thorns snagged at his Tuffy uniform jacket, and pulled little tufts of material from his brown twill uniform trousers. He was just thankful the needle-sharp thorns weren't pricking him.

He pushed through the bushes and found himself surrounded by another thicket. "Damn it to hell!" He pushed on. Going back now wasn't an option. He made it through the thicket to a small clearing and carefully pulled a branch of the wicked thorns away from his pants, sticking his finger in the process. He pulled his glove off, put the injured finger in his mouth, took a step, and stumbled over the body.

Chapter 31

Liddell was driving. "If we're going to Sonny's house, can we at least go by a drive-thru? There's a McDonald's on highway 41. I'm starving, pod'na."

Jack's stomach was screaming profanities too. "Okay. The warrant won't be ready for an hour at least. Drive-thru, Bigfoot. You pick the place. We need to get to Sonny's in case Sully is there. I don't want our guys to have to listen to his shit."

"Now you're talking, pod'na," Liddell said, and picked up speed. "If we're lucky, Uncle Marty will be there too."

Jack wasn't that optimistic. Murphy's Law says, *If something can go wrong, it will at the worst possible time, and screw you sideways.*

It took Bigfoot less than five minutes to pull into a spot at the Sonic on Covert Avenue. He ordered two number-five deals for himself, and a cheeseburger and drink for Jack.

"I said, drive-thru," Jack pointed out.

"Same thing," Liddell said, unclipped his seat belt, and loosened his belt.

He reminded Jack of a Sumo wrestler poised to do battle with a twenty-thousand-calorie meal. Their food arrived and Liddell tipped the girl an extra dollar. She put on a fake smile and said, "Gee. I guess college will have to wait." She walked away shaking her head.

Liddell didn't seem to notice. He was stuffing fries into his mouth when dispatch called on the car radio. "One David fifty-two."

"One David fifty-two, go ahead," Jack said.

"One David fifty-two, you are requested to call a Deputy Findlay, Henderson County Sheriff's Department ASAP."

"We're on a run. If it's not in reference to what we're working now can you get a phone number?" He wanted to serve the search warrant at Sonny's house. He didn't have time to deal with anyone else's needs.

"They requested you to call ASAP, Jack."

"Give me the number," he said, and punched the number dispatch relayed into his cell phone. He hit the send button.

The call was answered, "Go ahead."

Jack asked, "Is this Deputy Findlay?"

"Who's this?"

"This is Detective Murphy, Evansville Police Department, calling for Deputy Findlay, Henderson County Sheriff Department."

"Just messing with you," Findlay said. "This is Findlay. Your dispatcher gave me your cell phone number in case you didn't call me right back."

Jack put the call on speakerphone. "Sorry if I'm being a little short with you, Deputy. We're in the middle of something here and—"

"That's why I'm calling you," Findlay said. "I've got someone over here you want. An older gent named Martin Crispino."

Liddell pumped a big fist in the air. "Ba-boom! Something's going our way."

Findlay heard Liddell. He said, "Don't get too excited. This guy's maybe not going to talk to you."

"Did he ask for a lawyer?" Jack asked.

"No. He's unconscious. He's in ICU at Our Lady of Mercy Hospital. I've been here for two hours."

"What's going on? Is he under arrest?" Jack asked. They obviously had the EPD's All-Points Bulletin or they wouldn't have known to call Jack. What took them so long to call?

"No. He's not under arrest. I found him on the riverbank over here and we had a little problem identifying him. Let me start at the beginning."

Deputy Findlay explained getting dispatched to check out a report of a body on the riverbank. Findlay said Crispino was half in, half out of the water, fully clothed—shoes, overcoat and all. He felt for a pulse and didn't find one. He thought the guy was dead. He called for a detective, coroner, and AMR. He felt for a pulse again, thought he felt a weak one, but the guy wasn't breathing. He started emergency breathing and felt for a pulse again. Nothing. He performed CPR until the ambulance arrived and took over. The medics packaged the guy and beat feet for the hospital.

"This guy had a big gash on the back of his head, but he didn't seem to be injured anywhere else. He was suffering from hypothermia. Bled all over my damn coat and pants before the paramedics got to him. I damn near froze. Anyway, the ambulance got another run as they were dropping him off at the ER and left like their ass was on fire. They still had Crispino's clothes. Hence, the delay in calling you guys. When I got his clothes, his wallet was in his jacket pocket. He also had a holster on his belt for a handgun."

Liddell said, "He's got a 9mm Beretta. He showed us a carry permit from New York."

"Well, no gun. He must have lost it when he was thrown in the river. He's lucky he didn't die out there. But that's not the interesting thing. You're gonna love this."

Jack really doubted he was going to love anything to do with Marty.

Findlay said, "There was more than one ID in the wallet. Three driver's licenses in different names from three different states. Three concealed carry weapon permits. I ran all the names through records and that's when we came up with your APB on Martin Crispino."

Jack didn't know what to say. The handgun permit and driver's license they'd been shown had checked out. He was a little embarrassed that he'd been conned by Uncle Marty. Liddell wrote down Uncle Marty's other names that Findlay found.

"There was almost five grand in his wallet. Five grand! You believe someone carrying around that kind of money, gets knocked in the head, and they don't take his cash?"

Before Jack or Liddell could respond, Findlay said, "Hey. You think he will spring for a new coat and pants?"

"Is he expected to live?" Jack asked.

"Doc says he needs to warm up. He said hypothermia does different things to different folks, and I don't know how long he wasn't breathing before I got there. He's a tough old buzzard. He opened his eyes a few times. Who the hell have we got here?" Deputy Findlay asked.

"Can you do me a favor, Deputy Findlay?" Jack asked.

* * * *

Jack and Liddell were back on Highway 41 heading south toward Our Lady of Mercy. Deputy Findlay had given them the room number. He said the doctor was coming in and he would ask the doc if Crispino could be woken long enough to answer a few questions.

Jack called Captain Franklin and updated him on their progress. Captain Franklin said he would assign a detective to run down the type of vehicle and license plates for Marty's rental vehicle.

"It shouldn't take the deputy long to run Uncle Marty's prints through AFIS," Jack said. He had asked Findlay to take Crispino's latent fingerprints and have them run through AFIS. To Findlay's credit, that was already being done and he was waiting for the results.

AFIS, or the Automated Fingerprint Identification System, was managed by the FBI and was the most comprehensive fingerprint database in the world. If Crispino had ever been entered into the database, AFIS would get a match. Even with the technology available to hackers, it was almost impossible for an individual to change their identity and disappear from police records. Almost. It still took some heavy-duty connections and money to have three separate sets of identification that could pass law enforcement scrutiny.

They were just going over the Twin Bridges that separated Indiana from Kentucky, Evansville from Henderson when Liddell said, "I guess we can cross Uncle Marty off our list of suspects."

"Not necessarily," Jack posited.

"You think he gave himself a concussion and almost died from the cold?" Liddell asked seriously.

"The killer might not be working alone."

"Well, when you put it that way," Liddell said.

"Captain Franklin is going to have dispatch add Crispino's vehicle information to the BOLO. We can give it to Findlay and ask him to do the same thing here. Crispino had to get over here in something," Jack said.

"Unless he took a bus or a cab or swam."

"Bigfoot, you belong in a circus."

Liddell drove into Henderson and followed the signs for Mercy Hospital. They parked and met a deputy at the ER door, who took them to ICU and handed them off to Deputy Findlay.

Findlay caught a nurse as she came from the ICU and asked, "Is Dr. Ahmad still in there?" He was. Findlay said, "These are Evansville detectives. Tell Dr. Ahmad they're here?"

She didn't have to. The doors opened and a tall man in a white lab came out. He was blond-haired, blue-eyed, pale complexion, and not exactly what you would expect with the name Ahmad, but the nametag on his coat said he was.

Dr. Ahmad held a hand out and said, "You must be Detectives Murphy and Blanchard. You two have quite a reputation around here. Jack Murphy, Evansville's Clint Eastwood."

They shook hands and Ahmad said, "You are just in time. The patient is waking up. I must caution you that he will be in great pain. Imaging revealed a concussion and his core body temperature was eighty-nine degrees when he was brought in. He may not be able to talk, or make any sense of what you are asking. His MRI shows he may have a mild a TBI. He's strong, and he's a fighter or he wouldn't have made it this far."

"Do you expect him to make it further?" Liddell asked.

"I suspect he'll be able to go to prison if that's what you want with him. Deputy Findlay told me he's tied up in a murder investigation. I'll go in with you, but you must be brief."

"We understand," Jack said.

Dr. Ahmad opened the door and they followed him to a private room, more of a cubicle with curtains, and Jack could hear beeps and other noises he associated with his memories of spending time in hospital rooms just like this.

Dr. Ahmad pulled the curtain and went to his patient. Crispino's coloring was gray, his eyelids, lips and fingertips blue. The machines surrounding the back of the bed were active and none showed a straight line. Jack took that as a good sign. For Marty, at least.

"Mister Crispino," Ahmad said. "Martin."

Jack said a little louder, "Uncle Marty. It's me. Cubby."

Jack said to Ahmad, "Cubby's his favorite nephew."

Crispino's eyelids moved. His breathing became heavier. Jack wondered if Uncle Marty was going to live. He'd promised Frank Tunney that he could be present when Marty was found. It might be too late for that.

"Mr. Crispino," Ahmad said, and touched his shoulder. "Can you hear me? Can you open your eyes, please?"

Crispino moaned slightly, said, "Cubby." His eyes opened and came to rest on Jack. "Am I under arrest?"

Chapter 32

Whether if for medical reasons or if he was just being nosy, Dr. Ahmad insisted on staying in the room while they talked to Crispino.

"Do you know where you are, Mr. Crispino?" Ahmad asked.

"In a hospital," Crispino said. "I hope." He tried to smile but grimaced in pain instead.

"Do you know who I am?" Ahmad persisted.

"Never seen you before."

"Do you…"

Crispino said, "I know I'm getting tired of these questions. Why don't you tell me where I am and how I got here."

Jack took out his notebook and laid it on the foot of the bed. "He's his normal self," Jack said to Dr. Ahmad. "You don't want to answer my questions, Uncle Marty?"

"I can save you some time, Detective Murphy. I don't have a clue who hit me."

"I don't care who hit you," Jack lied, and this time Marty managed a tiny smile. "I want to know about the murder of Missy Schwindel."

Crispino's eyes gave him away, but he said, "Can I get something for the pain, Doc?" He shut his eyes tightly. Jack imagined Crispino's entire body must feel like it was being stuck with pins and needles as the nerves came back to life.

"Okay, that's it guys," Dr. Ahmad said. "You can come back when he's rested." He motioned toward the unit doors and the men headed that way. Deputy Findlay stayed outside the door and Ahmad walked Jack and Liddell to the elevators. "He's regained consciousness and he recognized you Detective Murphy. Both good signs."

"I shot someone for him," Jack said, and Dr. Ahmad's eyes widened. Jack explained, "The guy I shot had killed his nephew and…never mind."

Dr. Ahmad said, "He may have memory loss. Headaches. Chronic pain. Blurred vision. Emotional disturbance…"

"I had a TBI a couple of years ago, Doc. I'm familiar with the symptoms," Jack said.

"You've recovered well, Detective Murphy," Ahmad said. "Let's hope the same can be said of your friend in there."

He's not my friend, and I couldn't give a shit if he ever recovers. "He'll be in my prayers," Jack said.

"The hypothermia is my concern," Dr. Ahmad said. "He's going to hurt like stink on a June bug."

"Is 'stink on a June bug' your medical diagnosis, Doc?" Liddell asked.

"It's something my mother used to say. The nurse is medicating Mr. Crispino now. I don't expect him to wake again for several hours. Deputy Findlay can call you when he's awake."

Liddell said, "That's okay, Doctor. We've got places to go, people to meet. My partner hasn't shot anyone this week. But I'd like to know more about this hypo-stuff," Liddell said. "What did you call it?

Dr. Ahmad seemed happy to go off into a medical explanation that would have confused a NASA scientist. While Liddell was distracting Ahmad, Jack made a show of patting his pockets. "Forgot my notebook. Will it be okay if I go grab it? I'll just be a second."

"Go ahead," Ahmad said, and launched back into his description of the diagnosis, symptoms and other shit Jack didn't need or want to hear.

Deputy Findlay held the door open for Jack and whispered, "Smooth."

The nurse at the station asked Jack where he thought he was going.

He said, "Forgot my notebook. Dr. Ahmad said it was okay."

She turned her attention back to the twelve-inch sub that was begging for mercy. Jack hoped she wouldn't lodge a pepperoncini in her throat and tie him up doing the Subway-Sandwich Maneuver on her. He wasn't even sure he could get his arms around her.

Jack slipped inside the cubicle and saw Marty was wide awake and glancing at the beeping monitors. "Reminds you of slots in a casino, doesn't it?" Jack said.

"Yeah, but without all the cigarette smoke and half-naked women plying me with alcohol," Crispino said. "Knew you'd be back."

"Did the notebook trick give me away?" Jack asked.

"It was the name you said. I couldn't talk in front of Deputy Dawg. I don't know him."

"I want to know how Missy Schwindel is tied into this. And I want to know why the killer was after Sonny and Judge Knight. Apparently, he's after you too. What's his end game? You owe me that much. Remember Cubby?"

Crispino stared into space long enough Jack thought he'd passed out.

Crispino said, "Are you going to tell me I'm not going to make it?" He grimaced.

Jack noticed Crispino's pulse was low according to the monitors. The pain medicine they'd pushed was probably taking effect.

"I'm not going to lie to you, Marty. Your chances aren't too good. Just don't go into the light. Or get in a car with strangers," Jack said straight-faced, and inched the curtain back to see if he had a few more minutes alone with Crispino. The nurse was done with the sandwich, and was now turning her scowling face toward the cubicle. He'd have to hurry.

"You're full of shit, Murphy," Crispino said. "That's why I like you. And I always pay my debts." Crispino said. "The girl, Missy. She was a nobody. Little Bobby drugged her in a train station and took her to his apartment. He gets a little rough when he's drugged up. He calls it rodeo sex. You can imagine what that is.

"She must have come to and threatened to call the cops, or he was just being Little Bobby. He messed her up real good. He called Daddy to get the place cleaned up. Get rid of the girl. You know?"

"Bobby Touhey?" Jack asked.

Crispino said, "Big Bobby and Little Bobby. Little Bobby is his kid. Was his kid. Thank God for small favors." His voice was getting thick. "Big Bobby's clean-up crew took care of the body. I only know that she was burned to destroy evidence. Get rid of DNA. And I can tell you that kid spread his DNA like a virus. He would do a snake if he could hold it still."

"Who got rid of the body?" Jack asked.

"Big Bobby's guys. Sonny and Sully."

"Is that why you're here? Are you one of Big Bobby's cleaners?"

"I didn't kill Sonny, if that's what you're asking. You can thank someone else for that," Marty said, his eyes drifting like clouds. "When Little Bobby was killed, Daddy put the squeeze on a boatload of assholes. He wasn't satisfied with that. He had the idea that it was someone close to the operation—I mean the family. He told me he thought Sonny and Sully had something to do with getting his kid killed. Big Bobby was in a rage. The whole mess opened a bag of worms. Big Bobby should have kept a lid on it, but now he's afraid the cops will be all over him."

"You were here to—what?"

"I told you. I didn't kill Sonny. Me—I don't think Sonny or Sully had anything to do with Little Bobby's death. I think the girl who was killed is the reason for all of this. I'm supposed to find the guy that killed Little Bobby and give them a good talking-to," Crispino said.

"Looks like the killer found you first," Jack remarked. "Do you know who he is?"

"I was at Sonny's door. Came up behind me…" His words were slurring.

"Tracker," Crispino said. His eyelids were drooping, voice fading.

"Tracker? Is that his name? Marty?"

Crispino's head moved side to side slightly. His voice was a whisper. "Tracker…Jeep…Sully." He was asleep.

The nurse pulled the curtain open.

"Oh, here it is," Jack said. He picked up his notebook from the bed and showed her.

Chapter 33

Liddell drove north, across the Twin Bridges, back into Indiana.

"Tracker, Jeep and Sully? That's what you got?" Liddell asked. "Couldn't you shake him awake or slap more out of him? I'm disappointed, pod'na. Or should I start calling you Evansville's Clint Eastwood?"

"I wish you wouldn't. I have a hard enough time remembering who I am," Jack said. "But you can call me Supreme Commander if you want. That computer bitch on my phone does."

"You should learn to talk to Siri nicely, pod'na."

"At least we know his real name *is* Martin Crispino," Jack said.

Deputy Findlay told them AFIS had come back on Crispino's fingerprints. He was Martin Crispino, all right. He had one arrest for battery on a policeman.

"Still think he's a suspect?" Liddell asked.

"I haven't even eliminated you yet, Bigfoot."

"Marcie's my alibi, pod'na."

"She's having your baby. She doesn't count. She needs you to keep working so she can feed a baby Bigfoot."

"The baby's going to be a boy. I'll name him Jack."

"Yeah, yeah. After Jack Nicholson. I know."

"We're naming him after you, pod'na. He'll be my little pod'na."

The thought of a baby named after him gave Jack pause. He could feel his eyes getting moist. Now that he was back together with Katie, they had been talking around the edges of another pregnancy. They had lost one child, a girl—full term. The doctor had listened for the baby's heartbeat for an unusually long time. After that it was a blur of activity. Katie was rushed into the OR. Their daughter was stillborn. They were going to name her Caitlin. He'd not been allowed in the room while the doctors worked furiously to save them, but he was in the hall and saw everything. Jack's world collapsed and took his marriage with it.

Do we really want to risk it? Caitlin, I'm sorry I couldn't protect you.

"Whatcha thinking, pod'na?"

"I'm thinking I'd be honored. If it's a girl you can name her Jackie."

"That's better than my suggestion. Liddella Marcella."

Jack chuckled and his bad mood dissipated. "What do they call a female Bigfoot anyway?"

"She'll be mean. You don't call her anything."

They arrived at Sonny's house and several police units were parked in the driveway and in the frozen yard. A van with the logo "American Lock Service" was just leaving. Sergeant Walker came out and pointed at dark, round spots the size of a dime on the front mat, and a trail of dots leading toward the front drive.

"Blood," Walker said, and they followed him inside.

"Probably Crispino's," Jack said. "He told us he was at the front door when someone coldcocked him. Didn't see or hear anything. He said the gate was open."

"It was open when the uniformed officers got here as well," Walker said.

Jack said, "Crispino's in ICU at Mercy over in Henderson. He has a gash on the back of his head and was soaking wet, hypothermia. A deputy found him unconscious on the riverbank just across from here. We didn't know how he got there. Maybe we do now."

"You think he was thrown in?" Walker asked. "Even if he tried to swim across that's a long way in that cold water."

"He was fully clothed—gun missing—and soaked to the skin. Sonny's property meets the river," Jack said.

"Can you call Mercy and see if they'll collect a blood sample for me?" Walker asked. "I'll compare it with this blood."

"I'll call Deputy Findlay. He can get it," Jack said.

They carefully stepped over the blood trail and went inside. Walker shut the door behind them and in spite of his heavy jacket he was shivering. "I got here twenty minutes ago. No one was home. I called a locksmith. It's colder than a witch's kitty out there." Tony Walker never cursed. Well, almost never. He handed Jack the signed search warrant and Jack skimmed through it. It gave them permission to search the house, garage, vehicles, outbuildings, and anywhere that a poisonous substance could be found. The trail of blood was in plain view and led toward the river. They didn't need a search warrant to follow it to the river.

"Mindy's car is in the garage. There's a Harley in there with no license plates."

As Walker said this, one of his techs called from another room, "Sergeant Walker, you might want to see this."

Jack and Liddell followed Walker into the master bedroom. Women's clothes were carelessly cast on the floor, bed, chair and dresser top. The tech was holding open the door to a closet.

Walker let out a whistle. "Well, will ya lookie here?"

Jack and Liddell did. It was a spacious walk-in closet with racks of clothes and dressers on both sides. At the back was a ceiling-to-floor, wall-to-wall shelf of shoes. The shelf was swung away from the wall to reveal a tall safe. The safe door was open. Inside were several handguns, jewelry, and folders of paperwork.

"There's enough jewelry here to open a store. The guns are collector's items," Liddell said.

"No bottle with a skull and crossbones on the label?" Jack asked.

"We should be so lucky," Walker answered.

Jack knew they could photograph the safe and contents and document it, but their search warrant was for poison or anything related to poison. Not for guns. Not for jewelry. Not even the papers. These things may well have a bearing on their case, but at this point Jack couldn't think of any direct connection, hence a reason to seize them. Maybe Sonny was laundering his stolen drug money by purchasing jewelry and guns. Jack would need to apply for another warrant before seizing those items or the papers. That didn't mean they couldn't take pictures to prove they hadn't taken anything.

Jack and Liddell waited in the living room while Walker and the tech went back to their tasks. Walker was calling the prosecutor's office to start the search warrant for the contents of the safe.

"I've never seen this kind of stuff around your place," Liddell said. "You've got to be worth more than Sonny stole." He was referring to Jack's half-ownership of Two Jakes Restaurant and Marina. Jack's dad, Jake Murphy, was a street cop for thirty-five years. Jake's partner was Jake Brady. The two Jakes retired and bought several acres of Ohio riverfront that was little better than swampland. The two Jakes built a restaurant on an old docked barge, and little by little added on to their empire. When Jake Murphy died, he bequeathed his half of the business to Jack, knowing his other son, Kevin, would have nothing to do with it. Kevin was a scientist-type whose ambition was to travel the world and save zooplankton. Jack would always be a cop. When Jack was born, the doctor slapped his tiny bottom and Jack slapped handcuffs on the doctor.

"We're wasting our time here, Bigfoot. Even if they find the poison, I don't think there's anything here that will help us catch this guy. Even if Mindy was trying to kill Sonny, I don't think she would have the strength to hang his body like that."

Jack stopped Walker in the front foyer. "Tony, I think you can handle this. If you find something…"

"I'll let you know," Walker said. "By the way, we did find a mason jar on the kitchen counter half full of dried flower petals. The label on the jar said it's Cherry Blossom Tea. I'll collect some of the blossoms from the trees in the yard just in case."

"I guess we found our source," Jack said. "We have to find Mindy and see how much of this stuff she was feeding Sonny. If she was drinking it too, she needs to be seen by a doctor."

"I don't think anyone's planning on coming back here," Walker said.

"Maybe Sully got Crispino? It had to have happened before Sgt. Mattingly's guys got here. They've been out there watching the house for hours, pod'na."

Walker said, "Give me the deputy's number and I'll call. I can send someone to Mercy to pick up the blood sample. Oh, I forgot to tell you. Captain Franklin called. Crispino rented a white 2016 Jeep Cherokee at the airport Budget Rental. Captain Franklin added it to your BOLO and called the deputy in Henderson."

Jack thanked Walker and he and Liddell walked to their car. Liddell drove over the lawn to get around the police units. Jack rubbed his hands together in front of the heat vent. "Tracker, Jeep, Sully," he said. "He was referring to his Jeep? Maybe he put a tracker on Sully's car?"

"Is there any way to track a tracker?" Liddell asked.

Jack took out his iPhone and said, "Siri, find a Radio Shack near me."

Siri responded, "I'm sorry, Supreme Commander. I don't understand that command."

Jack gripped the phone. "You bitch!"

Liddell took the phone from Jack and said, "Radio Shack." Siri came back with a local Radio Shack. Liddell told Siri to call the number. Siri did. He handed the phone back to Jack while it was ringing.

"You have to talk nice to her, pod'na. You sound grumpy all the time."

"I do not," Jack said. The call was answered. Jack identified himself. The clerk sounded like he was twelve years old but he knew fluent GPS.

Jack finished the call and said, "This kid said we couldn't find a tracker because it has to be paired with another device. Uncle Marty must have put one on Sully's vehicle. If Sully caught him skulking around here, that would explain some things. Sully's suddenly much more interesting."

"We wait for Marty's Jeep to be found," Liddell said.

"Pretty much. Let's go back to headquarters."

"Hi-Yo, Silver, away!" Liddell said. "Don't you watch television? Me Tonto? You Lone Ranger?"

"Me Jack. You crazy."

Chapter 34

Zackariah Pugh was sheltered in the doorway of the old Sam's Market on Columbia Street. Down the block was St. Anthony's Church. The church and rectory were still used by the parish, but the school had been turned into a homeless shelter. Zack spent many a night at St. Anthony's Shelter when it was bitter cold like the last few days. He'd told Dayton he was still sharing an apartment with his dad. He couldn't bring himself to tell her the truth, tell her that he hadn't seen his dear old dad for over a year. Not conscious.

He preferred living in shelters, abandoned houses and buildings. One time he'd watched an old couple load their car with luggage and leave. They were going to be gone a while. He broke a glass pane in the back door and stayed in their house for a couple of weeks before they came home and called the police. He'd been placed with a foster family as a result of that, but he didn't stay long. He thanked the nice people and left as soon as the caseworker was out of sight.

He had learned a lot of useful skills while living on the street. He'd learned how to steal what he needed, how to take what he wanted, how to stay in someone's house while the owners were gone. A guy at the shelter had shown him that one.

He fingered the wad of bills in his pocket. Finding the money had been good luck. Dayton came in the room before he could go through the clothes, and ran out of the house screaming. The guy's boots were a little big, but when he put the socks on over his own they took up the extra room. He'd helped himself to the jacket. It was heavy, better than anything he'd ever owned. That's when he found the money, the badge, the ring and the gun. Whoever killed the guy had put all this in the coat pockets.

He started to run out the back, but there was no way he would leave Dayton in the shape she was in. He'd promised to take care of her. He kept his promises, but he had the problem of what to do with some of the stuff he'd found. A guy at the shelter had told him the best hiding place was in plain sight. He went quickly through the rooms. Nothing good. He went out the back and saw a cleanout plug for a sewer line. He was able to get the plug unscrewed and put the gun and some of the money inside the pipe before he heard a car coming. He screwed the plug back in, shoved some roofing shingles over it and ran out front in time to see a cop car coming down the street.

He'd kept the badge and the ring. He'd thought maybe he'd wear it. But it was big on him, like the boots and jacket. He probably shouldn't have taken the guy's badge. He knew that now, because that was what got him caught.

He didn't appreciate the way that detective had roughed him up. He'd been in lots of fights, beat up some old drunks, but the detective scared him. He didn't like the feeling. Besides, the cop had no right taking the ring from him. For all they knew it was his ring. Of course the cops wouldn't believe someone like him would have anything like that unless it was stolen. It was true he'd taken the boots and coat and money, but he needed them, and the dead guy didn't.

The cop had taken everything from him—even his socks and combat boots—and kept them. The blue jean jacket was the only one he owned. Socks and boots too, for that matter. The woman from CPS had given him a CPO jacket that was two sizes too big, dress socks and a pair of oxford loafers with pennies stuck in the strap on top. She'd bought him a hamburger from Wendy's and sent him on his way. He'd known they'd release him. They always did.

As soon as he'd left CPS he hotfooted it over to the house where he'd hidden the gun and money. There were still some cops wearing those white CSI clothes, but they were all inside or going back and forth to a wagon out front. He waited until only one cop was left, and snuck around back. The roofing shingles had been disturbed. At first, he was afraid they'd found his stash, but it was all there. He stuffed the cash in his coat pocket, stuck the gun in his waistband, put the cleanout plug back and walked away at a pace befitting the cold.

A few blocks down the street he had squatted between two wrecked cars on Dewig's Body Shop parking lot and counted the money. Ten thousand! His first thought was that he could buy airline tickets for himself and Dayton to fly to Hollywood. Hitchhiking in this cold was crazy. He scrapped that idea. He wasn't sure if they'd need some kind of identification to get tickets.

He didn't have anything. Not even a birth certificate. But at least he had the money. They could take a Greyhound.

He'd taken the gun from the back of his waistband and popped the ammo magazine. It was loaded. He read the name on the side. Glock. A .45-caliber. Big-ass gun. He didn't know how to shoot, but he probably wouldn't need to anyway. Just the sight of it was enough to make someone back off. With a psycho running loose, and every badge-wearing mofo in the city knowing he was the one that found the cop's body, he'd need the gun. The cops wouldn't have given two shits if it was him or one of his friends at the shelter that were killed.

He'd taken his booty and gone to the Army Surplus Store on First Avenue, where he boosted a fatigue jacket to wear over the shitty CPO jacket. He'd walked back streets until he got to the CVS on the corner and called Dayton. She didn't answer, but they'd made a plan. She knew to wait a few hours and meet him outside the little market when she could get away.

The sun was out, but the wind felt like little razor blades, slicing away at his face and the backs of his hands. He shoved his hands inside the pockets of the fatigue jacket and hoped like hell Dayton would show up soon. Maybe she wouldn't show up at all. If that prick father of hers caught her sneaking out, Zack knew the cops would show up instead. That would be bad. Bad for the cop that tried to stop him.

He lit a Camel cigarette, non-filtered, from a pack he'd lifted from Sam's Market. The jerk behind the counter didn't even look American. He had it coming. Zack stuck the cigarette in the corner of his mouth and the wind blew ashes into his eyes. He blinked and wiped at his eyes with the back of the coat sleeve, trying to be cool. He stuffed the Bic lighter and the pack of Camels into his coat pocket and buried his hands in with them.

He crowded into the doorway, trying to get out of the cutting wind. He was dancing from one foot to the other, eyes still burning and watering from the cold and the smoke. When he turned back around, a brand-spanking-new black sedan pulled to the curb. The windows were dark. Zack couldn't see the driver, but he figured the guy had to be an asshole. People who owned cars like that always were. The passenger window powered down and an old dude leaned across the seat. He was smiling at Zack.

"Whatever you're sellin', I'm not buyin', asshole," Zack said and flipped the half-burned cigarette at the car door. That was another thing he'd learned from the homeless guys at the shelter. Rich dudes were always trying to pick up young guys.

Zack reached inside his jackets and fingered the butt of the gun. He didn't want to threaten the old turd with it because that would just bring more cops. Where the hell was Dayton? The driver continued to smile at him. The passenger door popped open.

"Shit!" Zack said under his breath and wrapped his fingers around the grip of the .45. "If you don't shut that door, you'll be sorry," he said, making his voice as threatening as he knew how. He was an actor, so he had practiced it. It sounded pretty good.

The man's smile grew wider, and the back passenger window powered down.

"What the..." Zack said.

Dayton sat in the back of the car, unnaturally still, tears running down her cheek.

"You asked for it," Zack said. He leaned down in the car window with one hand on the gun and froze. The barrel of a gun pushed against his forehead.

"Give me the gun and get in, hotshot," Sully said.

"Please do what he says, Zack." Dayton's face had gone white, and he could see a long red mark across her forehead. A trickle of blood ran from one of her nostrils.

Zack slowly handed over the gun and slid into the passenger seat. He asked, "You okay, Dy?"

"She won't be if you say anything else," Sully said, and shoved the gun into Zack's ribs while he patted him down. Sully switched the gun to his left hand. "If you do anything I don't like I'll make you watch me kill your girlfriend. You understand?"

Zack nodded and said in a trembling voice, "What's going on? Who are you?"

"Shut up," Sully ordered, and Zack did. "Now put your seat belt on. Going without is not only illegal, it's unsafe."

Sully rested his left forearm across his lap, the gun's barrel pointed at Zack. Zack pulled the seat belt over his shoulder and clicked it in place. "Now sit on your hands and keep them there."

Zack put his hands under his buttocks.

"Ain't love grand?" Sully pulled away from the curb.

Chapter 35

A uniformed officer waylaid Jack and Liddell as soon as they entered the back doors of the detectives' office. "The chief's asking for you in the lobby."

"More meetings. Just what we need," Liddell said.

The officer said, "Not *the* Chief. Double Dick. He's in the lobby surrounded by reporters. I heard him promise an interview with you two."

"You didn't see us," Jack said and turned for the door.

"Too late," the officer said. "He heard you tell dispatch you'd be at Headquarters. He was standing ten feet away from me. Sorry."

"That's what happens when you keep your radio turned on. Rookie move," Jack said, and the officer grinned. "Let's get this over with, Bigfoot."

"Oh. Since I had my radio on," the officer said, "I heard a missing person run come in. It sounds like the girl you brought in this morning is gone again. Dayton Bolin, right?"

"How long ago?" Jack asked.

"Maybe thirty minutes."

"Who got the run? Please tell me it's not Jansen," Jack said.

"I think Sergeant Woehler took it."

"Great. Thanks," Jack said. "I take back all those nasty things I was thinking."

"Don't be nice to me, Jack. Scares me," the officer said and got out of the area quick.

Jack and Liddell entered the lobby. The officer had lied. Double Dick wasn't surrounded. Only a handful of reporters were present. Most had probably left when they heard Jack was coming. He was not known for his cooperation with the media.

Double Dick spotted Jack and Liddell. "Here's our investigators now. Detective Jack Murphy and Detective Liddell Blanchard," he said unnecessarily. "They can answer a few questions, but I'm sure they need to get back to work, ladies and gentlemen."

Someone from Channel 18 shoved a microphone in Jack's face. "Detective Murphy, are you making any progress in Sergeant Caparelli or Judge Knight's murders?"

A woman from Channel 12 asked, "Are the murders related? Have you talked to their families yet?"

That was newspeak for "Can we get film footage of someone in the family crying? Even a complete stranger crying will do."

Jack said, "I can't answer any questions concerning an ongoing investigation."

Jack and Liddell turned around and headed for their office.

"Very diplomatic, pod'na."

"Screw a bunch of media," Jack said loud enough for the reporters to hear. "They'd suck the blood out of a leech." *How's that for a sound bite?*

Deputy Chief Richard Dick said, "The detective is correct. It's not police department policy for the investigator to talk with the news media during an ongoing investigation." He glared at Jack's back. "I can't tie up the investigation, folks. I'll answer the questions I can. Please, one at a time."

Liddell punched Jack playfully on the shoulder and said, "Yea, though I walk through the valley of Double Dick, I shall fear no reprisal."

"Screw Double Dick," Jack said. "Twice."

"Feel better?"

"No."

They went to the office and Jack called Deputy Findlay to request a blood sample be taken from Uncle Marty. Findlay sent a nurse to get the blood sample. "Crispino's still out cold," he said. "Is it a good or bad thing that he's still alive?"

"Too early to say," Jack said, and disconnected the call. Jack put the phone on speaker and called Detective Woehler in the Juvenile Unit. He was out of the office. Jack called Woehler's cell.

"Woehler," the phone was answered.

"I'm on speakerphone. Don't say anything bad about Bigfoot," Jack said.

"Jack, I was wondering when I'd hear from you," Woehler said. "I just finished taking the report from Mr. and Mrs. Bolin and they're not happy. Ain't this the shits?"

"When did she go missing?" Jack asked.

"We don't know an exact time," Woehler said. "The parents picked her up here this morning and went home. Mrs. Bolin went to the store and Mr. Bolin had to go in to his office. When Mrs. Bolin came home an hour ago Dayton was gone. No note. Nothing. Dad is going postal. Mom needs a Xanax."

"Did she run off with Zack again?"

"No one has seen that kid all day. CPS took him home and dropped him off. I had officers check his neighborhood. We can't find his dad and we checked every bar around. But I did get something on Dayton. Let me pull over."

Jack waited and Woehler came back on the line.

"I checked with Dayton's neighbors. The woman across the street said a newer black car pulled up in front of the Bolin's house. A tallish man in a dark suit got out and went to the front door. Dayton followed him to the car and got in. He left. The neighbor thought it was one of Mr. Bolin's banker friends. She thinks that was around two hours ago."

"Did she have a better description of the man or his car?" Jack asked.

"White male, late forties to early fifties, thin, tall, expensive black suit. No beard or glasses that she could recall. The car was a Mercedes sedan. She remembers that because it's almost the same as Mr. Bolin's car."

"I don't expect she got the license plate number?" Jack asked.

"No luck there. Do you know who it is? I'm debating an Amber Alert, but wanted to give it a few more minutes to see if we can find Zack. What do you think?"

"I think I know who picked her up," Jack said. "I'll have Liddell text you the information. We already have a BOLO on this guy and his car. You should do the Amber Alert and mention this guy. His name is Vincent Sullis."

"Do we suspect he's the one that took her?"

"Yeah," Jack said. Liddell was already texting the information to Woehler's cell. "Put the Amber Alert out. He's an attorney from Boston. The car will have Massachusetts license plates that read SO SU ME.

Jack hung up and called Frank Tunney's cell phone.

"Jack. Glad you called. I heard you have Martin Crispino in custody," Tunney said.

"He's at Mercy Hospital in Henderson."

"Kentucky?" Tunney said.

"Yeah," Jack said. "Crispino was found unconscious on the river bank and doesn't know how he got there. He admitted being at Sonny's house, then waking up in the hospital. He's got a hell of a head wound and hypothermia. They're keeping him knocked out."

"How did he get hypothermia?" Tunney asked.

"Why don't you come by the office and I'll fill you in?"

"No can do," Tunney said. "I'm on my way to meet with someone. I won't be long."

Liddell said, "You don't have any friends. Where are you really going?"

Jack could hear sounds of traffic in the background. "I'll give you the brief version since your friends are more important to you than catching a multi-murderer." He filled Tunney in on the visit with Crispino.

"Crispino thinks these killings are revenge for the murder of a college student from five or six years ago?" Tunney asked. "If that's true, you have to ask yourself the question: What role do the monkey carvings and spikes play?"

Jack said, "I have an idea."

"Enlighten me."

"Crispino said this mobster's son raped and killed the girl. The mobster is Big Bobby Touhey. Ever hear of him?"

"Name doesn't ring a bell."

"Sonny and Sully were Boston detectives back then and worked for Touhey. Touhey had a kid, Little Bobby, who killed the girl, and Big Bobby asked them to get rid of the body. Sonny and Sully burned the body to destroy the evidence. The Boston detective I talked to said Little Bobby was killed a few weeks ago in Boston. He was cut open, his stuff was cut off and nailed to the floor with a railroad spike. They found another of these monkeys in his throat. Do No Evil this time. Hey, you ever heard of a Detective Yankowski?"

"No. I haven't been to Boston for quite a while. Did he say he knew me?"

"No. No," Jack said. "Yankowski said some creep came forward and confessed to killing the girl and burning her body. Yankowski didn't believe him, but he was convicted and given a five-year sentence. Guess who the Assistant D.A. was that made the plea deal?"

"Judge Knight," Tunney said.

"You should have been an FBI profiler," Jack said.

"Do they have any leads on this Little Bobby's killer?" Tunney asked.

"Not that Yankowski told me. He's digging on that end and will get back to me. Looks like we're looking for the same killer," Jack said.

"You're probably on to something there, Jack. You've connected the dots, but I say again, how are the monkeys and the spikes involved?"

"I thought you would tell me," Jack said.

"Okay. I'll be your Huckleberry. A monkey was found in the throats of all three victims. Sonny, Knight and Little Bobby. Each carving depicts a different part of the legend of the Wise Monkeys. See No Evil. That's Sonny. Hear No Evil, Knight. Do No Evil, Little Bobby. If we're right,

Sully will be next. Speak No Evil. I thought this guy Marty was interesting, but now I think he was just in the wrong place at the right time because he wasn't killed."

Jack asked, "What do you think of the old case Sonny and Sully were involved with in Boston? Knight gave the confessed killer a sweet deal. Maybe someone's getting even."

"It makes sense to me," Tunney said. "Any chance you can interview the guy that confessed to the girl's murder?"

Jack said, "He was killed in prison."

"Oh. Well, did Crispino see anything? Any leads there or is that just a coincidence?" Tunney asked.

Jack said, "Uncle Marty either didn't see who hit him, or he's lost some of his memory. The doctor said he could have memory loss. In any case, I don't think he wants to be involved anymore."

"And you say Sully and Mindy are missing. Are they answering their phones?"

"No. I put a BOLO out on them and Sully's car. Mindy's was left at the house. They left quickly. There's something else you need to know," Jack said. "I think Sully kidnapped one of the kids that found Sonny's body. This happened almost two hours ago. I'm not positive it was Sully, but he drives a black Mercedes sedan, and a witness across from the girl's house saw her leaving with a guy that matches Sully's description. In a black Mercedes."

Tunney was silent and Jack asked, "What are you thinking, Frank?"

"Oh, probably nothing," Tunney said.

"Come on. Give."

"Okay. I'm just thinking outside the box here," Tunney said. "What if Mindy and Sully are the ones behind all of this? You said Mindy called Sully to come to Evansville. Sully showed up at Mindy's several hours before Sonny's murder, to the best of your knowledge."

"That's right," Jack said.

"Now Sully and Mindy drop off the radar. Knight is found burned up in his car. And remember, Sully was in Boston—or in that area—when Little Bobby was killed. When he comes to Evansville you have two more murders. All with monkey carvings. All extreme violence. That kind of violence wouldn't bother a cop."

"Or an ex-cop," Jack added.

Tunney continued, "You said yourself that you thought Sonny was skimming from the money seized in drug raids. Maybe he's done it before but didn't get caught."

"If Big Bobby suspected Sonny of stealing he might have sent Sully to talk to his old partner," Jack said.

"And just maybe Sully wants what Sonny has. A big house, big money, expensive toys, and Mindy."

Jack agreed with him.

"Sully sounds sharp enough to set this up," Tunney said. "Maybe the monkeys were a diversion. Leaving the money behind was a ploy to make us think the motive for the killing was revenge. Maybe it was about the oldest motive in the world. Love, or sex, or whatever passes for a relationship these days."

Jack said, "Mindy couldn't leave Sonny without losing everything she has. The house was in her name, but I'm sure Sonny had a way around that if she left. Maybe something like a pre-nup."

Jack thought it over. It sounded right. "But why kidnap the girl?" Jack asked.

"I'm not sure, but I think he's wanting to eliminate any possible witnesses to Sonny's murder. He's not sure how much they really know," Tunney said. "This is all theorizing, Jack. It just makes me wonder why Sully's not dead. If he's not the killer, why hasn't the killer gotten to him?"

"Good point," Jack said.

"Jack, I've got to get off here. I'm almost to my meeting. Keep what we've talked about in the back of your mind. Better too much caution than not enough. If you find Sully, you should consider him armed and dangerous. He could be your killer. Mindy too, for that matter."

"Well, thanks for the brainstorming session. Enjoy your meeting," Jack said.

"I always do."

Chapter 36

Sully drove north into Vanderburgh County. He'd scouted this area before going to Mindy's, and was now glad he did. He didn't know if that detective was looking for him, but he definitely didn't want to be found now.

He pulled in behind The Peaks Inn and parked close to the door to the room he'd put Mindy in.

He pointed a finger at Zack. "Sit," he ordered, got out and walked around the vehicle. Sully opened Dayton's door and pulled her from the car by the arm. He opened Zack's door, grabbed him by the back of his coat collar and yanked him from the car.

"Listen to me, you little shit. You try anything, the first bullet goes into your girlfriend.

We're going in that door, straight ahead, single file, just like in school. You act up or talk, you get demerits." He shoved the gun in Dayton's back to press his point.

Zack went first and said over his shoulder, "People will be looking for us. That detective…"

Sully slapped the gun into the side of Zack's head. Zack staggered face-first into the brick wall of the inn. Sully put his arm around Dayton, grabbed a fistful of Zack's fatigue jacket and pulled them together. He shoved them toward the door.

Zack said, "If you touch her again, I'll kill you."

Sully shoved Dayton into the door and bounced her forehead against the door twice. No one came to the door.

"Shit. Mindy! You'd better not be passed out drunk."

To Dayton, Sully said, "Knock, bitch. Make it loud."

Dayton raised her hand and tapped on the door.

"I said loud," Sully said threateningly.

Dayton raised her hand again and knocked.

A woman's voice came from inside. "Who is it?"

Sully said, "Open the damn door, Mindy."

The latch turned and the door opened on the security chain. A pale face peeked through the crack. "Sully. I didn't know you was bringing visitors." The door closed, the chain came off and the door opened again.

Sully pushed Dayton and Zack inside, keeping a hand on Dayton's arm. He said to Mindy, "Put the chain on the front door."

Mindy stared at the gun in Sully's hand. "I don't understand…"

"Put the chain on the front door, dummy. Do it."

She seemed frozen.

"Now, Mindy!"

She walked to the front of the room with an obvious sway in her step. She had taken her sweater and shoes off and was in a see-through bra and tight jeans. Sully pushed them past the smelly bathroom toward a filthy kitchenette.

The kitchenette boasted a stove, mini refrigerator, counter and two barstools with backs. Two new rolls of silver duct tape were on the kitchenette counter. Sully forced Zack on one stool. Dayton climbed up on the other and sat without being told to. Sully kept the gun pointed at Zack and said, "Mindy, get the tape."

She looked confused. Sully said, "The tape, Mindy," and glared at her.

Mindy picked up the roll of tape and held it out to Sully.

"You do it," Sully said. "Do him first."

Zack held his wrists out and Sully said, "Put them behind your back, smart guy."

Mindy taped Zack's wrists. "Now her," Sully said, and Mindy obeyed.

Sully put his gun back in his holster and took the duct tape from Mindy. He wrapped the tape round and round Zack's legs and upper body, securing him to the barstool. He secured Dayton to the barstool in a similar fashion.

"I never seen you like this, Sully," Mindy said.

A malicious grin spread on his face.

"Don't you think you done enough—"

"Shut up and do what you're told," Sully snapped at her. "Go sit on the couch."

Mindy did as he said.

"What are you gonna do?" she asked.

He drew the gun. "Depends on what they have to tell me. If they lie, they die."

"He won't shoot—" Zack said. The blast was deafening in the small room, and a small hole appeared in the top of Zack's right boot. Zack's mouth hung open. Pain from a gunshot wound isn't immediate. It grows on you. When it did, Zack said, "Son of a…" and shut his mouth.

Dayton stared at Zack's face and then down at his bleeding foot.

"Now. Where were we?" Sully said. "Oh yeah. You're going to tell me everything you know. Everything."

Dayton continued to stare at Zack's boot.

Sully pointed the gun at Dayton's feet. "You first, girlie. Talk."

She did. Dayton told Sully everything she remembered, from meeting Zack on the street, to the police releasing her to her parents. "And then you came to my house and told me you were a cop and needed me to come downtown again to look at some pictures and I told you I didn't see anyone and you said I needed to come with you anyway and I told you I was meeting Zack again and…"

"Shut up," Sully commanded. He'd been watching Zack's face to judge the truth in the girl's words. He was good at spotting lies. "Now you," he said to Zack, the gun still trained on Dayton's feet.

Tears ran from the corners of Zack's eyes. The pain was unbelievable. He felt like he was going to pass out.

"I'll ask questions, you answer," Sully said. "Otherwise you and your girlfriend will have matching limps."

Zack said, "I'll tell you. Honest, mister."

"Yes, you will," Sully said. "First question."

Sully asked Zack how he came to pick the exact house there was a dead body in. He asked if Zack had seen any cars moving on his way to the house. He asked dozens of questions, and Zack's answers were basically the same as Dayton's, with the exception of the gun, and the ten thousand dollars. He hadn't seen any cars on the streets. He didn't know of Sonny Caparelli.

"The money I found was taken by the cops. I swear to God!"

Sully backhanded Zack with the gun and stuck the barrel against Dayton's head. "Is he telling the truth, honey? I'll know."

Dayton screamed, "Zack! Give him all the money if you really love me."

"Honest, mister. I ain't got any. I kept some from the cops, but a couple of those homeless guys by where you found me took it," Zack lied.

Sully slapped him across the face with the gun for the second time, leaving a gash under Zack's eye. "Don't lie to me. If I find the money on you, that's it for your girlfriend." To Dayton he said, "I guess he doesn't really love you."

"Okay. Okay. It's in my underwear. Ten thousand bucks," Zack said.

"Mindy," Sully said and looked back at her. She was sitting on the broken-down sofa. She had put her sweater back on but she was still barefoot.

"Get your ass over here. I got a job that was made just for you."

"Sully, I don't want to. Please don't make me. You're scaring me."

"You're not in one of these chairs," Sully said. "Get busy."

Mindy knelt in front of Zack and unzipped his jeans. She put a hand down in Zack's jeans and turned her face toward Sully. "What am I supposed to get?"

"You're not looking for his nuts. You heard the kid. The money's down in his crotch. You were always good at diving for money. Now dive."

She reached deeper and her hand came out with a wad of cash.

"You got some balls, kid," Sully said. "I'll give you that." He waggled the gun at Mindy and said, "Don't he have some balls?"

Mindy held the money out to Sully.

"Count it," Sully ordered. "I'm not touching something that's been up his crack."

Mindy counted agonizingly slowly. "Ten grand, Sully."

Sully said, "Go take a seat. Hang on to the money." He took the gun away from Dayton's head. "Telling the truth wasn't so hard, was it?" He smacked Zack in the nose with the butt of the gun.

Zack's nose gushed blood. Zack's face dropped and he shook his head, slinging blood across Sully's suit and shoes.

"You little son of a…"

"Stop it, Sully!" Mindy cried. "He's had enough. You got what you wanted. Just stop."

"You hear that, kid? She wants me to stop. Do you want me to stop too?" he asked Dayton.

Mindy doubled over, hands covering her mouth. "Sully, I think I'm gonna get sick."

"Not in here. Go outside. Get some air."

She headed for the door and he said, "Put your shoes on first, dumbass. I'll yell if I need you again."

She slid her shoes on and said, "Sure, Sully." She hurried outside.

* * * *

Mindy stepped out into the cold air and shut the door to the room. She was feeling kind of sick, but mostly she just wanted to get out of there. Sully was so focused on the two kids he didn't notice she had taken the keys to his Mercedes. She hurried around behind the motel, quietly unlocked the door of the Mercedes and slid behind the wheel. She waited until she heard a big truck coming down the road before starting the engine. She hoped the noise from the truck would mask the car starting. Her luck held.

She backed out and pulled onto New Harmony Road. She had no idea where she was going but she saw a sign for Diamond Avenue. She stayed on New Harmony Road and pulled smoothly into the light traffic on Diamond Avenue heading east. She remembered the airport was that way. She still had some cash. She had her credit cards, and her driver's license in a pocket of the jeans. She was thankful she had thought to grab all of that before Sully rushed her from her house.

Sully would be killing mad when he discovered she had left. Taken his car to boot. She'd seen what he did to that boy. That could be her. She'd always had a thing for Sully—even when she was with Sonny—but she had no illusions what she was to him.

"Just another whore," she said, and said it again, "Just a whore. That's what I am." She wanted to be angry, sad, anything but scared. "Screw you, Sully!" she said loudly, and tried to laugh, but it came out ugly and stiff with fright.

A white Jeep sat beside the road, exhaust plumes trailing out. The man sitting inside watched her closely.

Chapter 37

Zack grimaced in pain. Both eyes were swollen shut. The cut on his right cheekbone smarted and caused the eye to water constantly. Blood ran down his face and into his mouth. He was afraid to spit the blood out, fearing it would set the guy off again. He let it dribble down his chin. Sully had given up pistol-whipping Zack and slipped on leather gloves.

"I used to be a cop. You didn't know that," Sully said.

Zack had stopped listening. The pain was his world.

Sully landed a hard blow on Zack's ribs, driving the air from his chest. Zack gasped for air. The pain of broken ribs brought him back to the present.

"I kept some of my gear when I resigned—like these gloves. Three ounces of lead pellets in each one." Sully delivered a one-two punch to Zack's face and chest. Sully danced like a boxer and landed several more blows.

Zack's head lolled and hung to his chest. Sully could see the kid was barely breathing. There was no way this kid was still holding back. He'd already tried to say he was only getting rid of Sonny's body and it was his father who murdered him. He told Sully he was with the Narcotics Unit and was following Sonny. He would implicate his own mother if it stopped the beating. He knew the kid couldn't take much more, or it would kill him. He didn't care.

Sully pulled the gloves off, reached in his pocket and took out a switchblade. He yanked Zack's head back and put the tip of the blade under his chin. "You're running on empty, pal. I believe you. So now it's your punch's turn," Sully said, and pulled the blade through both sides of Zack's mouth. Zack passed out.

Sully went to the kitchen and rummaged around in the cabinets. He found a dented stew pot someone had left behind. He filled it with water and poured it over Zack's head. Zack came to sputtering. Dayton started screaming, and Sully said, "What's the matter, hon? You afraid I might do something like this?" Sully swung the pot into the side of Zack's head. He could hear something crunch. He threw the pot into the kitchen and said, "Listen kid, I want you to listen to your girlfriend beg you to tell me about the man who killed my friend. I don't want to hear any more made-up shit."

Zack mumbled. The words were garbled, but the implication was still there. "Touch her and I'll kill you."

Sully laughed out loud. "I almost like you, kid. You're tough as nails. You can take my admiration to the grave with you."

Sully slashed out with the knife, the blade cutting across the side of Dayton's face. She screamed and screamed, until Sully slapped her across the face. Hard.

Dayton stopped and said through puffy lips, "You don't have to do this, mister. We don't know who you are. I swear we won't tell anyone. Let us go and we'll just disappear. Please. Don't hurt us any—"

"Shut up!" Sully yelled, but for some reason the murderous excitement he'd felt while beating the boy was no longer there. He almost felt pity. He knew he'd gone too far to stop now. He had to kill them. He had to be able to tell Big Bobby that these two were no longer an issue. Big Bobby would expect that much if Sully wanted to keep his own life.

Suddenly he couldn't stand to see her face, those eyes pleading with him to stop. She was pretty and young and had her whole life ahead of her. Or she would have if she hadn't hooked up with the punk. Sully wanted to end this. Neither of them knew shit. And where the hell was Mindy?

He shook pillowcases from two flattened pillows on the bed and slipped them over the kids' heads. The girl began to panic, the cloth sucking in and out. He'd have to do her first.

He pulled his gun to shoot them both. The door behind him opened. "About effing time, Mindy! Where the hell have you been?"

An arm went around Sully's throat, drawing him back while another arm locked his head in a vise grip. Sully struggled. His breath was crushed from him, his strength was quickly fading, vision turning gray. His arms fell limp; the gun fell from his hand and clattered on the linoleum floor.

A man said in a kind voice, "Shhh. You're both safe now. Someone will come to get you soon. I promise."

"He's hurt real bad," Dayton said. "Please, mister. Please help us." There was no response. "Are you there?"

She heard a grunt, and scraping sounds, the door by the bathroom opened, scraping sounds again, and the door closed. A car engine started. She could hear the crunch of tires fading.

Chapter 38

Judy Mangold, the chief's secretary, stood in the doorway of Jack and Liddell's office. She was holding a thick sheaf of papers in front of her.

"Who uses a fax anymore?" she asked, as if this was akin to an alien spaceship landing in her office.

Jack took the papers from her. She turned and walked away without another word.

Jack glanced at the top sheet. "It's the stuff from Detective Yankowski." He handed pages to Liddell as he read them. He had only read a few pages when the phone on his desk rang.

"Murphy," he said.

"Don't you have your cell phone?" the police dispatcher asked.

"Sorry," he said. "What's up?" He'd left his phone in the car again.

"Deputy Findlay is trying to reach you."

Jack borrowed Liddell's cell phone and called Findlay. "What have you got?"

Findlay said, "Mr. Crispino came to and remembered something. He has a GPS tracker in his Jeep. You probably already know that. He said he put a device on Sully's car. If you find the Jeep, you'll find Sully if you're within a couple of miles. Have you found the Jeep?"

"Not yet," Jack said. "You put the BOLO on all of this out in Henderson, right?"

"Yeah. And Crispino said he was pretty sure it wasn't Sully who clocked him."

"Does he have any idea who it was?" Jack asked.

"No. But he said something else you might want to know. He asked if he could go into witness protection. He said he could name names if we could promise him that."

"Witness protection. Did he say the names were in reference to our murders?" Jack asked.

"He wouldn't say. He will only talk to a Federal Officer, and only if he gets a written guarantee signed by a U.S. District Attorney. He said he doesn't like the deals you make."

"I just happen to be working with a Fed on these murders," Jack said. "Special Agent Frank Tunney might be contacting you. I'll give him your number."

Jack found Tunney's number in Liddell's contacts and called. It rang several times and was picked up by voice mail. Jack left a message to call as soon as possible.

"He's not answering. I guess we'd better call Captain Franklin and fill him in on Crispino," Jack said, and handed the phone back to Liddell.

* * * *

Sully woke slowly. His throat was swollen and he couldn't swallow. He felt like his neck had been broken. He hurt everywhere. He tried to move his arms and discovered they were bound tightly behind his back. His chest felt tight, like it was being crushed, and bolts of pain shot from his shoulders to the tips of his fingers. He heard gravel crunching and tried to turn in the direction of the noise, but all that turned was his head, causing bolts of pain behind his eyes and more pain in his shoulders. He blinked. His eyes were open, but he could barely make out shapes in the darkness that surrounded him.

Suddenly a bright light flashed into his eyes. He squeezed them shut against the pain the light was causing. The light went out and he could see intermittent dots and flashes. He didn't know where he was. How he'd gotten here.

The crunching-gravel sound stopped and he heard a continuous rustling sound in the distance, like tires on pavement. He cut his eyes that direction and saw tiny dots moving. Headlights. A truck. A tractor-trailer. The pain behind his eyes receded. His senses worked again. He could smell mildew. No. The odor was dry, thick. Maybe he was in a farm field. He could smell oil mixed with the other. He heard something close. Off to his left.

"Who's there?" Sully asked.

"Is this going to be a knock-knock joke?" A man's voice startled him.

Sully struggled to turn toward the voice, but there was still that tightness across his chest. "Who are you? What is this? What the hell do you want from me?"

"Funny you should mention Hell, Sully."

The voice was coming from directly in front now.

"Where am I?" Sully asked. "What are you going to do to me?"

The voice now came from his other side. The man was moving around him. Like a predator sizing up his prey.

"Who the hell are you?" Sully demanded, but the panic growing in his gut told him who it was.

"Don't you know?"

Sully's mouth went dry. "You're crazy. That's who you are. A crazy man. Let me down from here. Let me down and face me like a man."

"A man? Is that what you think you are? No. You're not a man. You're the shit I wipe off my shoe in the grass. You're worse than Sonny was. He at least had someone to care for, and to care for him. But you? What do you have? What makes your life worth anything?"

Sully said nothing. He wouldn't beg.

"Remember Little Bobby?"

"I didn't have nothing to do with Little Bobby," Sully said. "If Big Bobby sent you, he's got the wrong guy. You must be Crispino. The Machine. I heard of you. You and me—we got something in common."

"Oh. What is that?"

"We both clean up Big Bobby's messes. Sonny, the judge, you—me. He uses us like hand wipes. We don't count for squat. He'll do to you what he told you to do me. You know that, don't you? We should work together. You and me."

"You and me," the voice repeated Sully's words.

Sully thought he heard interest in that voice, and a tiny glimmer of hope danced in his mind. "Yeah. You and me. We've got something Big Bobby needs. We've got skills, and the capacity to carry things to the end. You got rid of Sonny and the judge—even Little Bobby. That took some skill. You caught me out, big time. I gotta give you that. But it don't mean it's got to end this way."

The voice asked, "Doesn't it?"

Sully was on a roll, like a train with no brakes. "Hell no, it don't. You let me go and we'll work together. I've got almost half a million of Big Bobby's money. I can get that much more in jewelry. It's ours for the taking."

"If I wanted the money I could have taken it, Sully. But what you say interests me. Big Bobby does seem to attract people like us, doesn't he?"

Sully lifted his face even though it caused more pain. Sully was determined to get out of this. And when he did he was going to take this peckerwood's head off his shoulders. No. He'd bury this asshole and tell Big

Bobby where he could dig him up. Maybe Big Bobby would be satisfied. Sully could be a hero.

"He does. He'll use you to get me, and he'll send someone to take you out. Let me down from here and we'll make a plan. I think we should eliminate Big Bobby first," Sully said.

"I agree with you, Sully. Big Bobby needs to die."

"Cut me down," Sully said, trying to keep the pleading out of his voice.

The click of a switchblade opening next to his face startled Sully and his head jerked away from the sound. "Hey. No. Wait," he said.

"I took this from you. That was bad of me. Here, I'll give it back." The blade drove deep into Sully's groin.

"Oh shit! Oh shit!" Sully said. His words melded into the mewling hoarse whisper of impending death.

"You're not dying. Suck it up, Sully. I would say be a man, but you've wet yourself."

A wet stain bloomed across Sully's crotch.

"Okay, that might be blood. Come on, Sully. Convince me not to kill you. You can do better than tell me what I'm going to do next. You always were the planner in the bunch, weren't you?"

Sully's head hung forward. He lifted his face and screamed at the top of his lungs. "Help! Help!"

"Sonny was good at following orders. He didn't start out a greedy, corrupt cop. You made him that way. Bit by bit, you lured him into the slime of your world until it was too late to get free. I felt a little sorry for him, in fact. Left to his own means he might have led a boring little cop's life. Making runs, making arrests, writing citations. But that was never good enough for you, was it?"

"Someone will come. The cops will come," Sully said.

"No one can hear you except me. Well, maybe the squirrels or birds. No one is coming to help you, Sully. You're going to die like you lived. Alone."

Sully gritted his teeth. "You're him. You're the one Big Bobby wants dead."

The man put his face inches from Sully's, but there was no light of recognition in Sully's eyes.

"Listen to me. I don't know you," Sully said. He'd promised himself he wouldn't beg, but the next words that came from his mouth echoed the pleas he'd heard many times and ignored. "You can let me go and I won't say anything. I'll tell you where the money is. The jewelry. You can have it all."

"I can take anything I want."

The switchblade was yanked from Sully's groin and slashed across Sully's nose and cheek. Sully whipped his face side to side, trying to avoid the blade, but it came at him again and again, slicing flesh, scraping across teeth and bone until his face was a crisscross of bloody, gaping cuts. Screams filled the void his mind had retreated to.

The cutting stopped. Every beat of his heart pumped blood from his injuries. Blood poured down his throat, gagged him, and dribbled down his destroyed lips and chin.

"Your own mother wouldn't recognize you, Sully. You're a mess."

Sully couldn't speak. He just hung there, bleeding.

The man held a small, pale object close to Sully's eyes. "I'm sure you've heard the tale of the wise monkeys."

Sully recognized the voice. This was the man who had been calling him with the information on the investigation. The whole time the man was setting him up, driving him like a mouse into a trap.

He was beyond caring. He knew he was going into shock. His body was shutting down to preserve basic functions like breathing. He'd been taught at the police academy that shock could be temporarily countered by a burst of adrenaline. He had to get angry to hang on.

He spit blood through torn lips. "Kill me. I must have hurt you more than you've hurt me. I made you crazy." Sully tried to laugh but nothing came.

"We'll see," the man said. He bent over, then held a red plastic container high over Sully's head. The gasoline splashed down Sully's head, into his eyes, into the cuts, causing a burning pain beyond belief. A gloved hand grabbed Sully by the throat, shoving his head up and back, and squeezed until Sully's mouth popped open involuntarily. Something small, hard, was shoved past his teeth, past his tongue and deep into his throat."

Sully tried desperately to breathe, to expel the foreign item, to live. The last thing he saw on this earth was a flame that burst into life. It was him.

Chapter 39

It was fully dark out. A dusting of white flakes blew across the parking lot. Jack pulled his coat tight and went back inside. The cold air helped to clear his head, but what he really wanted was to clear this case. That, or four fingers of Scotch, neat.

Jack went back to the office and found Liddell leaned back in a chair in the corner, legs spread out in front of him, eyes shut. Jack stepped over Liddell's legs to get to his desk, and one of Liddell's eyes cracked open.

"I'm awake. Just thinking," Liddell said.

"Well, go back to sleep. I'll kick you if something breaks."

Liddell straightened in his chair. "I was thinking, pod'na. I do that sometimes, you know."

Captain Franklin came into their office.

"Nothing yet, Captain," Jack said. "Some interesting ideas, but we're pretty much waiting for our net to catch Vincent Sullis and/or Sonny's girlfriend, Mindy."

"Has Tunney been able to help?"

"He's helped a bunch," Liddell said.

"There's not much we can do until we catch up with Sully and Mindy," Jack said.

"You figure Mindy for the killings?" Captain Franklin asked.

"No," Jack said. "She's not capable of thinking this up, according to everyone that knows her."

"Don't discount her just because she's a woman, Jack. I've known some very devious people that put on a good front of being stupid."

"Yeah. Liddell, for instance," Jack said.

"Hey!" Bigfoot said. "I resemble that remark."

"Walker said he found some poisonous plant material at her house," Captain Franklin said.

"We were acting on information Dr. John gave us concerning the toxicology report on Sonny," Jack said. "Dr. John said the poison wasn't the cause of death, but if the level had increased in his system it could have killed him. I don't make Mindy for the botanist type, Captain. We had Walker seize her computer to see if she was cruising poison sites, but that's a long shot. Tunney thinks it's possible Mindy and Sully are an item, and she might be acting under his direction."

"What you're saying is that when the poison wasn't working fast enough, Sully came to help things along?" Captain Franklin asked.

"Something along those lines," Jack said. "Tunney thinks it might be for love...and money."

"Or the love of money," the captain said.

"Yeah." Liddell said. "When we talked to Mindy the first time, she said she suspected Sonny was cheating on her."

"I think that was a slip," Jack said. "She didn't stay on the script Sully wrote for her. He would know that would make her a suspect in the murder. He didn't want her to talk to us in the first place."

"It's odd that she just happened to have her attorney/family friend with her when her significant other is murdered," Captain Franklin said. "It's like they were waiting for the police to show up."

Captain Franklin stood in the office doorway, thinking. He said, "And you say Martin Crispino is in the hospital asking for the Witness Protection Program?"

"We've not ruled him out for Sonny's death. He was talking to us when the call came in about Judge Knight. Maybe to establish some kind of alibi."

"So he couldn't have killed Knight," Liddell said.

"I don't think he did that, but he may be working with someone else," Jack said.

"And they turned on each other? Maybe that's what sent Uncle Marty to the hospital, and he's not giving up his partner's name, waiting to take care of this himself?" Captain Franklin suggested.

"Possible," Jack said. "We'll know more when we pick up Sully and Mindy."

Captain Franklin said, "I hear the two juveniles that found Sonny's body are missing again? Is that involved?"

Jack wanted to get back to the stack of faxed papers from Detective Yankowski, go through them for the third time. But when your boss asks questions—at least if you respect him—you answer the questions. Captain Franklin was a man Jack definitely respected. Trusted? Sometimes. The man did have the hots for Jack's ex-wife, Katie, but hey, who wouldn't.

Jack said, "Woehler put an Amber Alert out on the missing kids. The boy, Zack, could be missing and no one would notice. The girl is a straight-A student from a good family, lots of friends, and up until she ran away she had a plan for her future."

"Ahh. Young love," Captain Franklin said. "You two have to catch this psycho. You're my best guys. Get it done. That's an order." He left.

"My best guys? Did he say that?" Liddell asked.

The phone rang. Jack picked up.

"Jack, you'd better get over here," Sergeant Mattingly said.

Chapter 40

The police officer working the ER desk at Deaconess Hospital was tired. He'd already put in a full shift, dealing with drunks and intervening in he-said she-said domestic squabbles. He came straight to his off-duty job at Deaconess, where he had to put up with another eight hours of the same. He didn't need what the ambulance had brought in on top of his already shitty day. When Jack and Liddell came through the ER doors, he led the way to the treatment rooms.

"The girl's in there. The doctor's with her."

The treatment rooms were aluminum and tempered-glass cubicles with curtains all around the inside. Four of these rooms lined one side of the hallway. Two of them had the curtains pulled closed. Jack could hear the doctor inside.

"How's the boy?" Jack asked. He could hear the girl, Dayton, answering the doctor's questions. She didn't sound too bad.

The officer said, "He's heavily sedated. I heard the ambulance crew say he had a gunshot wound and cuts, and took a world-class beating."

"Are any family members here?" Jack asked.

"They've been notified, as far as I know. One of the nurses said they can't find anyone for the boy."

The door to that room had been left open, and Jack walked down, slipped the curtain wide enough to peek in and saw a heavily bandaged and unmoving figure lying on the bed. He realized he really didn't like Zack. Apparently, someone else felt stronger about it than Jack.

"What about the girl?" Jack asked.

"AMR crew brought him in on a stretcher, but she was walking. She was a little hysterical. She's calmed down now."

Jack wondered how someone could be just "a little hysterical."

"Is Sergeant Mattingly coming?" Jack asked.

"Right here, Jack." Mattingly was coming down the hallway.

Mattingly had told them the kids were found at The Peaks Inn on the northwest outskirts of town. Jack knew the place. Cheap rooms, no Continental breakfast, but the bedbugs were free.

"Crime scene is going over the place now," Mattingly said. "I talked to the clerk and some of the residents around the area before I came here. There aren't any houses close to the place, and everyone was inside and didn't see anything helpful. The clerk didn't get a name, but the room was rented by a white male, forties to fifties, tall, dark suit. In fact, the guy rented the whole damn place and paid cash. I think Mr. Bolin is on his way, and he didn't sound too happy on the phone. Let's go to the break room."

They went down the hall to a room with one cheap chrome-legged table, two plastic chairs, and a full-size refrigerator with a note taped to the door that read, "Don't touch my food." It was signed by a doctor. If you left a note like that on the fridge in the detectives' office you risked coming back to find a tampon slipped into your sandwich by one of the heathens.

Mattingly said, "Dispatch got a call from a man saying two juveniles were hurt at The Peaks Inn and needed an ambulance. Dispatch tried to get more information but the caller hung up."

"Let me guess," Jack said. "The call came from a pay phone."

"Yeah. In the parking lot of the American Legion next door," Mattingly said. "My guys arrived and said they could hear a female screaming her head off. One of the room doors was open and they found the juveniles duct-taped to barstools. They were banged up real good, and the boy wasn't moving. I had one car follow the ambulance here, and the other stayed at the motel to wait for crime scene."

"Did the kids say anything to your guys?" Jack asked.

"The girl told him they'd been kidnapped by some guy and he shot the boy in the foot. He was going to shoot her too, and had put pillowcases over their heads. He was asking questions about Sonny and some money he thought they'd stolen."

"Did she see anyone else there?" Jack asked.

"Yeah. I think Mindy was there. Vincent Sullis?" Mattingly asked.

"Probably," Jack answered. "Can you stick around? I need to talk to the girl and I might need you."

Sgt. Mattingly said he would, and Jack and Liddell found the doctor in the hallway.

Jack asked, "Can we talk to Dayton?"

"Sure, Jack," the doctor said. "Hey, I thought you'd quit the department. Haven't seen you in here for a while. No slings, or crutches. Wow."

"I'm being more careful, but you should see the other guys."

"I never see the other guys. I don't work the morgue," the doctor said with a laugh. "She's been through a lot. Take it easy in there, Jack."

Jack and Liddell entered the cubicle and found Dayton propped up in a hospital bed. Her cheeks and jaw were black with bruises. A bandage covered the cheekbone under one eye.

"I want to go home," she said. "Is my daddy here?"

"Your parents are on their way," Jack told her. "Do you feel like answering a few questions before they get here?"

"Can I have my water, please?" she asked.

Jack handed her a cup of water from the bedside stand and she winced when she put the straw to her lips.

"Do you know who took you?" Jack asked.

She shook her head. "Is my mom coming too?"

"Dayton, I'm sure she is. I need you to answer my questions if you can. Shaking your head won't help me, okay?"

She nodded and then caught herself. "Yes."

"I won't keep you from your parents, I promise. They can take you home." He didn't tell her that he would have to question her at length later. She was pretty rattled as it was, and barely holding back the tears.

"Okay," she said, almost too softly for Jack to hear.

"Do you know the name of the person that took you away?" Jack asked again.

"She called him Sully. The woman in the room. He took us and she was in the room when we got there. She wasn't like him. I think she was scared of him too. Like us. Except she wasn't tied up or anything. He shot Zack in the foot. He just shot him!" Fresh tears spilled down her face. "He put pillowcases over our heads and said he was going to shoot me first. He kept asking Zack and me questions about the dead guy we found. He asked Zack where the money was."

"Did Zack have any money?" Jack asked.

"He had some stuck down his pants," Dayton said. "I didn't know. Honest."

"Sully found the money?" Jack asked.

"Yes."

"What else did he ask you about?"

"He asked Zack if the gun was the dead guy's. The guy we found this morning."

"What gun?" Jack asked.

"Zack had a gun when the guy took us. He took the gun from Zack when we were in his car. I can't believe Zack had a gun. I mean I don't know where he got it."

Jack said, "We'll get into the money and gun later. I have some other questions right now. Okay?"

She started to nod and said, "Sorry. Yes."

"Dayton, do you remember the woman's name?"

"She was old. Maybe thirty. I don't remember. I don't...I just want to go home. Please!"

"Anything you can remember will help me catch the guy that took you and Zack. If I don't, he might grab someone else. Shoot someone else."

"He was tall. Older. Wearing a suit and he had a big gun. He came to the door and said Zack was in big trouble and he needed me to come to the Police Department to vouch for Zack. He promised we'd only be gone ten minutes and my parents weren't home so I went with him. The guy, Sully, kept asking me where Zack was. I told him I didn't know."

"Did you know where Zack was?" Jack asked her.

"Zack called me and wanted to meet up and talk. I guess he still wanted to go to California. I asked the guy why he was asking me where Zack was, when he had said he was at the police station. That's when he pulled a gun out and told me to tell him where Zack was."

"You told him where you were supposed to meet Zack?" Jack asked. She nodded.

"It's okay," Jack assured her. "I would have told him too. You did the right thing."

Jack could tell by the look on her face that she didn't think she'd done the right thing at all. "What happened after that?"

"Zack was standing outside that little store—the one over by St. Anthony School—and the guy, Sully, stopped and made Zack get in the car."

"Go on."

"He pointed a gun at me and told Zack to get in. He took a gun from Zack and took us to that motel." She started crying and turned her face away.

"Dayton, it's okay. You're safe now. Zack is safe now. He's going to be okay. You did a good thing by yelling for help. That's why the policeman found you. You did good. You helped Zack."

She dabbed the sheet gingerly under her eyes. "Her name was Mindy. I remember he was mad at her. He slapped me and he cut me."

"Mindy? Are you sure?" Jack asked.

"Yeah. Mindy."

"Was Mindy hurt?" Jack asked. He was running out of time, but was afraid to push the girl too hard.

"She was scared. And drunk, I think. She didn't want that guy to hurt us. When he shot Zack, she freaked out and got sick. The guy told her to get out. She left us. Just like that."

"When Mindy left, what happened?" Jack asked.

"He put pillowcases over our heads. I couldn't see but I heard someone come in and he talked to her. Mindy."

"What were they talking about?" Jack asked.

"She didn't say anything. I heard the door open and Sully said something to her. Angry-like."

"Was he talking to Mindy?" Jack asked.

"I'm not sure. The guy said, 'I knew you'd be back,' or something like that. Then it sounded like someone was choking and I heard scraping sounds and the door opened. Another man said we were safe and someone would come and find us. Then I heard a door shut and there wasn't anything until the police came in and got us loose."

"You're doing fine, Dayton. Really. I'm proud of you. You're tougher than anyone I know. You did exactly right." Jack wanted to get her back from panic-land. If you need a woman to listen to you, compliment her. He got some tissues from the bedside stand and handed them to her.

"I was tough, wasn't I?" she said. She tried to smile and winced, putting a hand to her cheek.

"I'm sorry he hurt you, Dayton," Jack said.

"What else do you want to know?" she asked.

"Was it Mindy that the man, Sully was talking to?"

"I thought so, but I don't think so now. I remember Sully—or someone—making choking sounds. I thought he was killing the woman, Mindy. Then another man's voice told us we were safe. Why didn't he help us, Detective Murphy?" Dayton asked.

"It was a different man. Not Sully. You're sure?" Jack asked.

"I just remember it was a man. He sounded old, like you and Detective Blanchard."

Thanks. "Do you remember what kind of vehicle Sully was driving when he took you? What color?"

"It was a black like my dad's. My dad owns a Murano and his car was like it, but it wasn't a Murano, you know."

Jack could hear a commotion coming from the ER entrance.

"Your parents are here, Dayton. You can go home with them. You'll be safe now."

Mr. Bolin pushed through the curtain door of his daughter's room. He stopped at the foot of the bed and his breath caught in his throat. "Oh, baby, what happened?" Before she could answer, Mrs. Bolin came in, rushed to her daughter's side, and they began fussing over her.

Jack said, "Mr. Bolin, can you step down the hall a minute, please?"

Bolin followed Jack and Liddell toward the break room. "I've talked to your daughter. We are in a hurry to find the guy that did this," Jack said.

"Zack hurt my baby," Bolin said, no question in his mind who was guilty. Mr. Bolin's words were choppy. Jack knew he was a gnat's-hair away from exploding.

"It wasn't Zack," Jack said. "I have a good idea who the man is, and it wasn't Zack. He's in critical condition. The guy who took them shot Zack because he was trying to protect your daughter." Jack didn't tell him Zack was in the next cubicle. He was probably stretching the truth, but he didn't want Bolin going postal on Zack. At least not until the kid healed.

"Dayton told you who it was?"

"We were already searching for him," Jack said. "You can take Dayton home tonight. Someone will need to talk to her later on and show her some pictures."

"Did you arrest him?"

"We haven't found him yet," Jack said.

Bolin's muscles bunched, his hands turned to fists.

"Mr. Bolin, what your daughter told us leads us to believe the man is no longer a threat. I can't tell you more than that for now. I'll have a police car in front of your house tonight until we sort this out."

Bolin didn't seem to relax. "You're damn right you'll get someone to protect us," he said. "You told me this morning that she wasn't in danger."

Jack didn't want to argue with the man. He was right, and he was scared. "Why don't you go talk to her doctor? I don't think her injuries are too bad. Wait here until an officer escorts you home."

Bolin seemed to run out of adrenaline. "Sorry for that," he said. "Thank you for everything. Thank you for finding my baby girl. Anything you need from us…" Bolin gulped air, broke down and sobbed.

Liddell put a hand on Bolin's shoulder and led him back to his wife and daughter. The doctor was standing outside the cubicle.

The off-duty officer approached and said, "Dispatch on the phone for one of you."

Chapter 41

Jack was lost in thought as they got in Liddell's Crown Vic outside the ER.

"Is where we're going a secret, pod'na?"

"Sorry," Jack said. "New Harmony."

Liddell pulled onto Columbia Street and turned right on First Avenue, headed north to Diamond Avenue, which would take them to the little town of New Harmony.

Jack said, "A Posey County Sheriff's deputy called. He has another burned body."

"Sully?"

"Yeah," Jack said. "They found Uncle Marty's Jeep. Two semi-automatic handguns and a tracking device were in it. He found the wallet. Vincent Sullis, Boston driver's license. The Jeep's a rental."

"Tunney suggested Sully was the murderer," Liddell said. "Maybe this is some other poor bastard. Sully could have done it and left his wallet at the scene."

"Shit!" Jack said, and slammed his fist on the dashboard. "We're going around in circles. Sully's either the killer or he's dead and the real killer is long gone. This asshole is always one step ahead of us."

Liddell turned onto Diamond Avenue, crossed St. Joseph Avenue, and, seeing the road ahead was clear, he punched it. They were topping a rise just before they would reach Highway 69 when Jack saw flashing red, blue, and white lights in the distance. He heard sirens coming from the direction of New Harmony. Liddell topped the rise and Jack could see a half dozen emergency vehicles, including a two-tone brown Sheriff unit and Fire Department rescue and pumper trucks. The New Harmony town constable's rusting Chevy Caprice was there also, and coming from Highway 69 was a caravan of Civil Defense with blue lights blazing.

"Nothing much happens around here," Jack said.

Highway 69 was far in the distance and near total darkness had descended everywhere except under the floodlights from the emergency vehicles. A huge grain bin fed by a long conveyor belt was covered with white fire-retarding foam. As Liddell got closer, Jack could make out a foam-covered form in the shape of a man suspended from a metal strut of the conveyor belt. The shape's shoulders and head were slumped forward, arms behind its back.

Liddell pulled in behind a Posey County Sheriff car and a Smoky Bear hat approached.

"Deputy Stevens," the man said, introducing himself. He tilted the Smoky Bear hat toward the body. "Damn mess. I don't know how Crime Scene's going to get anything. If the cable wasn't strung under his arms, he'd have come apart like a baked chicken."

Having seen the results of a fire that afternoon, Jack had the same idea go through his mind.

"Any other injuries you could see? You mentioned some guns," Jack said.

"He was still on fire when I got here," Deputy Stevens said, unable to pull his eyes away from the body. "He was just hanging there like that. Burning like a wooden match."

The deputy was young. In his early twenties at most. Jack felt a twinge of compassion. The last big thing Jack could remember happening in Posey County was when two hired guns shot up the pharmacy in New Harmony, blowing the owner's head off.

"You say you found his wallet?" Jack asked.

The deputy led Jack across a partially frozen, partially mush and mud field to a Jeep that was hidden behind a work shack. The shack was painted white. The Jeep blended in perfectly. The driver's door stood open. Jack could see a pile of folded clothing on the front seat. A dark suit jacket, shirt, belt, shoes, and socks. The slacks were on top of the stack, and the wallet lay open on top.

"You opened the door and went through the clothes?" Jack asked.

The deputy said with a defensive look, "The door was open. The keys were in the ignition. The wallet was just like that. The two handguns are on the front floorboard."

"What about the GPS tracker?" Jack prodded.

"Yeah, I got that. It was on the ground over near the dead guy. I was afraid it would melt in the fire. I figured that was an exigent circumstance—you know—and I picked it up to keep it from being destroyed."

"You did the right thing, Deputy Stevens." Jack needed to keep this deputy friendly.

"Do you want to see it?" The deputy took it from his jacket pocket and put it in Liddell's hand.

Now there were two sets of fingerprints on the GPS, and not just the deputy's. Smart move.

Liddell said, "The GPS is still turned on."

The deputy said, "It was that way when I found it. I didn't turn it on, and that'll be in my report too."

"This is the Jeep. The guy who rented it is Martin Crispino. He's in the hospital in Kentucky. Vincent Sullis's car is still missing. It's a black Mercedes sedan with smoked windows and Massachusetts license plates."

"Yeah?" the deputy said. "I ran the plates on the Jeep and your BOLO came up saying you wanted this guy and a woman and the Jeep. What the hell's going on here, detectives?"

"Long story," Jack said. "If this really is Sully, you've ended our search. Did you see anything that might belong to a woman? A purse? Clothes? Shoes?"

"Not that I saw," the deputy said. "You still want the woman? Mindy something?"

"That's her. She was at a motel with Sully earlier."

The deputy started to ask a question but stopped himself.

"Sounds like you've got your hands full, Detective Murphy."

Liddell fiddled with the GPS tracker. "Nothing, pod'na. Either the one Uncle Marty put on Sully's car is turned off, or it's out of range."

The deputy said, "I've seen that type of tracker before. It has a range of, say, five miles max. I tried it before I called you and got nothing."

"You said you saw two handguns," Jack said.

"Three," Stevens said. "Two Glock .45 semi-autos and a Beretta 9mm. This guy was ready for a war. I haven't run the serial numbers."

"Can you do a couple of things for us?" Jack asked.

"Anything," Deputy Stevens said.

"First, can you see if there's a gun permit in the wallet?"

"I thought of that. None that I could see but I didn't want to mess with evidence too much."

"Not a problem," Jack assured him. "Do you have Crime Scene on the way?"

"I put a call in to the sheriff, but he's on vacation. Florida, lucky guy. We have a couple of guys do our forensics, but I need the sheriff's approval to call them in overtime like this."

Jack didn't think that would apply to something like a murder, but he said to Stevens, "You did right following policy, but I think you should go ahead and call them, give them a heads up." Jack knew the crime scene guys would probably come out anyway.

"Okay."

"And check the guns' serial numbers," Jack said. "Run them through the system for stolen, and call ATF. They will find the registered owners of the guns."

"I'll have to touch them to do that."

"It'll be okay to lean in the car and try to see the serial numbers," Jack said. "You need to put that in your report."

"Okay," Stevens said.

Liddell had been writing on a business card and handed it to the deputy. "This is the serial number for the Beretta 9mm Crispino was carrying. The other is for a Glock .45 that we think was stolen from our first victim. He was a cop."

"Sonny Caparelli," Deputy Stevens said. "I knew him. He was a good guy."

"The other .45 is probably Sully's. You'll need to run it through ATF."

"I'll do that right away and get back to you," the deputy said. "Anything else, detectives?"

"One more thing," Jack said. "I'm going to call Sergeant Walker. He's in charge of our crime scene unit. He can help you, and since our cases overlap we would like to have someone observe the scene here. Is that okay with you?"

"Sure. I'll take care of them personally."

"And one last thing," Jack said.

* * * *

Liddell drove east on New Harmony Road while Jack finished talking to an already stretched-thin crime scene sergeant.

"I didn't think the deputy would give the GPS to our crime scene," Liddell said.

"Why? I let him keep it until Walker's people can take it. It's a perfectly reasonable request." The last favor Jack had asked of Deputy Stevens was that he monitor the GPS and sign it over to the EPD crime scene techs when they arrived. He reasoned with Stevens that, except for this one, the murders had taken place in Evansville. It was more likely the killer would be heading back toward Evansville and that was why the GPS should be given to EPD.

"I'm not disagreeing with you, pod'na."

"We still don't know how the killer is getting around," Jack said. "Sonny's truck was left several blocks from that scene, keys in the ignition, and money under the seat. His gun and phone were missing. No clue as to what the killer was driving."

"Judge Knight was in his own car. Fire Department said the keys were still in the ignition. We don't know if anything was taken," Liddell added. "We don't know how the judge got to where he was killed or even if he was killed there. We don't know if the killer had a vehicle there to leave in. The judge was meeting someone where he was killed, would be my guess."

"Tunney may be right. The killer might have been working with Sully. That would explain why Marty's Jeep was found. The killer could have left in Sully's car."

"We're back to where…?" Liddell asked.

"Back to headquarters," Jack said. "We're missing something that should be obvious. I've had the feeling the answer is staring me in the face, but this guy doesn't quit. He's keeping us off balance reacting to his actions. I wish we could turn this around, but I don't have a clue as to how," Jack said. The truth was, Jack felt defeated. The guy with the monkey carvings was beating them. He wasn't after money, as Tunney had said. It was pure and simple revenge. The killer was someone who had crossed paths with the victims, or the victims had crossed the killer. Jack couldn't get Touhey out of his head. Big Bobby. Little Bobby. Yankowski. Sonny and Sully working for Big Bobby? And why did Crispino want witness protection? What did he know? The killer even had the mob scared.

Chapter 42

Mindy couldn't get the image of Sully shooting that kid out of her mind. She was sure Sully was going to kill all of them. She couldn't do the kids any good if she was dead. It had been hours ago, and she hadn't called the cops, but what would she say? If she ratted Sully out he would kill her for sure. He'd track her down and what he did to those kids would be nothing compared to what he'd do to her. He had a real sadistic streak.

She was certainly glad she'd put some warm clothes on before Sully told her to go outside if she was getting sick. She wanted out of the room. Away from him—from what he was doing—from what he was going to do. She really *was* feeling queasy when she told Sully she was going to get sick. That part wasn't a lie. And she didn't have a plan when she snuck his car keys off the table and headed out the door. But once outside, the frigid air shocked her out of a half-focused dream state where nothing was real and yet everything was too real. She felt—knew—she would have to get as far away from Sully as she could. As fast as she could.

She realized she was driving in the direction of her home as she passed The Old Mill Restaurant. It was a place where she and Sonny had eaten dozens of times. Sonny loved it. Said it reminded him of Danny-O's Bar in Boston, "where the faces never changed and the beer never got stale." Danny-O's was a stereotypical cop bar, where emergency lights scrounged from a wrecked cop car sat above the bar's mirror. Mindy had worked there. That's how she met Sully, who introduced her to Sonny. Sonny wasn't rich, but he'd been her ticket out of the crummy walk-up apartment she'd shared with two other girls. He'd been her ticket out of Boston.

New Harmony Road merged with Diamond Avenue heading east. A plan was developing. She knew she couldn't go anywhere near her house, the house she had put her time and love into. Sully had seen to that. Sonny too, to a certain degree. If Sonny hadn't gotten greedy they would still be living the good life. The life Sonny had promised her. She wasn't a young woman anymore, and she didn't know anyone in Evansville. Still didn't. All her friends were still in Boston and all of them were Sully's friends as well. Damn him!

She wanted to ditch Sully's car. Maybe go to the airport and park in the long-term lot. She could take the next flight out to anywhere. Sully would think of that. It was late and there might not be any flights. She couldn't sit in the airport all night.

She turned North on Highway 41, passing Dress Regional Airport, passing several motels near Interstate 64. She wanted some out-of-the-way place. Somewhere she could hide out for tonight. In the morning, she'd drive to the Louisville airport or go west to St. Louis. She had enough cash for a room, and she'd stuck a credit card in her pocket before Sully had rushed her out of her bedroom.

She turned east on I-64 without choosing one way or the other. Near Lynnville she saw a Red Roof Inn billboard advertising forty-four dollar room rates. Perfect. She would use Sonny's last name to check in. These kinds of places never checked ID. Sonny always said, "Cash is king." She felt a lump in her throat at the thought of Sonny and cheap motels. He had been married when they met. He'd taken her from her apartment and put her up in a string of motels, each successively cheaper than the last. When Sonny got divorced she thought he'd ask her to marry him, but he never did. He said they had it made. They didn't need a piece of paper to be loyal to each other. He was right in some ways. Wrong in others.

Tears ran down her cheeks, not from sadness or grief, but from anger—at herself. Why had she kept a relationship going with Sully? Sonny had been good to her, but she knew he couldn't protect her if push came to shove. Big Bobby always got what he wanted, and he thought everything was his.

She swiped at the tears blurring her vision and almost missed the exit for the Red Roof Inn. She swerved at the last minute, slowed down on the exit and followed the signs. She found a space behind the building where big construction trucks were gathered, and parked behind one of them.

Out of habit she reached behind the seat for the purse that wasn't there. Instead, she felt the handles of a duffel bag and her heart leapt. She lifted the bag. It was heavy. She set it on her lap and unzipped it. She didn't need a light to smell the money, to feel the bound stacks of one hundred-dollar bills she remembered Sully taking from her safe.

The panic she had been feeling was replaced with exhilaration, and tears of gratitude filled her eyes. She threw her arms up to the car's ceiling and let out a whoop. She'd not only stolen Sully's car, she'd stolen the money he planned to give Big Bobby to buy their lives. She would be able to go anywhere and no one could trace her. Sully could go to hell. When Sully didn't give Big Bobby the money, the blame would fall on Sully. He could tell any story he wanted, but he'd still be dead. She was alone, but she was alive and free. She had one more thing to do. Sully had left his cell phone in the car along with that detective's business card.

* * * *

"Detective Murphy?" Mindy said.

Jack recognized the voice immediately. "Mindy. Are you okay? Where are you?" He motioned for Liddell to slow down and he put the call on speakerphone.

"I'm not saying," Mindy said. "I'm okay. As okay as I can be, I guess, considering Sully was going to kill me." She'd started to call him at the Red Roof Inn but had changed her mind and drove on to Louisville. She needed time to think of what she was going to say.

"But you're someplace safe?" Jack asked. "Are you hurt? Do you need help?"

"I'm not hurt," Mindy said. "But you gotta get to The Peaks Inn and help those kids. Sully's got two kids there. He's gonna kill them. I'm sorry I didn't call sooner but I was out of my mind scared."

Jack hesitated to tell her they had Zack and Dayton. Or that they had reason to believe Sully was dead. But he'd have to tell her exactly that to get any answers from her.

"Mindy, I'm not going to tell you to come in to talk to me. I know you're scared. You had every reason to be. Sully was a dangerous man."

"What are you saying, Detective Murphy? You got Sully?"

"The kids are alive. Sully's dead. You don't have to be afraid. We'll get you home."

There was a long silence. Jack said, "Did you hear me, Mindy? You're safe now. The kids are safe. We found them. But I need you. You're the only one who can help me find out what the hell is going on." He waited.

She said, "You're a nice guy, Detective Murphy. My Sonny always said good things about you. He said you were tougher than anyone he knows and he knew some pretty tough guys."

"Sonny would tell you that you could trust me. You don't have to tell me where you are."

Silence again.

"Mindy?" Jack said.

"I'm thinking," she said. "You tell me something."

"Okay," Jack said. "If I can."

"Did Sully kill Sonny?

How do I answer this without frightening her even worse? "I think Sully was indirectly involved," Jack said. "Sonny would have told you, a case is never over until we know everything. Right, Mindy?"

Quiet.

"That's why I need to talk to you. You may have answers."

"Yeah. That's something my Sonny would say, too. He was a good detective, wasn't he, Detective Murphy?"

"The best, Mindy. He would be proud of you for helping me. He would tell you it's your duty, wouldn't he?"

"Yeah," she said. "But I still ain't going to tell you where I am. I've got to make a clean start. If Sully didn't kill Sonny, the guy that did is probably working for Big Bobby. Big Bobby will never quit until I'm dead."

Liddell had pulled off the shoulder and was giving Mindy's phone number to dispatch.

"I've heard about Big Bobby Touhey," Jack said. "I'm not positive he's behind this, but I do know that Sully and a guy named Crispino worked for him. Was Sonny working for Big Bobby?"

"That's what Sully told me. Sully's an asshole. He was supposed to be Sonny's best friend. But he was just using Sonny. He was using me. He's a liar."

"Mindy, do you have any idea who killed Sonny?" Jack asked. "Now that you know Sully's been killed, do you have an idea who else it could be?"

"Did Sully die like Sonny?" she asked. "I hope he died slow. Slow and painful."

"He was burned alive," Jack said, and was glad to tell her the truth at least about this one thing. Mindy was a gold-digging bitch, but she didn't deserve to die for it.

"Good. Good. He went straight to hell!"

"That he did, Mindy. Who do you suspect did that to him?" Jack asked.

"Sully has so many enemies it could be any of them. I mean, he did very bad things. I think he killed some people."

"For Big Bobby?" Jack asked, and saw that Liddell had turned on a digital recording device.

"Unh huh. When he was a cop," she said. "Sonny told me they done something really bad and that's why we had to leave Boston. Sully made Sonny help him get rid of a body and... Hey, didn't that judge get burned up too?"

"Judge Knight," Jack said. "Did you know him?"

"I never met him, but Sonny knew him back in Boston. Sonny took a lot of his police stuff to him here too. He seemed to trust him. Sully told me about him getting killed. I asked Sully if the judge had anything to do with all of this but he just told me to mind my business. Nobody tells me nothing."

Jack said. "Did Sonny tell you about the body he and Sully got rid of?"

"I know it was for Big Bobby. Some young girl. Younger than me even. Sonny had nightmares for a long time. He'd wake up yelling about her. "She's burning! She's burning!" he'd say, just like he was seeing it all again. He'd be soaked to the bone and shaking."

"How long ago was the girl burned?"

Mindy said, "Sonny got the job in Evansville a few months, maybe half a year later. I was glad we were moving because Sonny was drinking all the time and had those horrible nightmares. It was so bad I thought he was gonna kill himself. I mean, I told him he didn't kill the girl, so he didn't have to feel responsible. But you knew Sonny. He always took the world on his shoulders. He was a good man."

"He was like that," Jack lied. "We all miss him."

"They got the guy that killed her. Did you know that?" she asked.

"Did you know the killer?" Jack asked. "Did Sonny or Sully know him? Was it one of their acquaintances?"

"I didn't know him. Sonny said it was a CI of Sully's. That's a confidential information person."

"You said he had bad nightmares. Did Sonny work that girl's case?" Jack asked.

"Yeah. How come you're asking all these questions? Are you thinking Sonny had something to do with killing her? I told you they got the guy. He confessed."

Jack backpedaled. "I'm not saying that, Mindy. I just figured he'd catch that kind of case. He worked some serious stuff in Boston. Right?"

"Yeah. He worked it. He said it made him sick having to do it after he'd helped get rid of her body and all. The newspapers was all over Sonny, but he refused to talk to them. He said they were a bunch of sad—, sad—"

"Sadists," Jack helped her.

"Yeah. That's what Sonny said. I know you can take care of yourself, but you better watch out for Big Bobby. He's a psycho. He'd kill you for saying something against him. Don't matter you're here and he's there. That kid of his was crazy too."

"Do you think Sully killed the judge?" Jack asked.

"Nah. Sully was surprised as I was. He would have bragged about it if he had. He wouldn't have told me if he killed Sonny though. He needed me to get in the..."

Jack waited for her to finish the sentence but she was quiet. He could hear her breathing in the phone.

"Get in the what, Mindy?"

"You searched my house, didn't you?" Mindy asked.

"He needed you to open the safe? Is that what you were going to say?"

"Yeah. Sonny had this big safe hidden in the closet. He kept his *treasures* in there. That's what he called those guns. Treasures. Like they was made out of gold."

"You said Sully needed you to open the safe, Mindy. What did he take? There were guns still inside," Jack said. He had to be careful how he worded the next questions. He thought she was lying, but he didn't want to trap her in one. She had to have some wiggle room.

She was quiet.

Jack asked, "Was it money, Mindy? Is that what we're talking about?"

"You probably already know about the money, Detective Murphy. My Sonny said you was smart as a tick."

Sharp as a tack, Jack thought, but didn't correct her.

"Yeah, there was a bunch of money. Sully took it all. I didn't even know it was in there. I swear to God I'm telling the truth."

"I believe you," Jack lied. "Do you know how much money Sully found in Sonny's safe?" *Your safe.*

"It was a bunch, I can tell you. Filled a big bag with it. Sully probably has it hidden somewhere," she said. "Um...Did you find Sully's car?"

Jack now knew Mindy had Sully's car. She wouldn't tell him where she was. She was lying about the money. He could hear it in her voice. "The killer must have taken Sully's car," he said. "I thought maybe you had taken it. You were running for your life, Mindy. It would make sense."

She didn't deny it, which was as good as an admission. He could hear her breathing speed up. He'd hit a nerve. Probably not a good thing.

"Do you know how Sonny came by the money you said was in the safe?" Jack asked. She didn't answer. "There was a bunch of jewelry there too," Jack added. Still no response. "And the house and boat. That's a lot for a policeman, Mindy."

"It might have been an inheritance," Mindy said with little conviction.

"Mindy, I have to be honest with you. Sonny would want me to take care of you if I could. Don't take what I'm going to say now as a threat. I wouldn't harm you for a million dollars."

"I know you wouldn't. You're a good man, Detective Murphy. A real straight shooter..." she snorted like something was funny. "I didn't mean a *shooter*. That came out by accident."

"Yeah," Jack said and forced a chuckle. *Not funny, bitch.*

"Here's the bad news, Mindy," Jack said. "We know about the bank accounts. All of the accounts will be frozen. There will be a Federal investigation including theft, money laundering, and a bunch of other stuff I'd rather not burden you with. Until the investigation is over, they won't release any of it. The government will most likely take your house and any other valuables as proceeds of illegal acts. That includes Sonny's treasures and the jewelry, which I assume is yours."

"Sully told me that I could go back and get my stuff, that lying bastard. But I didn't have anything to do with any of this. I'm not a criminal. Sully said the money was the least of our worries. He was afraid of Big Bobby. He was a little afraid of you too. Not scared exactly, but you worried him."

"He should have been worried," Jack said.

"You and Sonny would have made a good team."

Jack didn't think so. He said, "Was Sonny still working for Big Bobby? Was Big Bobby the one giving him tips for the big drug busts?"

The line went dead. She'd hung up.

"Shit!" Jack said.

Liddell turned the recorder off and called police dispatch. He said to Jack, "They couldn't get anything on the cell phone number. It must be Sully's burner. Or maybe it was Sonny's burner. Oh hell, this just never ends."

"I think she took Sully's car and hightailed it out of town," Jack said. "That's why we can't get a fix with the GPS. At least we know she's still alive and we're not going to find her body somewhere. The bad thing is she might have several hundreds of thousands of dollars originally seized by the Feds. She was lying about the money."

"Unless Big Bobby sent more people than Sully and Uncle Marty. She didn't seem all that broke up about leaving a ton of jewelry behind, or losing the house and bank accounts. She might have four or five hundred grand in cash. Kind of a rags-to-riches story," Liddell said. "Where do you think she's going?"

"If she's smart, she'll use the money to get out of the country," Jack said. "We've still got the BOLO out on her and Sully's car. We may find her yet, but she's not really our target."

"What next?" Liddell asked.

"Donuts," Jack said.

"Now you're talking. That's why I love you, pod'na. Will you be little Jack's godparent?"

"Donuts in the office," Jack said.

"Sometimes you're just downright mean." Liddell pulled back onto the highway.

Chapter 43

Jack and Liddell pulled in behind police headquarters, and Jack saw Double Dick marching into the parking lot.

"Shit! What's he want?" Jack said.

Double Dick scowled as he approached. He was wearing a blue wool trench coat over his dress blue uniform. His cab driver's cap with gold braiding on the brim was cocked jauntily over one eye like an airline pilot. Jack didn't know whether to salute or give the man a boarding pass.

This is your captain speaking. Get your seat belts on. It's going to be a bumpy ride, folks.

"Deputy Chief," Jack said.

"Where have you been? I've been trying to reach you for hours, Murphy. Oh, never mind. Come inside. I'm freezing out here. I want to know what you've found out. You hear me? I'm tired of hearing everything on the grapevine. I know you hate the news media, but you really should make friends with those people. They can be very helpful."

Jack took his cell phone from his pocket and said to Liddell, "Do you remember the chief's home phone number, Bigfoot? He goes to bed late. He'll probably be up."

"What are you doing, Murphy?" Deputy Chief Dick asked, pulling the collar of his coat tighter around his face.

"Chief Pope gave me direct orders, Deputy Chief. He said he was not to be left out of *any* briefings, sir," Jack said. "I have to call him and tell him you want a meeting."

"But I'm the Commander of the Detectives' Unit," Dick protested. "You don't need permission...Oh, for God's sake. Don't bother the chief right now. I want you here bright and early. I'll call Chief Pope in the morning.

You and Blanchard will fill me in completely. Is that understood?" He stomped off toward the Executive Office parking spaces.

"Yes, sir. We're clear," Jack called after him.

Liddell said, "I heard Double Dick wants to be buried twenty feet deep when he dies." When Jack didn't bite, he said, "Because—way down deep he's really a nice guy. Get it?"

Jack ignored him and said, "We need to finish going through the file Yankowski sent, Bigfoot."

"Did the chief really give you an order?"

"No."

"You are one cool dude, pod'na."

"I'm one freezing dude."

They stepped inside the detectives' office and Jack said, "I never thought I'd say this, but Double Dick had a good thought out there."

Liddell put the back of his hand against Jack's forehead. "You're not feverish, and I haven't seen you imbibe."

"No. Really. The news media might be our friend and we didn't know it," Jack said.

Jack made a call. "Angelina," he said, and his side of the conversation went, "Yeah. I know what time it is. You wouldn't have talked to me that way when you worked for me. No. I don't want to explain anything to Mark. Quit busting my balls, Angelina. Remember when I asked you to get any news footage of the murders Detective Yankowski told us about? Yeah. You sent it? Well, we didn't get it. No, I didn't screw it up. Can you send the files to Liddell's email?" He listened and said, "Now would be good. We're in the office." He hung up.

A few minutes later Liddell's cell phone dinged. The message said, "Check your work email."

"Angelina?" Jack asked.

"That was quick," Liddell said. "Can you print all of it? I can't see anything on those tiny screens."

Liddell was already logging onto his system account. He pulled up a file and opened it.

"There's a dozen pictures here at least. We've got the *Washington Times*, *Baltimore Sun* and some other local Boston rags," Liddell said.

While Liddell printed the pictures, Jack called Sergeant Walker and asked him to send any crime scene photos that had civilians in the background. He then called Posey County Deputy Stevens.

Jack said, "Deputy Stevens, this is Murphy. I need to know what you found out on those guns."

Stevens said, "The 9mm came back registered to Martin Crispino. One of the .45s is registered to the Evansville Police Department. The other .45 is registered to a Vincent Sullis. Crime scene said the Jeep has been wiped clean of prints. I called the sheriff and he said to let your guys take the Jeep and anything else they thought would help. I've been watching the GPS tracker and there's nothing to report. It's all copacetic."

"Good job, Deputy," Jack said. "I'll let you know when the autopsy is scheduled."

Stevens responded, "I'll be ten-eight at the station for a few hours if you need me."

"Ten-four," Jack said and hung up.

Ten-eight is outdated police radio-speak meaning the officer is available for dispatched runs. Apparently, Posey law enforcement hadn't made the switch from *police secret radio codes* to *plain language*. The only code lingo you heard on the radio now might be a Signal-S, which means the officer is headed to the toilet. A Code-Three Signal-S is self-explanatory.

Liddell pulled a stack of pictures off the printer and they split them up while Jack told him what Stevens said about the handguns. Jack was flipping through pictures from news stories when Special Agent Frank Tunney walked in.

"I hear we've had more excitement. Did you forget I'm on the team?" Tunney asked.

"Sorry, Frank," Jack said. "I didn't forget, but things have changed."

Liddell walked over and sniffed Tunney's hair. "You smell like some girly shampoo, Frank. You got a girl in your room? Is that what the "meeting" was about?"

"You smell like barbeque and donuts," Tunney retorted.

"Touché. We just left another murder scene with a burned body. Not exactly BBQ, but close."

"Can we talk business, please?" Jack asked.

"I heard it might be Vincent Sullis," Tunney said. "That changes things a bit, doesn't it?"

"We thought the killer was Sully, but he got kidnapped by the real killer," Liddell said.

Tunney held up a finger. "Unless Sully was working with someone else, and they turned on each other like we discussed."

"We talked to Mindy Middleton. She told us that Sully kidnapped the kids and was going to kill them. That's nothing like the killer's M.O. The real killer saved the kids from Sully. Dispatch got an anonymous tip where the kids were. Another pay phone."

"Did Mindy see anyone? Another car?" Tunney asked.

"She was inside while he was torturing the kids. She said he was asking them if they had seen anyone around Sonny's murder scene. Maybe he was worried he'd been seen, or maybe he was trying to find the real killer," Liddell said.

Jack added, "Marty Crispino's Jeep was left at the scene where Sully was murdered. The GPS tracker was still in the Jeep along with three handguns. One was Crispino's, one was Sonny's and one was Sully's."

Tunney sat, quietly thinking. He said, "When is the autopsy scheduled for Vincent Sullis?"

"Little Casket is on her way to Posey County to get the body. She should be calling anytime now," Jack said.

"I guess we wait until Dr. John gets X-rays. See if there's another carving."

"We've got another avenue here," Jack said. "Mindy told me some things about Sonny and Sully regarding an old murder case and Bobby Touhey."

"That's interesting," Tunney said. "Tell me."

"She said Sully and Sonny helped get rid of a body once under the orders of Big Bobby Touhey. She said Sonny had nightmares afterward, where he would yell something about "She's burning!" She said he didn't want to talk about it, but it was getting to him. Detective Yankowski—the Boston detective—told me about an old murder case that Sonny was lead investigator on, and it fits. A young woman named Missy Schwindel was raped, mutilated and burned to death. Mindy said someone confessed to the murder and they thought it was over. A few months later, Sonny gets the job in Evansville. She said Sully was involved in that case too. And according to Yankowski, Judge Knight was involved. This could be it."

"You're suggesting that the killings are what? A retaliation for the old murder in Boston? Or are you saying they've been ordered by Bobby Touhey?" Tunney asked.

"Hell, I don't know what I'm saying," Jack said. "You're the analyst. Analyze."

Tunney laughed. "It doesn't work that way, Jack. But I'll try to help you if I can. It seems you have a real quandary on your hands."

"Yeah. Hey Frank. Detective Yankowski—the Boston detective—sent me a bunch of documents on that old murder, and some on the recent murder of Little Bobby Touhey. Angelina just sent us some news photos of that murder: at the courthouse, at the scene, that kind of stuff. We were about to go through it. Want to help?"

"Not really," Tunney said. "But let me make an observation here."

"Okay," Jack said.

"Whoever this guy is, if you find another monkey carving in Vincent Sullis's throat, it probably means the killer is finished. There are only four wise monkeys. Sullis would be the fourth."

Jack said, "Well, maybe he's done, but I'm not. Maybe he thought he was doing us a favor by killing a crooked cop and judge. He did us a favor by killing Sully and the mobster's kid. Doesn't matter."

"I'm agreeing with you, Jack. I just meant if he's done here, he's probably moved on by now. I'm afraid you may never know who this guy was."

"Frank, you know Jack," Liddell said. "He'll never let it go."

Tunney admitted, "He does have a rather impressive record with this sort of thing."

"You forgot about me. I'm good at this too," Liddell said.

"I could never forget you. Sometimes I wish I could, but there you are."

"Bite me, Frank."

"Oh, Jack," Tunney said. "I think I may have misspoke when I said there are only four wise monkeys. While I was researching, I found an ancient Japanese legend referring to a fifth monkey. I couldn't find an image of this one, if there is an image, but it is only referred to as Ten-Tei. Ten-Tei is the punisher. He's the one that metes out justice. If this guy thinks he's Ten-Tei and was passing judgment on the victims, he will be a formidable foe. Ten-Tei, by the accounts I've read, is fierce and swift in his punishment of wrongdoers. Who knows where he'll go next. Who he'll *punish*."

"So?" Jack said. "Monkey god versus .45 Glock."

"So proceed carefully, grasshopper," Tunney said.

"Thanks, Frank. I'll keep an eye out for your monkey god. He should be easy to spot. He'd make a good playmate for my mutt."

Tunney said, "Well, I wish you luck. I only stopped by to see what you turned up. I've got an early flight out tomorrow. D.C. has a case for me and I'd better get some sleep. You'll let me know what you come up with?"

"I thought your boss said we could have you for a while?" Jack asked. "This isn't about your meeting from earlier, is it?"

Tunney laughed. "Top secret," he said and winked. "Besides, I'm pretty sure your guy is done here."

"Yeah. I guess," Jack said. "Too bad you didn't know more about the murders in Boston. That's how we'll track this guy. I'm sure of it."

Tunney smiled. "Jack, I'm not consulted on every murder. If I was, I'd never have time to gamble or play golf—or go to meetings," he said, and left.

"Did you think he smelled kind of girly?" Liddell asked. "I wonder if he's got a girl back in his room."

"What makes you think that, Bigfoot?"

"Only two things make a cop wear cologne and give up on an interesting murder case. Sex and food."

"Bring your two-track mind back out of the feeding trough and get busy," Jack said.

The phone rang. It was Deputy Findlay calling from Henderson. "Glad I caught you," Findlay said. "I don't know how he could have done it. Man, I'm going ape shit trying to figure it out and my ass is hanging out in the wind like a single sheet of toilet paper."

"Findlay, what are you talking about?" Jack asked.

"Crispino's gone. I was outside his door the whole time, I swear on my mother's testicles."

"Shit!" Jack said. "Did you—"

"I put a BOLO out on him, and he ought to be easy to spot 'cause he's only got on a hospital gown and a smile."

"Unless he stole some clothes," Jack said.

"Screw me sideways and up and down!" Findlay said. "I'll get some help in here."

"Well, thanks for ruining my evening," Jack said.

"Glad I could help," Findlay said and hung up.

"I heard all of that," Liddell said. "Uncle Marty is one tough son of a gun."

"You're bad luck, Bigfoot."

"Me? What did I do?"

"Exactly," Jack said.

They divided up the photos sent by Angelina and the files sent by Detective Yankowski. Jack picked up one of the photos and stared at it. "Magnifying glass," he said to Liddell and held out a hand.

Liddell dug around in a drawer, found a magnifying glass and handed it over. The picture was outside a courthouse. Yankowski had marked this one as the murder of the guy who confessed to the killing from five years ago. Another was outside the police station at a news conference on the same date. Yankowski and his captain were circled in it. Jack picked up another photo. This one was a distant shot of the crime scene where Little Bobby was found gutted and hanging by wires. Apparently, some slick reporter had weaseled his way inside to get close enough to snap this one.

Jack focused the magnifying glass on one photo and then the other. He handed it to Liddell and put his finger beside one of the people in the background at Little Bobby's scene.

His phone rang. It was Angelina.

"Asshole. I couldn't go back to sleep," she said. "I went back through the pictures I sent you and guess what?"

Chapter 44

On their way to the Tropicana Hotel, Jack called Detective Yankowski's home telephone while Liddell drove. He spoke to a drowsy detective for only a few minutes. "Thanks again. Sorry to wake you," Jack said and disconnected.

"I couldn't hear over the pounding of my heart," Liddell said. "What did he say?"

"He confirmed it, Bigfoot. He spoke to him before Little Bobby was killed. There's no doubt."

"Do you think we're too late?" Liddell asked.

"Let's think positive."

"Okay. I'm positive he's gone," Liddell said. "I just have a hard time believing this, pod'na. I mean…we have no evidence. We can't arrest him. This may be the one that gets away."

Jack's phone rang. It was Little Casket.

"We haven't started the post mortem but it shows up on the X-ray," she said, and hung up without waiting for a reply.

"The body is Sully, Bigfoot. Our killer wouldn't waste one of the monkeys to throw us off track."

"We should call the captain," Liddell said. "Not just because it's the right thing, pod'na, but because this could go sideways on us and someone could get killed."

Jack said, "Let's hope the right guy gets killed. I'm not dying tonight. Neither are you."

"I'm serious, pod'na."

"I am too. I want you to stay downstairs and cover the front. I have a better chance if I go in al—"

"No way! If we go in together there's less chance he'll get squirrely. Safety in numbers, remember?"

"Okay. You've convinced me. You go in first," Jack said.

"I'll flip you for it."

"I'll go in first, Bigfoot. You're too big of a target and besides, you've always had my back. Trust me on this."

"If you're going to face him alone, I've got to tell you something first," Liddell said.

"Sure."

"A priest, an escaped convict and a mule go into a bar—" Liddell began.

"Just shut up," Jack said.

* * * *

The room number was on the card. Jack and Liddell rode the elevator to the fourth floor. The hotel was attached to the Blue Star Casino. The hallway wasn't entirely empty as they walked toward the room.

An older gent was weaving his way down the hall, swaying from wall to wall like a pinball, heading toward the casino. When he saw Jack and Liddell draw their .45s and check the magazines, the man stood ramrod straight, eyes to the front. As he passed he said, "Good evening, officers."

"Every day's a party," Liddell said.

"Not for everyone it ain't," the man said, and hurried to the elevator.

At the door to the room Jack took a breath and let it out. He wasn't nervous. He was scared shitless. Liddell was right. Chances were this wouldn't end well, but he didn't want another policeman to have to do this. He motioned for Liddell to stand to the side of the door. He reached up to knock and saw the glass peephole darken. The door opened a crack.

In a low voice Jack said to Liddell, "Cover me." Jack holstered his .45 but kept his hand on it. He pushed the door open and saw a partially packed suitcase on the side of the bed. A leather carry-on bag was next to it. Tunney smiled at them and said, "Come in, gentlemen. I wanted to get packed before I went to sleep. Old habits die hard."

Jack removed his hand from his .45 and entered the room. Liddell remained in the hall just outside the door, .45 in hand.

Tunney folded a shirt, and as he set it inside the suitcase Liddell shifted into an alert posture.

"What's going on?" Tunney asked, looking toward Liddell.

Jack could feel the tension in the air. He said, "Like Ricky Ricardo would say, 'Lucy, you got some splainin' to do.'" Jack smiled, and Tunney smiled in return.

Tunney put another folded shirt in his bag. "That's about it except for what I'm wearing when I leave." He was no longer smiling. "Just what kind of 'splainin' do you mean, Jack?"

"You know how I hate loose ends, Frank. Make me understand."

"It was her birthday," Tunney said. "She had just graduated with a degree in Criminal Justice. She wanted to celebrate both of these milestones with her father. I was supposed to pick her up at her apartment in Boston, but I was on a case in Manhattan and couldn't get away until late. She said she would come to me instead. She said it was her birthday, and she had always wanted to eat at Ecco, the Italian restaurant in Manhattan. She would take the train and meet me there. It would take a few more hours to get together, but what was a few hours compared to the twenty-two years that I had never known I had a daughter?"

"You have a daughter, Frank?" Liddell couldn't help asking.

With a bittersweet smile, Tunney said, "Yes, I had a daughter. We didn't know about each other until a week before her birthday. I met her mother when I was just starting out with the Bureau."

Tunney stared at something that wasn't there and spoke in a quiet voice. "I met Sue while I was on the job in Boston. I was young and fell in love. We spent every moment together for a month before I was transferred to California. I wanted Sue to go with me. My parents were both deceased. I'm an only child. Sue had no family. We were both alone. I thought it the perfect idea. She thought the idea was crazy. Sue had her life planned out, and her plans didn't include going to California for God knew how long."

He turned his attention to Jack and said, "She stayed in Boston. That was her decision. I moved to California. I couldn't give up the job. Sound familiar, Jack?"

It did.

"Anyway, we talked on the telephone a few times while I was in California, but you know how long-distance relationships are strained, to say the least. After a couple of months, I was so homesick for Sue I offered to come back to Boston. I said I'd take a job at Lowe's. I remember Sue crying. I thought it was tears of joy or relief and that she wanted me to come back. It wasn't. She said she didn't want me to quit. It wouldn't be the same."

Tunney distractedly folded a pair of slacks and laid them on the bed, lost in thought. He said, "I pushed. She withdrew even further. She finally told me she was pregnant and she wasn't keeping the baby. She said she was moving and I shouldn't try to find her.

"She was right. Nothing was the same after that. I was a father for the short length of that telephone conversation from across the states. She hung up, and I never heard from her again. I was heartbroken, but a few days later I put my considerable resources to work—and wasn't able to find her. It was like she'd dropped off the earth. Of course, if a woman marries and changes her name and doesn't go to work or drive a car it's almost impossible to locate them again. You know that."

Jack knew that was true. Today it was a little more possible, but twenty years ago they were working at a disadvantage.

"But then you found out you did have a daughter," Jack prompted Tunney, to get him talking about the case, how he was involved, and most importantly—although he had an idea of this last—what Tunney's motive was.

Tunney was quiet, folding and refolding a shirt, gathering his thoughts. "She took the train. I met it at the station near the Ecco. She wasn't on it." His eyes moistened and his words became thick. "I thought she had changed her mind. She wasn't ready to meet her old man. In our phone conversation, she had told me how she found me. Her mother, Sue, had pancreatic cancer. She left a letter for Missy when she died, and in it she explained what had happened and why she had never told her about me. She thought she was protecting Missy, but had a change of heart on her deathbed. Missy had seemed excited, happy about the idea of meeting me, but she was still a young girl and might have had cold feet. That's what I thought then.

"She had not given me her address. I only knew she lived in an apartment. I didn't know much about her but I always thought there would be time. I looked forward to each new revelation about the daughter I thought had been lost all those years."

"Missy Schwindel," Jack said, and a tear made its way down Tunney's cheek.

Neither Jack nor Liddell moved or spoke, allowing Tunney to come to the end of something that was of such import in his life it had driven a good man to kill mercilessly.

He wiped the wetness away with his sleeve and continued.

"I have a PsyD in Psychology." Tunney said. He stopped and looked at Jack. "Did you know I went to law school before I joined the FBI?"

"No. I never knew that, Frank."

"My daughter was following my career path. Do you know what that feels like? To have a family. To finally not be alone. I was overwhelmed with pride and a desire to meet this amazing child. I had made my mind up that she was going to attend the best schools. Have the opportunity to write her own ticket. Missy was my child, my family."

"I tried calling her cell phone over the next few days and got her voice mail each time. I became worried and called everywhere I could think of in both Boston and Manhattan. I checked the FBI databases. Manhattan and Boston had plenty of Jane Doe admissions, arrests, found bodies. None were Missy, of course. It was six weeks later I came to find out about the murder in Boston. Detective Yankowski had run the DNA and matched it to Missy. Because of the nature of the death, it was entered into VICAP and flagged to my attention."

"If I had only been there for her. Jack, you can't let the job ruin your life with Katie. You can learn from my mistake," Tunney said.

"You can't blame yourself, Frank," Jack said. "I know you think you should have picked her up at her apartment, but this is life. It's not always fair. In fact, it sucks sometimes."

A smile played at the corners of his lips, but his eyes remained alert, professional. "Spoken like a psychologist, Jack. Thanks. But it *was* my fault. I didn't have her address. She didn't give it to me. She was being careful and I don't blame her. She was her father's daughter, after all."

"Even you couldn't have predicted what would happen, Frank. You can't save everyone. Tell me how you got on to Sonny and the others. Did you find out who killed Missy?"

"It started to come together with Detective Yankowski. He's good. Almost as good as you two. He got the DNA match that identified Missy. But before he could get very far, a guy confessed. Sam Knight gave the guy a five-year deal. Five years in exchange for Missy's future—our future. Good doesn't always win out over evil, Jack. Sometimes it has to be helped along."

"Yankowski told me he couldn't disprove the guy killed Missy, Frank," Jack said. "The confession stood. The guy was killed. Case closed."

"For them. Not for me. Yankowski had taken DNA samples from Missy's apartment and matched them to the body, but the crime scene and coroner's reports said there was nothing else, no foreign DNA, the fire had destroyed everything. At the trial, the coroner reported there were signs, but no physical evidence to prove rape. The guy was never charged with rape. I thought the case was too pat. I mean, this guy shows up out of the blue and confesses to a murder. Knight gives him what amounted to a slap on the wrist. Then the guy conveniently is killed just before he is released from prison.

"It made me curious. I knew Yankowski was working a new homicide that he wasn't getting anywhere with. I offered to help. We convened at a cop bar, and while he drank Scotch I asked questions. Soon we were comparing cases and he started talking about Missy's murder and how he never thought the killer was caught. He told me about the suspicion that was hanging over Sonny's and Sully's heads before they both resigned. He said he thought the coroner's office knew more than they testified to in the trial.

"I visited the coroner and we had a heart-to-heart talk. I had to threaten a federal probe of misconduct before he would admit he hadn't reported everything from Missy's autopsy. He said there was a foreign sample from her remains that would have been evidence of the rape, but it was a small sample and so on. After more pressuring, he admitted that one of Big Bobby's guys threatened his family if he put it in the report. Knight had told the coroner this DNA would only confuse a good confession. The rape sample would point to the real rapist and killer, but Knight was running interference for Big Bobby. The coroner wasn't a bad man. He hadn't taken any money. He was just trying to protect his family."

"It was Little Bobby's DNA, wasn't it?"

Tunney said, "I collected the sample from the coroner and used a source of mine at the Bureau to run it discreetly. Robert Touhey Jr.—Little Bobby. I got him alone, and at first he didn't want to confess to raping and murdering my little girl. His testicles convinced him otherwise."

Jack waited for Tunney to continue.

"I'm not a killer, Jack. I track killers down. But these guys…"

Jack said, "I can understand doing Little Bobby. And Sully. Hey, I wanted to do Sully myself."

"I knew you'd understand," Tunney said. He refolded another shirt and held it.

"Did you know Sonny Caparelli and Sam Knight were in Evansville?" Jack asked.

"When I was here a few years ago, working with you on that case, I was introduced to Judge Knight by your captain. It was just a passing thing. I remembered the name from Boston in connection with the light sentence the killer was given. Yankowski had told me about Sonny."

"Sully was just icing on the cake," Jack said.

Tunney smiled. "I always said you would make a good profiler."

"No thanks," Jack said. "I already have a thankless job."

This made Tunney chuckle. He still had a hint of a smile on his face when he asked, "Am I under arrest, Detective?"

"Do you want to be?"

"Not really. No."

"Finish your story," Jack said. "I love a good story."

"This one doesn't have a happy ending, I'm afraid."

"Let me be the judge of that," Jack said.

Tunney placed the shirt in the suitcase and continued his story.

"While I was in Boston helping Yankowski on the other case, I reminded him he still wasn't satisfied with Missy's case. I offered to look through the file. Unofficially, of course. He had some photos from Little Bobby's funeral service. Good detective that he was. The pictures were damning. I was at the service, far, far in the background. It was foolish, but I couldn't help myself. I wanted to see the bastard in the ground. And I wanted to see who showed up. Sonny, Sully and Knight were all there. They pretended not to know each other, but it was a poor act. I shouldn't have lied to you. I told you I didn't know anything about Boston. My mistake. You know the rest, Jack. I had to kill them all. It wasn't a choice."

"The monkeys were a ruse?" Jack asked.

"It almost worked. Another hour and I would have been gone."

"And Big Bobby?"

"Big Bobby's not my problem, Jack. He's got syphilis. Like Al Capone. Elliot Ness didn't get Capone. Syphilis did. He'll be dead in a year, maybe less. He'll go painfully. Unless he takes the coward's way out."

"Were you really going to leave without saying goodbye?" Jack asked.

"I'm not going to jail. Only one of us is going to walk out of here."

Jack sensed Liddell winding up like a spring.

"I always admired you, Jack. I didn't want it to end like this." Tunney's hand reached inside the suitcase.

Jack drew his .45. Two deafening shots rang out. The room filled with the smell of burnt gunpowder.

Chapter 45

Japanese legend describes four wise monkeys. See No Evil. Hear No Evil. Speak No Evil. Do No Evil. Some say the wise monkeys are warnings. Others say the wise monkeys are an abstraction, a way of deciding if human behavior is acceptable when measured against the whole of society.

An even more ancient Japanese legend describes a fifth monkey, a Monkey King, Ten-Tei, whose job it is to mete out punishment for those who violate the teachings of the four wise monkeys.

Little Bobby Touhey, Sergeant Franco Caparelli, Judge Samuel Knight, Vincent Sullis. Each of these men had violated Ten-Tei's laws. Frank Tunney, with over twenty-five years of service with the FBI, having seen every type of depravity mankind can visit on its own, had meted out punishment appropriate for these men's crimes against a daughter he had never met.

A maxim of law enforcement teaches, "Anyone is capable of anything, given the right set of circumstances." Murphy's Law says, *Even the Devil was an angel once.* The fallout of Tunney's crimes affected many lives and brought no one back to life. Justice is incapable of truly righting a wrong.

Jack stood at the back of the "Celebration of Life" room at the funeral home and watched Katie and Marcie as they stood beside the casket, arms around each other, Marcie with one arm supporting her ready-to-burst stomach. Captain Franklin stood just behind the women, a hand on each of their shoulders. The room was large but full. It seemed the entire police department had turned out for the wake. Several men in suits, some FBI, ATF and DEA that Jack knew, several others he did not, stood in a group. It made Jack sad that even at a wake, there was still a separation in law enforcement.

Jack made his way through the mourners and stood beside the casket. He felt guilty. It was his fault. He was the one who insisted he and Liddell go charging in without backup. If he'd waited, maybe Frank would still be alive. Nothing about this body reminded him of the man he'd known.

Jack reflected back on that night at the Tropicana Hotel. He'd thought of little else since the shooting that night. It wasn't the first time he'd killed in the line of duty, Bigfoot either, for that matter, but Tunney was a friend and a lawman they both liked and respected. When Frank Tunney had pulled the gun from his suitcase, Liddell had shot without hesitation. Jack fired a split second later. Tunney never fired a shot. Tunney's weapon was not loaded.

Liddell approached, put a hand on Jack's shoulder, and leaned down to Jack's ear. "There's a guy in the back that wants to talk to you, pod'na." Liddell hooked a thumb in the direction of the gaggle of federal agents. "The older gent in the thousand-dollar suit. He's Donald Trump's doppelganger."

"He'll wait. Bigfoot, I want to ask you something. We did the right thing, didn't we?"

"Frank made the choice, pod'na. If it wasn't us, it would have been SWAT."

Jack wasn't so sure. He and Liddell still had to face the Shooting Board, Internal Affairs, and the Merit Board. Jack was a frequent flyer with all of them. "The Feds are having conniption fits. Frank was their best analyst. He's caught more serial killers, killers and mass murderers than our whole department combined. Did you know he was decorated by the president himself?"

"You've got to quit beating yourself up over this, pod'na. I was there too. It's just as much my fault—if there is any fault—as it is yours. I could have stopped you from confronting him. We didn't think we had a choice. He pulled a gun. We didn't know it wasn't loaded."

Liddell was wrong. He couldn't have stopped Jack. He knew he was like a dog with a bone.

Jack was told that Tunney had left his will with his boss back at Langley. In it, he requested Missy's body and Sue's remains be transferred to a mausoleum in Boston. He wanted his ashes put in the vault with them."

Jack touched Tunney's hand. It was cold, unreal. "You did the right thing, Frank. You got the bad guys. You're finished here. You can move on."

Jack and Liddell found their wives and walked to the doors. "I don't want to stay for the cremation," Jack said to them. He didn't say that he needed to get out of there before he had a meltdown, but Katie could sense it.

"We'll go outside, honey," she said. "But you need to stay."

Jack said, "I'm done, Katie. I'm really done."

Katie wrapped her arm in his. "You don't mean that. We'll go home. You need a Scotch and—"

"I need a lot of Scotch," Jack said. "It won't help. I just…" He couldn't finish. He felt sick. Sick of this life. Sick of damned police shit. Sick of everything. He looked at Marcie and wondered what they'd all do if it were Liddell in the casket. He felt sick. He had to get out of there. Get away by himself.

"I'm going to the cabin, Katie. I need some time," Jack said.

Before he could leave, the Fed that Liddell had pointed out approached them. The man didn't offer his hand. He said, "I'm Assistant Deputy Director Toomey with the FBI. I was Frank Tunney's boss."

Jack hung his head. He had expected this, but hoped he could make a clean getaway before the Feds came to tar and feather him and run him out of town on a rail. He felt like he deserved it.

"Look, Director Toomey. I can't tell you how bad this makes us all feel. If there was any other way I—"

"It's Assistant Deputy Director, and that's not why I wanted to meet you," Toomey said. "We need to talk. Not now." Toomey handed Jack a business card. "Call me next week. We need to talk."

Jack took the card. He didn't know what to say. Why wait until next week to chew Jack's ass out. "I don't think—" Jack said and the FBI man stopped him.

"Don't think. Call me. I'll be expecting it. I've already spoken with your chief." Toomey walked away without another word.

Marcie took Liddell's arm. "Honey?"

Liddell took the card from Jack and inspected it. "Shitfire, pod'na. I just hope it's not Larry Jansen."

Jack said, "What?"

"I hope my new pod'na isn't Larry Jansen."

Marcie said a little more insistently, "Liddell?"

"I'm not getting fired, Bigfoot," Jack said, but he wasn't too sure.

"If you go, I'm going too," Liddell said.

Marcie yanked on Liddell's arm and said, "I think it's time."

* * * *

Jack and Katie sat in the waiting room down the hall from the maternity ward. Jack had picked something up for his partner before they arrived, hoping they had time. It was Marcie's first child, so he didn't expect it to be quick. Katie was on the telephone with her sister, Moira, discussing baby gifts. Jack stared into space, half listening to his wife, and the other half thinking about Tunney. He wondered if Tunney had known what the outcome would be if he let Jack and Liddell into his room that night. Tunney knew they were coming. He proclaimed he'd never go to jail. He'd decided his own fate when he said only one of them would be leaving the room alive. It was a classic suicide-by-cop scenario.

A nurse stuck her head through the double doors and said to Jack and Katie, "You can come in now."

They followed her into the maternity ward, where the nurse opened a door for them. Bigfoot sat in a chair beside the bed, gripping Marcie's hand and grinning like a...well, a happy Bigfoot. The bundle on Marcie's chest was still and quiet, and Jack felt a moment of panic before he heard some noises only a newborn is capable of making.

"A girl pod'na," Liddell said, and tears welled up in his eyes.

Katie hugged Jack, kissed him squarely on the mouth, and did what any woman would do. She ignored the men completely and fussed over Marcie and the baby. That was the way life was. One new life brought into the world and another gone to the end of the path. He was glad to see Liddell immersed in the world of fatherhood, and not sunk into depression over what they'd had to do only a few days ago.

"I got you a present," Jack said to Liddell, holding something behind his back.

"I don't smoke cigars, pod'na. But if they're chocolate cigars, I'll split one with you."

Jack brought out a white paper sack and opened the top. He pulled out a long john with chocolate icing and handed it to Liddell.

"Hey, thanks pod'na." Liddell said, "Look, babe. He put 'It's a Girl' on the top."

"That's nice, Jack," Marcie said.

"Nice?" Liddell said. "He's the best!" He waggled the donut toward the baby saying, "You want one, don't you? You're just like your daddy. Say donut."

Jack laughed at him. Katie and Marcie ignored him. The baby just made sounds. To Jack she was saying, "Feed me, Daddy."

Liddell bit off half the long john and asked, "What would you have done if the baby was a boy? Huh?"

Jack reached in the bag and pulled out another long john. Iced on top were the words, "It's a Boy."

"Always prepared. Just like the Boy Scout motto, pod'na."

Jack said, "The Boy Scout motto is 'Don't touch me there.' Come out in the hall."

Liddell got up and followed Jack into the hallway and asked, "Did Yankowski call you back?"

"I talked to his captain. He said Big Bobby was nowhere to be found. The Feds are looking for him on money-laundering charges, Boston PD wants him in relation to the murder of Missy Schwindel, Narcotics wants to see if he's ready to make a deal. The only ones who don't want him are you and I, Bigfoot."

"Speaking of Feds," Liddell said, "Did you find out what the FBI Director wanted?"

"Assistant Deputy Director," Jack corrected him. "No. I haven't called, and so far he's left me alone. Maybe he's got someone else he hates worse."

"How about Mindy?" Liddell asked. "Any luck finding her yet?"

"In the wind," Jack said. Mindy had completely disappeared. Jack figured she had left the country with the money Sonny had stashed in the safe. Good for her. He knew Sonny had been poisoned, but he still believed she didn't know the tea contained deadly amounts of cyanide. Lots of people drank the stuff. Just another ditzy blonde. He heard the FBI weren't actively seeking her, so he wished her well. He wished Sonny hadn't been crooked. He wished Sully hadn't been such an asswipe. He wished Frank would have done this differently. He wasn't sure he wanted to do this anymore.

Maybe he could quit and help manage Two Jakes Restaurant. Hell, he didn't even have to work, with the money he was making off the business. He could stay home. Have beer-eal for breakfast. Have regular sex. Drink Scotch. Drink more Scotch. Maybe he'd even think seriously about having a baby like Bigfoot. Well, not like Bigfoot, but a baby.

Liddell and Marcie had decided on a name. Jane. They were naming her after Marcie's mother. Jack wasn't too disappointed, although he liked the name Jackie more than Jane.

Katie's sister, Moira, showed up and joined the other women in ignoring the men. Jack wouldn't have it any other way.

Epilogue

Three months later...

Mindy watched the ocean wash onto the white sands of the beach in Barbados. This was her life now, and it was a good one. She had the sun, she had the sand, she had a house with beachfront, and she'd even bought a new identity. Cash really was king, just like Sonny had said.

She finished her drink, picked up her bag, folded her chair, and walked up the beach to her house. She'd always wanted a house with a glass front with a view of the beach. She could watch the sunset every day if she wanted. At last, she could relax. She had outrun everyone. It had been three months since Sonny's death and she'd held her breath every single day. But not now. Now she was Jillian Wozniak. It was the name of a friend she knew from grade school. It was a stupid name, but it was the one she'd given the guy who made her a passport and Colorado driver's license. She'd even had a birth certificate made in case she wanted to get a driver's license here.

She opened the sliding doors and admired her tan legs. She thought about Sonny and how careless he had become at the end. She was the one who figured out how they could skim money off the drug busts. She knew Big Bobby would catch on sooner or later, and that was why she had started poisoning Sonny. It was slow to work, but if he died from that particular poison no one would be the wiser. She'd get everything, he'd get the blame.

She wasn't sorry that asshole FBI guy killed everyone. It made her plan that much better. She was a victim her whole life. But she wasn't stupid like Big Bobby and Sonny and Sully and even those detectives had thought. Big Bobby thought Sully took the money. Sully got dead. She got away. And she read online that Big Bobby had died of something. Couldn't happen to a more deserving guy.

She reluctantly turned away from the gorgeous vista that was her new life and walked into her kitchen. She opened a bottle of wine, poured half of it in a Big Joe glass, walked into her front room and stopped dead in her tracks.

An older gentleman with white, slicked-back hair sat on her sofa. He ran a hand through his hair and wiped it on the white slacks of his Panama suit.

"Hello, Mindy," Uncle Marty said. "Big Bobby's wife sends her regards."

The Deadliest Sin

Don't miss the next exciting Jack Murphy thriller by Rick Reed

Coming soon from Lyrical Underground,
an imprint of Kensington Publishing Corp.

Keep reading to enjoy a page-turning excerpt . . .

Chapter 1

Coyote sat in the booth, drinking stale coffee, eating a crust of cherry pie and writing in a five by nine inch ring notebook. He had to record his thoughts, his feelings. That's what his shrink said. His shrink was an asshole, but at two Benjamin's a session Coyote didn't want to waste the advice.

The gray-haired waitress shuffled over in dirty house shoes.

"Coffee?" she asked.

Coyote looked around the shabby cafe. It was narrow, with a six-foot counter on one side, and two ramshackle booths on the other, one with duct tape holding a leg together, and no customers. The coffee in the bottom of the carafe was black and thick as syrup. *This's what she calls this drain cleaner.*

He was polite. "No," he said. His voice was gruff, deep for a man barely five and a half foot tall. He was wearing a Stetson, crisp white shirt with imitation pearl snaps, creased blue jeans and Western boots. His trench coat lay on the bench beside him. He was not a big man by any standard, but only a few men had made the mistake of seeing him as small.

The woman said, "Closing in five."

He ignored her as her shoes scuffed across the stained black and white tiles. He dug deep in a pocket and pulls out a crumpled twenty. He slid it under his cup and reads what he'd written so far:

I'm tired. Tired of everything and everyone. People disgust me. Food doesn't taste good. There's no happiness anywhere for me. I see people pretending to sing, their words full of hate and anger and violence. They dance with faces showing hate and confrontation. What are they so unhappy about? Why do they want to disrespect everything they got for free? They won't work. They think they can be rich and happy taking drugs. They dishonor their parents and each other. They fight from a safe distance with texts and computers and phones. Cowards.

Everyone is out for themselves and the only thing they can agree on is that their elders were wrong, racist, or homophobic. They don't see why 'elders' always talk about the past, about the lessons that took a lifetime to learn. They are confused about who they are, who anyone else is, angry that their elders didn't give them more. Why should they take any blame or responsibility?

This is where my mind goes when I'm on the road. Alone, thank God. My dreams are visions, premonitions of things to come. Slackers, drug addicts, and alcoholics, irresponsible, arrogant, pretenders surround me. They have created a world where they matter, but they don't. If the last three or four generations were wiped from the face of the earth, we wouldn't notice. They contribute nothing. They do nothing. They want everything. They're using my air.

"Time," the old woman said.

Coyote got up. He couldn't wait to leave. The smell of putrid coffee mixed with the odor of fried onions was enough incentive to go. He walked out the door, his boots crunching on rock salt. He pulled his coat tighter against the frigid air, looked down the street at the Impala with the fogged up windshield. The asshole had made Coyote wait. Coyote respected that.

He turned down the alleyway, slipping something from his pocket.

* * * *

The old-model VW sat halfway down the street, lights off, engine running. The man inside was tall and lean. He was bent like a pretzel, stuffed into the driver's compartment, knees touching the dashboard, his upper body bent forward over the steering wheel, head almost touching the roof while he watched the man inside the coffee shop. They made him spend two days driving in circles, St. Louis to Chicago to Louisville and back to Evansville. He waited another two days to meet this man they called Coyote, to whom he was to turn over his load and get paid.

He didn't trust them, nor believe them. He'd made this same run dozens of times over the last five years and each time took the same route. They were worried about something or they wouldn't have changed things. That meant he had to worry too. He'd deliberately missed the delivery to Coyote. They wouldn't get delivery until he got paid, double the original amount, and he'd taken steps to ensure they wouldn't double cross him.

The cramped quarters of the VW were claustrophobic compared to the big cab of the Ryder truck but it wouldn't be long now. The VW was the only thing he could steal on short order before this meeting, and it didn't stand out in his surroundings.

He was late for this meeting with Coyote but one thing a life of crime had taught him—caution. He'd driven around, randomly passing by the meeting spot he'd selected, and watched the man in the cowboy hat go inside. He didn't know Coyote by sight, but the description he'd been given matched this little guy to a tee. Coyote sat down in a booth and didn't move except to drink something, probably coffee, and eat a piece of pie.

Several times he'd driven past the University of Evansville, with its sweeping lawns, water fountains, concrete benches, fraternity houses, bookstores and libraries and labs. He'd had thoughts of going to school once upon a time. He'd given those ideas up before he made it to high school and joined his father in the family business instead. Stealing and stripping cars brought in money and you didn't need a degree to do it. That's how he was in possession of this car. He wondered how different his life would have been if he hadn't...

Coyote came out, glanced down the street, looked directly at the VW with the engine running, turned and walked into the alleyway. Coyote had seen him. He hadn't been as careful as he thought. But he had to get his money. All of his own was spent keeping his mom in that goddam nursing home in Florida. He owed her. She'd kept him alive in between the beatings his drunken bum of a father had given him.

He watched the last light go out in the shop. The old woman that had waited on Coyote came out wearing what looked like a long bathrobe. She was thin as a rail and he could see her S-shaped spine pushing against the back of the thin garment. She made her way down the street, stopping and turning around several times, as if someone would be desperate enough to molest her wrinkled ass.

She was swallowed by the darkness down the block. The neighborhood was dark. The only light came from the campus parking lots and it barely spilled over onto the streets. Three blocks north was a scattering of little one-bedroom houses. It was from one of these that he'd 'borrowed' the car.

He turned to the dog in the back seat. "Stay, uh..." He hadn't given the dog a name. Maybe he'd keep him. Maybe not. He'd never had a dog. Wouldn't have this one but he couldn't leave it behind. Too damn cold in the truck. He couldn't do that to the mongrel. It was his soft spot. "Spot. I'll call you spot," he said to the dog. "Okay? You like Spot?"

The dog's head cocked to one side, its mouth opening as if smiling. The dog was a pup really, maybe a shepherd mix. "Stay," he said softly to the dog. It cocked its head to the other side and its dark seemingly pupilless eyes locked on his. It gave a short whine, as if to say, "You can call me anything. Just take me with you."

He laughed. When he got paid he could afford for both of them to eat better than dog food. His little pun made him laugh again.

He exited the VW. The hinges creaked long and loud. He didn't want to leave the door ajar because the dome light would stay on and even though there seemed to be no one around, it would attract attention. He had to slam the door twice to make it latch. It didn't really matter if Coyote heard it. Coyote knew he was there. Knew he was coming to meet him in the alleyway. He just didn't want some asshole to steal the car. And his dog. A dome light was like a bug light. It attracted thieves.

The dog whined again. He turned back to the car and put a finger to his lips. The dog settled back in the seat. *Smart boy. Good boy.*

A cold wind smacked his face as he approached the alleyway. It was pitch black. At the end of the alleyway he saw a dull glow about waist level. *A cigarette.*

He stopped halfway and said, "It's me. I want my money, or you can tell your boss he don't get the truck. Pay me and I'll tell you where you can find the keys."

The cigarette didn't move. Coyote didn't speak.

His legs trembled but he forced himself to move forward a few more steps. He had to be firm on this. After this he would be out of the business, but that didn't matter.

He took another few steps and stopped dead still. The glow *was* from a cigarette, but it was sitting on top of a crate with no one holding it. Too late, he stepped back when an arm went around his neck pulling him backward and down. Coyote's breath was in his ear and smelled like coffee and cigarettes. There was a pressure and sharp pain in the side of his chest. The pain found its way deeper until his legs turned to rubber. There were several sharp stings to his chest and the arm relaxed, released him. He fell to the ground. It was cold on his cheek. Something stung his neck.

"You'll get what the boss wants you to have, asshole," a gruff voice said. A long slender blade entered the side of his throat. He could feel it push through, but it felt like pressure and not pain.

The Coyote stood up and said, "You've been paid."

His last thoughts weren't of dying. They were of the dog. He'd never had a dog.

Chapter 2

Detective Jack Murphy, third generation Irish-American cop, ducked under the yellow crime scene tape blocking the mouth of the alleyway. About once a month he and his partner worked weekends in the detectives' office. This weekend was their turn. He covered his mouth and nose with a gloved hand to keep the freezing cold out and bemoaned the fact that if the run had come in thirty minutes earlier, this shit would have been third shift's responsibility. Such was the luck of the Irish.

Jack and his partner, Liddell Blanchard, were assigned to Homicide, but investigated almost every type of violent crime. Their specialty was serial violent crime; serial rapes, multiple robberies with injury, home invasions with injury, or deaths where homicide was suspected. Liddell joked that he and Jack were actually personal injury lawyers with badges and guns. From what dispatch told Jack, this death was more than suspected.

Jack was almost six feet tall, sturdily built, with dark hair, short on the sides and spiked in the front, and gray eyes that could turn stormy. He liked redheads, Scotch, Guinness, and long walks on the beach, minus the long walks.

His partner, Liddell Blanchard, aka Bigfoot, was talking to the first officer on the scene. Liddell stood over six and a half feet and weighed in at a full-grown Yeti. Breaths issued forth like cartoon dialogue balloons from the law enforcement officers working the scene.

An ambulance was pulling away. Its emergency equipment was silenced. There was no need.

Sergeant Tony Walker approached, bundled against the cold and wearing an oversize Tyvek suit with the hood pulled over a ski mask. It made him look like the Stay Puft Marshmallow Man in the *Ghostbusters* movie, or a fat, white commando.

"It's a mess back there, Jack," Walker said.

"What have we got?" Jack asked.

Walker was his previous partner in the investigations unit. Then Walker got himself promoted to Sergeant and was transferred from Detectives to the Crime Scene Unit. Walker was an excellent detective and an even better Crime Scene analyst.

Walker tilted his head toward the end of the alley where a body lay crumpled like a bloody paper towel.

"White male in his late forties," Walker said. "Several puncture marks in his jacket. He was stabbed in the side, chest and neck. The weapon was a thin bladed knife. He's been down at least overnight because some of the blood is frozen. We're just now patting his clothes down for a wallet."

Walker signaled one of his techs to continue while he talked to Jack. "The owner of the coffee shop next door found him this morning. She didn't touch him. She called it in as a drunk, possible mugging. She said there've been other muggings back there once or twice. An officer and an ambulance arrived about three minutes after she called, about seven a.m., and found him like that, felt for a pulse but otherwise didn't touch anything. There's a lot of blood. His throat was punctured in three places that I can see. The killer wanted to make sure he was dead."

The tech held a key out. "This was in his shoe. I don't think there's anything else. Can we turn him over, Sarge?"

"Let's do it," Walker answered. He handed Jack a medical mask. "Coroner's on the way,"

Jack was grateful for the mask. The tip of his nose was freezing. "What's the temperature?"

The tech, a Corporal named Morris, said, "A balmy five degrees. It was three below overnight."

The deceased's waist-length quilted jacket, once tan, was now painted deep red. He had on tan desert-style military boots, no gloves, no hat, and a Black Watch plaid scarf tucked down in the jacket. No jewelry. His hair was blond, going on gray, going on bald. His cheeks were sunken. *False teeth? Missing?* He didn't have a mustache but there was a two or three day growth of grayish facial hair. His upper lip carried the deep lines of a heavy smoker. The middle and index finger were yellowed. *He was a smoker and he was left-handed.* Jack put his age nearer sixty. Ice crystals had formed on the ridges of the jacket, around the cuffs and around the bottoms of the jeans. Tony was right. He'd been down a while.

"Anyone find a weapon, Tony?" Jack asked Walker.

"Not yet."

Crime scene had turned the body on its back. Jack counted three punctures in the outer jacket. He had worked some stabbing deaths less than a month ago. The cold temperatures were about the same as today. Those bodies displayed frozen blood, too. He remembered from the autopsy report that blood contained chemicals that slowed the freezing process. This guy had obviously been killed here and left here. Maybe the Coroner could give an accurate time of death.

The face was flattened like a coin on the side that had lain against the ground. Grit was frozen into the skin. Morris said, "We'll have to wait until the Coroner gets him to the morgue to search him better, but he doesn't have anything on him. Wallet, change, nothing except the key."

"I guess we can't rule out robbery as a motive," Jack said. "Maybe it started out as a mugging and he fought back. Any marks on his hands?"

Walker answered that one. "It doesn't look like he fought his attacker. We'll have to wait for the autopsy. I'll call you when I know more."

Jack asked, "What do you think the key goes to?"

Morris showed it to Jack. Imprinted in the metal were the capital letters ABUS.

"ABUS," Jack said. "Is that a padlock? A toolbox?"

"I'll look it up," Morris said. "I don't really know."

"Stay in touch," Jack said to Walker and headed back to the street.

Liddell came from the direction of the University bookstore and Jack met him on the sidewalk. "No luck, pod'na. The bookstore's closed up tight on Saturday. The sign in the door says it closed at seven yesterday evening. Opens Monday morning at eight. Officers are going door to door."

"Did you talk to the first officer on scene?"

"Yeah. Officer Steinmetz," Liddell said. "Gladys Rademacher owns The Coffee Shop. She called 911 at seven saying someone was passed out in the alley beside the shop. Steinmetz arrived five minutes later. Ambulance arrived when he did. He saw someone laying face down in the back of the alleyway and walked down to check. It looked to him like a drunk passed out wearing a red coat. He said he's found a few college students passed out from partying too hard and thought it was one of them until he got close. One of the ambulance crew checked the guy and determined he was dead. Steinmetz called crime scene, dispatch and the Coroner."

"Mrs. Rademacher?" Jack asked.

"Yeah. I talked to her for a minute. She's inside. Said she closed up at midnight. She had one customer from about ten until closing. The guy just sat there and had one cup of coffee and pie that he barely touched. She said he left when she locked up, so that would have been about five after midnight. When she went out the customer was nowhere in sight. She saw a car down the street with its engine running. She doesn't know what kind of car and couldn't see if anyone was in it. She described the customer as a white man but couldn't give a description, guess his age or remember what he was wearing. She said he wasn't talkative. But neither is she. I had to drag that much information out of her. Maybe you'll have better luck. The ladies like you, pod'na."

Jack looked up and down the streets. Dozens of cars were parked at the curbs. None with the engine running. It was still early. The university across the street wasn't awake yet. College students slept in on weekends. Jack called out to the officer holding the crime scene log. "Can you ask someone doing the neighborhood canvass to write down license plate numbers and car descriptions? We need to know what's parked and how long it's been there."

The officer got on his portable. Jack and Liddell went to interview the owner of The Coffee Shop. The door was unlocked and warm air blasted them. A bell over the door rang when Jack and Liddell came in but the woman paid no attention. She was behind a small wood-topped counter, pouring water into a Mr. Coffee on a small table next to an iron stove possibly as old as the woman herself. She finished the coffee and bent over the oven, taking out several freshly baked pies. The mouthwatering aroma filled the room.

Liddell said, "Mrs. Rademacher, this is Detective Murphy. He'd like to ask you a few questions if you have time."

"I don't," she said.

"Mrs. Rademacher..."

The woman's shoulders dropped. "Oh, go ahead. I guess you won't leave me alone. I don't know who killed that guy out there but it wasn't me."

"Why would you think you're a suspect, Mrs. Rademacher?" Jack asked.

She grinned. Most of her top teeth were missing. "I watch Cold Case Files and CSI New York. The last to see 'em alive is always the prime suspect."

Jack had experienced CSI's effect on the public. He'd learned to interview these crime show addicts a little differently from other people.

"We don't think you killed the murder victim. You're not our prime suspect," Jack said.

"Unh huh," she said as if she didn't believe him.

"But you are our best witness. You might be able to break this case wide open for us. What time do you open your business, Mrs. Rademacher?" Jack asked. He hoped to enlist her. Civic duty to help the police was a thing of the past.

"Depends," she said and offered nothing else.

Time to change tactics.

"What time did you open this morning?" Jack asked again, this time in a less friendly manner.

"Why?" she asked. "I told you I didn't kill him. Are you going to arrest me?"

Jack said, "It's warm in here. This building is maybe eighty years old. You don't have central air or heat. Even in one with good insulation it would take that stove of yours about two hours to get to this temperature. I'm guessing you've been here since about five this morning."

"Five thirty," she said. "Stove's a good 'un. They don't make 'em like this no more. Don't need central heat."

"You got in at five thirty. You called the police at seven," Jack pointed out. "Why didn't you call police immediately, Mrs. Rademacher?"

"It's none of my business who's drunk or where they pass out."

"But, in fact, you *did* call the police," Jack said.

"Wouldn't you?" she asked.

Jack pretended to be impatient, "We can do this here, or we can do it downtown. You'll have to start talking or lock up and come with us."

She looked at him and snorted.

"That's a good 'un. Cops have to read you Miranda rights first."

"Are you gonna talk or do I have to get rough?" Jack asked and winked at her.

She grinned and crossed her arms. She was wearing a ratty pair of cloth house shoes. Her ankles were bare. A plaid nightgown stuck out of the bottom of a long house coat. She didn't care. She was having fun. How she could be enjoying this encounter considering there was a dead man outside was beyond Jack.

She said, "You boys might as well have coffee and a piece of pie. I don't have any donuts." She nodded toward one of the booths.

Jack remained standing and Liddell squeezed into a seat.

"Mrs. Rademacher," Jack said and she held a hand up.

"Name's Freyda. I never did like being called by my married name. Mr. Rademacher, curse his hide, is dead. Dying was the only good thing he ever did for me."

Jack found a couple of chairs by the counter and pulled them over to the booth. He motioned for the woman to sit. She ignored him and went behind the counter, brought back two mugs of coffee and handed them to Jack and Liddell.

"Want some cherry pie?" Without waiting for an answer, she brought a pie, plates, and silverware to the table.

"Thank you, ma'am," Liddell said and scooped half a pie onto a plate.

She slid into the booth beside Liddell and said, "Ask your questions."

"Okay. Freyda. If you were the detective, what questions would you ask such a fine, observant woman as yourself?"

Freyda snickered. "Fine woman. That's a hoot. You must be blind as a bat, but let me think. I guess I'd ask about that car down the street. And I guess I'd ask who the customer was that left here."

"That's good thinking," Jack said. "And what do you think you would say to the detectives?"

"You haven't tasted your coffee," she said to Jack, getting off topic once again.

"You aren't drinking the coffee," Jack pointed out.

"Are you kidding?" she said. "This is too strong for a 'fine woman' such as myself."

Jack took a sip. She was right. He could strip paint with this stuff. "So, what did the witness tell you about the car and your customer, Freyda?"

"The witness wasn't talking to the cops. She, or he, was afraid of getting whacked. Killers always return to the scene of the crime. That's what that hunk on CSI New York says. Gary Sinise knows his killers."

Chapter 3

Liddell asked for seconds on the pie and a second cup of coffee. Freyda said, "You like my pie."

Liddell grunted with a mouthful.

"That guy last night didn't eat his pie or drink his coffee. Sat there writing in his notebook and looking out the window," Freyda said.

"You said there was a car down the street with the engine running," Jack prompted her. "Did he come up in that car?"

"I was in here when he came in. Can't see down the street from here."

"Tell us about your customer. Anything you can remember," Jack said. He got up and warmed up his coffee. It grew on you.

"I remember better now," she said. "Like I said he was a white guy. Maybe fifty or less. I can't tell much about these young people anymore. Younger than sixty looks like babies to me. He came in around ten last night. I didn't see him park so I don't know anything about what he was driving. I don't think it was the car down the street that I saw with the engine running, but I couldn't tell you why. Just a feeling. You know. Like cops get that gut feeling."

"Okay," Jack said.

"Well, I left a few minutes after he did, but I didn't see him on the street and the only car I saw was the one I told you about."

"Okay," Jack said. "Tell us more about the customer."

Liddell pushed his plate away and took out a notebook and pen. "Can you tell us what your gut told you about the customer?"

"He was a white man, like I already said. He was about four inches shorter than me and I'm five foot ten. He was wearing a dark colored spy coat. You know? A heavy trench-looking coat, like they wear in those old spy movies."

"A Burberry," Liddell suggested.

"It wasn't a berry anything," Freyda said.

Liddell took out his phone and pulled up pictures of Burberry coats. He held it where she could see and he flipped through the pictures. She stopped him at one.

"That's it. That's the same coat. Only his was charcoal colored and shiny. Some kind of leather."

Liddell showed the picture to Jack. The coat cost a thousand dollars. The customer had expensive taste. So what was he doing in this hole at that time of night? Or any time of night for that matter.

"Go on," Jack said.

"He looked a little undernourished. Should'a ate the pie. Didn't look like he ate much of anything. Except he looked hard. Like he'd seen some things. Done some things, if you know what I mean."

"Have you had other customers like him?" Jack asked.

"Never. He just looked odd," she said.

"How so?" Jack asked.

"He was wearing that coat, but he was wearing jeans and cowboy boots, and a rodeo kind of shirt—white with them pearl buttons—and a cowboy hat. These kids around here don't give a shit what they look like but he really stood out. He wasn't a college student, I can tell you that. And he wasn't a professor or anything like that. I would have seen him before. His voice was froggy like one of them chain smokers. He gave me the creeps."

"What did he say?" Jack offered.

"I asked if he wanted anything else. He said "No." I told him I was closing. He left a twenty to pay a three-dollar tab and didn't wait for change. I looked around when I left because I was scared he was after something else. Know what I mean?"

Jack didn't want to know. The thought of it made him vomit in his throat just a little. "I can see where you would think that," he lied.

"You're so full of it," she said and gave that mostly toothless smile again.

"Did anyone else come in?" Jack asked.

"Too cold," she said, motioning toward the university dorms. "Them kiddies stay inside smoking their wacky-weed and fornicating all day like rabbits. Bunch a' dummies. I hired one or two of them over the years, but they couldn't even make change without getting on them damn phones."

Jack changed the subject. "The car down the street with its engine running," he prompted

"Yeah. I locked up and checked my surroundings—a woman can never be too aware. Plus I had the day's money in my pocket. No one was on the street but there was that car half way down the block. That way." She pointed south. "The engine was running and someone was in it. Maybe two people. I couldn't see if it was man, woman or child."

Jack asked for a description of the car and was surprised at how succinct the answer was.

"Seventy-four puke green Volkswagen Beetle," Freyda said.

"You're sure?" Liddell asked.

"Asshole husband owned one. I sold the damn thing the day after he died. Got me a Cadillac convertible. Always wanted one but asshole said it wasn't in the budget. He was so tight he'd squeeze a penny until old Abe's gums bled."

Jack remembered seeing a faded green older model VW down the street when they arrived. He was getting on his radio when an officer came in.

"Detective Murphy, we've got a car down here that was stolen overnight," the young officer said. "Stolen close to here. The owner is coming over. I thought you'd want to know."

"Thank you," Jack said.

"Wait a minute," Freyda said. She went to the stove and came back with the remains of the cherry pie wrapped in aluminum foil.

Liddell said, "For me?"

Freyda answered, "You might as well take it. Won't be many customers today."

Jack turned at the door and asked, "Where was the customer sitting?"

"The other booth," Freyda said. "Ain't cleaned it yet. You think there might be some latent fingerprints you can run through that Automatic Fingerprint machine?"

Jack looked at the condition of the floor and countertop. In the back of the shop was another room with no door. "What's back there?" he asked.

"Supplies," Freyda answered. "And trash."

"Freyda, is there any chance you didn't wash the dishes?"

"Maybe. The pie he didn't eat is in the trash can." Her eyes widened. "DNA. You guys are almost as good as Mark Harmon. Want me to see if I can find them dishes and stuff?"

"I'll have a crime scene detective come in and you can let him do that. You'll need to show him where to look. Can you do that?" Jack asked.

Another toothless grin. "Will there be a reward?"

* * * *

Jack and Liddell followed the officer down the street to the stolen car. It matched the description Freyda had given them, except there was a dog inside this one. A black and white border collie jumped at the driver's window, snarling and showing his displeasure at having three men leering in the windows.

"When I called the owner he said he didn't have a dog. I've called Animal Control," the officer said.

While the officer kept the dog's attention on the driver's side, Jack went to the passenger side and saw the ignition had been torn out. He said to the officer. "Be sure no one touches anything before crime scene can do their thing."

"You think this car is involved?" the officer asked.

Jack had only seen the young officer around recently. Only a rookie would ask that question.

"Possible until we find out different," Jack said. "Can you interview the owner when he shows up?"

To Jack's disappointment the officer replied, "I don't think he'll know anything except his car got stolen."

"You got something else important to do...?" Jack looked at the officer's nametag. "Officer Keene."

"I got off an hour ago, Detective Murphy. My wife's pregnant and she's sick, sir. I'm sorry but I didn't think I'd be here this long."

Jack wanted to say something like "That's the job you signed up for kid," but he said, "Wait until Animal Control gets the dog and you can go home. I'll tell the Sergeant I dismissed you. I'll take the report. Give me the guy's name and such."

Officer Keene handed Jack a page from his notebook and said, "The car owner's name is Samantha Lee."

"You'll need to write up a detailed report of what you did here. When you were dispatched, etc. And tell Animal Control to keep the dog by itself. Don't hurt it. When crime scene gets here, and the dog is gone, you can leave. Got it?"

"Got it," the officer said.

Jack and Liddell headed back to The Coffee Shop when they heard a curse come from behind them. Jack turned in time to see Officer Keene on the ground and the Collie bouncing off his chest, coming their way fast.

"What the shit?" Liddell said as the dog flew past them and turned down the alleyway.

Keene ran after the dog. "Sorry, detectives. I was just checking to see if the car was unlocked and the damn thing came out."

Jack rounded the corner. The dog was sitting beside the body, its haunches against the dead guy, teeth bared at the crime scene techs as they backed away.

"I guess we know whose dog it is," Liddell said.

Keene put his hand on the butt of his gun and Jack put a hand on Keene's arm. "Do not shoot the dog. Animal Control will be here. I need the dog alive and talking."

Liddell muttered, "You old softie."

"Bite me, Bigfoot."

Jack's cell phone buzzed and he pulled it from inside his heavy coat. To Liddell he said, "We need to get Freyda to ID the car."

Jack answered the phone and the dispatcher said, "Jack, you and your partner are wanted behind the old sheet metal works off Fountain Avenue. That's near the railroad tracks just across the creek."

"We're kind of busy here," Jack said. "Can you send someone else? Call Captain Franklin. He'll call someone in to take that run."

"Captain Franklin knows what you're on. He said to send you and Blanchard."

When it rains it pours. "Okay. We'll leave here in about five or ten minutes."

"You need to go now, Jack. There's multiple dead, and—"

Jack hung up on her. "We need to go."

Bigfoot headed to their car.

"Who's going to pick this one up?" Liddell said. It was a Saturday. They were the only detectives were working weekends and Captain Franklin had ordered both of them to go to the other scene.

"You call Walker, Bigfoot," Jack said. "I'll drive. I want to get there before the Earth cools. You drive like an old woman."

"Do not," Liddell said and made the call.

They jumped in the Crown Vic and headed toward the Fountain Avenue Bridge. Jack got on his cell and called dispatch. "Have the officer call my cell phone right away."

His phone rang. "What have you got?"

The female officer's voice was trembling like she was crying or was about to. "Oh God, Jack!"

Jack recognized the voice. It was Crime Scene Tech Joanie Ryan. He could hear voices in the background giving commands to "Stand back. Move back." He stepped up his speed and was there in just minutes.

He turned onto a gravel easement, drove over some railroad tracks and behind a warehouse where several police cars had formed a circle around a large Ryder box van. Outside of these cars were several news vans with antennae raised like ants surrounding their prey. A uniformed officer was talking to the driver of a news van by gestures that brooked no argument. The driver backed away from the scene, and the officer moved on to the next van, shooing them away.

Sergeant Mattingly directed the stringing of crime scene perimeter tape. He and his team were forcing the gawkers and news hawkers back almost to Fountain Avenue. In Jack's world, there were two different sets of Constitutional rules. One for police. A different set for the news media. If police stood in someone's yard or filmed through the window of their house there would be a lawsuit and criminal charges. The news media called it their First Amendment right.

Jack and Liddell made their way over to Crime Scene tech Joanie Ryan. She had composed herself but stood, camera in hand, an uncertain look on her face.

"Are you okay, Joanie?" Jack asked.

The words meant as comfort brought the tears flowing. "I never…"

"Show me," Jack said. He took her arm and walked her toward the Ryder truck that was backed almost into the trees that lined Pigeon Creek. The doors of the truck were open. A cut padlock lay on the ground. Even without prior knowledge of what he would find, Jack could smell the contents before he rounded the back of the truck.

Inside, scattered in piles, were over a dozen bodies. A number of these were huddled along the back wall of the truck, nearest the cab. They appeared to have been clinging to each other for warmth. All were unmoving.

Jack asked Joanie, "Who cut the lock?"

"I did," Sergeant Mattingly said as he approached them.

"Can you get the bridge closed off?" Jack asked Mattingly.

"I've got cars securing the road on both sides of it."

Jack said, "Can you spare someone to go across the other side of the creek from here and keep the news from trying to film the back of the truck?"

"The buzzards are circling," Mattingly said, and moved away to give the orders.

Jack said, "Before I forget, at the other murder I told Officer Keene he could go home to his wife."

Mattingly said, "Keene's not married."

"The lying little shit," Liddell said out loud.

Jack held a hand up and said, "Shhh. Listen." He listened and looked for any signs inside. In the pile of bodies at the back, near the truck's cab, the fingers of a small hand moved and the sound came again.

"Someone's alive!" Jack shouted and hoisted himself into the opening.

Acknowledgments

Writing fiction is akin to lying with permission. I've been asked if I ever have writer's block. My response is always, "No. But I have liar's block. I can't remember what lie I just told." This novel is a work of fiction and is not intended to reflect negatively on any law enforcement agency. Any resemblance to persons, places, or events is unintentional and a figment of your overactive imagination. Shame on you.

I want to acknowledge the Evansville Police Department for allowing Jack Murphy and Liddell Blanchard work among their ranks.

A very good friend, Marty Crispino, was the inspiration for the Uncle Marty character in this book. Another good friend, Mindy Middleton, graciously allowed me to use her name for one of the main characters. The real Marty doesn't break legs to collect debts and the real Mindy is not an airhead.

Writing a series is difficult work. I could not do it without the help of my editor, Michaela Hamilton, and Kensington Books' expert staff of marketing, publicity, designers, proofers, copy editors, legal professionals, and all the others that work the magic of publishing. When I was a teen I worked in a donut shop making the dough (not money). The bakers would then transform this glob of stuff into wonderful donuts and pastries. My relationship with Kensington is just that. I make the dough, they make the donuts.

I thank all of you who have read, written to me and/or written reviews of my books, either to praise or to critique.

Meet the Author

Photo by George Routt

Sergeant Rick Reed (Ret.), author of the Jack Murphy thriller series, is a twenty-plus-year veteran police detective. During his career, he successfully investigated numerous high-profile criminal cases, including a serial killer who claimed thirteen victims before strangling and dismembering his fourteenth and last victim. He recounted that story in his acclaimed true-crime book, *Blood Trail*.

Rick spent his last three years on the force as the commander of the police department's Internal Affairs Section. He has two master's degrees, and upon retiring from the police force, took a full-time teaching position with a community college. He currently teaches criminal justice at Volunteer State Community College in Tennessee and writes thrillers. He lives near Nashville with his wife and two furry friends, Lexie and Belle.

Please visit him on Facebook, Goodreads, or at his website, www. rickreedbooks.com. If you'd like him to speak at your event, or online, you can contact him at his website or at bookclubreading.com

Printed in the United States
by Baker & Taylor Publisher Services